The Face of Death

Also by Cody Mcfadyen

Shadow Man

Cody Mcfadyen

THE FACE
OF DEATH

HODDER &
STOUGHTON

Grateful acknowledgement is given for permission to reproduce the following:
'Self-pity' by D H Lawrence, copyright © The Estate of Frieda Lawrence Ravagli.
Reproduced by kind permission of Pollinger Limited and the Proprietor.

A CIP catalogue record for this title is available from the British Library

Hardback ISBN 978 0 340 84008 5
Trade Paperback ISBN 978 0 340 84009 2

Set in Minion by
Rowland Phototypesetting Ltd,
Bury St Edmunds, Suffolk

Printed and bound by Clays Ltd, St Ives plc

Hodder Headline's policy is to use papers that are natural,
renewable and recyclable products and made from wood
grown in sustainable forests. The logging and manufacturing
processes are expected to conform to the environmental
regulations of the country of origin.

Hodder & Stoughton Ltd
A division of Hodder Headline
338 Euston Road
London NW1 3BH

For Brieanna,
my 'Little B'

ACKNOWLEDGMENTS

To Liza and Havis Dawson, as always, for the great support, advice, encouragement, and representation. To Danielle Perez and Nick Sayers, my editors at Bantam and Hodder respectively; this was a tough book, and they refused to let me call it done till it was done. To Chandler Crawford for her great foreign representation. Finally, to my family and friends for putting up with me while I wrote this book. I don't know about all writers, but I know this particular writer can be hard to live with when the writing is going rough.

Book One

Down at the Watering Hole

(WHERE THE DARK THINGS DRINK)

1

I dream of the face of death.

It's an ever-changing face, worn by many at the wrong time, worn by all eventually. I have looked into this face, over and over and over.

It's what you do, dummy.

A voice in my dream tells me this.

The voice is right. I am in the Los Angeles branch of the FBI, and I am responsible for hunting the worst of the worst. Child killers, serial killers, men (and sometimes women) without conscience or restraint or remorse. It's what I have done for over a decade and if I haven't seen death in all its guises, I've seen it in most. Death is endless and erosive. Its unfettered face wears on a person's soul.

Tonight, the face changes like a strobe in a fog, moving between three people I once knew. Husband, daughter, friend. Matt, Alexa, Annie.

Dead, dead, and dead.

I find myself facing a mirror with no reflection. The mirror laughs at me. It hee-haws like a donkey, it lows like a cow. I hit it with my fist and the mirror shatters. A purple bruise blossoms on my cheek like a rose. The bruise is lovely, I can feel it.

My reflection appears in the mirror shards.

The voice again: Broken things still catch the light.

I wake from this dream by opening my eyes. It's a strange thing, going from a deep sleep to full awareness in the space of a blink. But at least I don't wake up screaming anymore.

I can't say the same for Bonnie. I turn on my side to look at her, being careful not to jostle. I find she is already awake, staring into my eyes.

'Did I wake you up, honey?' I ask.

She shakes her head. *No*, she's saying.

It's late, and this is one of those times where sleep still beckons. If Bonnie and I are willing, it will draw us back down again. I open my arms to her. My adopted daughter moves close to me. I hug her tight, but not too tight. I smell the sweetness of her hair and darkness claims us with the whisper of an ocean tide.

When I wake up, I feel great. Really and truly rested, in a way I haven't for a long time. The dream has left me feeling cleansed. Gently scoured.

I feel unrushed and distant and peaceful. I don't have anything in particular to worry about, which is strange; worry is a phantom limb for me. This is like being in a bubble – or maybe the womb. I go with it, floating for a little while, listening to my own white noise. This is a Saturday morning, not just in name, but as a state of being.

I look over to where Bonnie should be, and see only rumpled sheets. I cock an ear and hear faint patterings. Ten-year-old feet, moving through the house. Having a ten-year-old daughter can be like living with a fairy. Something magical.

I stretch and it feels glorious and catlike. Just one item is needed to make this morning a thing of perfection. As I think it, my nose twitches.

Coffee.

I bound out of bed, and head down the stairs to the kitchen. I note with satisfaction that I'm wearing nothing but an old T-shirt and what I call my 'granny panties,' along with a pair of ridiculous fluffy slippers in the shape of elephants. My hair looks like it just

4

went through a hurricane. None of it matters, because it's Saturday, and no one else is here but us girls.

Bonnie meets me at the bottom of the stairs with a cup of coffee.

'Thanks, munchkin.' I take a sip. 'Perfect,' I say, nodding. And it is.

I sit down at the dining table, sipping my coffee. Bonnie drinks a glass of milk, and we look at each other. It's a very, very comfortable silence. I grin.

'This is some great morning, isn't it?'

She grins back, and that smile steals my heart again, nothing new. She nods.

Bonnie does not speak. Her muteness is not a result of any physical defect. It's the result of her mother getting butchered while she watched. And of the killer then tying her to her mother's corpse, face-to-face. She was there for three days like that. She hasn't spoken a word since.

Annie – her mother – was my best friend in the world. The killer came for her to hurt me. At times, I know that Annie died because she was my friend. Most of the time I don't know this. I pretend it isn't there, something just too huge and dark and crushing, a shadow the size of a whale. If I were to know that truth too often, it would break me.

Once, when I was six, I was angry at my mother for some reason. I can't even remember why. I had a kitten that I'd named Mr Mittens, and he came up to me with that empathy animals can have, knowing I was upset. Mr Mittens approached me with unconditional love, and my response was to give him a little kick.

He wasn't hurt, not permanently. Not even temporarily. But he was never really a kitten again. He would always flinch first when you went to pet him. To this day, if I think about Mr Mittens, I'm consumed with guilt. Not just a twinge, but a feeling of pure *awfulness*, a kind of crippling of the soul. It was an evil act. I did permanent harm to something innocent. I never told anyone what I did to Mr Mittens. It's a secret I plan to take to my grave, a sin I'd rather go to hell for than confess.

Thinking about Annie makes me feel like I kicked Mr Mittens to death. So I'm comfortable not knowing, most of the time.

Annie left Bonnie to me. She is my penance. It's not fair, because Bonnie is magic and wonder and sunny days. Muteness, night screams, and all. Penance should involve suffering; Bonnie brings me smiles.

I think about all this in an instant, looking at her. Thought moves fast.

'How about we hang out and be lazy for a few hours, and then we go shopping?'

Bonnie considers this for a moment. This is one of her traits. She doesn't blithely respond to anything. She gives it real thought, makes sure that when she answers, it's the truth. I don't know if this is a product of what she went through, or a quirk of character she was born with. She lets me know what she's decided with a smile and a nod.

'Coolio. Want breakfast?'

This requires no consideration, food being a consistent exception to that quirk. Affirmation is instant and enthusiastic.

I putter around, making bacon, eggs, toast. As we munch, I decide to broach the coming week with her.

'I told you I took a few weeks off, didn't I?'

She nods.

'I did it for a lot of reasons, but one in particular. I wanted to talk to you about it because . . . well . . . it'll be a good thing, but it might be a little bit hard too. For me, I mean.'

She leans forward, watching me with a steady, patient intensity.

I sip my coffee. 'I've decided it's time to put some things away. Things like Matt's clothes, his bathroom stuff. Some of Alexa's toys. Not the photos or anything like that. I'm not talking about erasing them. It's just . . .' I'm looking for the words. I find them, and they form a simple sentence: 'It's just that they don't live here anymore.'

Succinct, a single line. Filled with all of the meaning and knowledge and fear and love and hope and despair in the world. Spoken after crossing a desert of darkness.

6

I am the head of the Violent Crimes Unit in Los Angeles. I'm good at my job – real good. I oversee a team of three other people, all hand-selected by me, all exemplary law-enforcement professionals. I could be modest, I suppose, but I would just be lying. The truth is, you *really* don't want to be the psycho that my team is after.

A year ago, we were hunting a man named Joseph Sands. Nice guy to his neighbors, loving father of two, bearer of just a single flaw: He was hollow inside. He didn't seem to mind, but I'm sure the young women he tortured and murdered did.

We were hot on his trail – close to figuring out that it was him, in other words – when he changed my world. He broke into my home one night and, using just rope and a hunting knife, ended the universe as I knew it. He killed my husband, Matt, in front of me. He raped and disfigured me. He pulled my daughter, Alexa, up, using her as a human shield to catch the bullet that I had fired at him.

I returned the favor by filling him up with every bullet in my gun, and reloading to do it all again. I spent six months after that deciding whether I was going to go on living or blow my brains out.

Then Annie got killed, and Bonnie was there, and somewhere along the way, life got a firm grip on me again.

Most people can't truly conceive of being in a place where death might be preferable to life. Life is strong. It grips you in many ways, from the beating of your heart, to the sun on your face, to the feel of the ground beneath your feet. It grasps you.

Its grip on me was as thin as a thread. A strand of spider's silk, holding me over the edge of the chasm of forever. Then it was two threads. Then five. Then it was a rope. The chasm began to recede, and at some point I realized that life once again had a grip on me. It had snared me back into the moment to moment of drawing breath and pumping blood, and I cared about it all again. The chasm was gone, replaced by a horizon.

'It's time to make this a real home again, honey. You understand?'

She nods. I can tell she understands it in every way.

'Now – here's the part you might like.' I give her a small smile. 'Aunt Callie took some time off, and she's going to come stay with us and help out' – this elicits a smile of pure delight from Bonnie – 'and Elaina is going to be coming over too.'

Her eyes become lighthouses of happiness. The smile is blinding. Definite approval. I grin. 'Glad it makes you happy.'

She nods, we get back to eating. I'm woolgathering when I realize she is studying me again, head cocked. She has a soft, quizzical look on her face.

'You wonder why they're coming?'

She nods.

'Because . . .' I sigh. It's another single, simple sentence: 'Because I can't do it by myself.'

I'm resolute about this, about moving forward. But I'm a little bit afraid of it too. I've spent so much time being fucked up, I'm suspicious of my recent bout of stability. I want friends around to support me if I get a little bit wobbly.

Bonnie gets out of her chair, comes over to me. I feel such softness in this child. Such goodness. If my dreams contain the face of death, then this is the face of love. She reaches up and traces the scars that cover the left side of my face with a light finger. Broken pieces. I am the mirror.

My heart fills and empties, fills and empties.

'I love you too, sweetheart.'

Quick hug, canyon of meaning, back to breakfast. We finish and I sigh with contentment. Bonnie burps, huge and loud. A shocked silence follows – and then we both break out in laughter that comes straight from the belly. We laugh until we cry, it subsides to giggles, ends in smiles.

'Want to go watch some cartoons, munchkin?'

A blazing smile, like the sun on a field of roses.

I realize that this is the best day I have had in the last year. The very, very best.

8

2

Bonnie and I are going through the glendale galleria – mall to end all malls – and the day has only gotten better. We stopped into a Sam Goody's to look at the music selection. I got a CD set – *Best of the Eighties* – and Bonnie got the newest Jewel CD. Her current musical interests seem to match her personality: full of thought and beauty, neither unhappy nor joyous. I look forward to the day that she asks me to buy her something because it makes her toes tap, but today I could care less. Bonnie's happy. That's all that matters.

We buy some giant salted pretzels and sit down on a bench to eat them and people-watch. Two teenagers wander by, oblivious to anything but each other. The girl is in her mid-teens, brunette, homely, slender on top, heavy on the bottom, wearing low-slung jeans and a halter top. The boy is about the same age and adorably un-cool. Tall, skinny, gangly, sporting thick-lensed glasses, lots of acne, and hair down past his shoulders. He's got his hand in the back pocket of her jeans, she has her arm around his waist. They both look young and goofy and awkward and happy. Two square pegs, they make me smile.

I catch a middle-aged man goggling at a beautiful twentysome-thing. She's like an untamed horse, full of an effortless vitality.

9

Perfect jet-black hair down to her waist. Flawless tanned skin. Perky smile, perky nose, perky everything, exuding confidence and a sensuality that I think is more unconscious than purposeful. She walks by the man. He continues to catch flies with his open mouth. She never even notices him. The way of things.

Was I like that once? I muse. Something beautiful enough to lower the male IQ?

I suppose I was. But times change.

I get looks now, it's true. But they're not looks of desire. They are looks ranging from curiosity to distaste. Hard to blame them. Sands did some of his best work when he cut my face.

The right side is perfect and untouched. All the really grisly stuff is on the left. The scar starts at my hairline in the middle of my forehead. It goes straight down to between my eyebrows, and then it rockets off to the left, an almost perfect ninety-degree angle. I have no left eyebrow; the scar has replaced it. The puckered road continues, across my temple, arcing in a lazy loop-de-loop down my cheek. It rips over toward my nose, crosses the bridge of it just barely, and then turns back, slicing in a diagonal across my left nostril and zooming one final time past my jawline, down my neck, ending at my collarbone.

There is another scar, straight and perfect, that goes from under the middle of my left eye down to the corner of my mouth. It's newer than the rest; the man who killed Annie forced me to cut myself while he looked and hungered. He loved watching me bleed, you could see it in his eyes, an exaltation. It was one of the last things he felt before I blew his brains out.

Those are just the scars that are visible. Below the neckline of whatever blouse I happen to be wearing, there are others. Made by a knife blade and the cherry-end of a burning cigar.

For a long time, I was ashamed of my face. I kept my hair forward on the left, trying to obscure what Joseph Sands had done to me. Life got its grip on my heart again and my view of those scars changed. I keep my hair back these days, tight against my head in a ponytail, daring the world to look.

The rest of me is not too bad. I'm a shorty, four foot ten inches tall. I have what Matt used to call 'mouth-sized boobs.' I'm not thin, but am in shape. I have a not-small ass, more of a bubble butt. Matt used to love it. Sometimes he would fall down on his knees when I was in front of the full-length mirror, grab my butt, and look up at me. In his best Gollum voice he would go, 'My preciousssss . . .'

It never failed to give me a case of out of control giggles.

Bonnie pulls me out of this idle reverie with a tug on my sleeve. I look to where she is pointing. 'You want to go into Claire's?'

She nods.

'No problem, munchkin.' Claire's is one of those places that was designed for the mother/daughter experience. Cheap but stylish jewelry for young and old, hair scrunchies, brushes emblazoned with glitter.

We walk in and a twentysomething turns out to be one of the salespeople. She comes up to us with a patented retail smile, ready to help and sell. Her eyes widen as she gets a good look at me. The smile falters first, then shatters.

I raise an eyebrow at her. 'Problem?'

'No, I –' She continues to stare at my scars, flustered and horrified. I'm almost sympathetic. Beauty is her deity, and so my face must look like a victory for the devil.

'Go help the girls over there, Barbara.' The voice is sharp, a slap. I look over and see a woman in her forties. She's beautiful in that way that beautiful women can have when they get older. Salt-and-pepper hair, along with the most striking blue eyes I've ever seen. 'Barbara,' she repeats.

The twentysomething snaps out of it, flings out a single 'Yes, ma'am,' and races away from me as fast as her perfectly pedicured feet can carry her.

'Don't mind her, sweetheart,' the woman says. 'She's big on smiles, but a little lacking in the IQ department.' The voice is kind and I open my mouth to reply when I realize that she's not talking to me, but to Bonnie.

I look down and see that Bonnie is staring daggers at the twentysomething. Bonnie is protective of me; she had not been amused. She responds to the woman's voice, turning to her, giving her a very frank look of appraisal. The frown is replaced by a shy smile. She likes the salt-and-pepper lady.

'I'm Judith, this is my little shop. What can I help you ladies with?'

Now she is speaking to me. I give her my own look of appraisal, and see nothing false here. Her kindness is unforced, more than genuine. It's innate for this woman. I'm not sure why I ask it, but the words fly from my lips before I can stop them. 'Why aren't you bothered like she was, Judith?'

Judith gives me a look with those oh-so-sharp eyes, follows it with a soft smile. 'Honey, I beat cancer last year. It required a double mastectomy. The first time my husband saw the results, he didn't even blink, just told me he loved me. Beauty is a highly overrated commodity.' She winks. 'So, can I help you . . . ?'

'Smoky,' I reply. 'Smoky Barrett. This is Bonnie. We're just looking around, and you already helped us a lot.'

'Well, enjoy and you just let me know.'

One last smile, a small wink, and she's off, trailing kindness behind her like a fairy glow.

We spend a good twenty minutes in the shop, loading ourselves down with trinkets. Half of them will never be used, but boy were they fun to buy. Judith rings it all up, and we murmur goodbye, and leave with our loot. I look at my watch as we stand outside the store.

'We should get back, babe. Aunt Callie is going to be showing up in an hour or two.'

Bonnie smiles and nods, takes my hand. We exit the mall into a perfect day of California sunshine. It's like walking into a postcard. I think about Judith, and glance at Bonnie. She doesn't see me looking at her. She seems carefree, like a child should.

I put on my sunglasses and think again: This is a great day. The best in a long while. Maybe it's a good omen. I'm clearing the house of ghosts, and life keeps getting better. It makes me certain I'm doing the right thing.

I know when I go back to work that I'll remember: There are predators out there, rapists and murderers and worse. They're walking with us under that same blue sky, basking in the heat of that same yellow sun, always watching, always waiting, brushing up against the rest of us and quivering when they do, like dark tuning forks.

But for now, the sun could just be the sun. Like the dream-voice said: We broken things, we still catch the light.

3

The living room couch holds us in a soft, relaxed grip. It's a slightly battered old couch, light-beige microfiber, spotted in places by the past. I see wine drops that wouldn't come out, something food-related that probably dates back years. The loot from the mall waits in bags on the coffee table, which also shows signs of past misuse. Its walnut was shiny when Matt and I bought it; now its top is marred and scarred.

I should replace them both, but I can't, not yet. They've been loyal and comfortable and true, and I'm not ready to send them off to furniture heaven.

'I want to talk to you about something, honey,' I say to Bonnie.

She grants me her full attention. She senses the hesitation in my voice, the conflict inside me. *Go ahead*, that look says. *It's okay.*

This is another thing I hope to put behind us, someday. Bonnie reassures me too often. I should be guiding her with my strength, not the other way around.

'I want to talk to you about you *not talking*.'

Her eyes change, going from understanding to troubled.

No, she's saying. *I don't want to discuss this.*

'Honey.' I touch her arm. 'I'm just concerned, okay? I've spoken with some doctors. They say if you go too long without speaking, you could lose the ability to talk for good. If you never talk again,

14

I'll still love you. But that doesn't mean that's what I want for you.'

She crosses her arms. I can see the struggle going on inside her but I can't define it. Then I get it.

'Are you trying to figure out how to tell me something?' I ask.

She nods.

Yes.

She stares at me, concentrating. She points at her mouth. She shrugs. She does this again. Points. Shrugs. I puzzle about it for a moment.

'You don't know *why* you're not talking?'

She nods.

Yes.

She holds up a finger. I've come to learn that this means 'but' or 'wait.'

'I'm listening.'

She points at her head. Mimes being thoughtful.

Again, it takes me a moment.

'You don't know why you're not talking – but you're thinking about it? Trying to figure out the reason?'

I can tell by the relief on her face that I've hit the mark. It's my turn to be troubled.

'But, honey – don't you want some help with that? We could get you a therapist –'

She jumps up from the couch, alarmed. Cuts her hands in the air.

No way, no how, uh-uh.

This one needs no explanation. I understand in a flash.

'Okay, okay. No therapists.' I put a hand on my heart. 'Promise.'

This is another reason to hate the man who murdered Bonnie's mother, dead or not. He was a therapist and Bonnie knows it. Bonnie watched him kill her mother, and he killed any potential trust of his profession along with her.

I reach out, grab her, pull her to me. It's clumsy and awkward but she doesn't resist.

'I'm sorry, babe. I just ... worry about you. I *love* you. I'm afraid of you never talking again.'

She points at herself, and nods.

Me too, she's saying.

Points at her head.

But I'm working on it.

I sigh.

'Fair enough, for now.'

Bonnie hugs me back, showing me that it's fine, the day isn't ruined, no harm done. Reassuring me again.

Accept it. She's happy, right now. Let her be.

'Let's dig through all this cool junk we got, what do you say?'

Wide grin, big nod.

Yeah.

Five minutes later the trinkets have distracted her from the earlier discussion.

They distract me less, of course. I'm the grown-up. I don't get to soothe my worries with nail polish.

There are things I haven't told Bonnie about this two-week break. Omissions, not lies. A parental right. You omit so your child can be a child. They'll grow up and shoulder the weights of an adult soon enough, and inevitably.

I have some choices to make about my life, and I have two weeks to decide what I'm going to do. That's a self-imposed deadline. I need to make a decision, not just for me, but for Bonnie as well. We both need stability, certainty, a routine.

This has all come to a head because I was summoned to the Assistant Director's office ten days ago.

I have known Assistant Director Jones for the entirety of my FBI career. He was my original mentor and career rabbi. Now he's my boss. He didn't arrive at his current position through politics; he moved up through the ranks by being an exceptional agent. In other words, he's real, not a suit. I respect him.

AD Jones's office is windowless and austere. He could have chosen a corner office with great views, but when I'd queried him

16

on it one time, his response had been something along the lines of 'A good boss shouldn't spend much time in his office anyway.'

He'd been seated behind his desk, a big, hulking, gray-metal anachronism that he's had for as long as I've known him. Like the man himself, it screams, 'If it's not broke don't fix it.' The desk's surface was covered, as always, by multiple stacks of folders and papers. A worn wood and brass plaque announced his title. No awards or certificates adorned the walls, though I happen to know he has plenty he could put up.

'Sit down,' he'd said, indicating the two leather chairs that are always there.

AD Jones is in his early fifties. He's been in the FBI since 1977. He started right here in California and worked his way up the chain of command. He's been married twice and divorced twice. He's a handsome man, in a hard, carved-from-wood kind of way. He tends to be terse, gruff, and unapologetic. He's also a formidable investigator. I was lucky to have worked under him so early in my career.

'What's up, sir?' I'd asked.

He'd taken a moment before answering.

'I'm not big on tact, Smoky, so I'll just lay it out. You've been offered a teaching position at Quantico, if you want it. You're not required to accept it, but I am required to tell you about it.'

I'd been dumbfounded. I'd asked the obvious question:

'Why?'

'Because you're the best.'

Something in his demeanor had told me there was more to it than that.

'But?'

He'd sighed. 'There is no "but." There's an "and." You *are* the best. You're more than qualified and more than deserving based on merit.'

'What's the "and"?'

'Some higher-ups in the Bureau – including the Director – feel that you're owed it.'

17

'Owed it?'

'Because of what you've *given*, Smoky.' His voice had been quiet. 'You've given the Bureau your family.' He'd touched his cheek. I didn't know if it was an unconscious gesture or apropos of my scars. 'You've been through a lot because of your job.'

'So, what?' I'd asked, angry. 'They feel sorry for me? Or are they worried about me cracking up down the road?'

He'd surprised me with a grin. 'Under normal circumstances, I'd agree with that line of thinking. But no. I talked to the Director himself and he made it clear: This isn't a politicized payoff. It's a reward.' He'd given me an appraising look. 'Have you ever met Director Rathbun?'

'Once. He seemed like a straight shooter.'

'He is. He's tough, he's honest – as honest as the position allows him to be – and he tells it straight. He thinks you're perfect for the job. It would come with a pay raise, you'd have stability for Bonnie, and you'd be out of the line of fire.' A pause. 'The thing is, he told me it was the best the Bureau was going to be able to do for you.'

'I don't understand what that means.'

'There was a time you were being considered for Assistant Director – my job.'

'Yes, I know.'

'That'll never be on the table again.'

Shock had coursed through me.

'Why? Because I got thrown for a loop when Matt and Alexa died?'

'No, no, nothing like that. That's way too deep. Think shallower.'

I had, and understanding had arrived. On one hand, I hadn't believed it. On the other, it was Bureau, through and through.

'It's about my face, isn't it? It's an image issue.'

A complicated mix of pain and anger had flared up in his eyes. This had died away to weariness.

'I told you he gives it straight. It's a media-driven age, Smoky. There's no conflict with you running your unit and looking the way you do.' His lips had twisted into a sardonic smile. 'But apparently the consensus is that it wouldn't work in a director-level position. Romantic if you're the hunter, bad for recruitment if you're a Director or Assistant Director. I think it's crap, and so does he, but that's the way it is.'

I'd searched for the outrage I'd expected to feel, but to my surprise had found it absent. I could only summon up indifference.

There was a time when I had been as ambitious as the next agent. Matt and I had talked about it, even planned for it. We'd assumed that I'd climb the command ladder as a matter of course. But things had changed.

Part of this was pragmatism. Personal feelings aside, the powers-that-be weren't wrong. I was no longer fit to be the administrative face of the FBI. I was good as a soldier, scarred and scary. I was fine to train others, the grizzled veteran. Photo ops with the President? Never going to happen.

The other part was possibility. Teaching at Quantico was a plum position that many aspired to. It came with good pay, regular hours, and a lot less stress. Students didn't shoot at you. They didn't break into your home. They didn't kill your family.

All of this had passed through my mind in an instant.

'How long do I have to give my answer?' I'd asked.

'A month. If you say yes, you'd have plenty of time to make the transition. Six months or so.'

A month, I'd thought. Plenty of time and no time at all.

'What do you think I should do, sir?'

My mentor hadn't missed a beat.

'You're the best agent I've ever worked with, Smoky. Hard to replace. But you should do whatever is best for *you*.'

Here in the present, I glance at Bonnie. She's engrossed in her cartoons. I think about today, about relaxed mornings and breakfast burps and trips to Claire's.

What's best for me? What's best for Bonnie? Should I ask her?

Yeah, I should. But not now.

For now I was going to continue with the current plan. I was going to pack Matt and Alexa away. Gone but not forgotten.

We'll see what things look like after that.

I didn't feel stressed by the need to decide. I had choices. Choices meant future. Future here, future in Quantico, it was all forward motion, and motion was life. All of that was better than six months ago.

You keep telling yourself that. But it's not that simple, and you know it. Something's hiding behind that indifference, something dark and nasty and fang-ful.

Fang-ful isn't even a real word, I reply to myself, scornful.

I put all of this out of my mind (or try to) and snuggle closer, letting Saturday be Saturday again.

'Cartoons rock, don't they, babe?'

Bonnie nods without looking away from the TV.

Yes, she agrees. *They do.*

Not fang-ful at all.

4

'Don't you both look lazy and pleased about it,' Callie says.

She stands in the kitchen, posed. Burgundy-painted fingernails tap the black granite countertop of the kitchen island. Her copper hair contrasts with the white-oak cabinets behind her. She arches a single perfect, disapproving eyebrow.

Bonnie and I grin at each other.

If there was a patron saint of irreverence, it would be Callie. She is indelicate, sharp tongued, and has a habit of calling everyone 'honey-love.' Rumor says that she has a written reprimand on file for calling the Director of the FBI 'honey-love.' I don't doubt it; it is Callie to the core.

She is also beautiful in a way that the twentysomethings envy, because it is a permanent beauty, a movie-star beauty, undeterred by age. I have seen pictures of Callie at twenty, and I can honestly say that she is more beautiful now at thirty-eight. She has flaming red hair, full lips, long legs – she could have been a model. But instead of packing a hairbrush, she packs a gun. I think one of the things that makes her even more beautiful – if that's possible – is her absolute disinterest in her own physical perfection. It's not that she has a poor self-image (far, far from it), it's that her beauty isn't a meaningful trait to her.

Callie is hard as nails, smarter than the scientists at NASA, and the most loyal friend a person could ever hope to have. None of this is self-evident. Callie is not a touchy-feely girl. I've never gotten a greeting card or a birthday present from her. Her love shines through her actions.

It was Callie who found me in the aftermath of Joseph Sands. Callie who took my gun away from me, even as I pointed it at her, and pulled the trigger, firing on empty, click-click-click.

Callie is a member of my team; we have worked together for ten years. She has a master's degree in forensics to go along with a mind made for what we do. Callie has a certain brutality to her when it comes to investigative work. Evidence and truth are her higher power. If the evidence points to you, she'll turn on you and devour you, regardless of how well you got along before that point. She won't feel guilty about it either. The simplest solution: Don't be a criminal and you'll get along with her just fine.

Callie isn't perfect, she just wears her bruises better than the rest of us. She'd gotten pregnant at fifteen and had been forced by her parents to give up the child for adoption. Callie had kept this a secret from everyone, including me, until six months ago. A killer had forced it into the open. People could envy her beauty, but she'd fought and suffered to become the person she is.

'We *are* pleased,' I say, smiling. 'Thanks for coming.'

She waves her hand in a gesture of dismissal. 'I'm here for the free food.' She gives me a stern look. 'There *will* be free food, won't there?'

Bonnie answers for me. She goes over to the refrigerator, opens the door, and comes back holding a Callie favorite: a box of chocolate donuts.

Callie mimes wiping away a tear. 'Bless you.' She smiles down at Bonnie. 'Want to help me polish off a few?'

Bonnie smiles back, more sun and roses. They get milk, an important ingredient. I watch them down some donuts and I reflect on the fact that this, this simple minute, brings to me a burst of happiness that is almost a perfect thing. Friends and donuts and smiling daughters, the elixir of laughter and life.

'No, honey-love,' I hear Callie say. '*Never* eat without dunking first. Unless no milk is available, of course, because that's the first rule of life, and never forget it: *The donut always trumps the milk.*'

I stare at my friend in wonder. She's unaware of it, engrossed in doling out her donut-lore. This is one of the things that makes Callie one of my favorite people. Her willingness to have fun. To grab, guiltless, at the low-hanging fruit of happiness.

'I'll be back in a minute,' I say.

I pad up carpet-covered stairs to my bedroom and look around. It's a good-sized master. Plantation shutters on the front wall can be configured to let the sunshine in by increments, or in force. The walls are painted in off-whites, the bed coverings are a bright splash of light-blue color. The bed dominates the room, four-poster, king-sized, top-of-the-line, heaven-sent mattress. Heaps of pillows, mountains of pillows. I love pillows.

There are two matching chests of drawers, one for Matt and one for me, all in dark-colored cherrywood. A ceiling fan churns away, quiet, its low-slung hum my longtime sleep companion.

I sit down on the bed and look around, taking it in as a whole.

I need a moment, before it all starts. A moment to see it for what it was, not what it's going to become.

Great things and terrible things and things banal, all happened here, on this bed. They run through me like raindrops through tree leaves. A quiet thundering on the roof of my world.

Memories eventually lose their sharp edges and stop drawing blood. They quit cutting you and start *stirring* you. That's what my memories of my family have become, and I'm pretty happy about that. There was a time when a thought of Matt or Alexa would double me over in pain. Now I can remember and smile.

Progress, babe, progress.

Matt still talks to me from time to time. He was my best friend; I'm not ready to stop hearing his voice in my head.

I close my eyes and remember moving this bed into this room, after Matt and I bought it at some mom-and-pop furniture store.

This was our first home, purchased by cleaning out our bank accounts for a down payment and praying for an understanding lender. We bought a home in an up-and-coming area of Pasadena, a newer two-story (no way could we afford one of the hundred-year-old Craftsman homes, though we eyed them wistfully). It wasn't so close to work, but neither of us wanted to live in LA proper. We wanted a family. Pasadena was safer. The house looked like every other one around it, yes, it lacked identity, true – but it was ours.

'This is a home,' Matt had said to me in the front yard, hugging me from behind as we both looked up at the house. 'We're going to make a life here. I think a new bed fits that. It's symbolic.'

It was silly and sappy, of course. And I agreed, of course. So we bought the bed, and struggled it up the stairs ourselves. We broke a happy sweat assembling the headboard and frame and baseboard, grunted getting the box spring and mattress on. We sat on the floor of the bedroom, panting.

Matt had looked over at me and smiled. He'd bobbed his eyebrows up and down. 'Whatcha say we slap some sheets on the bed and engage in some horizontal mambo?'

I had giggled at his crudity. 'You sure know how to charm a girl.'

His face had grown mock-serious. He'd placed a hand on his heart, while raising the other. 'My father taught me the rules of bedding a wench. I promise, as always, to live by them.'

'What are they again?'

'Never wear your socks during sex. Know the location of the clitoris. Cuddle her to sleep before falling asleep yourself. No farting in bed.'

I nod, solemn. 'Your father was a wise man. I agree to your terms.'

We mamboed all afternoon, and into the dusk.

I look down at the bed. Feeling it more than seeing it.

Alexa was conceived on this bed, in some sweaty, tender moment, or maybe during something rougher and more acrobatic, who knows. Matt and I came together two and parted three. A successive joy, divine addition.

I spent sleepless nights on this bed while I was pregnant. Ankles swollen, back aching. I blamed Matt for everything. Blamed him with a bitterness you can only achieve at three in the morning and 210 days. I loved Matt for everything too. A depthless love that was a mixture of real joy and hormones gone berserk.

Most people start out, really, too selfish for marriage. A pregnancy will beat that right out of you.

The day after we brought her home, Matt and I set Alexa down in the middle of this bed. We lay on either side of her, and wondered at the fact of her.

Alexa was made here. She cried here sometimes. She laughed here, she was angry here, I think she even vomited here once after Matt let her eat too much ice cream. I cleaned up the bed, Matt slept on the couch.

I have learned lessons in this bed. Once, Matt and I were making love. Not having sex – *making love*. It had been preceded by wine and candles. We had the perfect CD playing at the perfect volume – loud enough to create an atmosphere, low enough not to distract. The moon was lush and the night breeze was temperate. We had just enough sweat going to keep us slippery in a scxy, non-sticky way. It was sensuous defined.

And then, I farted.

It was a ladylike toot, sure – but a fart nonetheless. We both froze. Everything seemed to hang in a long, agonizing, embarrassed moment.

And then, the giggling started. Followed by laughter. Followed by howls that we smothered with pillows, until we remembered Alexa was staying at a friend's. Followed later by a different kind of sex. It was no longer storybook, but it was more tender and more true.

You can have pride, and you can have love, but you can't always have both. In this bed I learned that love was better.

It wasn't all farts and laughter. Matt and I fought in this bed too. God, did we have some good fights. That's how we referred to them – 'good fights.' We were convinced that a successful marriage required a healthy knockdown, drag-out every now and then. We took great pride in some of our 'better efforts' – retrospective pride, of course.

I was raped in this bed, and I watched Matt die while I was tied to this bed. Bad stuff.

I breathe in, breathe out. The raindrops fall through the tree leaves, soft but inexorable. The basic truth: You get wet when it rains, no way around it.

I consider the bed and think about the future. About all the good things that could still happen here, should I decide to stay. I didn't have Matt, and I didn't have Alexa, but I did have Bonnie, and I did have me.

Life as it used to be, that was the milk. But *life* in *general*, was pure chocolate donut, and the donut trumps the milk.

'So this is where all the magic happens.'

Callie's voice startles me from my reverie. She's standing in the doorway, her gaze speculative.

'Hey,' I say. 'Thanks for coming. For helping me do this.'

She walks into the room, her eyes roving. 'Well, it was this or reruns of *Charlie's Angels*. Besides, Bonnie feeds me.'

I grin. 'How to catch a wild Callie: chocolate donuts and a really big mousetrap.'

She comes over, plops down on the bed. Bounces up and down on it a few times. 'Very nice,' she judges.

'I have a lot of good memories here.'

'I've always wondered . . .' She hesitates.

'What?'

'Why did you keep it? This is the same bed, isn't it? Where it happened?'

'The one and only.' I run a hand over the comforter. 'I thought about getting rid of it. I couldn't sleep in it for the first few weeks after I came home. I slept on the couch. When I got up the courage to try, I couldn't bear sleeping anywhere else. One terrible thing

26

happened here. That shouldn't outweigh all of the good times. I loved people here. My people. I'm not letting Sands take that away from me.'

I can't decipher the look in her eyes. Sadness. Guilt. A little bit of longing?

'See now? That's the difference between us, Smoky. I have a single bad moment in my teens, sleep with the wrong boy, get pregnant, and give up my child. I make damn sure forever-after that I never have another committed relationship. You get raped in this bed, but its strongest memories for you are the moments you shared with Matt and Alexa. I admire your optimism, I really do.' Her smile is just short of melancholy. Her lips curve in self-mockery. 'As for me? My cup runneth under.'

I don't reply, because I know my friend. She's sharing this with me, but that's all she's capable of. Words of comfort would be embarrassing, almost a betrayal. I'm here so she can say these things and know someone heard her, nothing more.

She smiles. 'Know what I miss?' she asks. 'Matt's tacos.'

I look at her in surprise. Then I smile too.

'They were great, weren't they?'

'I dream about them sometimes,' she replies, melodramatic longing in her eyes.

I couldn't cook with a gun to my head. I could burn water, as the saying goes. Matt, as always, as in all things, was the whole package. He bought cookbooks and tried things and nine times out of ten the results were amazing.

He'd learned how to make tacos by hand from someone, I don't know who. Not the kind with the icky store-bought shells, but the kind where you begin with a supple tortilla and transform it on the spot into a stiff yet chewy half-moon of deliciousness. He added some kind of spice to the meat that literally made my mouth water.

Callie too, it seems. She loved food, and invited herself to dinner three or four times a month. I can see her in my mind, scarfing down tacos, chewing her food while talking out of the side of her mouth. Saying something that made Alexa giggle till her milk went the wrong way and spewed out of her nose. Which was, of course, the height of hilarity, the apex of thigh-slappers for Alexa.

'Thank you,' I say.

She knows what I mean. *Thank you for that memory, that forgotten bit of bittersweet, that punch in the gut that hurts and feels wonderful all at once.*

This is Callie, spinning in close to hug my soul, spinning back out to regain her haughty distance.

She gets up from the bed and heads for the door. She looks back at me and smiles, a mischievous smile.

'Oh, and so you know? You don't need a mousetrap. Just drug the donuts. I'll *always* eat the donuts.'

5

'How are you doing, Smoky?'

Elaina is asking me this. She showed up about twenty minutes ago, and after going through the requisite hugs with Bonnie, she'd maneuvered me off so that we were sitting alone in my living room. Her gaze is frankness and kindness and klieg lights. She faces me head-on, piercing me with those brown eyes. 'No bullshit allowed,' that look says.

'Mostly good, some bad,' I say without hesitation. Being less than honest with Elaina never occurs to me. She is one of those rare people, the ones who are kind and strong at the same time.

She softens her gaze. 'Tell me about the bad.'

I stare back at her, trying to find words for my new demon, the devil that romps through my mind while I sleep. I used to dream about Joseph Sands, he chuckled and chortled and raped me again and again, killed my family with a wink and a smile. Sands has faded; the nightmares now center around Bonnie. I see her sitting on a mad-man's lap, a knife at her throat. I see her lying on a white rug, a bullet hole through her forehead, a crimson-angel spreading beneath her.

'Fear. It's the fear.'

'What about?'

'Bonnie.'

Her forehead clears. 'Ah. You're afraid something's going to happen to her.'

'More like terrified. That she's never going to talk and end up nuts. That I'm not going to be there when she needs me.'

'And?' Elaina asks, nudging me. Pushing me to put the real terror, the guy at the bottom of that dark barrel, into words.

'That she's going to die, okay?' It comes out sounding snappish. I regret it. 'Sorry.'

She smiles to show me it's fine. 'All things considered, I think your fear makes sense, Smoky. You lost a child. You know it *can* happen. For goodness' sake, Bonnie almost died in front of you.' A gentle touch, her hand on mine. 'Your fear makes sense.'

'But it makes me feel weak,' I reply, miserable. 'Fear is weakness. Bonnie needs me to be strong.'

I sleep with a loaded gun in my nightstand. The house is alarmed up the wazoo. The dead bolt on the front door would take an intruder an hour to drill through. All of it helps, but none of it dispels.

Elaina gives me a sharp look and shakes her head once. 'No. Bonnie needs you to be *present*. She needs you to love her. She needs a mother, not a superhero. Real people are messy and complicated and generally inconvenient, but at least they are there, Smoky.'

Elaina is the wife of one of my team members, Alan. She's a beautiful Latin woman, all gentle curves and poet's eyes. Her true beauty comes from her heart; she has a fierce gentleness to her that says 'Mom' and 'Safe' and 'Love.' Not in some silly, Pollyanna way – Elaina's goodness is not sappy-sweet. It's inexorable and undeniable and full of certainty.

Last year she was diagnosed with stage-two colon cancer. She'd had surgery to remove the tumor, followed by radiation and chemo therapy. She's doing well, but she's lost the hair that had always been so thick and unstoppable. She wears this indignity the way I've learned to wear my scars: uncovered and on display. Her head is shaved bald and isn't hidden by a hat or bandanna. I wonder if the pain of this loss hits her out of the blue sometimes, the way the absence of Matt and Alexa used to hit me.

Probably not. For Elaina, hair-loss would take a backseat to the joy of being alive; that kind of straightforwardness of purpose is a part of her power.

Elaina came to see me after Sands took away my family. She barreled into my hospital room, shoved the nurse aside, and swooped down on me with her arms wide. Those arms captured and enfolded me like an angel's wings. I shattered inside them, weeping rivers against her chest for what seemed like forever. She was my mother in that moment; I will always love her for it.

She squeezes my hand. 'The way you feel makes sense, Smoky. The only way you could be free of fear altogether would be to not love Bonnie the way you do, and I think it's too late for that.'

My throat tightens up. My eyes burn. Elaina has a way of getting to simple truths, the kind that are helpful and provide freedom, but carry a price: You can't unlearn them. *This Truth* is ugly and beautiful and inescapable: I'm stuck with my fear because I love Bonnie. All I have to do to be stress-free is un-love her.

Not gonna happen.

'But will it stop being so bad?' I ask. I heave a frustrated sigh. 'I don't want to screw her up.'

She takes both my hands, gives me that unswerving look. 'Did you know I was an orphan, Smoky?'

I stare, surprised.

'No, I didn't.'

She nods. 'Well, I was. Me and my brother, Manuel. After Mom and Dad died in a car accident, we ended up being raised by my *abuela* – my grandmother. A great woman. I mean that as in "greatness." She never complained. Not once.' Her smile is wistful. 'And Manuel – oh, he was such a wonderful boy, Smoky. Big-hearted. Kind. But he was frail. Nothing specific to point to, but he was always the first to catch anything going around and the last to get over it. One summer day my *abuela* took us to Santa Monica beach. Manuel got caught by the undertow. He died.'

The words are simple, and spoken plainly, but I can feel the pain behind them. Quiet sorrow. She continues.

'I lost my parents for no reason at all. I lost my brother on a beautiful day, and his only sin was that he couldn't kick hard enough to get back to shore.' She gives me a shrug. 'My point, Smoky, is that I know that fear. The terror of losing someone you love.' She pulls her hand away, smiles. 'So what do I do? I go and fall in love with a wonderful man who does a dangerous job, and yes, I've lain awake at night, afraid, afraid, afraid. There have been some times that I took it out on Alan. Unjustly.'

'Really?' I am having trouble reconciling this with the pedestal I have Elaina perched on; I can't imagine her as less than a perfect person.

'Really. Sometimes years pass without a ripple. I don't even think about losing him, and I sleep fine. But it always comes back. To answer your question: *No*, for me, it never goes away for good, but *yes*, I'd still rather love Alan, fear and all.'

'Elaina, why didn't you ever tell me any of this? About you being an orphan, about your brother?'

The shrug is perfect, almost profound.

'I don't know. I suppose I spent so much time not letting it define me that I forgot to tell the story when I should have. I did think of it once, when you were in the hospital, but I decided against telling you then.'

'Why?'

'You love me, Smoky. It would have added to your pain more than it would have helped.'

She's right, I realize.

Elaina smiles, a smile of many colors. The smile of a wife who knows she's lucky to have a husband she actually loves, of a mother who never had a child of her own, of a bald Rapunzel who's happy to be alive.

Callie appears with Bonnie at her side. They're both appraising me. Looking for the cracks, I imagine.

'Are we ready to get this show on the road?' Callie asks.

I force a smile. 'Ready as I'll ever be.'

'Explain what it is we're doing,' Elaina says.

I gather myself up into an imaginary fist and will it to hold on to the slippery, quivery parts of me. 'It's been a year since Matt and Alexa died. A lot has happened since then.' I look at Bonnie, smile. 'Not just for me. I still miss them, and I know I always will. But . . .' I use the same phrase I gave to Bonnie earlier today. 'They don't live here anymore. I'm not talking about erasing their memories. I'm keeping every picture, every home movie. I'm talking about the practical things that don't have use anymore. Clothes. Aftershave. Golf clubs. The things that would only get used if they were here.'

Bonnie gazes at me without hesitation or reserve. I smile at her, and put my hand over hers.

'We're here to help,' Elaina says. 'Just tell us what to do. Do you want to split up the rooms? Or do you want everyone to go from room to room together?'

'Together, I think.'

'Good.' She pauses. 'Which room should we start in?'

I feel glued to the couch. I think Elaina senses this. So she's prodding. She's making me move, telling me to *stand up*, to get into motion. I find it irritating and then feel guilty for *being* irritated, because I've never been irritated with Elaina before and she doesn't deserve it now.

I stand in a single motion. Like jumping off the high board without thinking about it first. 'Let's start in my bedroom.'

We put a bunch of boxes together, a startling cacophony of ripping tape and scraping cardboard. Now it's silent again. Matt and I each had our own closet in the master bedroom. I'm looking at the door to his closet and the air is getting heavy.

'Oh for God's sake,' Callie says. 'It is just *too* damn serious in here.'

She stalks over to the windows and yanks open the plantation shutters on one, then another, then the last. Sunlight comes rushing into the room, a flood of gold. She opens the windows in decisive, almost savage, motions. It takes a moment before a cool breeze begins to eddy, followed by the sounds of the *out there*.

'Wait here,' she growls, heading toward the door of the bedroom.

Elaina raises an eyebrow at me. I shrug. We hear Callie tromp down the stairs, followed by some sounds from the kitchen, and now she's tromping back up to the bedroom. She enters holding a small boom box and a CD. She plugs in the boom box, puts in the CD, and hits play. A driving drumbeat begins, mixing with an electric guitar riff that is catchy and a little familiar. This is one of *those* songs: I can't name it, I've heard it a thousand times, it always gets my foot tapping.

'*Hits of the Seventies, Eighties, and Nineties,*' she says. 'It won't deliver on *substance*, but it'll deliver on *fun*.'

Callie has transformed the room in the space of three minutes. It has gone from shadowed and somber to bright and frivolous. Just another bedroom on a beautiful day. I think about what she said earlier, about her inability to commit, and realize that avoiding the serious in her personal life has had at least one good side effect: She knows how to have fun at the drop of a hat.

I look down at Bonnie, raise my eyebrows. 'Think we can boogie our way through this, babe?' I ask.

She grins at me and nods.

'Yeah,' I reply back. I take a breath, walk over to the closet, and open the door.

6

The music and sunlight worked, at least in my bedroom. We went through Matt's closet without me feeling too sad.

We packed away his shirts and slacks, his sweaters and shoes. The smell of him was everywhere, and the ghost of him. It seemed like I had a memory for every piece of clothing. He'd smiled wearing this tie. He'd cried at his grandfather's funeral in this suit. Alexa had left a jam handprint on this shirt. These memories seemed less painful than I had expected. More rich than depressing.

Doing good, babe, I'd heard Matt say in my head.

I didn't reply, but I had smiled to myself.

I thought about Quantico and that possibility too. Maybe it would be good to leave this place behind.

If I do, it needs to be about choice, not retreat. I need to embrace my ghosts and lay them down, because they'll follow me wherever I go. That's what ghosts do.

We got through the closet and the bedroom and then the bathroom, and I floated through it all, the pain there but tolerable. *Bitter-sweet, waitress, heavy on the sweet.*

We filed down the stairway together with the boxes, moved into the garage, then up into the attic above the garage, dropping them

35

off and pushing them back into corners where I knew they'd sit in the dark and gather dust.

Sorry, Matt, I thought.

They're just things, babe, he replied. *The heart doesn't get dusty.*

I guess.

By the way, Matt says, out of nowhere, *what about 1forUtwo4me?*

I don't answer. I stand on the ladder, in the attic from the waist up.

'Smoky?' Callie calls from the doorway of the garage.

'Be there in a sec.'

Yes, I think. *What about 1forUtwo4me? What's the plan there?*

I had learned, doing what I do, that good men and women can still have secrets. Good wives and husbands can still cheat on each other, or have secret vices, or turn out not to have been so good after all. And, I had learned, it all comes out once you die, because once you're dead, others are free to root through your life at their leisure and you can't do a darn thing about it.

Which brings me to 1forUtwo4me. It's a password. Matt had explained the concept of picking secure passwords to me once after a family e-mail account had been compromised.

'You want to include numbers with letters. The longer the better, obviously, but you want to pick something you can memorize and not have to write down. Something that'll be mnemonic. Like . . .' He'd snapped his fingers. 'One for you, two for me. That's a phrase that sticks in my mind. So I change it a little and add some numbers and come up with 1forUtwo4me. Silly, but I'll remember it, and it'll be hard for someone to guess by accident.'

He'd been right. It was like gum on your shoe. 1forUtwo4me. I'd never have to write it down. It would always be accessible.

A few months after Matt died, I'd been sitting at his computer. We had a home office, and we each had our own PC. I was feeling numb and looking for something to awaken an emotion inside of me. I scrolled through his e-mail, dug through his files. I came upon a directory on the computer labeled *Private*. When I went to open the directory, I found that it was password protected.

1forUtwo4me, there it was, trotted out before I had to really think about it. My fingers had moved to the keyboard. I was about to type it out. I stopped.

Froze.

What if? I'd thought. What if private really does mean private? Like, private from me?

The thought had been appalling. And terrifying. My imagination went into overdrive.

A mistress? Porn? He loved someone else?

Following these thoughts, the guilt.

How could you think that? It's Matt. Your Matt.

I'd left the room, tucked away Mr 1forUtwo4me, and tried not to think about it.

He popped up every now and then. Like now.

Well? Truth or denial?

'Smoky?' Callie calls again.

'Coming,' I reply and clamber down the ladder.

I still feel Matt.

Waiting.

1forUtwo4me.

Packing away the past, it occurs to me, is messy stuff.

We're standing in the doorway of Alexa's room. I can feel discomfort looming in the not-far-off. Pain is a little sharper here, though still tolerable.

'Pretty room,' Elaina murmurs.

'Alexa liked the girly-girl stuff,' I say, smiling.

It is a little girl's dream room. The bed is queen-sized, with a canopy, and it's covered with purples of every possible hue. The comforter and pillows are thick and lush and inviting. 'Lie down and drown in us,' they say.

One quarter of the floor is covered in Alexa's stuffed animal collection. They range from small to big to huge, and the species run the gamut from the identifiable to the fantastic.

'Lions and tigers and heffalumps, oh my,' Matt used to joke.

I take it all in, and a thought comes to me. I wonder at the fact that it never occurred to me before.

Bonnie has slept with me since the day I brought her home. I don't think she's ever entered this bedroom.

Be accurate, I chide myself. You never brought her in here, that's the truth. Never asked her if she might want a king's ransom of stuffed animals, or a purple explosion of bedsheets and blankets.

Time to fix *that*, I think. I kneel down next to Bonnie. 'Do you want anything in here, sweetheart?' I ask her. She looks at me, her eyes searching mine. 'You're welcome to whatever you want.' I squeeze her hand. 'Really. You can have the whole room.'

She shakes her head. *No, thank you*, she's saying.

I've put away childish things, that look says.

'Okay, babe,' I murmur, standing up.

'How do you want to handle this room, Smoky?' Elaina's gentle voice startles me.

I run a hand through Bonnie's hair as I look around the room.

'Well,' I start to say – and then my cell phone rings.

Callie rolls her eyes. 'Here we go.'

'Barrett,' I answer.

Sorry, I mouth to them.

A deep voice rumbles. 'Smoky. It's Alan. Sorry to bother you today, but we got a situation.'

Alan is overseeing the unit while I'm on vacation. He's more than competent; the fact that he's felt the need to call me raises my antennae.

'What is it?'

'I'm in Canoga Park, standing in front of a house. Scene of a triple homicide. *Bad* scene. Twist is, there's a sixteen-year-old girl inside. She's got a gun to her head and says she'll only talk to you.'

'She asked for me by name?'

'Yep.'

I'm silent, processing.

'Really sorry about this, Smoky.'

'Don't worry about it. We were just about to take a break,

anyway. Give me the address and Callie and I will meet you there soonest.'

I jot down the address and hang up.

The man had gotten it wrong: Death *doesn't* take a holiday, apparently. Par for the course. As always, I am living my life on multiple levels: Make this a home, decide if I am going to leave this home and go to Quantico, go stop a young woman from blowing her brains out. I can walk and chew gum at the same time, hurrah for me.

I look at Bonnie. 'Sweetheart –' I begin, but stop as she nods her head. *It's okay, go*, she is saying.

I look at Elaina. 'Elaina –'

'I'll watch Bonnie.'

Relief and gratitude, that's what I feel.

'Callie –'

'I'll drive,' she says.

I crouch down, facing Bonnie. 'Do me a favor, sweetheart?'

She gives me a quizzical look.

'See if you can figure out what we should do with all those stuffed animals.'

She grins. Nods.

'Cool.' I straighten up, turn to Callie. 'Let's go.'

Bad things are waiting. I don't want them to get impatient.

7

'All tucked away,' Callie muses as we pull onto the suburban street in Canoga Park.

She's talking to herself more than to me, but as I look around, I understand the observation. Canoga Park is a part of Los Angeles County. Los Angeles doesn't provide a lot of distance between the suburbs and the city proper. You can be on a street lined with businesses, drive two blocks, and find yourself in a residential neighborhood. It was a casual transformation; traffic lights gave way to stop signs and things just got more *quiet*. The city hustled nearby, never stopping, always there, while the homes were here, 'tucked away.'

The street we'd turned onto was in one of those neighborhoods, but it has lost that quiet feeling. I spot at least five cop cars, along with a SWAT van and two or three unmarked vehicles. The obligatory helicopter is circling above.

'Thank God we still have daylight,' Callie remarks, looking up at the helicopter. 'I can't stand those blinding spotlights.'

People are everywhere. The braver ones are standing on their lawns, while the more timid peek out from behind window curtains. It's funny, I think. People talk about crime in urban areas, but all the best murders happen in the suburbs.

Callie parks the car on the side of the street.

'Ready?' I ask her.

'Born ready, bring it on, pick your cliché,' she says.

As we exit the car, I see Callie grimace. She places a hand on the roof of the car to steady herself.

'Are you all right?' I ask.

She waves away my concern. 'Residual pain from getting shot, nothing I can't handle.' She reaches into a jacket pocket and pulls out a prescription bottle. 'Vicodin, today's mother's little helper.' She pops the top and palms a tablet. Downs it. Smiles. 'Yummy.'

Callie had been shot six months ago. The bullet had nicked her spine. For one very tense week we weren't sure she was going to walk again. I thought she'd recovered fully.

Guess I was wrong.

Wrong? She carries her Vicodin around with her like a box of Tic Tacs!

'Let's see what all the shouting is about, shall we?' she asks.

'Yep,' I reply.

But don't think I'm going to let this go, Callie.

We head over to the perimeter. A twentysomething patrolman stops us. He's a good-looking kid. I can sense his excitement at being a part of this law-enforcement cacophony. I like him right away; he sees the scars on my face and almost doesn't flinch.

'Sorry, ma'am,' he says. 'I can't let anyone in right now.'

I fish out my FBI ID and show it to him. 'Special Agent Barrett,' I say. Callie does the same.

'Sorry, ma'am,' he says again. 'And, ma'am,' he says to Callie.

'Don't sweat it,' Callie replies.

I spot Alan standing in a cluster of suits and uniforms. He towers above them all, an imposing edifice of a human being. Alan is in his mid-forties, an African-American man who can only be described as *gargantuan*. He's not obese – just *big*. His scowl can make an interrogation room seem like a small and dangerous place for a guilty man.

Life loves irony, and Alan is no exception. For all his size, he is a thoughtful man-mountain, a brilliant mind in a linebacker's body. He combines meticulous precision with near-infinite patience. His attention to detail is legendary. One of the best testaments to his character is the fact that Elaina is his wife, and she adores him.

Alan is the third member of my four-person team, the oldest and most grounded. He told me when Elaina had been diagnosed with cancer that he was considering leaving the FBI so that he could spend more time with her. He hasn't brought it up since, and I haven't pushed him on it, but I am never really unaware of it.

Callie popping pills, Alan thinking of retiring – maybe I should leave. Let them rebuild the team from scratch.

'There she is,' I hear Alan say.

I start to catalogue the various reactions to my face and then let it go. Take it or leave it, boys.

One of the men steps forward, putting a hand out to shake mine. The other hand, I note, grips an MP5 submachine gun. He's dressed in full SWAT regalia – body armor, helmet, boots. 'Luke Dawes,' he says. 'SWAT commander. Thanks for coming.'

'No problem,' I reply. I point to Alan. 'Do you mind if I have my guy fill me in? No offense intended.'

'None taken.'

I turn to Alan and push aside all my own internal chatter, letting the simplicity of action and command take over. 'Hit me,' I say.

'A call came into 911 about an hour and a half ago from the next door neighbor. Widower by the name of Jenkins. Jenkins says that the girl – Sarah Kingsley – had stumbled into his front yard, dressed in a nightgown, covered in blood.'

'How did he know she was in the front yard?'

'His living room is in the front of the house and he keeps his drapes open until he goes to bed. He was watching TV, saw her out of the corner of his eye.'

'Go on.'

'He's shook, but he musters up enough courage to go out and see what the problem is. Said she was unfocused – his word – and mumbling something about her family being murdered. He tries to get her to come into his house, but she screams and runs off, reenters her own home.'

'I take it he was wise enough not to follow her?'

'Yeah, the heroics only went as far as his own front yard. He ran back inside, made the call. A patrol car happens to be nearby, so they come over to check it out. The officers' – he checks his note-pad again – 'Sims and Butler, arrive, poke their heads in the front door – which was wide open – and try to get her to come back out. She's unresponsive. After talking it over, they decide to go in and get her. Dangerous maybe, but neither of them are rookies, and they're worried about the girl.'

'Understandable,' I murmur. 'Are Sims and Butler still here?'

'Yep.'

'Go on.'

'They enter the home and it's a fucking bloodbath from the get-go.'

'Have you been inside?' I interrupt.

'No. No one's been in there since she got hold of a weapon. So they go in, and it's obvious that something bad happened, and that it happened recently. Lucky for us, Sims and Butler have dealt with murder scenes before, so they don't lose their heads. They give anything that looks like evidence a wide berth.'

'Good,' I say.

'Yeah. They hear noise on the second floor, and call out for the girl. No answer. They proceed up the stairs, and find her in the master bedroom, along with three dead bodies. She's got a gun.' He consults his notes. 'A nine mm of some kind, according to the officers. Things change fast at that point. Now they're nervous. They're thinking maybe *she's* responsible for whatever happened here, and they point their weapons at her, tell her to drop the gun, etc., etc. That's when she puts it to her own head.'

'And things change again.'

'Right. She's crying, and starts screaming at them. Saying, quote, "I want to talk to Smoky Barrett or I'll kill myself!" End quote.

They try to talk her down, but give it up after she points the gun at them a few times. They call it in and' – he opens his arms to indicate the overwhelming presence of law enforcement around us – 'here we are.' He nods his head toward the SWAT commander. 'Lieutenant Dawes knew your name and got someone to get ahold of me. I came here, checked things out, called you.'

I turn to Dawes, study him. I see a fit, alert, hard-eyed professional policeman with calm hands and brunet hair in a crew cut. He's on the short side, about five-nine, but he's lean and coiled and ready. He radiates calm confidence. He's a SWAT stereotype, something I always find comforting whenever I encounter it. 'What do you think, Lieutenant?'

He studies me for a few seconds. Then shrugs. 'She's sixteen, ma'am. A gun's a gun, but . . .' He shrugs again. 'She's sixteen.'

She's too young to die, he's saying. *Definitely too young for me to kill without it ruining my day.*

'Do you have a negotiator on-site?' I ask.

I'm asking about a hostage negotiator. Someone trained in talking to unbalanced people carrying guns. *Negotiator* is a bit of a misnomer, actually; they usually operate in three-man teams.

'Nope,' Dawes replies. 'We currently have three negotiating teams in LA. Some guy decided today was the day he was going to jump off the top of the Roosevelt Hotel in Hollywood – that's one. There's a dad about to lose custody of his kids who decided to put a shotgun to his head – that's two. The last team got T-boned in an intersection this morning on their way to a training seminar, if you can believe that.' He shakes his head in disgust. 'It was a truck that hit them. They'll live, but they're all in the hospital. We're on our own.' He pauses. 'I could handle this all kinds of ways, Agent Barrett. Tear gas, nonlethal ammo. But tear gas is going to fuck up what sounds like a murder scene. And nonlethal ammo, well . . . she could still shoot herself even after getting hit with a beanbag.' He smiles without humor. 'Seems like the best plan involves you going in there and talking to a crazy teenager holding a gun.'

I give him my best sucking-lemons sour-face. 'Thanks.'

He gets serious. 'You gotta wear body armor and have your weapon out and ready to fire.' He cocks his head at me, interest sparking in his gray eyes. 'You're some kind of *super shooter*, right?'

'Annie Oakley,' I reply.

He looks doubtful.

'She can put out candle flames and shoot holes through quarters, honey-love,' Callie says to him. 'I've seen her do it.'

'Me too,' Alan growls.

I'm not trying to brag, and this is not bravado. I have a unique relationship with handguns. I really *can* shoot out candle flames, and I really *have* shot holes through quarters thrown into the air. I don't know where this gift came from – no one in my family even *liked* guns. Dad was gentle and easygoing. Mom had an Irish temper, but she still covered her eyes during the violent parts of movies.

When I was seven, a friend of my father's took me and my dad to a shooting range. I was able to hit what I wanted with minimal instruction, even then. I'd been in love with guns ever since.

'Okay, I believe you,' Dawes says, raising his unencumbered hand in a gesture of surrender. His face grows serious. His eyes get a little distant. 'Targets are one thing. Have you ever shot a person?'

I'm not offended by him asking this. Since I *have* shot and killed another human being, I understand why he asks, and know that he's right to ask. It *is* different, and you can't know just how different until you've done it.

'Yes,' I respond.

I think the fact that I don't offer any further details convinces him most. He's killed too, and knows it's not something you feel like bragging about. Or talking about. Or thinking about if you can help it.

'Right. So . . . body armor on, gun out, and if it comes down to a choice between you and her, do what you gotta do. Hopefully, you can talk her down.'

'Hopefully.' I turn to Alan. 'Do we have any idea – at all – why she's asked for me?'

He shakes his head. 'Nope.'

'What about her – any details on who she is?'

'Not much. People here are into the "good fences make good neighbors" philosophy. The old guy, Jenkins, did say that she was adopted.'

'Really?'

'Yeah. About a year ago. He's not close with the family, but he and the dad talked to each other from their driveways every now and then. That's how he knew who the girl was.'

'Interesting. She could be the doer.'

'It's possible. No one else had anything substantial to offer. The Kingsleys were good neighbors, meaning they were quiet and minded their own business.'

I sigh and look toward the house. What had started out as a beautiful day was turning into a bad one fast.

I turn to Dawes.

'If I'm acting as negotiator, that means I have command for now. Any problems with that?'

'No, ma'am.'

'I don't want anyone getting trigger-happy, Dawes. No matter how long it takes. Don't go behind my back and start rappelling from the roof or anything cute.'

Dawes smiles at me. He's not offended. This is standard fare. 'I've been to a few of these, Agent Barrett. Contrary to popular belief, my guys aren't itching to shoot someone.'

'I've worked with our own SWAT, Lieutenant. I know all about getting pumped up for a call.'

'Even so.'

I study him. Believe him. Nod.

'In that case – do you have some body armor I can borrow?'

'You don't have your own?'

'I did, but it was recalled. Mine and four hundred others in the same lot – faulty composition resulting in them being overly brittle, or something like that. I'm waiting for a replacement.'

'Ouch. Good catch on their part then, I guess.'

'Except that I had reason to wear it three times before they figured out that it might not actually stop a bullet.'

He shrugs. 'Vest won't protect you from a head shot, anyway. It's all a roll of the dice.'

With that encouraging observation, Dawes goes off to get my Kevlar.

'He seems calm enough,' Alan observes.

'Keep an eye on things anyway.'

'They'll have to go through both of us,' Callie says. 'I'll flash them a little leg, Alan will terrify them, end of problem.'

'Just worry about what to do once you're inside,' Alan says. 'You ever done any negotiation?'

'I've taken the class. But no, I've never dealt with a "situation."'

'Key is to listen. No lies unless you're sure you can get away with them. It's about rapport, so lies are a deal breaker. Watch for emotional triggers and give them a nice, wide berth.'

'Sure, simple.'

'Oh yeah, and don't die.'

'Very funny.'

Dawes reappears with a vest. 'I got this off a female detective.' He holds it up, looks at me, frowns. 'It's going to be big.'

'They all are unless I get them custom.'

He grins. 'No height requirement, I take it, Agent Barrett?'

I grab the vest from him with a scowl. 'That's Special Agent Barrett to you, Dawes.'

The grin fades. 'Well, be careful in there, Special Agent Barrett.'

'If I was going to be careful, I wouldn't go in there at all.'

'Even so.'

Even so, I think. What a great turn of phrase. Short and sweet, but fraught (another great word) with meaning.

You could die in there.

Even so.

8

I'm standing in front of the home's open front door. I'm sweating and scratchy in the ill-fitting body armor I've thrown over my shirt. I have my Glock out and ready. The day is moving toward dusk, shadows are starting to stretch, and my heart is pounding like a drummer on speed.

I glance back at the law-enforcement presence behind me.

Barricades have been erected in front of the home, starting at the street. I count four patrol cars and the SWAT van. The uniforms are standing guard at the barricades, ready to speak one phrase, and one phrase only: 'Go away.' The SWAT team waits inside the perimeter, a deadly group of six, black helmets gleaming. The lights on the patrol cars are all on, and they're trained on the house.

On me.

Law enforcement is a dirty job. It's about body fluids, decay, and people at their worst. It's about life and death decisions made with too little information. The most trained cop or agent is still never trained enough to deal with everything. When crisis comes (and it *always* comes), it's often solved the way we're solving it now: an agent with a two-week class in hostage negotiation, called away from her vacation, wearing a loose-fitting Kevlar vest, doubting her ability to do what she's about to do. In other words, we do our best with what we have.

I shut it all out and peer through the door.

A few drops of sweat pop out on my forehead. Salty pearls.

It's a newer home for this area, a two-story with a stucco and wood exterior, topped by a clay-tile roof. Classic Southern California. It looks well cared for, possibly repainted in the last few years. Not huge, the owners weren't rich, but nice enough. A middle-class family home not trying to be anything else.

'Sarah?' I call in. 'It's Smoky Barrett, honey. You asked to see me, and I'm here.'

No answer.

'I'm going to come in to see you, Sarah. I just want to talk to you. To find out what's going on.' I pause. 'I know you have a gun, honey. I need you to know that I have one too, and that I'm going to have it out. Don't be scared when you see it. I'm not going to shoot you.'

I wait, and again, there's no answer.

I sigh and curse and try to think of a reason to keep from walking into this house. Nothing comes to mind. Some part of me doesn't want anything to come to mind. This is a not-so-secret truth of law enforcement: These moments arc terrifying, but they are also when you feel most alive. I feel it now, adrenaline and endorphins, fear and euphoria. Wonderful and awful and addictive.

'I'm coming in now, Sarah. Don't shoot me or yourself, okay?' I'm going for light humor, I come off sounding nervous. Which I am.

I squeeze the gun butt, take a deep breath, and walk through the front door.

The first thing I smell is murder.

A writer asked me once what murder smells like. He was looking for material for a book he was writing, some authenticity.

'It's the blood,' I'd said. 'Death stinks, but when you smell blood more than anything else, you're usually smelling murder.'

He'd asked me then to describe the smell of blood.

'It's like having a mouthful of pennies that you can't get rid of.'

I smell it now, that cloying copper tang. It excites me at some level.

A killer was here. I hunt killers.

I keep walking. The entryway floor is red hardwood over concrete, quiet, polished, squeak-free. To my right is a spacious living room with medium-thick beige carpet, a fireplace, and vaulted ceilings. A two-section matching beige couch is arranged in an L-shape facing the fireplace. Large double-paned windows look out onto the lawn. Everything I can see is clean and nice but unimaginative. The owners were trying to impress by blending in, not by standing out.

The living room continues on the right toward the back of the house, meeting the dining room seamlessly. The beige carpet follows. A honey-colored wooden dining table sits under a light hanging from a long black chain attached to the high ceiling. A single white French door beyond the table leads into the kitchen. Again, all very unsurprising. Pleasing, not passionate.

Ahead of me is a stairway, zigging right to a landing, then zagging left to take you to its destination, the second floor. It's covered with the same beige carpet. The walls on the way up the stairs are filled with framed photographs. I see a man and a woman standing together, smiling and young. The same man and woman, a little older now, holding a baby. The baby, I assume, grown into a teenage boy, handsome. Dark hair on all of them. I scan the photos and note no pictures of a girl.

To the left of the stairs is what I assume to be a family room. I can see thick sliding glass doors leading from that room into the now shadowy backyard.

I smell blood, blood, and more blood. Even with every light in the house blazing the atmosphere is heavy and jagged. Harm happened here. Terror filled the air here. People died violently here, and the feel of it all is stifling. My heart rate continues to rat-a-tat-tat. The fear is still there, sharp and strong. The euphoria too.

'Sarah?' I call out.

No answer.

I move forward, toward the stairs. The smell of blood gets stronger. Now that I can see into the family room, I understand why. This room also has a couch, which faces a large-screen television. The carpet is *soaked* in crimson. Blood came out here by the pints, more than the pile or fabric could absorb. I can see puddles of it, dark, thick, and congealing. Whoever bled that much there, died there.

No bodies, though.

Means they were moved, I think.

I look, but I don't see any blood trails, any evidence of bodies being dragged. All the blood is pooled, self-contained, except for the large, jagged patch nearest to me.

Maybe they were picked up.

That would mean someone strong. A human adult body, at deadweight, is a formidable thing to lift, much less carry. Any fireman or paramedic will tell you this. Without the leverage a helpful and conscious person provides, carrying a grown man's body can be like carrying a six-foot bag of bowling balls.

Unless the blood came from a child, in which case the lift and carry would not have been as difficult. Wonderful thought.

'Sarah?' I call out. 'I'm coming up the stairs.' My voice sounds overloud to me, cautious.

I'm still sweating. Air-conditioning is off, I realize. Why? I'm noting a thousand things at once. Fear and euphoria, euphoria and fear.

I grip my gun with both hands and start to move up the stairs. I reach the first landing, and turn left. The smell of blood is even stronger now. I smell new scents. Familiar odors. Urine and feces. Other, *wetter* things. Guts, they have an aroma all their own.

I can hear something now. A faint sound. I cock my head and strain my ears.

51

Sarah is singing.

The hairs on the back of my neck stand up. My stomach does a single loop-de-loop as the adrenaline overwhelms the endorphins and fills me with the clangy-jitters.

Because this is not a happy sound. It's a horror sound. It's the kind of song you'd expect to hear coming out of the earth in a graveyard, at night, or maybe from the shadowy corner of a cell in a mental institution. It's a single word and a single note, sung in a monotone.

'Laaaa. Laaaa. Laaaa. Laaaa.'

Over and over, that single word, that single note, in a voice just above a whisper.

I start to worry in a way I hadn't before, because this is the sound of insanity.

I move up the last flight of stairs in quick strides, passing all those smiling faces in the photographs. Their teeth seem to glitter in the light.

Look at that, I think when I reach the top, more beige carpet.

I'm standing in a short hallway. A bathroom is at the end of the hall. Its lights are on, its door flung wide. I can see *(surprise!)* a beige tile floor, more evidence of the uninspired tastefulness I've come to expect from this home.

The hallway turns to the right at the bathroom, and I surmise that a bedroom door is just beyond that turn.

More beige, I'll bet.

My heartbeat hammers, and *God* am I sweating.

To my immediate right is a set of white double doors. The entrance, I'm sure, to someplace terrible. The smells have all become stronger. Sarah's horrible singing tickles my skin.

I reach out a hand to open the right door. It pauses just above the brass handle and trembles.

Girl with a gun on the other side of that. Girl with a gun, covered in blood, in a house that smells like death, singing like a crazy person.

Go on, I think. The worst thing she can do is shoot me.

No, moron. The worst thing she can do is look right at me and then blow her brains out or smile and blow her brains out or –

Enough, I command.

Silence inside. My soul goes quiet.

My hand stops trembling.

A new voice comes, one familiar to soldiers and cops and victims. It doesn't offer comfort. It offers certainty. It speaks the hardest words and it never, ever lies. The patron saint of impossible choices.

Save her if you can. But kill her if you must.

My hand drops and I open the door.

9

The room is decorated in death.

It's an extra-large master bedroom. The king-sized bed has a large wooden hutch and a mirror behind it, and still takes up less than a third of the floor space. There is a plasma TV mounted on the wall. A ceiling fan hangs, turned off, its silence anointing all the other stillness in this room. The beige carpet is present, almost comforting under the circumstances.

Because blood is *everywhere*. Splashed on the ceiling, smeared on the off-yellow walls, beaded on the ceiling fan. The smell is overpowering; my mouth fills with still more pennies and I swallow my own saliva.

I count three bodies. A man, a woman, and what looks like a teenage boy. I recognize them all from the photographs on the stairway walls. They are all naked, all lying on their backs in the bed.

The bed itself has been stripped bare. The blankets and sheets lie on the floor, wadded and blood-soaked.

The man and woman are on either side, with the boy in the middle. The two adults have been disemboweled, in the worst sense of the word. Someone cut them from throat to crotch and then reached into them and *pulled*. They have been turned inside out. The throats of all three have been slit like hogs, sopping grins from ear to ear.

'Laaaa. Laaaa. Laaaa. Laaaa.'

My eyes go to the girl. She's sitting on the windowsill, looking out into the night and what I can only guess is the backyard. I can see the dim silhouettes of other rooftops in the distance. It's a twilight world, caught between the dying sun and the awakening streetlamps. Apropos.

The girl has a gun in her hand, and she's pressing the barrel against her right temple. She hadn't turned around at the sound of the door opening.

I can't blame her. I wouldn't want to turn around either.

Even as my heart hammers, the clinical part of me takes notes.

The blood on the walls was put there by the killer. I know this because I can see patterns. Slashes, swirls, and curlicues.

He played here. Used their blood like finger paint to make patterns. To say something.

I look over at Sarah. She continues to gaze out the window, unaware of me.

She's not the perpetrator. Not enough blood on her, and the corpses are all too big. She'd never have gotten any of them up the stairs by herself.

I move forward into the room, trying not to step on evidence. I give up; I'd have to levitate.

Too much blood, but none of it in the right places. Where's the murder scene?

Every bit of blood evidence I could see was purposeful. None of this was the result of a throat being slit.

Focus.

The investigator in me is a detached creature. It can view the worst of the worst with dispassion. But detachment isn't what I need right now. I need empathy. I force myself to stop examining the scene, to stop calculating, and focus all of my attention on the girl.

'Sarah?' I keep my voice soft, unthreatening.

No response. She continues to sing in that awful monotone whisper.

'Sarah.' A little louder now.

Still no reaction. The gun stays at her temple. She keeps on singing.

'Sarah! It's Smoky. Smoky Barrett!' My voice booms, louder than I'd intended. I startle myself.

Startle her too. The singing stops.

Quieter: 'You asked for me, honey. I'm here. Look at me.'

This sudden silence is as bad in its own way as the singing had been. She's still looking out the window. The gun hasn't moved from her temple.

Sarah begins turning toward me. It's a montage of slow, jerky motions, an old door opening on rusted hinges. The first thing I notice is her beauty, because of its contrast with the horror around her. She is ethereal, something from another world. She has dark, shimmering hair, the impossible hair you see on models in shampoo commercials. She's Caucasian, with an exoticness about her that speaks of European roots. French, perhaps. Her features have that ideal symmetry that most women dream of having, and too many living in Los Angeles go under the knife to get.

Her face is the mirror opposite of mine, a counterpoint of perfection to my flaws.

She has blood splattered on her arms and face, and soaked into the short-sleeved long white nightgown she's wearing. She has full, cupid-lips, and while I'm sure they're normally a beautiful pink, right now they are the pale white of a fish belly.

I wonder about that nightgown. Why had she been wearing it in the afternoon?

Her eyes are a rich blue, heart-stopping. The look of defeat I find in them is so profound, it makes me queasy.

Pressed to all that beauty, the barrel of what I can now tell is a nine-mm Browning. This is no weak twenty-two. If she pulls the trigger, she'll die.

'Sarah? Can you hear me now?'

She continues to look at me with those defeated, blue-flame eyes.

'Honey, it's me. Smoky Barrett. They said you asked for me, and I got here as fast as I could. Can you talk to me?'

She sighs. It's a full-body sigh, straight from the pit of her stomach. A sigh that says, *I want to lie down now, I want to lie down and die.* No other reply, but at least she keeps looking at me. I want this. I don't want those eyes to start roaming, to remember the bodies on the bed.

'Sarah? I have an idea. Why don't we walk out into the hallway? We don't have to go anywhere else – we can sit at the top of the stairs, if you want. You can keep that gun pointed right where it is. We'll just sit down, and I'll wait until you're ready to talk.' I lick my lips. 'How about it, sweetheart?'

She cocks her head at me, a casual motion that becomes horrifying because she keeps the gun barrel against her temple *as* she does it. It makes her seem hollow. Puppet-like.

Another deep sigh, even more ragged sounding. Her face is expressionless. Only the sighs and the eyes show me what's going on inside her.

Located somewhere in hell, I'd say.

A long moment passes, and then she nods.

I am almost thankful, at this moment, for Bonnie's muteness. It's made me comfortable with nonverbal communication, able to understand nuanced meaning regardless of words.

Okay, that nod says. *But the gun stays, and I'll probably still use it.*

Just get her out of this room, I think. That's the first step.

'Great, Sarah,' I reply, nodding back to her. 'I'm going to put away my gun.' Her eyes follow my hands as I do this. 'Now, I'm going to back out of the room. I want you to follow me. I want you to keep your eyes on mine. That's *important*, Sarah. Only on me. Don't look right or left or up or down. Look at me.'

I start to move backward, going in a straight line. I keep my eyes locked on hers, willing her to do the same. I stop when I'm standing in the doorway.

'Come on, honey. I'm right here. Walk to me.'

A hesitation, and then she slides off the windowsill. Kind of *pours* off it, like water. The gun is still at her head. Her eyes stay on mine as she moves toward the doorway. They never stray to the bed, not once.

Good, I think. Nothing like looking at that mess to make you want to kill yourself.

Now that she's standing, I can tell that she's about five foot two inches. In spite of her shock, her movements are graceful and precise. She glides.

She looks small surrounded by the murdered dead. Her bare feet are splashed with blood; she either doesn't notice, or doesn't care.

I walk back to let her move through the doorway. She plods past me, keeping her eyes on my hands. A watchful zombie.

'I'm going to reach over and close the door. Okay, honey?'

She nods. *I don't care*, the nod says. *About living or dying or anything at all.*

I close the door and allow myself a moment of relief. I wipe sweat from my forehead with a trembling hand.

I take a deep breath and turn to Sarah. Now let's see if I can get her to give me that gun.

'You know what? I'm going to sit down.'

I take a seat so the bedroom doors are at my back. I do this without breaking eye contact. *I'm here, I see you, you have all my attention*, I'm saying.

'It's a little hard to talk while you're up there and I'm down here,' I say, squinting up at her. I indicate the space in front of me. 'Why don't you take a seat?' I examine her face. 'You look tired, sweetheart.'

That eerie head-cocking gesture again. I lean forward and pat the carpet.

'Come on, Sarah. It's just you and me. No one is going to come in here until I tell them to. No one's going to hurt you while I'm here. You wanted to see me.' I pat the carpet again, still maintaining eye contact. 'Sit down and relax. I'll shut up and we'll wait here until you're ready to tell me whatever it is you wanted to tell me.'

She moves without warning, stepping backward and then lowering herself to the floor. It's done with the same pouring-of-water grace that she displayed as she slid off the windowsill. I wonder idly if she's a dancer, or perhaps a gymnast.

I give her a reassuring smile. 'Good, honey,' I say. 'Very good.'

Her eyes stay on mine. The gun is still glued to her right temple.

As I consider my next move, I remember one of the key lessons my negotiations instructor gave:

'Speaking when you want, not speaking when you want, it's all about control,' he'd observed. 'When you're dealing with someone who's refusing to speak, and you don't know what buttons to push – don't know much about them personally, in other words – you need to shut up. Your instinct will be to fill that silence. Resist it. It's like letting a phone ring – it makes you crazy, but it'll stop ringing sooner or later. Same thing here. Wait them out, and they'll fill that silence for you.'

I keep my face calm, my eyes on hers, and I stay silent.

Sarah's face is a superlative of stillness, and absence of motion, formed from wax. The corners of her mouth don't twitch. I feel like I'm having a staring contest with a mannequin that blinks.

Her blue eyes are the most 'alive' part of her, and even they seem glassy and unreal.

I examine the blood on her as I wait.

The spatter on the right side of her face looks like a collection of sideways teardrops. Elongated, as though each drop hit her skin with force and then was stretched by inertia.

Flung there, maybe? By fingertips soaked in blood?

Her nightgown is a mess. The front is soaked. I see spots at the knees.

As if she knelt. Maybe she was trying to revive someone?

My train of thought derails when she blinks, sighs, and then looks away.

'Are you really Smoky Barrett?' she asks. It's a tired voice, filled with defeat and doubt.

Hearing her speak is both elating and surreal. Her voice is dusky and subdued, older than she is, a hint of the woman she'll become.

'Yep,' I reply. I point to my scars. 'Can't fake these.'

She keeps the gun to her head, but as she looks at my scars, sorrow replaces some of the deadness in her face.

'I'm sorry,' she says. 'For what happened to you. I read about it. It made me cry.'

'Thank you.'

Wait for her. Don't press.

She looks down. Sighs. Looks back up at me.

'I know what it's like,' she says.

'What, honey?' I ask in a soft voice. 'You know what what's like?'

I watch the pain rise in her eyes, like two moons being filled up with blood.

'I know what it's like to lose everything you love,' she says, her voice cracking, then dropping to a whisper. 'I've been losing things since I was six.'

'Is that why you wanted to see me? To tell me about what happened then?'

'When I was six,' she says, continuing as though I hadn't said anything, 'he started it all by murdering my mother and my father.'

'Who is "he," Sarah?'

She locks eyes with me, something in them flares up for a moment before dying back down.

What was that? I wonder. Sorrow? Anger?

It was something huge, that's for sure. That was no minnow that had swum to the surface before diving back down into deeper waters, it was a soul-leviathan.

'He,' she says, her voice flat. 'The Stranger. The one who killed my parents. The one who kills anything I love. The . . . *artist.*' The way she says 'artist,' she could be saying 'child molester' or 'shit on a hot sidewalk.' The revulsion is strong and pure and palpable.

'Did The Stranger do this, Sarah? Was he here, in this house?'

Her sorrow and fear are swept away by a look of cynicism that rocks me. It's far, far too terrible and cunning for a sixteen-year-old girl. If that dusky voice belongs to a twenty-five-year-old woman, this look belongs to a world-worn hag.

'Don't *humor* me!' she cries, her voice high-pitched and derisive. 'I know you're only listening to me because of' – she wiggles the gun – 'this. You don't really believe me!'

What just happened here?

The quiet air between us starts to hum.

You're losing her, I realize. Fear thrills through me.

Do something!

I gaze into those rage-filled eyes. I remember what Alan said.

Don't lie, I think. Truth. Only truth. She'll smell a lie from a thousand yards away right now and then it's game over.

My words come from somewhere effortless, almost extemporaneous. 'I'll tell you what I care about right now, Sarah,' I say, my voice strong. 'I care about *you*. I know you didn't do what happened here. I know that you're very close to killing yourself. I know you asked for me, and that means that *maybe* I have something to give you, something to tell you, that will keep you from pulling that trigger.' I lean forward. 'Honey, I don't know enough about anything going on here to *humor* you, I promise. All I'm trying to do is understand. Help me understand. Please. You asked for me. Why? Why did you ask for me, Sarah?' I wish I could reach out and shake her. I plead instead. 'Please tell me.'

Don't die, I think. Not here, not like this.

'Please, Sarah. Talk to me. Make me understand.'

The words work: The anger leaves her eyes. Her trigger finger relaxes and she looks away.

Thank God, I think, fighting down a bubble of semi-hysteria, a bout of the

(*clangy-jitters*)

When she looks back, anguish has replaced the rage.

'You're my last hope,' she says. Her voice is small and hollow.

'I'm listening, Sarah,' I urge her. 'Tell me. Last hope for what?'

'Last hope . . .' She sighs, and it rattles in her throat. 'Of finding someone that'll believe I'm not just bad luck,' she whispers. 'That'll believe The Stranger is real.'

I stare at her, incredulous.

'*Believe* you?' I blurt. I yank a thumb behind me, indicating the bedroom and what's inside. 'Sarah, I know something happened here that you didn't have anything to do with. And I'm willing to listen to whatever you have to say.'

I think she's caught off guard by the fact that my response comes as such a reflex action and that I seem so genuinely astonished at the idea of *not* taking her seriously. Hope lights up her eyes and wars with that terrible cynicism. Her face twists, her mouth wrenches. She looks like a fish drowning in the air.

'*Really?*' she asks in an agonized whisper.

'*Really.*' I pause. 'Sarah, I don't understand what's happened to you up to this point. But from what I've seen so far, the person responsible for this had to be strong. Stronger than you. Or me, for that matter.'

A kind of fearful wonder runs through her eyes. 'Did he . . .' Her lower lip trembles. 'Do you mean that you can *tell* he was here?'

'Yep.'

Is that so?

But there's another possibility, yes? Maybe she made the father do all the heavy lifting at gunpoint. She could still be the one.

I dismiss the thought with an imaginary wave of my hand.

Too advanced, too dark. She's too young to have honed her tastes to that degree.

'Maybe,' Sarah whispers, more to herself than me. 'Maybe he screwed up this time.'

Her face crumples, then smoothes back out, crumples, then smoothes back out. Hope and despair battle for the steering wheel. She drops the gun. She brings her hands to her face. A moment later, that raw, naked anguish again. It bursts from her, piercing, primal, terrible, pure. The sound of a rabbit in the jaws of a wolf.

I grab the gun from the carpet, say 'Thank God' to myself once, safety it, and stuff it into the waist of my jeans. I grab Sarah as she shrieks, and stuff her into the space between my arms and my chest.

Her grief is a hurricane. It pounds against me.

I hold her tight, and we ride out the storm.

I rock and croon and say wordless things and feel helpless and miserable and yet relieved.

Better crying than dead.

When it's over, I'm soaked with tears. Sarah clings to me, semi-boneless. She's exhausted.

In spite of this, she struggles and pushes away from me. Her face is swollen from crying, and pale.

'Smoky?' she says. Her voice is faint.

'Yes, Sarah?'

She looks at me, and I'm surprised at the strength I see, swimming up through the exhaustion that's pulling her down.

'I need you to promise me you'll do something.'

'What?'

She points down the hall. 'My bedroom is back there. In a drawer by the bed is my diary. Everything is in it, everything about The Stranger.' She grips my arms. '*Promise* me you'll read it. *You* – not someone else.' Her voice is fierce. '*Promise me.*'

'I promise,' I say without hesitation.

At this point, you couldn't keep me from it.

'Thanks,' she whispers.

Her eyes roll up into her head and she passes out in my arms.

I shiver once, an after-reaction. I unclip the radio from my belt and turn it on.

'All clear in here,' I say into it, my voice steadier than I feel. 'Send in a medic for the girl.'

10

Night has officially fallen in Canoga Park. The house is lit up by patrol cars and streetlamps, but SWAT is getting ready to leave and the helicopter has gone. The neighborhood is quiet again, though I can hear the sounds of the city just a few blocks away. Windows are lit up along the street, families are inside, every curtain is drawn. I imagine if I checked them, I'd find every door locked too.

'Good work,' Dawes said to me as we watched the EMTs load an unconscious Sarah into the back of an ambulance. They were moving fast; she'd started to turn gray and her teeth were chattering. Signs of shock.

'Thanks.'

'I mean it, Agent Barrett. This could have turned out a lot worse.' He pauses. 'We had a hostage situation six months ago. A meth-freak dad with a gun. He'd beat up his wife, but what really worried us was the fact that he was waving that gun around with one hand while he cradled his five-month-old daughter in his free arm.'

'Bad,' I say.

'Real bad. Add to it that he was high, I mean flying. You ever see a meth-freak when they're wigging out? It's a combination of hallucinations and paranoia. Not much for a hostage negotiator to work with.'

'So what happened?'

Dawes looks away for a moment, but not before I catch a glimpse of the grief in his eyes.

'He shot the wife. Without warning. He was jabbering away and then he just stopped talking mid-sentence, pointed the gun at her, and . . . *blew . . . her . . . away.*' He shakes his head. 'You could have heard a pin drop in the command van. Suffice to say, it forced our hand.'

'If he could shoot the wife without preamble . . .'

Dawes nods. 'Then he could do the same with the baby. Our sniper already had a shot lined up, and he got the green light and he took it. It was righteously accurate, dead in the forehead, no fuss, no muss. Perfect.' He sighs. 'Problem is, Dad dropped the baby girl and she landed on her head and died. That sniper shot himself a week later.' His look is more piercing this time. 'So, like I said, it could have turned out a lot worse here, Agent Barrett.'

'Call me Smoky.'

He smiles. 'All right, I will. Do you believe in God, Smoky?'

The question startles me. I give him my most honest answer.

'I don't know.'

'Yeah. Me neither.'

He shakes my hand, gives me a sad smile and a slight nod, and he's gone. His story remains behind, echoing inside me, a tale of impossible choices.

Thanks for sharing, Dawes.

I sit down on the curb in front of the house and try to gather myself. Callie and Alan are both on their cell phones. Callie finishes and comes over, plopping down next to me.

'Good news, honey-love. I called Barry Franklin, and he agreed, after much grumbling, to ask for this case. He'll be here shortly.'

'Thanks,' I say.

Homicides, with some exceptions, are not federal crimes. I'm not allowed to walk into a jurisdiction and take over a murder just because I feel like it. Everything we do involves and requires liaison with the locals to be on the up-and-up. Like most agents (and local cops) I prefer to engineer my 'liaison relationships.' This is where Barry comes in. Barry is a homicide detective for the LAPD, one of the elite few to reach the rank of Detective First Grade. If he wants a case, it's his.

I met him on the very first case I had as a unit head in Los Angeles. A crazy young man was torching homeless people and taking their feet for trophies. Barry had asked the Bureau to help with a profile. Neither of us had cared about politics or credit. We just wanted to catch the bad guy and we did.

The pragmatic end of things: He's an excellent investigator, he won't deny me access to the crime scene, and if I ask him nicely, he'll utter the magic words, *request for assistance*. Those words open the door to full and unfettered involvement on our part. Until then, we are legally no more than observers.

'How are you doing, honey-love?' Callie asks.

I rub my face with my hands. 'I'm supposed to be on vacation, Callie. The whole thing in there . . .' I shake my head. 'It was surreal. And fucked up. The day started out great. Now I feel crappy and . . . yuck. Too many messy cases in a row.'

People think every murder is a bad one, and while they're technically right, horror comes in degrees. The gutting of an entire family is a jolt.

'You need a dog,' she says.

'I need a good laugh,' I reply, forlorn.

'Just one?'

I give her a wry smile. 'Nope. I need something on a *trend*. A *series* of good laughs. I need to wake up and smile, and then I need to do it again the next day, and again the day after that. *Then* I can have a shitty day, and it won't feel so bad.'

'True,' she muses. '"Into every life a little rain," and all that – but you've taken it to a new level.' She pats my hand. 'Get a dog.'

I laugh, as she'd intended.

Quantico, Quantico, a voice sings inside my head. No Sarahs, no up close and personal, no clangy-jitters there.

Alan heads toward us, still talking on his cell phone. When he gets to us, he holds the phone away from his ear. 'Elaina wants to know the outlook on tonight. As far as Bonnie goes.'

I think it through. I need Barry to arrive. I need him to get his Crime Scene Unit onto processing the house. I need to go through the home and soak in the scene.

It isn't officially ours yet, but I'm not willing to just walk away. I sigh.

'It's going to be a late one. Can you ask her if she minds taking Bonnie for the night?'

'No problem.'

'Tell Elaina I'll be in touch tomorrow.'

He puts the phone to his ear and walks away, delivering the news.

'What about me?' Callie asks.

I give her a tired grin. 'You get to work on your vacation, just like me. We're going to meet Barry, check things out . . .' I shrug. 'And then we'll see. Maybe it will be back to vacation-time, maybe not.'

She sighs, an overdramatic, long-suffering sigh. 'Slave driver,' she mutters. 'I want a raise.'

'I want world peace,' I reply. 'Disappointment abounds. Get used to it.'

'Bonnie's covered,' Alan says as he returns. 'So what's the plan of action here?'

Time to take command.

This is my primary function, above all others. I run a group, really, of luminaries. Everyone has an area they shine in. Callie is a star when it comes to forensics. Alan is a legend in the interrogation room, and he's the best there is when it comes to beating feet and canvassing an area. He's tireless and he misses nothing. You don't get people like that to follow you because they like you. They have to respect you. It requires just a touch of arrogance. You have to be willing to acknowledge your own strengths, to be a star in your own area and know it.

Where I excel is in the understanding of those we hunt. In *seeing* a scene, not just looking at it. Anyone can walk through a murder site and observe a body. All the skill is in the reverse-engineering. Why that body? Why here? What does that say about the killer? Some are skilled at it. Some are very skilled. I'm gifted, and just arrogant enough to acknowledge it.

My personal talent in my chosen field is my ability to understand the darkness that makes up the men I hunt.

Lots of people think they understand the mind of serial killers. They read their true-crime books, perhaps they steel themselves and give a series of gory crime photos an unblinking eye. They talk about predators, the psychosexuality of it all, and they feel enlightened.

All of that is fine, there's nothing wrong with it – but they miss the boat by a mile.

I tried to explain this once in a lecture. Quantico was doing their version of career day, and various guest speakers were giving command performances to rooms full of bright young trainees. My turn came and I stared out at them, at their youth and hope, and tried to explain what I was talking about.

I told them about a famous case in New Mexico. A man and his girlfriend had spent years hunting and capturing women. They would bring the abductees into a specially equipped room, filled with restraints and instruments of torture. They'd spend days and weeks raping and torturing their victims. They videotaped most of what they did. One of their favorite implements was a cattle prod.

'There is video,' I'd said, 'where you can see smoke pouring out of a young woman's vagina because they used a cattle prod to penetrate her.'

Just this, this tiny bit of information, far from the worst available, silences the room and turns some of those young faces white.

'One of our agents, a woman, had the job of making a series of detailed drawings of all the whips and chains and saws and sex toys and other perversities that this couple had used on the women they'd brought into that room. She did her job. She spent four days doing it. I've seen the drawings and they were good. They were used in court, actually. Her superior praised her and told her to take a few days off. To go home, see her family, clear her head.' I had paused, letting my eyes roam over all those young faces. 'She went home and spent the day with her husband and her little girl. That night, while they were asleep, she crept downstairs, got her service pistol out of the gun safe, and shot herself in the head.'

There had been a few gasps. There had been a lot of silence.

I had shrugged. 'It would be easy to take that strong young woman and classify her and not think anything more about it. We could call her weak, or say that she must have already been depressed, or decide that something else was going on in her life that no one knew about. And you're welcome to do that. All I can tell you is that she'd been an agent for eight years. She'd had a spotless record and had no history of mental illness.' I'd shaken my head. 'I think she looked too much, went out too far, and got lost. Like a boat on the ocean with the shore nowhere in sight. I think this agent found herself floating on that boat and couldn't figure out a way to get back.' I had leaned forward on the podium. 'And that's what I do, what my team does: We look. We look and we don't turn away, and we hope that we can deal with that.'

The administrator running the program hadn't been all that happy with my talk. I hadn't cared. It was the truth.

I wasn't mystified by the act of that female agent. It wasn't the seeing that was the problem, not really. The problem was the *un-seeing* and the *stop seeing*. You had to be able to go home and turn off the images that wanted to giggle through your mind, all sly feet and whispers. This agent hadn't been able to do that. She'd put a bullet in her head so she could. I empathized.

I guess that's what I was trying to tell those fresh-scrubbed faces: This isn't fun. It's not titillating, or challenging, or a roller-coaster scare.

It's something that must be done.

It's my gift, or my curse, to understand the desires of serial killers. To know why they feel the way they do. To feel them feeling it, just a little, or just a lot. It's something that happens inside me, something based in part on training and observation, based in greater part on a willingness to become intimate with them. They sing to themselves, a song only they can hear, and you have to listen the way they listen if you want to hear the tune. The tune's important; it dictates the dance.

The most important component is thus the most unnatural act: I don't turn away. I lean in for a closer look. I sniff them to catch their scent. I touch them with the tip of my tongue to catch their flavor. It has helped me capture a number of evil men. It's also given me nightmares and moments where I wondered at my own hungers: Were they mine? Or had I just understood too *much*?

'Barry is coming,' I tell Alan. 'It's his scene. It may not become ours, but let's proceed as if it's going to be. Callie, I want you to walk the scene with me. I need your forensic eyes. Alan, I want you to re-canvass the neighborhood. Barry won't have a problem with that. Let's find out what the neighbors know.'

'You got it,' he replies, pulling out a small notepad from his inside jacket pocket. 'Ned and I will dig in.'

Alan has always called his notepad 'Ned.' He told me his original mentor said the notepad was a detective's best friend, and that a friend should have a name. He'd demanded that Alan come up with one, and thus Ned was born. The mentor was long gone, the name was forever. I think it's a form of superstition, Alan's version of a baseball player's lucky socks.

Callie squints at a black Buick that has just been let past the cordon lines. 'Is that Barry?' she asks.

I stand up, and recognize Barry's heavy, bespectacled face through the windshield. I feel a kind of relief run through me. Now I could *do* something.

*

'I'd give you a hard time about the date you pulled me away from,' Barry says as we approach, 'but you look like you're having a shitty night yourself.'

Barry is in his early forties. He's heavy without being fat, he's bald, he wears glasses, and he has one of the more homely faces I've seen – the kind of homely that becomes cute in the right light. In spite of these handicaps, he's always dating pretty, younger women. Alan calls it the 'Barry phenomenon.' Supreme confidence, without being arrogant. He's funny, smart, and larger than life. Alan thinks a lot of women find that combination of self-assurance and a big heart irresistible.

I think that's just a part of it. There's a hint of unyielding strength in Barry that rolls through all that amiability like thunder in the distance. He's seen it all, he knows that evil is a *real* thing. Barry is a hunter of men, and at some level, right or wrong, that's always going to be sexy in an animal-scent kind of way.

I know his grumbling is all for show; we've lost track of who really owes a favor to whom, and in truth, neither of us really cares.

'Anyway,' he says, pulling out a notepad, his own Ned, ready now to get down to business. 'What have you got for me?'

'Ritual slaughter. Evisceration. An ocean of blood. The usual,' I say.

I fill him in on what I know. It isn't much, but it begins the back-and-forth rapport that works so well for us. We'll walk the scene and talk as we go, bouncing observations off each other, honing our conclusions. It might seem aimless to an observer, but it's method, not madness.

'Three dead?' he asks.

'Three that I saw, and I'm pretty sure that's it. Patrol cleared the house, and they didn't mention any other bodies.'

He nods, tapping his pen on the notepad. 'You're sure the girl didn't do it?'

'No way,' I say, emphatic. 'She didn't have enough blood on her. You'll see what I mean when we go inside. It's . . . messy. I'm also fairly certain that one of them was killed downstairs and then carried into the bedroom. Carried, not dragged. She doesn't have the strength for that.'

He looks toward the house, thinking. He shrugs. 'Doesn't really play for me, anyway,' he says. 'The girl doing it. What you described sounds like advanced killing. Not to say that sixteen-year-olds aren't doing some bad things these days, but . . .' He shrugs again.

'I sent Alan off to interview the neighbors. I didn't think you'd mind.'

'Nope. He's the man when it comes to that stuff.'

'So when can we go in?' I ask.

I'm anxious now, reenergized. I want to start looking at this killer.

He glances at his watch. 'I expect the Crime Scene Unit here any minute – another favor you owe me. Then we can slip on our paper booties and get to work.'

I start outside the house. Barry and Callie wait, patient, listening.

I examine the front of the home. I look up and down the street, at the homes on either side. I try to imagine what it would have been like in the daytime.

'This is a family neighborhood,' I say. 'Crowded. Active. It was Saturday, so people would have been at home. Coming here, today, was a bold move. He's either overconfident or very competent. Not likely a first-timer. I'm guessing he's killed before.'

I walk forward, moving up the walkway and toward the front door. I imagine him, moving up this same path. He could have been doing it while I was shopping with Bonnie, or perhaps while I was clearing out Matt's master-bedroom closet. Life and death, side by side, each one unaware of the other.

I pause before walking through the front door. I try to imagine him here. Was he excited? Was he calm? Was he insane? I come up blank. I don't know enough about him yet.

I enter the home. Barry and Callie follow.

The house still smells like murder. Worse now, as time has passed, and the odors have begun to deepen.

We move to the family room. I stare down at the blood-soaked carpet. The CSU photographer is busy taking pictures of it all.

'That's a hell of a lot of blood,' Barry observes.

'He cut their throats,' I say. 'Ear to ear.'

'That'd do it.' He looks around. 'Like you said. No blood trails.'

'Right. But all of this tells us things about him.'

'Such as?' Barry asks.

'He likes what he does. Using a blade is personal. It's an act of anger, sure, but on another level, it's an act of joy. The way you kill a lover. The only thing more intimate is using your bare hands. It can also be the way you kill a stranger that you love. A sign of respect, a thank-you for the death they're giving you.' I indicate the bloody room with a sweep of my hand. 'Bloodletting can be intimate or impersonal. Blood is life. You cut the stranger you love so you can be close to the blood when it starts flowing. Blood is also a path to death. You drain pigs of blood pretty much the same way. Which way did he see them? As pigs, or lovers? Were they nothing, or everything?'

'Which do you think?'

'Don't know yet. The point is, however he viewed them, there wasn't any *doubt*. You don't kill with a knife if you're conflicted. It's an act of certainty. A gun gives you distance, but a knife? A knife has to be used up close. A knife is also evidence that the manner of death is as important to him as the death itself.'

'How's that?'

I shrug. 'A gun is quicker.'

Callie is walking around the room, looking at the blood and shaking her head.

'What's wrong?' I ask.

She indicates a dark puddle near her feet. 'This is wrong.' She points at another pool off to the left. 'That's wrong.'

'Why, Red?' Barry asks.

'Blood-spatter analysis is a mix of physics, biology, chemistry, and mathematics. No time for a detailed course here, but suffice to say that physics, blood viscosity, and the carpet material itself tell me these two puddles are likely here by design.' She walks closer to us, points to the much larger blood patch near the entrance to the family room. 'Note the lines here.' She leans forward, indicating a line of blood that widens as it moves away from us, ending in a somewhat rounded head with jagged edges. 'See how it almost looks like a giant tadpole?'

'Yes,' I reply.

'You see this all the time on a smaller scale. Castoff spatter produces a long, narrow stain with a defined, discernible head. The sharper end of the stain, or the "tail," always points back to the origin point. This is simply a larger version of that, and fits with someone getting their throat cut.' She points. 'You see it here, and here. And note the blood on the wall nearby?'

I look. I see more tadpoles, only smaller, along with a number of drops, big and little. 'Yes.'

'Think of blood in the body as contents under pressure. Poke a hole in the container and it flows out. Blood spatter is caused by the force of the flow outward, which determines speed and distance. Cutting an artery produces a lot of force. Smashing a hammer into a head creates a lot of force. However you slice it – pun intended – blood leaves the body, moves outward with greater or lesser force, until it impacts a surface, at which point it transfers that motion and energy to the surface, thereby creating a pattern against it. The results are your tadpoles, your droplets with scalloped edges, and so on, blah-de-blah.' She points again to the carpet and nearby wall. 'You can see evidence of arterial spray near the baseboard, and in the lines of blood on the carpet. Spontaneous motion, with directionality created by force. This is murder. Those other two are not. If I had to guess, I'd say that blood was *poured* onto both those spots. From a container of some kind. They are pools, not castoff or spatter. The directionality would have come from above, and the size of the pools, as well as the lack of spatter near their edges, indicate a leisurely pour. Very little force.'

Now that she's pointed it out, I can see it. The puddles in question are too orderly, too aesthetically proper, too round. Like syrup onto pancakes.

'So . . . he kills someone down here,' Barry says, 'and then . . . what? He decides he didn't get the room bloody enough?'

Callie shrugs. 'I can't tell you why he did it. I *can* tell you that those two spots came last. They're wetter than the kill-spot and more congealed.'

'Huh.' He looks at me. 'What do you think? The victim killed down here was the last to die? Or the first?'

'I think the last,' I say. 'When I arrived, the blood here was still fresh, while the blood on the walls upstairs looked dry.'

Something about the sliding glass door has caught my eye. I walk toward it.

'Barry,' I say. 'Look at this.'

I point at the latch. It's unlocked, and the door is open a crack. Hard to see unless you are right on it as we are now.

'That's probably the point of entry,' Callie muses.

'Get some shots of this before I open the door,' Barry says to the CSU photographer.

The CSU – a studious-looking guy I know as Dan – snaps pictures of the latch area and the door.

'That should do it,' Dan says.

'Thanks,' Callie says, smiling.

Dan turns red and looks down at the carpet, smiling but tongue-tied. I realize that he's been made speechless by a combination of his own natural shyness and Callie's formidable beauty.

'You're welcome,' he manages, before trotting off.

'Cute,' Callie says to Barry.

'Uh-huh.' He's distracted by his examination of the latch. 'Looks broken,' he muses. 'Definitely forced by something. I can see tool marks.'

He straightens back up and uses his gloved hands to open the door. It moves from right to left as we're facing it now. From the outside, coming in, it would be left to right.

A right-handed killer would probably have opened it with his left hand, as his right would have been filled with . . . what? A knife? A backpack?

We step through the door into the backyard. It's dark, but I can tell the yard is large, and I can see the shadowy outlines of a square-shaped swimming pool. A single medium-sized palm tree to the far left reaches for the night sky.

'Is there a light back here?' Barry wonders.

Callie fumbles around on the wall near the sliding glass door in the family room, looking for a switch. When she finds it and flips it, all the banter we've been using to distance ourselves from this tableau dissipates.

The switch had been set to turn on not just the yard lights, but the pool lights, as well.

'Jesus,' Barry mutters.

The light blue bottom of the pool combines with the underwater lights to create an island of shimmering brightness in the dark. The blood in the water stands out against this brightness, a suspended crimson cloud. It floats on the top, in places a mix of clots, pink foam, smooth oil.

I walk over to the side of the pool and peer into the water.

'No weapon or clothing in here,' I say.

'Lot of blood though,' Barry notes. 'Can't even see the bottom from some angles.'

I look around the yard. It's walled on every side by actual six-foot-high concrete and brick, a rarity in suburban Los Angeles. Ivy grows along the top and combines with tall bushes in this and adjoining yards to create tremendous privacy. The house itself may have been built to let the light in, but the backyard was all about keeping out prying eyes.

I think about the room upstairs, splashed with blood.

He took his time up there, I think. Playing and painting and having a ball. That would have been messy work.

76

'The killer *used* the pool,' I say.

Callie raises her eyebrows. Barry gives me a quizzical look. I realize that I'm a step ahead; I've seen the bedroom, they haven't.

'Look, he's doing this midday. It's a Saturday, so people in this neighborhood are home. Even more significant: It's a beautiful, sunny Saturday. People are out in their yards, riding their bikes, enjoying the weather.' I point toward the master-bedroom window. 'He played in the bedroom. Blood's everywhere on the ceiling and walls – but it's not spatter from the killings. It's there because he *put* it there. He would have been covered in blood. He'd have to wash it off somehow, and he wanted to do it here. Liked doing it here.'

'Why not use the bathroom inside?' Callie asks. 'Quite a risk, coming into the yard, don't you think? Privacy or not – he has to leave the house proper. Someone could come knocking while he's out here, or come home, and he'd never know it.'

'For one thing, it's smarter,' Barry says. 'He probably knows that we'll be checking the drain traps in the bathrooms. It's going to be a lot harder to find anything that belongs to him in the pool filtration system. And chlorine isn't exactly investigation friendly.'

I examine the pool. It's about twenty feet long and appears to be a uniform depth all the way across. A single set of steps leads down into the water. Glossy clay tiles surround it and form a deck.

'Tile is wet in places,' I observe.

'We need to get out of here,' Callie says, her voice sharp. 'Right now.'

Barry and I look over at her, surprised.

'*Why* is it wet?' she asks.

I get it. 'Because he walked around out here, probably naked, probably barefoot, and probably left footprints. That we'll probably destroy if we keep tramping around.'

'Right,' Barry says. 'Oops.'

'They're going to have to go over this entire area with an ultraviolet light,' Callie says. 'Inch by agonizing inch. Thank goodness that's someone else's job tonight.'

Trace evidence, including latent prints, semen, and blood, can fluoresce under ultraviolet light. Callie is right. If he was nude out here and walking around with impunity, this is a potential hot spot for evidence.

We move back through the sliding glass door, but continue gazing out into the yard.

'You said you think the pool was about more than washing away evidence?' Barry asks.

'I think . . .' My voice trails off. It comes to me the way it always does: swimming from out of some dark place, fully formed. 'I think he liked the fact that he could do something dark out in the open. He killed this family in the middle of the day, he all but bathed in their blood, and then he stripped down and took a nice, long swim while their bodies began to bake in an unventilated home. In the meantime, the people in this neighborhood held their kids' birthday parties and clipped their hedges and barbecued their steaks, not knowing that he was here, enjoying the day in his own way.' I look at Barry. 'The feeling of triumph must have been overwhelming. Like a vampire walking around in the daylight. This scene is about power and ownership. Confidence in coming here during the day, confidence in his use of knife as the murder weapon. It fits.'

'Sick fuck,' Barry says, shaking his head. He sighs. 'So, he does a few laps in the pool, maybe lies around listening to the neighbors while he pats himself on the back. The question though is sequences. You say the scene downstairs was fresh. I'll buy that, but how does it play? He kills two vics upstairs, creates a little abstract art with their blood, comes and swims, then kills the third victim? And what's Sarah doing while all this is happening?'

I shrug. 'We don't know yet.'

'I hate when they make me work for it.' He sighs. 'Hey, Thompson!' he bellows, startling me. As if by magic, the twentysomething uniform who had tried to prevent our entrance earlier today appears.

'Yes, sir?' he asks.

'Don't let anyone into the backyard unless the head of CSU says so.'

'Yes, sir.' He takes his place by the sliding glass door. He's too young. Still excited about getting to be here.

'Ready to see the bedroom?' Barry asks us.

It's a rhetorical question. We're sniffing the trail, making things happen, putting the picture together in our heads.

Get it while it's hot.

We leave the family room and head up the stairs, Barry taking the lead, Callie behind me. We reach the top. Barry peers into the room.

'Is it necessary for both of you to come in?' a critical voice asks. 'To tramp all over everything?'

This sourness belongs to John Simmons, head of this shift's LAPD Crime Scene Unit. He's crabby, crusty, and absolutely untrusting of anyone but himself when it comes to handling the evidentiary part of a homicide. These traits are forgivable; he's one of the best.

'Three, actually,' Callie says, moving forward so that he can see her too.

Simmons is not a young man. He's been doing this for a very long time, he's in his late fifties, and it shows. Smiles, for him, are like diamonds: rare, and only worn on the right occasions. Callie, it appears, merits one.

'Calpurnia!' he cries, grinning from ear to ear. He moves toward us, shoving Barry and me out of the way to embrace her.

Callie smiles and hugs him back while Barry looks on, bemused. I have seen this behavior before, and know its source. Barry does not.

'I did an internship under Johnny while I was getting my degree in forensics,' Callie explains to Barry.

'Very gifted,' Simmons says, fondly. 'Calpurnia was one of my few successes. Someone who truly appreciates the science.'

Simmons looks over at me now. His study of my scars is frank, but it doesn't bother me. I know the basis of his interest is judgment-free curiosity.

'Agent Barrett,' he says, nodding.

'Hello, sir.'

I've always called John Simmons 'sir.' He's always seemed like a 'sir' to me, and he's never disabused me of the fact. Callie is the only person I know of who calls him 'Johnny,' just as he's the only person I can imagine getting away with calling her 'Calpurnia,' the given name she hates with such ferocity.

'So, Calpurnia,' he says, turning back to Callie, 'I trust you'll watch over my crime scene? Ensure nothing gets trampled or touched that shouldn't?'

Callie raises her right hand, puts her left one on her heart. 'I promise. And, Johnny?'

She tells him about the backyard. He favors her with another fond smile.

'I'll get someone onto that directly.' He gives Barry and me a last, suspicious look before stepping aside.

We enter the room. Simmons heads downstairs to crack the whip, leaving us alone. For all his grumbling, he understands this part of it – the need to soak it in. He's always given me the space I need to do this, never crowding me or peering over my shoulder.

Now that I don't have my attention fixed on Sarah, I stop and really *look*.

Mr and Mrs Dean and Laurel Kingsley, as I now know them to be, fall easily into the 'fit-forties' niche. They are tanned, with good-looking faces, muscular legs, and a certain polish about them, a vitality I can still sense, even in these circumstances.

'God, he was confident,' I say. 'Not just in coming here on the weekend and in the daytime. He subdued two fit, healthy parents and two teenage children.'

Dean's eyes are wide and turning into the eyes of the dead, gray and filmy, like soap scum in a bathtub. Laurel's eyes are closed.

Both of them have their lips pulled back, reminding me of a snarling dog, or someone being forced to smile at gunpoint. Dean's tongue protrudes, while Laurel's teeth are clenched together.

Forever now, I think. She'll never pull her teeth apart.

Something tells me that this carefully cared for woman would have hated that.

'He would have used a weapon to intimidate them, and it wouldn't have been just a knife,' I say. 'Not threatening enough for so many victims. It would have been a gun. Something big and scary looking.'

From the collarbone down, it's as if they each swallowed a hand grenade.

'A single long slice on each of them,' Barry says. 'He used something sharp.'

'Probably a scalpel,' I murmur. 'Not clean, though. I see signs of hesitation in the wounds. Note the ragged spots?'

'Yep.'

He cut them open with a halting, trembling hand. Then he reached into them, grabbed hold of whatever he touched, and pulled, like a fisherman cleaning a fish. Standing over Mrs Kingsley now, I'm able to make out the middle third of her spine; key organs aren't there to block my view of it.

'Hesitation cuts are odd,' I murmur.

'Why?' Barry asks.

'Because in every other way he was confident.' I lean forward for a closer look, examining the throats this time. 'When he cut their throats, it was clean, no hesitation.' I stand up. 'Maybe they weren't hesitation marks. Maybe the cuts were uneven because he was excited. He might have come to orgasm slicing them open.'

'Lovely,' Callie says.

In contrast to Dean and Laurel, the boy – Michael – is untouched. He's white from blood loss, but he was spared the indignity of being gutted.

'Why'd he leave the boy alone?' Barry wonders.

'He either wasn't as important – or he was the most important one of all,' I say.

Callie walks around the bed at a slow pace, examining the bodies. She casts looks around the floor, squints at the blood on the walls.

'What do you see?' I ask.

'The jugular veins of all three victims have been severed. Based on the color of the skin, they were bled dry. This was done prior to the disembowelment.'

'How can you tell that?' Barry asks.

'Not enough blood pooled in the abdominal cavities or visible on the exposed organs. Which is the general problem: Where's the rest of the blood? I can account for place of death for one of the victims – the family room downstairs. What about the other two?' She gestures around the room. 'The blood in here is primarily on the walls. There are some blotches on the carpet, but it's not enough. The sheets and blankets from the bed are bloody, true, but the amount seems superficial.' She shakes her head. 'No one had their throat cut in *this* room.'

'I noticed the same thing earlier,' I say. 'They were bled out somewhere else. Where?'

A moment passes before we all gaze down the short hallway that leads from the master bedroom to the master bathroom. I move without speaking; Barry and Callie follow.

Everything becomes clear as we enter.

'Well,' Barry says, grim, 'that explains it, all right.'

The bathtub is a large one, made for lazing around in, built with languor in mind. It's a little over one-quarter full of congealing blood.

'He bled them out in the tub,' I murmur. I point to two large rusty blotches on the carpet. 'Pulled them out when he was done and laid them there, next to each other.'

My mind is moving, my perception of the connectedness of things picking up speed. I turn without speaking and walk back into the bedroom. I examine the wrists and ankles of Dean and Laurel Kingsley. Callie and Barry have followed and look at me with their eyebrows raised.

I point at the bodies. 'No marks on their wrists or their ankles. You have two adults. You get them to strip naked, you put them into a tub, one at a time, you slit their throats, one at a time, bleed them out, one at a time – does that make any sense?'

'I see what you mean,' Barry says. 'They would have been fighting back. How does he get it done? I don't think saying "Take a number, I'll kill you next" would've cut it.'

'Occam's razor,' I reply. 'The simplest answer: They *weren't* fighting back.'

Barry frowns, perplexed, and then his face clears and he nods. 'Right,' he says. 'They were out cold. Maybe drugged.' He makes another note on his pad. 'I'll have them look for that during autopsy.'

'You know,' I say, shaking my head, 'if that's true, then that makes three bodies he had to carry, including one he'd had to have moved up the stairs.' I look at Barry. 'How tall would you say Mr Kingsley is? Six feet?'

'Six or six-one.' He nods. 'Probably weighs one-ninety.'

I whistle. 'He'd have to muscle Kingsley into the tub, drugged . . .' I shake my head. 'He's either tall or strong or both.'

'Helps.' Barry nods. 'We're not looking for a little guy.'

'Of course, there could have been two of them,' Callie says, glancing at me. 'We know about tag teams, don't we?'

She's right. Partnerships in murder are not uncommon. My team and I have chased more than one twisted killing club.

'No visible evidence of sexual violation,' Barry notes, 'but that doesn't mean much. We won't know for sure until the medical examiner gets a good look at the bodies.'

'Have them check the boy first,' I say.

Barry raises a single eyebrow at me.

'He wasn't gutted.' I point to Michael's body. 'And he's clean. I think the killer washed him, postmortem. It looks like he combed his hair. It might not have been sexual – but there was something going on there. Less anger at Michael, for whatever reason.'

'Gotcha,' Barry says, jotting in his notepad.

I gaze around the room, at the streaks of blood on the walls and ceilings. In some places it seems splashed, like an artist had tossed a can of paint onto a blank canvas. But there are intricacies as well. Curls and symbols. Streaks. The most obvious thing about it is that it is everywhere.

'The blood is key to him,' I murmur. 'And the disembowelment. There's no evidence of torture on any of the victims, and they were bled out prior to being cut open. Their pain wasn't important to him. He wanted what was inside. Especially the blood.'

'Why?' Barry asks.

'I can't say. There's too many possible paradigms when it comes to blood. Blood is life, you can drink blood, you can use blood to tell the future – take your pick. But it's important.' I shake my head. 'Strange.'

'What?'

'Everything I've seen so far points to a disorganized offender. The mutilation, the blood painting. Disorganized offenders are chaotic. They have trouble planning and they get caught up in the moment. They lose control.'

'So?'

'So how is it that the boy wasn't gutted and Sarah is still alive? It doesn't fit.'

Barry gives me a considering look. Shrugs.

'Let's go see her room,' he says. 'Maybe there'll be some answers there.'

11

'Wow,' Callie remarks.

The reason for this soft exclamation is twofold.

First, and most obvious, the words written on the blank wall next to the bed.

'Is that blood?' Barry asks.

'Yes,' Callie confirms.

The letters are large. The slashes that form them are angry, each one a mark of hate and rage.

THIS PLACE = PAIN

'What the hell is that supposed to mean?' Barry gripes.

'I don't know,' I reply. 'But it was important to him.'

Just like the blood and the disembowelment.

'Interesting that he wrote it in Sarah's bedroom, don't you think?' Callie asks.

'Yeah, yeah, puzzle puzzle cauldron bubble,' Barry grumbles. 'Why can't they ever write anything useful. Like: "Hi, my name is John Smith, you can find me at 222 Oak Street. I confess."'

The second reason for Callie's 'wow' can be found in the décor. The memory of standing in Alexa's room earlier today comes to me by comparison. Sarah's room is about as far from froufrou girly-girl as you can get.

The carpet is black. The drapes on the windows are black and they're pulled shut. The bed, a queen-sized four-poster, isn't black – but the pillowcases, sheets, and comforter on it are. It all contrasts with the white of the walls.

The room itself is a good-sized room for a child. It's about half as big as the standard-sized 'kids' room' in most homes, perhaps ten by fifteen. Even with the large bed, a dresser, a small computer desk, a bookshelf, and an end table with drawers next to the bed, space remains in the center of the room to move around in. The extra space doesn't help. The room feels stark and isolated.

'I'm no expert,' Barry says, 'but it looks to me like this kid has problems. And I'm not just talking about a bunch of dead people in her house.'

I examine the wooden end table next to the bed. It's about the height and width of a barstool. A black alarm clock sits on top of it. Its three small drawers are what interest me the most.

'Can we get someone in here to fingerprint this?' I ask Barry. 'Now, I mean?'

He shrugs. 'I guess. Why?'

I relate the end of my conversation with Sarah. When I finish, Barry looks uncomfortable.

'You shouldn't have made that promise, Smoky,' he says. 'I can't let you take the diary. Period. You *know* that.'

I look at him, startled. He's right, I do know it. It goes against the chain of evidence, and at least a dozen other forensic rules, the violation of which would probably send John Simmons into some kind of apoplectic seizure.

'Let's get Johnny up here,' Callie says. 'I have an idea on how to handle this.'

Simmons looks around Sarah Kingsley's bedroom. 'So, Calpurnia. Explain to me what it is you're trying to accomplish here.'

'Obviously, Johnny, Smoky can't take the diary. My idea was to make a copy via photographs of each page.'

'You want my photographer to spend time – now – taking a picture of every page in the girl's diary?'

'Yes.'

'Why should I give this a particular priority?'

'Because you can, honey-love, and because it's necessary.'

'Fine, then,' he says, turning away and heading toward the door. 'I'll send Dan up.'

I stare after him, bemused at his instantaneous and complete capitulation.

'How was that so easy?' Barry asks.

'The magic word was "necessary,"' Callie says. 'Johnny won't tolerate wasted motion on his crime scene. But if something is needed from his team to clear a case, he'll work them for days.' She gives us a wry smile. 'I speak from experience.'

The diary is black, of course. Smooth black leather and small. It's not masculine or feminine. It's functional.

Blushing Dan the Photographer Man is here, camera ready.

'What we want is an image of each page, in sequence, large enough to be printed out on letter-sized paper and read.'

Dan nods. 'You want to photocopy the diary with the camera.'

'Exactly right,' Callie says.

Dan blushes, again. He coughs. This proximity to Callie seems to be overwhelming him. 'No – uh – problem,' he manages to stammer out. 'I have a spare one gigabyte memory card I can use and let you take with you.'

'All we need then, is someone to prop it open.' She holds up her hands, showing the surgical gloves she's already slipped on. 'That would be me.'

Dan calms down once he's back and safe behind his camera lens. Barry and I watch as he shoots. The room is quiet, punctuated by the sound of the camera firing and by Dan murmuring for Callie to turn the pages when needed.

I glimpse Sarah's handwriting and at last see a hint of femininity.

It's precise without being prissy. A smooth, exacting cursive, written in – *surprise* – black ink.

There's a lot of it. Page after page after page. I find myself wondering what a girl who surrounds herself with the color black writes about. I find myself wondering if I want to know.

This is a lifelong battle for me: the struggle to 'unknow' things. I am *aware* of the beauty of life, when it exists. But I'm also never *unaware* of how terrible life can become, or how monstrous. Happiness, in my estimate, would be an easier state to achieve if I didn't have to reconcile these opposing forces, if I never had to ask the question: 'How can I be happy when I know, right now, at this very moment, that someone else is experiencing something terrible?'

I remember flying into Los Angeles at night with Matt and Alexa. We were coming home from a vacation. Alexa had the window seat and as we'd come down through the clouds, she'd gasped.

'Look, Mommy!'

I'd leaned over and looked through the window. I'd seen Los Angeles below, outlined in a sea of lights that stretched from horizon to horizon.

'Isn't it pretty?' Alexa had exclaimed.

I'd smiled. 'It sure is, honey.'

It had been pretty. But it was also terrifying. I knew right then, at that very moment, that sharks were swimming down there in that sea of lights. I knew that as Alexa smiled and goggled, women were getting raped down there, children were being molested, someone was screaming as they died too soon.

My dad once told me, 'Given a choice, the average man would rather smile than hear the truth.'

I had found that to be true, in victims, and in myself.

It was all just wishful thinking, that hope of 'unknowing.' I would read the diary and I'd let that black cursive writing take me wherever it wanted to take me, and then I'd know whatever it wanted me to know.

The sound of the camera fills the room, startling me each time it goes off, like gunfire.

It's not quite nine o'clock when I head downstairs. John Simmons sees Barry and me and motions us over. He's holding a digital camera in his hand.

'I thought you'd be pleased to know,' he says, 'that we were able to lift a set of latent footprints from the tile. Very clean.'

'That's great,' I reply.

'Too bad there's no database to run it against,' Barry remarks.

'Even so, the prints *are* noteworthy.'

Barry frowns. 'How's that?'

Simmons hands over the camera. 'See for yourself.'

It's a digital 35mm SLR camera, with an LCD screen on the back so that you can preview the photos taken. The resolution on these cameras is significant enough these days that they are the primary tool used to record raised prints. The photo on the screen is small, but we can see what John is referring to.

'Are those scars?' I ask.

'I believe so.'

The sole of the foot is covered with them. They are all long and thin and horizontal, going from one side of the foot to the next, none of them lengthwise.

Barry hands the camera back to Simmons. 'You seen anything like that before?'

'I have, in fact. I've done volunteer work for Amnesty International on three occasions, assisting in postmortem examinations of possible torture victims as well as evidence collection from suspected torture sites. These scars resemble the kind created when the soles of the feet are caned or switched.'

I wince. 'I take it that's painful?'

'Excruciating. Done inexpertly – or expertly depending on your goal, I suppose – it can be crippling, but it is generally done to punish, not to maim.'

'These on both feet?' Barry asks.

'Both.'

We're silent, considering this turn of events. The possibility that our perpetrator had been tortured sometime in his life was germane to his profile, if nothing else.

'It fits with the picture of him as a disorganized offender,' I remark.

Even if other things don't.

'Caning of the feet is rare here,' Simmons says. 'Its use is predominant in South America and parts of the Middle East, as well as Singapore, Malaysia, and the Philippines.'

'Anything else we should know about?' Barry asks.

'Not as yet. We'll be capturing the contents of the filtration system, of course, so we'll have to wait and see.'

Forensic handling of a crime scene is a process of *identification* and *individualization*. Individualization occurs when a piece of evidence comes from a unique source. Fingerprints are individualized to a single person. Bullets can, in most cases, be individualized to a specific weapon. DNA is the ultimate in individualization.

The vast majority of evidence can only be identified. Identification is the process of classifying evidence as coming from a common – but not unique – source. Metal shavings are found in the crushed skull of a victim. The shavings are examined and identified as a metal commonly used in making hammers. Identification.

The paths can cross. We have a suspect. We check to see if the suspect owns a hammer. He does. Marks on the victim's skull match the claw of the suspect's hammer *and* further investigation finds the victim's DNA on the edges of the claw. We fingerprint the handle and find only the suspect's prints on it. Identification and individualization, back and forth, conspiring to seal his fate.

It's a laborious process, one that requires not just technical expertise, but the ability to apply logic and connect the dots. I had observed the visible, the blood in the pool water, and surmised that our suspect took a swim. Callie processed this information, saw the wet tile, and led us to an invisible footprint.

The precision of Sherlock Holmes is a nice fantasy. The reality is that we are thinking vacuums. We suck up everything and then we parse it and hope we'll understand what we find.

I'm standing on the lawn with Barry, waiting for Callie to wrap up with Photographer Dan. It's been a long day, and the thinking vacuums are in there sucking away. Alan should be wrapping up soon. I ache to leave.

Barry pulls a pack of Marlboros from his front shirt pocket. My old brand, I think, wistful.

'You want one?' he asks, offering the pack to me.

I fight the omnipresent urge to accept. 'No, thanks.'

'You quit?'

'I'll have to live vicariously through you.'

'Hey,' he says, magnanimous, as he strikes a match. 'I'll even blow some smoke into your face, if you ask me nice.'

He brings the flame close, gets his cherry tip, and takes a deep, satisfying drag.

I watch him blow the smoke out. It forms a huge cloud that hangs in front of us, no breeze available to move it along. My nostrils flare. The sweet smell of addiction, yum, yum, yum.

'I'm gonna go see the girl in the morning,' Barry says. 'Be helpful if you came along.'

'Call me early on my cell.'

'You got it.' He puffs again, indicates the house with a nod. 'How do you see it so far?'

'A lot of it is confusing. The one thing that's clear is that there's a message behind his actions. The question is: Is it a message for us, or just for himself? Does he want us to understand what all that blood means, is that why he left the words on the wall? Was that a calculated act? Or was he doing it because voices in his head told him to?' I turn so I'm facing the house. 'We do know he's confident and bold and competent. We don't know if he's an organized or disorganized offender. We don't know what he fears, yet.'

Barry frowns. 'Fears? What do you mean?'

'Serial killers are narcissists. They lack empathy. They don't choose their method of death or torture based on what they think their victims will fear. That would *require* empathy. They choose their methods and their victims based on what *they* fear. A man who fears rejection from beautiful blond women kidnaps and tortures them with lit cigarettes until they tell him they love him, because beautiful blond Mommy burnt his penis with her menthols. That's oversimplified, but it's the basic truth. Method and victim are everything. The question I still need to answer is: Who was the victim here? Sarah or the Kingsleys or both? The answer to that will lead us to everything.'

Barry stares at me. 'You got some dark shit going on in that mind of yours, Barrett.'

I'm about to reply when my cell phone rings.

'Is this Agent Barrett?' A man's voice, vaguely familiar to me.

'Who's this?'

'Al Hoffman, ma'am. I'm on the hotline.'

The 'hotline' is what we call the LA FBI's 24–7 version of an answering service. They have the contact numbers for everyone from the Assistant Director on down. If someone from Quantico wants to talk to someone here, for example, and it's after hours, they call the hotline.

'What's up, Al?'

'I just got a weird anonymous call for you.'

My hackles go up.

'Male or female?'

'Male. Voice was muffled, like he was holding something over the mouthpiece.'

'What did he say?'

'He said, quote: "Tell the bitch with the scars that there's been another killing, and that this place equals justice." He gave me an address in Granada Hills.'

I'm silent.

'Agent Barrett?'

'Did you get a trace on the number, Al?'

This question is a formality. The hotline had automatic tracing installed post 9/11, but that's supposed to be classified information.

'It's a cell phone. Probably cloned, stolen, or untraceable disposable.'

'Give me the number anyway. And the address, please.'

He reads off the address. I thank him and hang up.

'What's going on?'

I tell Barry about the call.

He stares at me for a moment. 'Fuck and shit and all the rest!' he exclaims. 'You kidding me? You think it's for real?'

'"This place equals justice"? That's too close, too coincidental. It's for real.'

'This nut really knows how to ruin a Saturday night,' he mutters. He tosses his cigarette into the street. 'Lemme tell Simmons I'm leaving. You grab Red and I guess we'll go and see what the difference between pain and justice is for this guy.'

Alan is still nowhere to be seen. I call him on his cell phone.

'I'm three doors down eating cookies with Mrs Monaghan,' he says. 'A very nice lady who also volunteers with the neighborhood watch.'

Alan is inhumanly patient when it comes to witness interviews. Unfazeable. His 'nice lady who volunteers with the neighborhood watch' probably translates to 'cranky, nosy woman who watches everybody with a sharp eye and talks about them with an even sharper tongue.'

I fill him in on the phone call from the hotline.

'Want me to come with?' he asks.

'No, you and Ned eat your cookies and finish the canvass.'

'We will, but call me and let me know what happened. And be careful.'

I consider using the same 'If I was going to be careful, I wouldn't be going' quip I'd given Dawes but decide against it. Alan's voice sounds too serious.

'I will be,' I reply instead.

12

We've taken the 118 freeway heading east. The road is half-packed, neither busy nor deserted, the constant state of freeways in Los Angeles.

I feel tense and crabby and dark. This day continues to fall farther and farther down the rabbit hole.

'Why you?' Callie asks, startling me from my self-pity party.

'Why me what?'

'Why did Mr Bad Man call you?'

I consider this.

'It could have been planned, I suppose, but I don't think so. I think he was there.'

'Come again?'

'I think he was there. Watching. He saw us arrive and he recognized me.'

It's a staple of profiling and criminal investigation that perpetrators will return to the scene of a crime. The reasons are myriad. To find out how the investigation is going. To relive the experience. To feel powerful.

'I think he always planned to tell us about the second crime scene. He decided to hang around, see what happened, and call it in. It just happened to be us.'

'So he recognized you.'

'Unfortunately.' I sigh.

'Barry's signaling to exit.'

Barry knows the area we're going to, an apartment complex.

'Not a total shit hole, but not a great place either,' he'd said. 'I caught a suicide there about four years ago.'

I follow and we turn right onto Sepulveda Boulevard. Things become busier here than on the freeway. It's Saturday night, and people have places to go, things to do, the hamster wheel of life.

'I wonder if this scene will be fresher than the last one,' she says. 'Do you think he's going on a spree? Making a night of it?'

'I really don't know, Callie. This guy is puzzling. He guts a family, but he leaves the boy alone and Sarah gets to live. He paints the room with their blood, but he plans well enough to drug them. On the one hand he seems psychotic and disorganized, on the other he's purposeful and controlled. It's weird.'

She nods in agreement. 'Swimming in the pool was impulsive.'

Killers are human, and humans are complex. But over the years, we've learned that there are patterns to look for. All serial killers are driven by the compulsion to kill. The how and why of it can be worlds apart.

Organized killers, the Ted Bundys of the world, tend to follow a plan. They are the icemen, the ones with clarity. They're careful and cold-blooded until the moment of the act itself. They don't necessarily have a need to depersonalize their victims, and they can be consummate actors, blending in with the rest of us, their sickness undetectable.

Disorganized killers are different. They are the Jeffrey Dahmers, the Son of Sams. They have difficulty assimilating with others. They often trouble their neighbors or coworkers with odd behavior. It's hard for them to control their compulsions and they thus find it difficult to stick to any long-term plan. In the methodology of the disorganized killer you find victims of opportunity and over-the-top mutilations. This is the realm of on-site cannibalism, of women with their breasts or genitals ripped away.

Of a husband and a wife, gutted like deer.

Full-blown disembowelment represents a frenzy. It would be very unusual for a killer in that state to be able to *make* the choice to keep Sarah alive. And yet he did.

'He seems to have a plan,' Callie says. 'Perhaps things aren't as they seem.'

'What Sarah said would seem to indicate that she was his intended victim. So why so much violence to the others? Things don't add up.'

'They will.'

Callie is right. They will, they always do. Serial killers may not always get caught, but they are never – ever – original, not when you get down to the basics of what makes them tick. They might be cleverer than we're used to, or more horrifying, but in the end, they are all driven by compulsion. A pattern is inevitable. This is an absolute and they can't escape it, no matter how sane or smart they are.

'I know. So what's up with the pain and the pain pills?' I ask, blurting it out before really thinking about it.

Callie glances at me, eyebrow raised. 'There's an abrupt change of subject.' I make a right turn, following Barry. 'The doctors think it's a result of some minor nerve damage. They say it could heal, but they're not as hopeful as they had been. It's been almost six months, after all.'

'How bad is the pain?'

'It has sharp moments. That's not the real problem. It's the constancy of it. Low-key pain that never goes away is worse, in my humble opinion, than occasional agony.'

'And the Vicodin helps?'

I see her smile in profile. 'Smoky, we're friends for many reasons. One of them is that we only speak the truth to each other. Ask what you really want to ask.'

I sigh. 'You're right. I'm worried about the addiction end of things, obviously. Worried for you.'

'Understandable. So here's the truth: Addiction is inevitable. I imagine if I stopped taking them now, it would be difficult. In another three months, it'll probably be worse. The truth is, if this never resolves, I'll be on some form of pain medication forever, which will mean the end of my career. So, Smoky my friend, you're right to be worried, and you're not alone in worrying. I give you permission to ask me about it once a month, and I promise to be honest about where things stand so you can make the right decisions. Beyond that, I don't want to discuss it, agreed?'

'Jesus, Callie. Are you doing everything the docs are telling you to?'

'Of course I am.' She sounds tired. 'Physical therapy is the main thing. I want to lick this, Smoky. I have five things in my life: my job, my friends, my daughter, my grandson, and my frequent, very satisfying sexual encounters. I'm fairly happy with that. Losing this job?' She shakes her head. 'That would leave a rather large hole. And that's about as much "me talk" as I can stand for now.'

I stare at her, sigh. 'Fair enough.'

I let it go, but file it under 'urgent.' Just another thing that'll never be far from my mind. I should report her and put her on desk duty, but I won't and she knows it. Callie is as ruthless with herself as she is with the truth of evidence. If she feels she's become a liability, I won't have to sideline her. She'll do it herself.

Of course, if I go to Quantico, the professional end of it won't be my problem . . .

Barry turns left onto another one of those quieter, residential streets. I follow him for a block, we turn left at a stop sign, and make an immediate right into an apartment parking lot.

'I see what he means about this place,' Callie remarks, looking through the windshield.

This is an old apartment complex of a type raised in the seventies, a two-story built around a courtyard with perhaps forty units. It's trimmed in brown wood, and the stucco over the concrete is dirty and cracking. The pavement in the parking lot is cracked, and there are no paint-lines to delineate the boundaries of the parking spaces. Two large blue trash Dumpsters are pushed up against the building. Both are close to overflowing.

We get out of the car and meet Barry.

'Nice, huh?' he says, indicating things.

'I've seen worse,' I reply, 'but I wouldn't want to live here.'

'Yeah, well, the courtyard used to be okay. What's the apartment number?'

'Twenty.'

'Second floor. Let's go.'

Barry's right; the courtyard is *okay*. Not great, but better than the exterior. It has a centerpiece of trees and grass, well kept up. All of the apartment doors face into the courtyard, two floors of them, forming one big square. You can hear the city here, but there's a degree of insulation. It was meant to be an oasis of privacy, but it was designed on too small and too cloistered a scale. It feels like a trap now, or a cage. Wagons circled against the coming, inevitable siege of the city.

'Apartment twenty is on the upper left corner,' Barry says.

'Take the lead,' I reply.

We un-holster our weapons and make our way up the stairs. I can see lights on in most windows. Everyone keeps their drapes drawn here; there's no other way to achieve any privacy. We reach the top of the stairs. The door to apartment twenty is two doors to our right.

Barry hugs the wall as he makes his way to the door, moving fast. We follow. He reaches out with his free hand and knocks, loud. Copknocking.

'LAPD. Open the door please.'

Silence.

Silence, in fact, all the way around. TVs had been on, radios had been playing. Now everything has gone quiet. I can sense the other residents, listening. Circling those wagons.

Barry knocks again, louder.

'Open up, please. This is the Los Angeles Police Department. If you don't open the door, we'll be forced to enter the premises.'

We wait.

Again, no response.

'Phone call gives us probable cause.' He shrugs. 'Let's see if the door is unlocked. If not, we'll have to dig up the manager.'

'Go ahead,' I tell him.

He reaches over and tries the knob. It turns in his hand. He looks back at us.

'Ready?'

We nod.

He flings the door wide with a single motion, moving to the right of it as he does so. His gun comes up in a two-handed grip. I fill the space on the left and do the same.

We're looking into a living room butted up next to a kitchen. The carpet is a medium weave, old and dirty, an unattractive brown. A black leather sofa sits against a wall in the small space, facing a cheap entertainment center housing a thirty-inch television. The TV is on, the volume down. An infomercial for some kind of business opportunity murmurs.

'Hello?' Barry calls.

No reply.

A cheap and battered wooden coffee table sits in front of the leather couch. I see various adult magazines spread across it, and what appears to be a jar of Vaseline. An ashtray, overflowing with butts, sits to the right.

'Smells like feet and ass in here,' Barry mutters.

He moves into the apartment, gun still at the ready. I follow. Callie comes in behind me. We see nothing in the kitchen as we approach it other than a ceramic-lined sink full of dirty dishes. An old-fashioned split-level refrigerator hums.

'Bedrooms are in the back,' Barry says.

It's a very short walk through a very small hallway to get to the bedrooms. We pass a single bathroom on the right. I see white tile, a white tub. It's small and dirty and smells of urine. Nothing to speak of on the counter around the wash-basin. The mirror is specked and unclean.

The bedrooms are situated next to each other. The door to the one on the right is open and I see what appears to be some kind of a home office. There's a computer on an old metal desk, a nineteen-inch flat screen monitor, and a bunch of shelves made from cinder blocks and one-by-six boards. The shelves are almost empty, filled with a few paperback books and adult videotapes. A bong sits on the top of one, a quarter-full of murky pot-water.

It occurs to me that this is a sad, strange place. The only things of value I've seen have been the couch, the television, and the computer system. Everything else is cheap and salvaged and time-worn, with a layered hint of seedy degradation.

'I'm smelling something now,' Barry murmurs, nodding toward the door to the other bedroom, which is closed.

I move closer and there it is: that cloying tang, pennies in my mouth.

'I'm going to open it,' Barry says.

'Go ahead,' I reply, gripping my weapon. My heart hammers away. Barry and Callie look as tense as I feel. *I* probably look as tense as I feel.

He grips the knob, hesitates for a moment and throws it wide. He raises his weapon in a single motion.

The smell of blood rushes out to greet us, along with the odors of sweat, feces, and urine. I see the promised words, on the wall above the bed:

THIS PLACE = JUSTICE

They seem proud and bold, almost joyous to me.

Below the words, something that used to be a man. Next to the man lies a girl, her skin an unnatural alabaster.

We all lower our weapons. The threat was here, but it has come and gone.

This bedroom continues the apartment's motif, small and sad. Dirty clothes lie on a floor in the corner. The bed is a double, consisting of just a mattress on a box spring on a metal frame. No headboard or baseboard. No chest of drawers.

On the bed is a naked man with his insides torn out. He's Hispanic. He's a small man; I put him at approximately five foot seven inches, and he's skinny – too skinny. He's probably the smoker. His dark hair is flecked with gray and I'm guessing his age to be somewhere between fifty and fifty-five.

The girl is Caucasian, and looks to be in her early to mid-teens. She has a pretty enough face, with dirty-blond hair. Small, pert breasts. Freckles on her shoulders. Her pubic area has been shaved. Other than the slash across her throat, she's uninjured. I note that her eyes, like those of Laurel Kingsley, are closed. She doesn't look like she'd be related to the man, and I wonder about her presence here, in this sad place with this older man and his coffee table decorations of girlie mags and Vaseline.

I wonder about something else, a more subtle similarity between this scene and the Kingsleys': The fact that he left both the children intact, while all the adults have been disemboweled.

He kills the kids but he doesn't mutilate them. Why?

'This area is too small,' Callie says. 'I don't recommend entering the room prior to CSU.'

'Roger that,' Barry says, holstering his gun. 'Definitely the same guy, Smoky, wouldn't you say?'

'Without a doubt.'

The man's face is frozen in a shout, or maybe a scream. The girl's face is calm, passive, which I find a lot creepier and a little more depressing.

'Well, Smoky, I'm officially overburdened now, and I'm officially requesting assistance.'

I force myself to turn away from the dead girl's too-bland features. 'You know what that means,' I say to Callie.

She sighs, a puff of the cheeks. 'I'll wake up Gene and we'll get going on this.'

Gene Sykes is the head of the LA FBI's Crime Lab. He and Callie have worked together in the past. They'll work together now to handle this scene, and I know they'll find anything that's there to find.

'Wait,' I say as a thought comes to me. 'What timeline do you see between this and the Kingsley murders?'

'Based on the state of the corpses, I would guess this scene is approximately a day old,' she says.

'So he killed here first, and then went right to doing the Kingsleys. Strange.'

'How's that?' Barry asks.

'Ritual serial homicide follows a cycle. Murder is the peak of the cycle. Depression follows the act. We're not talking about feeling a little down, we're talking deep, debilitating depression. And yet our perp killed here, woke up the next day, and murdered the Kingsleys. It's not impossible, but it's unusual.'

'Everything about this sucks,' Barry observes.

As Callie contacts Gene, I get a call from Alan.

'I'm done here. Everything go okay?' he asks.

'That depends on your definition of "okay."' I fill him in on the second scene.

'He did us the big favor.'

'The big favor' is our way of saying that the perpetrator gave us a second scene without us having to think about it first. Many times, the first scene we get simply doesn't provide enough evidence to lead us to a perp. In those cases, all we can do is wait for him to strike again, and hope he's more careless the second time around. Or the third. Or the fourth. It's disheartening and guilt-creating. 'The big favor' is sarcastic – and yet it's not. He's provided us with a second scene and we don't have to feel guilty about it because it happened before it was our responsibility. Everything from this point forward is on us.

'Yep. What did you find out?'

'Nothing. No one noted anything unusual. No strange vehicles, no strange people. But this is one of those neighborhoods. Middle of the middle.'

Alan is referring to a study he forwarded to me recently. It was an application of sociology to criminal investigation. It made a note of how changes in technology and perception of rising crime, coupled with economic factors, conspired to make our jobs harder.

Neighborhoods used to tend toward community. People as a rule knew their neighbors. The result, in terms of non-forensic investigation, was a more observant witness pool and an environment where the outsider stuck out as such.

Time marched on, things changed. Women went to work. The access to information about crime and criminals expanded as the reach of television grew. People began to realize that a neighbor could be a child molester, the high school quarterback could be a date rapist, and in general they began to circle the wagons.

These days, the study found, most middle-class neighborhoods – the 'middle of the middle' – lack that old sense of community. The vast majority of residents know the names of the neighbors on either side, but that's it.

Poorer neighborhoods, in contrast, tend to be more tight-knit. Wealthy neighborhoods tend to be more security conscious and watchful. The study concluded that the best place for a criminal to work was in the 'middle of the middle,' where every home was an island, and that in those neighborhoods, forensics were more likely to solve a crime than witnesses.

'Even so,' Alan continues, 'there was a birthday party just three houses down. Lots of kids and parents around.'

'Which tells us he doesn't stick out.' I consider this. 'He might have worn a uniform.'

'I don't think so. I asked, no one remembered seeing anyone from the gas, electric, or phone companies. On a weekend, that wouldn't have been the smartest move anyway.'

'It would stand out more than it would blend in.'

'Right.'

'He's so damn bold, Alan. During the day, when everyone would be home. Why?'

'You think it means something.'

'I know it. You don't take a risk like that without a reason. He likes messages and he was sending one by coming for them when he did.'

'What?'

I sigh. 'I don't know yet.'

'You'll figure it out. What's the game plan?'

'Barry asked for our help, so we're on it – but go ahead and go home. We'll pick this up again tomorrow.'

'You sure?'

'Yes. I'm going to do the same myself. I have too much information and not enough answers. I need space to think and forensics needs time to work.'

'Call me tomorrow.'

I exit the apartment. Barry is outside, leaning up against the railing. The sky is clear tonight; I can see more stars than usual. The beauty escapes me.

What's that smell? Oh, yeah – it's me. I smell of death.

'Made any sense of this yet?' Barry asks.

'No answers, just more questions.'

'Such as?'

'Connections. How do the Kingsleys tie in with the two corpses in there? What is it about the children, why doesn't he disfigure them? Why does he only close the eyes of the females? Why did he leave Sarah alive, and what's *her* connection to this scene? Is there one?' I throw up my hands, frustrated.

'Yeah. So how do you want to proceed?'

'Callie and Gene and company will process things here. You have Simmons at the Kingsleys'. We have Sarah to interview tomorrow, and we have the diary.' I stop, turn to him. 'I'm going home.'

He arches his eyebrows, surprised. 'Really?'

'Yes, really. My head's spinning, I kept a teenage girl from blowing her brains out and I've seen five too many dead people. My head's packed with information about our perpetrator, most of it contradictory. I need a shower and some coffee and then I'll take another look at it.'

104

He holds his hands up in a 'don't shoot' gesture. 'I come in peace.'

I chuckle against my will. Barry is almost as good at that as Callie is. Almost. 'Sorry. Can you do me one last favor tonight?'

'Sure.'

'Find out who they are. The man and the girl. Maybe it will help me figure some things out.'

'No problem. I'll call you on your cell. I'll also get some uniforms over here to assist with whatever.'

'Thanks.'

Callie comes out of the apartment.

'Gene and team are on their way, sleepy-eyed and grumpy.'

I fill her in on the conversation between Barry and me.

'Vacation-time is over, I suppose?'

'Long gone.'

13

How much life can you live in a single day?

I'm at home now, alone. Bonnie is spending the night with Elaina and Alan. It would have been cruel to wake her just so she could keep me company. I'm freshly showered and I'm sitting on my couch, facing a TV that's not on, my feet on the coffee table, staring at nothing.

I'm having trouble putting the day away.

It's a trick I had to force myself to learn early: how to leave a scene behind when I came home. How do you separate these two worlds, the dead and the living? How do you keep them from bleeding over into each other? These are questions every cop or agent has to answer for themselves. I wasn't always successful, but I managed. It usually began with forcing myself to smile. If I could smile, I could keep smiling. If I could keep smiling, I could laugh. If I could laugh, I could leave the dead where they lay.

My cell phone rings. Barry.

'Hey,' I answer.

'I have some information for you on the vics in the apartment. I don't know how it ties in with anything else, but it's interesting.'

I grab a notepad and pen from the coffee table.

'Tell me.'

'Male's name is Jose Vargas. He's fifty-eight years old and hails from sunny Argentina. He's not a solid citizen. He's done time for burglary, assault, attempted rape, and statutory rape.'

'Nice guy.'

'Yeah. He's been suspected but not convicted of pimping, pandering, child molestation, and animal abuse.'

'Animal abuse?'

'Of a sexual nature, apparently.'

'Oh. Yuck.'

'There was suspicion in the late seventies that he might be involved in human trafficking, but nothing ever came of it. That's what I know about Mr Vargas so far. He won't be missed.'

'The girl?'

'Nothing on her yet. No ID in the apartment. I did see a tattoo on her left arm that had some Cyrillic lettering on it, for what that's worth.'

'Russian?'

'Seems so. Though it doesn't mean she *is* Russian. One other thing. She's got scarring on the bottom of her feet. Same type we saw at the Kingsleys'. Newer, though.'

A brief surge of adrenaline shoots through me.

'This is important, Barry. The scars are key.'

'Yep. I agree. That's all I've got, for now, though. Callie and Sykes are going to town here. I'm heading back over to the Kingsleys'. I'll call you in the morning.'

'Bye.'

I lean my head back and gaze at the ceiling. It's covered with that acoustic 'popcorn' that was so normal at one time and is so despised today. Matt and I had planned to get rid of it but had never gotten around to it.

Scars, I think. Scars and children. These things are important. How?

Without an eyewitness or a confession or a video of the perpetrator committing the crime, we are left with one avenue: Collect everything, collect it as fast as humanly possible, and then examine it, align it, and attempt to understand it. Investigative

107

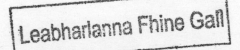

arcs shouldn't go wider and wider, they should become smaller and smaller.

I slide down so that I am sitting on the floor in front of the coffee table rather than on the couch. I rip pages from the notepad and lay them out horizontally.

It's time to organize my thoughts on this. I need to write everything down, put it there in front of me so I can actually *see* the connections in this case.

Across the top of one page I write: PERPETRATOR

I chew on the pen, thinking. I begin to write:

Methodology: He cuts the throats of his victims. This is an intimate act. Drains them of blood, and blood is important to him, representative. He disembowels the bodies of the adults postmortem. Possibly drugs them first to control them.

Behaviors: Doesn't mutilate the children, only the adults. Why?

Less anger at females than males, as evidenced by the fact that he closes their eyes. He wants the men to see it all, but not the women. Why?

Is he gay?

I think about this one. It's far too early and we have too few facts for me to make a decisive determination. But the mere fact that he goes easier on the women than the men is telling. Ritual serial murder almost always includes a sexual component, and the gender of the victims generally follows the sexual orientation of the killer. Dahmer was gay, so he killed gay men. Straight men kill women. And so on.

'You murder those who enrage and frustrate you,' an instructor once noted. 'Who better to incite rage and frustration than the object of your desire? Or,' he continued, 'to put it more crudely: When he closes his eyes and masturbates, what sex does he see – a man or a woman? The answer will be the gender of his victims.'

I nod. Something to think about. I continue with my notes.

Perp attacked during the day. Why take the risk? There's a reason for this.

Perp left Sarah alive.
Communicates with law enforcement. A Planner.
HE HAS SOMETHING TO SAY.

Message left at the Kingsley Scene in Sarah's bedroom:
This Place = Pain. Message left at the Vargas scene:
This Place = Justice.

(Note to self: Why 'PAIN' for Sarah, and 'JUSTICE' for Vargas? This is significant.)

Appears Disorganized.

I look at this line. Tap the pen against my teeth. I make a decision. I add some emphasis and two words:

APPEARS Disorganized — But Isn't.

(Theory: The disembowelment in this case is NOT indicative of a loss of control. It's a part of his overall message, as is the blood and the day-time attack.)

Conclusion: Perpetrator = Organized. Components that appear disorganized are simply a part of his message.

Occam's razor strikes again. An organized killer can appear disorganized at times. The reverse will not be true. He held himself to a script, demonstrated planning and control and resolve. Organized.

Known Characteristics: Soles of his feet are scarred. Possibly a result of torture (caning), which is indigenous to South America, the Middle East, Singapore, Malaysia, Philippines.

(Note: Vargas is from Argentina. Coincidence?)

Oh, yeah, I think, sarcastic. Coincidence. You bet.

(Note: Unidentified teenage female at Vargas scene had similar scars on her feet. What's the connection here?)

I remember something else from the Kingsley scene. I move back up to where I had written *Methodology* and add:

Evidence of hesitation cuts on Mr and Mrs Kingsley. Result of sexual excitement?

Uncertainty is the sign of a novice, a hunter who hasn't calmed down yet or found his stride. This doesn't fit the man I'm seeing in my mind. I don't think he hesitated; I think his hand shook because he was too aroused to control it.

He protects the women by closing their eyes, even though he still kills them and disembowels them. He kills the children but he doesn't close their eyes or disembowel them.

I read this paragraph again. And again. Something is tapping on the door of my mind, something that wants to be let in. I am familiar with this feeling and know I need to be quiet and let it come.

Why the gradations? Men are worse than women but women are worse than children.

The knocking stops as the door swings wide.

He has been hurt by men. He has not been directly harmed by women, but left unprotected by them. Both of these things happened to him when he was a child.

There is no proof of these conclusions, nothing to put under a microscope or up on a screen, but I know they are correct. I feel it. I feel him.

Men are the object of his fear and his rage. He leaves their eyes open so they can see everything that happens to them. Women die, and deserve it, but there's a nod to tenderness there in the closing of the eyes.

A mother, maybe? Who didn't protect him from an abusive father? If she was abused by the father as well, the killer would hate her and empathize with her at the same time.

The children aren't mutilated but their eyes are left open so they can *see*.

See what I did to him, see what the world does to us.

The girl at Vargas's apartment was a mix of the two, eyes closed but not disemboweled. Was this a reflection of her age? Almost a woman, still mostly a child? Did this confuse him?

What's it all about? Two sets of murders on back-to-back days. Hatred of men, anger at women, empathy for children. This place = pain. This place = justice . . .

A revelation appears, a rush of wind in my head. I blink at the realization.

I write it down.

This is about revenge. Revenge for actual wrongs, not imagined abuse . . .

Pain for some, justice for others. Both add up to vengeance. It fits with his victims and methodology.

I consider this, excited.

This is why he comes in the middle of the day. He's saying to his victims, to the objects of his vengeance, 'You're not safe anywhere. I can bring justice to you even when the sun is out, even in a home surrounded by strangers.'

Because justice is righteous, and the righteous are invincible.

He may or may not be gay, but the sexual component isn't in the present, it's in the past. He's getting revenge for abuse that was almost certainly sexual in nature.

Abuse by men.

My building excitement derails as it hits the unexplained.

What about Sarah? Why leave her alive and in pain as opposed to killing her? More relevant: Revenge is personal. What is Sarah's connection to him?

I accept that I have no answer for these questions. The rest still feels right.

Vengeance. This is his motivation, this is the reason behind his choice of victim and his method of murder. Sarah is just a puzzle piece I haven't found the fit for yet.

I think some more, decide there's nothing else I can add to this page for now.

Examine his victims.

I grab another page and write across the top:

VICTIM JOSE VARGAS:

Fifty-eight, originally from Argentina.
(Note: Find out how long he's been in the US and how he got here.)
Behaviors: Ex-con. Violent offender, including crimes against children.

I consider the obvious connection here. Had Vargas abused the perpetrator?

Suspected of human trafficking sometime in the seventies.

Manner of Death: Throat was cut. He was disemboweled postmortem.

Question: Was Vargas connected to either Sarah or the Kingsleys in some way? Or was Vargas connected only to the killer?

A lack of connection between the two sets of victims would indicate that the killer was finally starting on something he'd been planning for a while and hitting it fast.

Making a list, checking it twice . . .

Vargas appears to have continued to abuse minors. (Found with an unidentified female companion who was not of age.)

I consider the page, set it aside. I grab another and across the top I write:

SARAH KINGSLEY:

Adopted daughter of Dean and Laurel Kingsley (So what's her real last name?).
Sixteen years old.
Left alive by the Perpetrator. (Why?)
Says her birth parents were murdered. (Verify)

Addendum: Says her birth parents were murdered by THIS perpetrator.

Oddity: Claims the Perp has been stalking her for years.

I turn my gaze back to the ceiling. Sarah's importance is glaring and obvious. She's the only living witness, and she claims to have knowledge of the perp. She also represents a significant anomaly in the perp's behavior: He didn't kill her. He left her alive as part of his vengeance plan.

If what Sarah says is true, he's been at this for a good long while. He's not delusional, he's capable of differentiation of desires, and he's very, very smart. All bad for us. Planned vengeance killers are harder to catch than sexual sadists or ritual murderers. They aren't crazy enough.

But why the intimacy?

In vengeance murders, you generally see more anger than joy. It's about destruction. What I had seen at the Kingsleys' was an almost equal balance. The messages on the wall, the disembowelments, these were compelled by rage, they fit. The blood

113

paintings didn't. They were a sexual act. Memories to masturbate to.

That's just noise, I realize. The investigatory key is the vengeance motive. The other is an anomaly, but the human condition is filled with those. Interesting but not conclusive – or what we call probative.

I turn back to the page.

> Sarah asked for me at the Kingsley crime scene, but had already planned to contact me before it happened. (Why me?) Wrote a diary she claims is probative.

I can feel myself flagging. I want to continue, but I'm about to hit the end of my rope for today.

Concentrate. What's the assignment of resources for tomorrow?

> Barry and I to interview Sarah Kingsley.

> Callie and Gene to finish processing the Vargas crime scene.

> Get everyone a copy of the diary with orders to read it.

> It will have to wait till Monday, but we need deep background checks on Sarah and all victims. Find the connections!

I read what I've written, nod to myself, satisfied. We still have a long way to go, but I can see him now. I've begun to feel him, and that's bad for him. A muted satisfaction purrs through me.

Less than a day's gone by, and I already know why you do what you do.

I put the pen down and let myself go slack.

God, I'm tired. At more levels than just the physical.

My cell phone rings. I look at the caller ID. Tommy. Something in me lifts a little.

Tommy Aguilera is more than a friend, but less than a husband. Not just a lover, but not someone I need beside me, night after

114

night. Tommy is a possibility; that's the ten-words-or-less summary.

He's an ex–Secret Service agent who now works as a private security consultant. We'd met when he was still in the Service. I'd been investigating a case involving a California senator's son who'd decided he liked rape and murder. Tommy was assigned to protect the senator, who was pro-life and had been getting a ton of death threats. In the events that followed, Tommy was forced to shoot this Fortunate Son. My testimony saved Tommy from a political firestorm that could have ended his career.

He'd told me then to let him know if I ever needed anything. I'd taken him up on this six months ago, and afterward, something interesting had happened: I'd kissed him, and he'd kissed me back. Better still, he'd undressed me and had wanted me bad, scars and all. It made me cry and helped me heal. Matt was the love of my life. He was my soul mate. He was irreplaceable. But I needed a man to tell me I was beautiful, and to prove it with sweat, not words. Tommy had done this with gusto.

We sleep together three or four times a month. I'm busy, he's busy, it's comfortable. The perfect arrangement, for now.

I answer the phone. 'Hey, Tommy.'

'Hey. Thought I'd call you. Not too late, is it?'

Tommy gives new meaning to the word *laconic*. It's not that he's uncomfortable talking to people, or lacks a vocabulary. It's his way. He prefers to listen.

'Nope. I just got in, actually. I got called out to a scene.'

'I thought you had time off. Packing and stuff.'

Tommy knew what I was doing this weekend, and knew that he needed to stay away while I was doing it. His ability to understand this kind of thing was just another hint of the depth beneath his stoicism.

'I did, but there was a girl at the scene. She had a gun to her head and was asking to see me. I had to go.'

'Turned out okay?'

'It was bad, but the girl lived.'

'Good.' A long pause. 'I knew what you were doing today. Didn't want to intrude, but wanted to see how you were doing.'

Yes, I think, how are you doing?

I sigh. 'I'm doing crappy. Can you come over?'

'On my way.'

He hangs up.

Action, not words, Tommy's way.

Tommy knocks on the door and I let him in. He takes a look at me and leads me over to the couch without saying a word. He sits us down and gathers me up in his arms, and I sigh and lean into him.

There's no hair stroking or words of comfort with Tommy. Instead, there's strength and certainty, as if he's saying, *Whatever you need, even if it's just this.*

I stay there, head against his chest, and wonder at the feel of him. It's like lying against a rock encased in velvet. Tommy is somewhere in between rugged and pretty, a dark-haired Latin man with the lithe muscled body of a dancer and the rough hands of a killer. He's the male version of Callie; women are drawn to him like lemmings to a cliff, yearning to jump off into those dark and guarded eyes. He's no model – he has a large scar at his left temple, an imperfection that only adds to his appeal – but he is handsome to the bone.

He pushes me away, gentle.

'Want to tell me about it?'

I tell him. About the morning and afternoon and Sarah and the gutted bodies of Dean and Laurel Kingsley, the tub full of blood, the murders of Vargas and his as-yet-unknown companion.

'Gross,' he offers.

'Yeah. It got to me.'

He nods toward the notepad pages on the coffee table. 'That about the case?'

'Uh-huh.'

'Mind if I look?'

'Go ahead.'

He picks up and scans each page. Puts them all back down and shakes his head.

'Sounds complicated,' he observes.

'It always starts out that way.' I look at him, smile. 'Thanks for coming over. I feel better. A little.'

'No problem.' He looks around. 'So . . . where's Bonnie?'

'She's at Alan and Elaina's for the night.'

'Hmmm.'

I look up at him, see a small smile playing on his lips. I grin and punch him in the chest. 'Sheesh! All I said was I feel a *little* better, and you're already imagining me with my clothes off!'

Another small smile. 'Actually, I'm always imagining you with your clothes off,' he says.

Banter and playfulness, but I realize as I look at him that there's more to it than what's on the surface. Tommy likes to listen, and not just to what's being said. He listens with his eyes and with his mind, and he's been listening to me. He's offering sex *because* he's listened, and he knows I need contact, comfort, distraction.

I angle my head up, he angles his down, and our lips meet. My desperation makes the contact electric, and need surges through me, emotional, mental, physical, impossible to separate. I grab the sides of his head and stick my tongue in his mouth. I taste Tommy, with a dash of beer.

I move into him so that I'm straddling his lap. He moves a hand up under my shirt, under my bra, a single motion. The feel of his callused fingers on my nipple is exquisite. I moan, and feel him go hard against me.

One of the reasons I've always been a fan of sex is that you can mix the primal with the tender, you can get just a little bit *ugly*, a little bit *animal*, and have it all turn out okay in the end. If you're already feeling dirty and conflicted and a little bit savage, as I am right now, sex can keep pace, right beside you.

I pull my face back from Tommy's, still holding his head between

117

my hands. His fingers continue to knead my nipple, his cock continues to throb, and his eyes are clouding up with lust.

'Fuck me right here,' I say, my voice husky. 'Tear off my clothes, bend me over the couch, and fuck me now.'

He halts everything for a moment, the fingers going motionless, as his eyes search mine. He seems to find the permission-based-on-sanity that he needs.

He picks me up and off him, sits me down, and grabs my shirt, lifting it in a rough motion, bringing my arms over my head. The shirt comes off, is tossed aside, and he doesn't slow, reaching behind me, unsnapping my bra, yanking it from my shoulders.

He pauses for a moment, looking down at my breasts, and he pushes me on my back, and his hands grab and squeeze, rough without being painful, perfect, making me arch my head back and gasp. He brings his mouth to each one, sucking and licking just long enough to make me want him bad before he backs away.

Now he undoes the button of my jeans, pulls down the zipper, and yanks the jeans down my waist, down my legs, taking my panties with them. I end up with my legs spread, fully naked now, wet, feeling like Jezebel-squared.

His mouth comes down between my legs, and I come immediately, crying out, explosions shivering across my belly, down my thighs. Time gets rubbery, and the world gets vague, and I'm rolling around in the sensation of it all, shameless, Eve with the apple, a cat in heat.

His mouth leaves me, and he stands up, and I watch, dazed, as he undresses himself. When his cock springs free, I growl, and it's Jezebel-cubed, I'm reaching out for him as he slides on a condom. He grips my wrists, pulls me toward him, and then he grabs me around the waist, lifts me in the air, carries me over to the arm of the couch, and places me there, belly on the couch arm, hands against the cushions, ass in the air.

I feel him maneuvering behind me, and then he's inside me, one hand on my flank, the other gripping my shoulder, thrusting, fulfilling my request.

118

It's animal, it's primal. It's what I need: an irresistible force, a tidal wave, something to sweep over me, to drown me, and to take the corpses out to sea with it when it recedes.

I give myself over to it, and take what he's offering – guiltless sublimation. I have more than one orgasm as he works toward his own, and when it arrives for him, his fingers dig into me, as his whole body tenses, not enough to bruise, just enough to hurt a little, a brief, sweet pain.

Then it's over and we come apart, collapsing onto the couch, curling into each other, spent, satisfied, a little bit shaky.

Tommy looks over at me after a moment or two. 'Wow,' he says.

'Wow back.' I smile. I look into his eyes. 'Thanks, Tommy.'

'Anytime.' I see that smile tugging at his lips again. 'And I do mean *anytime*.'

I grin, kiss him on the cheek.

The shakiness of earlier is gone. I can still hear the dead whispering, but I have some distance now.

Tommy disentangles and heads into the kitchen. I admire his backside going and his front-side as he returns, a beer in hand for him, bottled water for me. He sits back down and we re-entangle.

I take a drink of water. Sniff the air. 'Smells like sex.'

'What's sex smell like?'

'Like . . .' I tilt my head and smile, the words coming to me. 'Like new sweat and a clean cock.'

He takes a swig of his beer. 'Racy and literate at the same time.' He kisses the back of my neck. 'Sexy.'

'Are you admitting that you love me for my mind?'

'Nope. I love you for your *behind*. I *like* you for your mind.'

'Ass.'

'What?'

'You said "behind." It makes you sound like a four-year-old. Say "ass."'

'Can't.'

I turn and look at him, arch an eyebrow. 'Are you kidding?'

'Nope.'

I search his eyes, realize he's really not kidding. I snuggle back into him. Giggle.

'What a Boy Scout you are, Tommy. I had no idea.'

'Eagle Scout, actually.'

I can't help it; I dissolve into laughter at this. The movement my laughter creates turns into something else, and Tommy shows me that he definitely got his sex merit badge if nothing else.

An hour later. We're each lying naked, backs on the carpet, feet propped up on the coffee table.

'I think that's it for me,' Tommy says. He sounds pleased about it.

'A bad day has to be good for something.'

'Speaking of that,' he says. 'I had a thought. Or two.'

I turn over onto my side so I can see him in profile.

'What's that?'

'When you described the scene. Bodies bled out in the bathtub. You know they'd still have to be alive for that, right?'

'Uh-huh.'

No blood flow when you're dead. The heart stops.

'But he still had to restrain them somehow. You mentioned drugs as a possibility. I think you're right. I'd bet he used some kind of a muscle relaxant. That way they'd know what was going on while it was happening. More thrill for him.' He shrugs. 'Just a thought.'

I run a finger through the curls of his chest hair. He's not a bear; there's just enough hair there to provide visual and tactile input when needed.

Tommy's right, I realize. I'd given him a bare sketch of the day, but from it, he'd extrapolated a sense of the doer, of the doer's hungers, of the *way* the doer hungers. I'd thought of drugs, but muscle relaxant as a specificity . . . it was worth considering.

When did you consider it, Tommy-mine? Before we had sex or after? During?

I'm ready again, and I only wonder why for a moment. Most

of the people I met today were dead. I'm not. Sex is a way to feel alive.

I move my hand down farther and grab hold of something.

'I'll check that hunch out tomorrow,' I say. 'Now I want you to dig deep, muster up that Secret Service training, and do your duty.'

He tweaks one of my nipples, puts down his beer, and we spend another hour or so proving that we're alive.

Exhausted. Spent. Happy.

'I had another thought,' Tommy says, breaking the comfortable silence.

'You sure seem to do a lot of thinking while we're having sex.'

'I do all my best thinking when I'm naked.'

'So?'

'There's a motivation that encompasses both *pain* and *justice*.'

'Yeah, I know.'

He raises an eyebrow. 'Really?'

'The oldest one of all,' I say. 'Revenge.'

'Thought I might have the jump on you with that one.'

I kiss his cheek. 'Don't feel bad. When exactly did you have time to think of that, anyway?'

He grins at me. 'Orgasms clear the brain.'

'So what you are saying, basically, is that this *came* to you?'

He rolls his eyes.

It occurs to me that I feel better. A lot better. I'd felt bad, he'd called, he'd come. We'd had sex and talked about work and –

I jolt inside as a whole new thought comes to me.

Oh my God – are we a couple?

It's an idea as strange and alien as it is comforting and familiar. One of the things about being married for many years is the feeling of security that develops, the certainty of knowing that you always have someone in your corner. If everyone else fails you, or dies on you, or betrays you, you always have that other person. You are never really alone. To lose that is to lose a part of yourself. The empty space in the bed itches in the night like a phantom limb.

Have we crossed that line? The one that says 'casual' on one side and 'couple' on the other?

'What?' Tommy asks.

'Just . . .' I shake my head. 'Just thinking about us. Never mind.'

'Don't do that.'

'What?'

'Don't think something and say it's nothing. You don't have to tell me what it was, but don't tell me it's nothing.'

I search his eyes. Find no anger there, only honesty, concern.

'Sorry,' I say. 'I was just wondering . . .' I swallow, once. Why is this so hard to get out? 'Tommy, are we a couple?'

He smiles at me. 'Is that all? Of course we are.'

'Oh.'

'Look, Smoky, I'm not saying it's time for us to move in together, or to get married. But we're together. That's how I see it.'

'Oh. Wow.'

He shakes his head in amusement. 'You were married for a long time. You're used to "together" meaning love and marriage. I don't love you.'

Something in my stomach tumbles and I feel sick. 'You . . . you don't?'

He reaches out, strokes my cheek. 'Sorry, I didn't mean that the way it sounded. What I mean is, I'll never say it unless I mean it, and I'm not ready to say it yet. But I can see a point coming where I will. If we keep going the way we're going, I'm going to wake up one day and love you. That's the road we're headed down. We're together.'

More butterflies now but not the nausea-inducing kind.

'Really?'

'Truth.' He squints at me. 'How do you feel about that?'

I snuggle into him. 'I like it,' I say, realizing it's true.

I do like it. Better, it's guiltless. I don't feel any disapproval from Matt's ghost.

But what about Quantico? Gonna make him fall in love with you and leave him flat?

It's another factor to take into account, I reply to myself, stubborn. More choices. Choices are good.

Except it's not that simple and I know it. I could hurt Tommy with what I decide. The simplicity of a 'new start' is an oversimplification of my life. I know that Alan and Callie and Elaina would back me to the hilt should I decide to take the position. Everyone would be sad, but the bonds there are too old and too strong. We wouldn't lose each other.

You can have a long-distance relationship with friends and family. Not with a guy who loves you.

Don't forget about your mute foster-daughter, your pill-popping friend, and 1forUtwo4me! Don't forget about a restless house you haven't finished packing away and a friend who just beat cancer and the fact that Matt's and Alexa's gravestones are here, not in Virginia. Who'll place the flowers?

'Know what I want?' I whisper, willing my ghosts away, for now.

He shakes his head.

'I want you to take me upstairs and help me sleep.'

He lifts me into his arms without a word and carries me up the stairs. We move past Alexa's room, but I don't think about that, and then we're in my bed, and he's got me, he's there, and I'm able to start drifting away, while he keeps me safe, my guardian against the dead.

14

'I talked to the hospital this morning,' Barry tells me as we walk through the parking lot. 'They said that the girl was treated for shock, and she had some bruising on her wrists and ankles, but that otherwise there's nothing physically wrong with her.'

'Well, that's something, I suppose.'

I fill him in on my thoughts of last night, including my theory regarding vengeance as motive.

'Interesting. What doesn't add up, though, is Sarah. If we cut her and the Kingsleys out of the picture, it makes sense. Vargas is into kids, has been for a long time. Maybe he likes torture too, caning their feet. One of the kids grows up, comes and kills him. It even explains why he went easy on the girl. Closing the eyes. No disembowelment.'

'Yes.'

'But Sarah and the Kingsleys? I don't see where that fits in.' He shrugs. 'Still, I do like the revenge motive.'

'Perhaps Sarah can shed some light on things.'

'Hang on a sec,' Barry says as we get near the entrance, nervous. 'I need a smoke before we go in.'

I smile at him. 'You don't like hospitals either?'

He shrugs as he lights his cigarette. 'Last time I was in one, I was watching my dad die. What's to like?'

124

Barry looks bleary-eyed. I notice he's wearing the same clothes he had on last night.

'Did you ever go home?' I ask.

He puffs a few times and shakes his head. 'Nope. Simmons didn't wrap up until almost seven A.M. I had to call in a couple of software experts too. They're still there.'

'Why?'

'The boy, Michael? His computer has some kind of super-duper protection program installed on it. They gave me the technical rundown, but it's over my head. Enter the wrong password and it wipes the hard drive clean. That part I understood.'

Hey, try 1forUtwo4me. You never know!

I suppress an eye twitch. 'Interesting.'

'It gets better. They say it's a custom job, very advanced, and – get this – they don't think the boy put it on the computer.'

'Why?'

'Too advanced. Something about the level of encryption provided. We're talking beyond military-grade.'

'It could have been put there by the perp then.'

'That's my thought.'

'It would make sense. He has something to say to us. That's why the writing on the wall at both scenes, why he called me to tell me about Vargas. He's telling us something, but he's doing it at his own pace.'

'I like it when they get all clever like that. It means they're ripe for fucking up.'

'Was anything else found?'

'We have the footprints and the computer. No prints, no hairs, no fibers. The feet are good though. We catch him, we can definitely get a match. Like I said – fucking up. Bodies went to the medical examiner, we'll see what happens there. Did you hear anything from Callie?'

'I haven't talked to her yet. I'll call her when we're done here.'

'Maybe he was dumb there too.' He takes another deep drag on his cigarette. 'About the girl. I don't have much yet, but here goes:

125

She's been with the Kingsleys for a little over a year, real name is Sarah Langstrom.'

Sarah Langstrom, I think, trying the name on for size.

'I checked for a record,' Barry continues. 'She was arrested for drug possession when she was fifteen – smoking a joint on a bus bench in broad daylight. Nothing else came up. I'll get her file from Social Services tomorrow.'

'She said her parents were murdered. When she was six.'

'That's great. I love a happy ending.' He sighs. 'How do you want to handle interviewing her?'

'Strictly straight and narrow. This girl . . .' I shake my head. 'If she feels like we're not being honest with her, or we're not taking her seriously – she'll stop trusting us. And I don't think she trusts us much anyway.'

'Fair enough.' He takes a final drag on his cigarette before flicking it into the parking lot. 'I'll follow your lead.'

Sarah has a private room in the children's wing of the hospital. Barry has a guard posted outside the door. Young Thompson again. Tired looking but still excited.

'Any visitors?' Barry asks him.

'No, sir. No one.'

'Sign us in.'

It's nice enough, as hospital rooms go, which as far as I'm concerned is like saying that it's the best one available at the Bates Motel. The walls have been painted a warm beige, and the floor is some kind of faux-wood. Better than white linoleum and institution-green, I admit to myself. There's a large window, and the drapes are pulled open, allowing the sunlight to pour in.

Sarah's in a bed near the window. She turns her head to see us as we enter.

'Aw, geez,' I hear Barry say under his breath.

She looks small and pale and tired. Barry is appalled. This is another reason I like him. He's not jaded.

126

I walk up to the side of her bed. She doesn't smile, but I'm happy to see less *deadness* in her eyes.

'How are you?' I ask.

She shrugs. 'Tired.'

I indicate Barry with a nod of my head. 'This is Barry Franklin. He's the homicide detective in charge of your case. He's a friend of mine, and I asked him to take on your case because I trust him.'

Sarah looks at Barry. 'Hi,' she says, disinterested. She turns back to me. 'I get it.' She sighs, her voice resigned and bleak. 'You're not going to help me.'

I blink, surprised.

'Whoa, honey. The local police are always involved. It's how things work. That doesn't mean I'm not a part of it.'

'Are you lying to me?'

'Nope.'

She stares at me for a few seconds, eyes narrowed and suspicious, gauging the truth of what I'm saying. 'Okay,' she says, reluctant. 'I believe you.'

'Good,' I reply.

Her face changes. Hope, mixed with desperation. 'Did you get my diary?'

I choose my words carefully. 'I couldn't take the original diary. We have rules about how we handle things at a crime scene. But' – I raise my voice as I see her face begin to fall – 'I had a photograph taken of every single page in it. Someone is going to be printing those photographs out for me today, and I'll be able to read them. Just as if they were the pages from your real diary.'

'Today?'

'I promise.'

Sarah gives me another long, suspicious stare.

There's no trust in this girl, I think. No trust at all.

What had it taken to make her this way? Did I want to know?

'Sarah,' I say, keeping my voice even and gentle, 'we need to ask you some questions. About what happened in your house yesterday. Are you ready to do that?'

The gaze she gives me is filled with too much experience, a kind of empty indifference I've seen before in victims. It's easier to be indifferent than it is to care.

'I guess.' Her voice is flat.

'Do you mind if Barry is here while we talk? I'll ask all the questions. He'll just sit away from us and listen.'

She waves a hand. 'I don't care.'

I pull up a chair next to her bed. Barry sits down in a chair near the door. More of our easy dance. He'll be able to hear everything, but he'll remain unobtrusive. It won't be hard for Sarah to forget that he's even there.

There's an intimacy to victim recollection. It's personal. A sharing of secrets. Barry knows this, and he knows that Sarah is going to be most comfortable sharing those secrets with me.

She's turned her head back to the window. Away from me, toward the sun. Her hands are folded. I see black nail polish on every nail.

Let's get this row on the shoad, inner-me says.

'Sarah, do you know who did this?' The key question. 'Do you know who it was that killed the Kingsleys?'

She continues staring out the window. 'Not in the way you mean. I don't know his name, or what he looks like. But he's been in my life before.'

'When he killed your parents.'

She nods.

'You said you were six when that happened.'

'June 6,' she says. 'On my birthday. Happy birthday to me.'

I swallow, stumbling inside for a moment at this revelation.

'Where did that happen?'

'Malibu.'

I glance at Barry. He nods, makes a quiet notation in his notepad. We'll be able to track down all the details of this earlier murder, if it happened.

'Do you remember what occurred back then? When you were six?'

'I remember all of it.'

I wait, hoping she'll elaborate. She doesn't.

'How do you know the man who killed the Kingsleys yesterday is the same man who killed your parents ten years ago?'

She turns to look at me, a faint expression of resignation and muted anger on her face. 'That's a stupid question.'

I regard her for a moment. 'Well, then ... what's a good question?'

'*Why* is he the same man?'

I blink. She's right. That's the most incisive question of all.

'Do you know why?'

She nods.

'Do you want to tell me?'

'I'll tell you a little. The rest you'll have to read about.'

'Okay.'

'He ...' She struggles with something. Maybe to find the right words. 'He said to me once, "I'm making you over in my own image." He didn't explain what that meant. But that's what he said. He said he looked at me and my life the way an artist looks at clay, and that I was his sculpture. He even had a name for the sculpture, a title.'

'What was it?'

She closes her eyes. '*A Ruined Life.*'

The scritch-scratch of Barry's pen pauses. I gaze at Sarah, trying to digest what she's just said.

Organized, I think to myself. Organized but driven by something specific and obsessive. Revenge is the motive, and destroying her is a piece of it. A big piece.

She continues talking. Her voice is a little bit faint and faraway. 'He does things to change my life. To make me sad, to make me hate, to keep me alone. To change *me*.'

'Has he ever told you why?'

'He said, when it all started: "Even though it's not your fault, your pain is still my justice." I didn't get it then. I don't get it now.' She looks at me, searching, inquisitive. 'Do you?'

'Not specifically. We think this is about some kind of revenge for him.'

'For what?'

'We don't know yet. You said he does things to change your life. To change you. What kind of things?'

A long, long pause. I can't tell what's moving through her eyes. I only know that it's sorrowful and huge and that it's not new to her.

'It's about me,' she says, her voice small and quiet. 'He kills anyone who is good to me or could be good to me. He kills the things I love and that love me back.'

'And no one's caught on to this before?'

She goes from calm tones to a low roar in an instant, startling me. Those blue eyes are blazing. 'It's all in my diary! Just *read* it. How many times do I have to tell you? God! God! God!'

She turns away, back to the sun once more, trembling and twitching and overflowing with rage. I can feel her pulling away, going inside herself.

'I'm sorry,' I say, soothing. 'And I promise, I will read it. Every page. What I need to know now is what happened yesterday. In the house. Anything you can remember.'

Another long pause. She's not angry anymore. She looks tired, right down to her molecules.

'What do you want to know?'

'Start at the beginning. Before he came to the house. What were you doing?'

'It was mid-morning. About ten o'clock. I was putting my night-gown on.'

'Putting it on? Why?'

She smiles, and that old hag Sarah keeps inside herself is back in full force, chuckling and ugly.

'Michael told me to.'

I frown. 'Why did Michael tell you to?'

She cocks her head at me.

'Why, so he could fuck me, of course.'

15

'You and Michael were having sex?'

I'm proud of myself. I've managed to keep my voice steady and judgment-free at this revelation.

'No, no, no. Sex is something that happens between two people that are equal. I was *fucking* Michael. So he wouldn't lie to Dean and Laurel and make them send me away.'

'He was forcing you?'

'Not physically. But he was blackmailing me.'

'With what? What had you done?'

She shoots me a look of incredulity. 'Done? I hadn't done *anything*. But that wouldn't have mattered. Michael was the perfect son. Straight As, track team captain. Never did anything wrong.' The bitterness in her voice is like acid. 'Who was I? Just some stray they'd taken in. He said if I didn't have sex with him, he'd plant pot in my room. Dean and Laurel were nice people, and they were good to me – but they didn't have much tolerance for anything . . . unusual. They would have sent me away. I figured I could hold out for another two years, till I was eighteen, and then I'd be a legal adult and I could leave.'

'So you . . . had sex with him when he asked you to.'

'A girl's gotta eat.' Her voice drips with sarcasm, and a hint of self-loathing that makes my heart ache. 'He just wanted me to blow him and he liked fucking me.' She looks down at her hands. They tremble in counterpoint to the hard face she's showing me. 'Hey, I haven't been a virgin for a long time. What's the big deal?'

'The Kingsleys didn't suspect?'

Sarah rolls her eyes. 'Please. I told you, they were good to me – but they *really* liked thinking that everything in their life was perfect.' She hesitates. 'Besides . . . they *were* good to me. I didn't want them to know about Michael. It would have hurt them. They deserved better.'

'So, you were putting your nightgown on. What happened then?'

'He showed up at my bedroom door.'

'Michael?'

'No, The Stranger. He just appeared there. No warning. He was wearing panty hose over his face, like he has in the past.' She chews her bottom lip for a moment, caught up in a memory. 'He had a knife in his hand. He was happy, smiling, relaxed. He said hello, acting all jolly and normal, and then . . . he said he had a gift for me.' She pauses. 'He told me: "Once upon a time, a man deserved to die. He was an amateur poet, this man, a gifted one. He made pretty words, but he was darkness inside. One day I came to the man, I came to him and I put a gun to his wife's head and I told him to write her a poem. I told him it would be the last thing she'd ever hear before I blew her brains out. He did what I said and I killed them, praise be to God. Once they were dead, I pulled their insides out, so the world would see their darkness."'

The message, I think. He disembowels them so that we will see who they really are.

I note the religious bent as well. Fanaticism in serial killers is nearly always a sign of insanity.

But not in this case. His faith wasn't sparked by his desire for revenge. It's something he grew up with.

'Did he give you this poem?' I ask. 'Was that the gift?'

'A copy, yeah. He said he retyped it for me. I put it in the pocket of my nightgown after he made me read it.' She nods toward the table next to her hospital bed. 'It's in the drawer. Go ahead. He was right, it's pretty good, when you consider the circumstances.'

I reach over and open the drawer. Inside is a folded square of nondescript letter-sized white paper. I unfold it and read:

IT IS YOU

When I breathe
It is you
When my heart beats
It is you
When my blood flows
It is you
When the sun rises
When the stars shine
It is you
It is you.

I'm a barely casual reader of poetry, unqualified to judge what I've just read. I only know that I like its simplicity, and I wonder about the moment in which it was written.

'It's true, you know,' Sarah says.

I look up. 'What's true?'

'If he says it happened that way . . . then it happened that way.' She closes her eyes. 'The Stranger told me that the ink on the original is smudged because the poet cried while he was writing it. It also has his wife's blood on it. "Beautiful pinpoint drops," he said, "because the blood misted from her head when I shot her."'

'Go on,' I say. 'What happened next?'

She looks off, her voice faint.

'He asked me how I liked the poem. He seemed genuinely interested. I didn't answer. He didn't seem to mind. "It's good to see you again," he said. "Your pain is more beautiful than ever."'

'Sarah, how accurate is your memory of the way he talks and what he says? Don't be offended.'

133

'I have a gift for voices and what people say. It's not a photo-graphic memory or anything. I can't remember it exactly, not word for word, not like that. But I'm pretty good. And I really concentrate on him when he's speaking. The way he talks. The things he does.'

'That's good, it will help,' I encourage her. 'How tall is he?'

'A little over six feet.'

'Is he black or white?'

'White and clean shaven.'

'Is he a big man? By that, I mean, is he fat or skinny? Muscular or weak?'

'He's not fat, but he's not thin. He's very strong. He has a perfect body. *Perfect*. Not a flaw on it. He must work out like crazy. He's well built without being all pumped up.'

I hear Barry's pen scratch away.

'Go on,' I say. 'What happened next?'

'"I'm almost done sculpting you, Sarah," he said. "Ten long years, full of ups and downs and twists and turns and sorrow. I've watched you bend and break. It's interesting, isn't it? How many times a human being can shatter and still keep moving forward? You're not the same little girl you were when we began this journey, are you? I can see the cracks, the places where you had to glue yourself back together."' Sarah shifts in the bed, restless. 'This isn't exact, okay? It's not word for word, but basically it's what he said and how he sounded.'

'You're doing fine,' I assure her.

She continues. 'He had a bag with him. He opened it and pulled out a small video camera and pointed it at me.'

'He's done that before, hasn't he?' I ask.

She nods. 'Yes. He says he's documenting my ruin. That it's important, that without it there's no justice.'

Killers collect trophies. The video is his.

'What did he do next?'

'He focused on my face, and he said: "I want you to think of your mother."' She turns to me. 'Want to see what he saw?'

134

Before I can tell her no, I really don't, her eyes change and I forget to breathe.

They fill up with a grief and yearning as vivid as a sunrise. I see hope unfulfilled, a fundamental loss of heart.

She turns away. I can breathe again.

But how can she?

'What then?' I push out, a little shaky.

'He just sat for a little bit, watching me through the camera lens. Then he started to talk to me. "Do you know what one of the most exciting parts of this is for me, Sarah? *The things I can't control.* Take this place, for instance. A family that is kind to you without being truly warm. A son who shows the world a perfect face, but blackmails you so you'll suck his cock. It's amazing. On the one hand, all chance. I didn't make this home. On the other hand, you are only here because of me. Did you ever think of that while Michael's cock was in your mouth? That you were there, looking up into his eyes, because of the things I've done?"'

Sarah gives me a sardonic smile. 'The answer is yes. I did think about The Stranger, some of those times.' I note that her hand is still trembling.

'Go on,' I encourage her.

How'd he know Michael was abusing her? A mental note I keep to myself, for now. I don't want to break her rhythm.

'He got nasty, then.' She stares off, remembering. 'He said: "Do you know what Michael made you, Sarah, the moment you got down on your knees in exchange for his silence? He made you a whore."'

Sarah's hands fly up to her face, startling me. She covers her eyes and her shoulders tremble.

'Are you okay?' I ask her in a soft voice.

She heaves out a single deep breath, almost a sob. A moment passes and she drops her hands back into her lap.

'I'm fine,' she says, toneless.

She continues putting a voice to the man she calls The Stranger.

'"Chance, but not really," he said. "All I had to do was place

135

you on the road, as God willed me to. I knew I could count on human nature to make your journey hard, as long as I was there to remove the kind ones. The ones that care are always a minority, Little Pain. A raindrop in a storm."' She looks at me. 'He's right. He may have stacked the deck and given my life a push, but the people that did bad things to me?' She rubs her arms as though she's cold. 'He didn't *make* them do those things. They did them on their own.'

I want to comfort her, to tell her that not everyone is bad, that there are good people in the world. I've learned to stifle this instinct. Victims don't want sympathetic words. They want me to turn back time, to make it *not have happened.*

'Go on,' I say.

'He kept on talking. He likes to hear himself talk. "Our time together is going to be done soon. I'm almost ready to complete my work. I've found the last few pieces I've been searching for, and soon, I'll reveal my masterpiece." He stuffed the camera back into the bag and stood up. "It's time for the next leg of your journey, Little Pain. Follow me."'

'Why does he call you "Little Pain"?' I ask.

'It's his pet name for me. His "Little Pain."' The look in her eyes is savage. 'I *hate* it!'

'I don't blame you,' I murmur. 'What happened next?'

'I started to move toward the door, like he asked, but then I stopped. Useless, I know, but I felt like I needed to make him force me to walk out that door. Like it meant something that I didn't go on my own. Silly.'

Maybe, I think, but it gives me hope for you.

'What then?'

'"Don't be difficult," he said, and he grabbed me by the arm. He was wearing thick gloves, but I could still feel how hard and strong his hands were. He led me down the hall to Dean and Laurel's bedroom.' She gives me a wistful look. 'That window I was sitting at when you came in? I remember seeing it then, thinking what a beautiful day it was.'

136

'Go on,' I coax her.

'He pushed me down the hallway that leads to their bathroom.' She shivers. 'That's where he had them. Dean and Laurel.'

'Were they alive?'

Her gaze at me is weary. 'Of course they were. They were naked, and they were alive. They weren't moving. I didn't know why until he told me. "Drugged," he said. "I gave them an injection." Miva-something chloride he called it. I can't remember the exact name. He said it kept them aware, that they could feel pain and hear us but that they couldn't move much.'

Score one for me on the drugs, and one for Tommy on the muscle relaxant, I think.

Something occurs to me. 'Sarah, his voice – would you recognize it if you heard it? Not just the words or the way he speaks, but the tone of it?'

She nods, somber. 'I can't forget it. I dream about it sometimes.'

'Go on.'

'He had Dean facedown. Laurel was on her back. He set his camera on a tripod, and put it on record. Then he picked Dean up like a baby, no effort at all, and stood him in the bathtub. "Come here, Little Pain," he said to me. I walked over to the tub. "Look into his eyes," he told me. I did.' Sarah swallows. 'I could see that he'd told the truth. Dean was . . . *there*. He knew what was going on. He was aware.' She shivers. 'He was also terrified. You could see it in his eyes. He was so scared.'

'Then what happened?'

'The Stranger told me to step back. He angled Dean's head forward, so his chin stuck out.' She cranes her own neck, showing me. '"When you know the moment of your own death, you know the meaning of both truth and fear, Mr Kingsley," he said. "It makes you wonder what comes next: the glory of heaven or the fires of hell? I tortured a student of philosophy not long ago, a bad, evil man. I cut him, I burned him, I shocked him. I was waiting. I had told him before we began: If he could come up with a single original observation about life, I would end the pain. On the morning of the second day, while I was castrating him, he screamed: '*We are all living in the moments before our own death!*' I kept my promise, and gave him release. I remember that truth before I kill someone."'

Sarah swallows. 'Then The Stranger cut Dean's throat. Just like that.' Her voice sounds distant and amazed. 'No warning. So *quick*. The blood spurted out. The Stranger kept Dean's neck angled so the blood would go into the tub. I remember thinking that I couldn't believe how much of it there was.'

About five or six quarts in the average human body. Not even enough to fill up a kitchen sink halfway, but blood is supposed to *stay inside*, so six quarts can seem like sixty.

'What happened then?'

'It went on for a while. The blood was spurting at first, then it was dribbling. Then it stopped. "Look into his eyes again," he told me. I did.' She closes her own eyes. 'Dean was gone. Nobody home.'

She's quiet for a moment, remembering.

'He lifted Dean out of the tub and laid him down on the carpet.'

A long silence.

'And then?' I prod.

'I know what you're thinking,' she whispers.

Her voice is filled with self-loathing, and she can't meet my eyes.

'What, Sarah? What am I thinking?'

'How could I just stand there while he did these things and not try to get away?'

'Look at me.' I put some force into my tone and make her face me. 'I wasn't thinking that. I know: He could move fast. He had a knife. You didn't think you'd be able to get away.'

Her face twists, once. She shudders, a wave, head to toe, involving the whole of her.

'That part is true, but . . . it's not the only reason.'

Once again, she can't meet my eyes.

'What's the other reason?' I keep my voice gentle, free of judgment.

138

It's a sad little shrug. 'I knew he wouldn't kill me. I knew if I just stood there and watched, and did what he said, and didn't try to get away, he wouldn't hurt me. Because that's how he wants me. Alive and in pain.'

'In my opinion and experience,' I say, after a moment, my voice careful, 'alive and in pain is better than dead.'

She appraises me. 'You think so?'

'I do.' I point at my scars. 'I have to look at these every day, and remember what they mean. It hurts. I'd still rather be alive.'

A bitter smile. 'You might not feel that way if you had to go through it all again every few years.'

'I might not,' I say. 'But the important thing is that, right now, *you* still do.'

I can see her considering this. I can't tell what she decides.

'So,' she continues, 'he stood over Laurel for a minute, just looking down at her. Her body didn't move, she didn't even blink – but she cried.' Sarah shakes her head, her expression haunted. 'A single line of tears from the corner of each eye. The Stranger smiled at her, but it wasn't a happy smile. He wasn't making fun of her or anything. He almost seemed sad. He leaned forward and he closed her eyes with his fingers.'

We hadn't known until now that he closed their eyes pre-mortem. It confirms my belief that men are his primary target. He closed Laurel's eyes because he didn't want her to see what was coming.

Big deal – he still killed her.

I park these thoughts, for now.

'And then?' I ask.

Sarah looks away from me. Her face changes, along with her voice, becoming wooden, mechanical. When she speaks, it's a staccato. 'He stood up. Picked her up, stood her in the tub. He slit her throat. Bled her out, dropped her on the rug.' She's trying to hurry through this memory. It takes me a moment to realize why.

'You were closer to Laurel than you were to Dean, weren't you?' I ask softly.

She doesn't cry, but she closes her eyes tight for a moment.

'She was nice to me.'

'I'm sorry, Sarah. What happened next?'

'He had me help him move their bodies into the bedroom. He didn't really need my help. I think he just wanted to keep my hands occupied so I couldn't run away. We carried Dean in first, and then Laurel. He grabbed them under their arms, I took them by the feet. They were so pale. I've never seen a person white like that. Like milk. We laid them on the bed.'

She goes silent.

'What, Sarah?'

I see a little bit of that same emptiness I'd seen in her last night. Some of the girl at the window, gun to her head, singing a one-note song.

'He had a long leather case in his pocket. He opened it up and took out a scalpel. He handed it to me, and he told me . . . he told me . . . he told me . . . how to cut them. "Throat to waist," he said. "One slice, no hesitation. I'm letting you do this, Sarah. Letting you expose what they really are, inside."' Her eyes are a little glazed. 'It's like I wasn't really there. Like I wasn't in myself. I just remember thinking, "Do what you have to do to stay alive." Thinking that, over and over and over, as I took the scalpel and I went over to Laurel and cut her open and I went over to Dean and cut him open and I peeled their skin back because The Stranger told me to and there was muscle, and he made me cut that too, and peel that away and now there's bone and guts and he made me put my hands inside and *pull* and *pull* and *pull* and it was like rubber Jell-O and wet and it smelled and then it was' – her head slumps forward – 'over.'

The words had rushed out of her, not stopping, a flood. Emptying her and filling me, sewer water, a death-river, horror at high tide. I want to stand up and run away and never see or hear or think of Sarah again.

But you can't. She's got more to say.

I look at Sarah. She's gazing down at her hands.

'"Do what you have to do to stay alive," that's what I kept thinking,' she whispers. 'He just smiled and filmed the whole thing. Do what you have to do to stay alive. To stay *alive*.'

'Should we stop?' I ask.

She turns to me, dreamy-eyed but confused.

'What?'

'Should we stop? Do you need a break?'

She stares at me. She seems to come back to herself. She presses her lips together and shakes her head.

'*No*. I want to get through this.'

'You're sure?'

'I'm sure.'

Maybe, maybe not. But I need to hear the rest of it, and I think she needs to tell it.

'Okay. What happened next?'

She rubs her face with her hands. 'He told me to come downstairs with him. I followed him, down to the family room. Michael was there, sitting on the couch, naked. He was paralyzed too.

'The Stranger laughed, and patted Michael on the head. "Boys will be boys. But you already knew that, didn't you, Little Pain? Michael was a nasty boy. He had a video camera going while you were down on your knees. I found the tapes on one of my prior trips here to reconnoiter. Don't worry though, I'll be taking them with me. It can be our little secret." He yanked Michael off the couch and dragged him across the rug.' She frowns. 'I still had the scalpel. He hadn't taken it away from me. That's how sure he was that I wouldn't try anything.' She shrugs, miserable. 'Anyway. He dragged Michael over to me, and he told me it was my turn. "Go on," he said. "You saw how I did it upstairs. Ear to ear, a big red grin." I told him no.' She shakes her head, a gesture of despair. 'Like it mattered. Like it would make a difference.' Her smile is pained and crooked and full of self-hate. 'In the end, one thing you can count on about me – I'll do what it takes to survive. "Do it," he said, "or I'll cut the nipples off your breasts and feed them to you."' She pauses, looking down at her lap. 'I did it, of course,'

141

she says in a small voice. She looks up at me, fearful of what I might think. 'I didn't *want* him to die,' she says, her voice quavering. 'Even though he blackmailed me and made me have sex with him and all those things, I didn't want him to die.'

I reach over and take her hand. 'I know you didn't.'

She lets me hold the hand for a moment before pulling it away.

'*God.* Michael just bled and bled and bled. *God.* And then The Stranger had me help him carry the body upstairs. He put him on the bed, in between Dean and Laurel.

'"It's not your fault," he said. I thought he was talking to me, but then I realized he was talking to Michael. I was afraid he was going to make me cut him open too, but he didn't.' She pauses. 'I started to get mad. I think he saw it, thought I might actually try to do something, because he told me to drop the scalpel. I did think about trying to stab him. I really did. In the end, I did what he told me to.'

'And you're here and alive,' I say, trying to encourage her.

'Yeah.' Tired again.

'What happened next?'

'He told me to come into the bathroom with him. He went over to the tub, and dipped his hand down into the blood. He started flicking it at me, saying, "In the name of the Father and the daughter and the Holy Spirit." He got blood on my face and other parts of me.'

The teardrop spatter I'd seen last night, I think.

'Is that exactly what he said? "In the name of the Father and the daughter and the Holy Spirit"? Not "Father and the Son"?'

'That's what he said.'

'Go on.'

'Then he told me it was time to get busy. He said he needed to express himself. He took off his clothes.'

'Did you notice anything about him?' I ask her. 'Any birthmarks, scars, anything at all?'

'A tattoo. On his right thigh, where no one would ever see it unless he was naked.'

142

'Of what?'

'An angel. Not a nice angel, though. It had a mean face and a flaming sword. Kind of scary.'

An avenging angel, maybe? Is that how he sees himself, or is it just a symbol of what he's doing?

'If I had a sketch artist work with you, could you describe the tattoo?'

'Sure.'

I don't see this perpetrator settling for a design selected from a book. He would have had the tattoo done to his custom and exact specifications. It's possible we could track down the artist.

'Anything else about him?'

'When I saw him naked, I could tell that he shaves his body. Armpits, chest, legs, his cock, everywhere.'

This isn't uncommon for a clever, organized offender. Most make a study of basic forensics and work to reduce their chances of leaving trace evidence behind. Shaving body hair is something serial rapists do all the time.

'What about moles? Scars?'

'Just the tattoo.'

'That's good, Sarah. When we find him, that's going to help us nail him.'

'Okay.' She seems listless.

'He took his clothes off. Then what?'

'He was hard.'

'You mean he was erect?'

'Yeah.'

I bite my lower lip, ask the question I'm dreading. 'Did he . . . touch you?'

'No. He's never fucked me, or tried to.'

'What did he do next?'

'He took two pairs of handcuffs out of the back pockets of his pants. "I need to lock you down now," he said, "so I can do my work without worrying about you running off." He cuffed my hands behind my back, and then he cuffed my ankles. He carried me into the bedroom and sat me on the floor. I didn't fight him.'

'Go on.'

'He went downstairs and came back up with a big pot.'

'A cooking pot?'

'Yes. He filled it with blood from the tub and then . . .' She shrugs. 'You saw the bedroom.'

He'd had himself a little party. Splashed the walls, finger paints from hell.

'How long did that go on?'

'I have no idea,' she says, toneless. 'I just know that when he was done, there was blood everywhere. He was covered in it.' She grimaces. 'God, he was so *proud*! He finished up and he stood in front of the window for a second, looking out. "A beautiful day," he said. "God made this day." He slid it open and stood there, naked and covered in blood.'

'He went swimming after that, didn't he?'

She nods. 'He left me there, left the room, and a few minutes later I heard him splashing around in the pool.' She looks at me. 'I was starting to get fuzzy by then. Starting to go in and out. Getting crazy.'

Who wouldn't?

'Anyway.' She sighs. 'I don't know how much time went by. I just remember lying there, and I felt like I was falling asleep and then waking up, but I wasn't *really* falling asleep – I don't know. It's like I was fainting, over and over and over. One of the times I woke up, he was back.' She shivers. 'He was clean again, no blood on him. He was looking down at me. I fainted again. When I woke up, I was downstairs, and he was dressed. He had that pot in his hands. "A little here," he said. And he tipped it, let some blood spill onto the rug in the family room. Then he said, "A little there," and went into the backyard and dumped the rest of the blood from the pot into the pool.'

'Do you know why he did that?' I ask her.

The hard, too-old eyes are back. 'I think . . . it seemed right to him. Like a painting. That spot on the rug, the water in the pool, they needed a little more *red* to be just right.'

I stare at her for a moment before clearing my throat. 'Fair enough. What happened next?'

'He sat down in front of me with the camera, pointed it at me. "You've been many things, Little Pain. An orphan, a liar, a whore. My pain-angel. Now you're a murderer. You just killed another human being. Think about that for a minute." He went quiet then, just pointing the camera at my face and recording away. I don't know how long it went on. I was out of it.

'He undid the handcuffs and told me he was leaving. "We're almost there, Sarah. Almost at the end of our journey. I want you to remember, it's not your fault, but your pain is my justice."

'Then he was gone.' She gazes at me. 'I went in and out for a little while. Things went black. The next thing I remember is talking to you in the bedroom.'

'You don't remember asking for me?'

'No.'

I cock my head at her. 'Why did you?'

She gives me a measured look of consideration that reminds me, for a moment, of Bonnie.

'Since I was six years old, a man has been coming into my life, taking away anything and anyone I love. And no one believes he exists.' Her eyes move across my face, dancing along my scars. 'I read about what happened to you, and I thought, Maybe she'd believe me. I could tell you knew what it was like. To lose every-thing. To be reminded of it, every day. To wonder whether dying might be better than living.' She pauses. 'I got the diary a few months ago and I wrote it all down. Every ugly thing. I was going to find a way to contact you and give it to you.' The shrug is small and bleak. 'I guess I did.'

I smile at her. 'I guess you did.' I bite my lower lip. 'Sarah, what he said to you, about you being a murderer . . . you know that's not true, right?'

She begins to shiver. The shivers turn into shakes, full-body trembles, her eyes wide, her face pale, her lips white and pressed flat together.

'Barry, get the nurse!' I say, alarmed.

'N-n-no!' Sarah says.

I look at her. She shakes her head as an underscore and crosses her arms over her chest, hugging herself and rocking back and forth. I watch, poised to hit the call button. A half-minute goes by and the shaking subsides back to shivers, the shivers die away. Color comes back into Sarah's face.

'Are you okay?' I ask, feeling stupid for asking. It's an impotent question.

She moves a lock of hair away from her forehead.

'It happens sometimes,' she says in a voice that's surprisingly clear. 'Bubbles up out of nowhere, like a seizure.' Her head snaps around, her eyes meeting mine, and I'm startled by the clarity and strength I see in them. 'I'm almost done, do you understand? This is it. Either you find him and stop him or I'm going to take away the thing he wants the most.'

'What's that?'

Her gaze is steady but haunted. Firm yet lost. 'Me. More than anything, he wants me. So if you can't catch him, I'm going to take me away for good. Do you hear me?'

She turns back to the window, back to the sun, and I could argue with her, I could protest, but I realize she's gone away from us for now.

'Yes,' I reply, my voice soft. 'I do hear you.'

'So what'd you think about all that?' Barry asks.

We're back outside, in the parking lot. He's smoking and I'm wishing that I could do the same.

'I think that was a horrible, horrible story.'

'Got that right,' he mutters. 'If she's telling the truth.'

'What do you think?'

'I've heard some crazy tales in my time. Seen a lot of lying. This didn't feel like that.'

146

'I agree.'

'What did you think about the suicide threat?'

'It's real.'

That's all I say, all I need to say. I can tell Barry agrees with me.

'What about our guy?'

'I'm still fuzzy on this perp. Revenge is the motive to a near one hundred percent certainty. And it's everything to him. He was willing to give up personally mutilating the bodies so that he could force Sarah to do it. Hurting her was more important, more fulfilling, than cutting them open himself.'

'But not killing them,' Barry observes.

'Except when it came to the boy. Again, making her do it, his observation of her pain, was enough. But murder, according to her, gives him an erection. Playing with the blood . . . that's ritual, that's sexual. Watching her do it seems too cerebral.' I rub my face with my hands, try to shake myself into a semblance of normality. 'Sorry, I'm not being helpful.'

'Hey, we've worked a few of these together. This is how it goes for you.'

He's right, this is how it goes. Observe, observe, observe, think, correlate, feel, and do it all again until the killer's outline goes from fuzzy to focused. It's chaotic and jumbled and contradictory, but this is how it goes.

'Can you get a sketch artist over here?' I ask. 'The tattoo will be distinctive, unique.'

'I'll make it happen.'

'I'll reach Callie and see what occurred at the Vargas scene. I'll make sure she calls you and fills you in too. Barring a big forensic break, I think the most productive path is going to be digging into everyone's past, with special attention to Vargas. That's where the answer lies. Based on the vengeance motive, and the way he treats the bodies of the children, I'm interested in the human-trafficking angle.'

'That's one for you then.'

'Why?'

'Apparently, the trafficking beef was federal all the way. FBI, in fact.'

'Here?'

'Californi-yay. But I'll start rooting around in the Kingsleys' lives. Sarah's too. I'll check out her parents, see if they really were murdered. Oh yeah, and I'll follow up with the medical examiner. Damn, I'm busy.'

'I'll make sure Callie gets you a copy of the diary.'

We both stand there, thinking. Making sure we've covered all the bases.

'Guess that's it then,' Barry says. 'I'll be in touch soon.'

'That apartment was a disgusting pigsty, honey-love.'

'I know. What did you find?'

'Let's see, where to begin? Method of death was the same as the Kingsley family. Throats were cut, blood drained into the tub in the bathroom. Mr Vargas was disemboweled. No hesitation cuts on him, however.'

I tell her about Sarah.

'He made *her* cut them open?'

'Yes.'

Silence. 'Well, that would explain it then. Moving on. The young lady wasn't mutilated – as you saw. We don't have an ID on her yet, but she was young. My guess would be somewhere between thirteen and fifteen. We found a tattoo of a cross, with Cyrillic writing underneath it that translates to "Give thanks to God, for God is love."'

'Seems odd that an American girl would have Cyrillic writing tattooed on her. She's either Russian or local Russian. Which makes sense.'

The Russian mob has become a huge player in human trafficking, including underage sex workers.

'The scarring on her feet is very similar to what we saw on the footprints recovered at the Kingsleys', except these are fewer in number by far. They also seem relatively fresh. The ME estimated, based on color and fading, that they're about six months old.'

'Odd coincidence, don't you think? Both her and the perp having the same kind of scarring?'

'No, because I don't believe it's a coincidence. All the prints we recovered matched the two victims. We have a ton of hair and fibers. We also have a lot of semen stains, but they're all old and dry. You know, flaky.'

'Thank you for that visual.'

'I've only given the computer a cursory once-over, but I did see e-mail and various documents on it, as well as lots and lots of porn. Lots of porn. I'm having the computer brought back to the office, where I'll be going through it. Did I mention lots of porn? Mr Vargas wasn't a nice man.'

'Did the perp play with their blood?'

'If you mean, did he enjoy another round of finger painting, then no.'

He gave up the mutilation of the Kingsleys to Sarah. Maybe the blood-painting was a substitute. A kind of consolation prize.

'What about the diary?'

'I'm off to the office, I'll print it out there.'

'Call me when you have.'

I reach James on his cell phone.

'What do you want?' he answers.

This kind of greeting doesn't surprise me anymore. This is James, the fourth and final member of my team. He's oil to everyone else's water, a saw blade against the grain. He's irritating, unlikable, and infuriating. We call him Damien when he's not around, after the character in *The Omen*, the son of Satan.

James is on my team because he's brilliant. His intellect is blinding. A high school graduate at fifteen, perfect SAT scores, he had a PhD in criminology by the time he was twenty, and joined the FBI at twenty-one, the goal he'd been striving toward since he was twelve.

James had an older sister, Rosa. Rosa died when James was twelve, at the hands of a serial killer wielding a blowtorch and a smile. James helped his mother bury Rosa, and he decided at her grave what he was going to spend the rest of his life doing.

I don't know what else drives James besides the job. I don't know anything about his personal life, or if he really has one. I have never met his mother. I have never known him to go out to the movies. He's always turned the radio off when I've been a passenger in his car, preferring silence to song.

He's beyond careless when it comes to the emotions of others. He can flip between scalding hostility, or a thoughtlessness that embodies the ultimate in 'I don't need to know how you feel, and in the final analysis, I really – *truly* – don't care.'

He's brilliant, though. An undeniable brilliance, blinding as an arc light. He has another ability as well, one that he shares with me, that binds us together, however unwillingly. He can peer into the mind of a killer and not blink. He can gaze at evil full in the face and then pick up a magnifying glass to get a closer look.

In those times, he is invaluable, a companion, and we flow together like boats and water, rivers and rain.

'We have a case,' I say.

I brief him on everything.

'What does this have to do with my Sunday?' he asks.

'Callie will have the diary couriered to you today.'

'And?'

'And,' I say, exasperated, 'I want you to read it. I'm going to do the same. Once we're done, I want to compare notes.'

A long pause, followed by a longer sigh, very put-upon. 'Fine.'

He hangs up without saying another word. I stare at the phone for a moment and then I shake my head, wondering why I'm surprised.

16

'How's things, sweetheart?' I ask Bonnie.

I had realized, in the parking lot, that everyone was in motion, everything necessary was being done. Which meant I could go be Mom for a little while. This was a skill you had to learn in law enforcement: how to make the time. The cases you are responsible for are important. Literally matters of life and death. You still have to get home for dinner sometimes.

We're in Alan and Elaina's living room. Alan's off running errands. I'd briefed him on the case in general, but have no duty for him at the moment. Elaina is bustling about in the kitchen, getting us something to drink. Bonnie and I are on the couch, staring at each other for no particular reason.

She smiles and nods. *Good*, she's saying.

'Glad to hear it.'

She points at me.

'How am I doing?'

She nods.

'I'm fine.'

She frowns at me. *Stop lying*.

I grin. 'I should be allowed to have some secrets, babe. Parents aren't supposed to tell their kids everything.'

She shrugs. A simple motion with specific meaning: *Well, we're different.*

Bonnie's body is ten years old, but that's where it ends. I feel more often like I'm living with a teenager than with a young girl. I used to ascribe this to what she's experienced, the things she's gone through. I know better now.

Bonnie is gifted. Her gift doesn't lie in child-genius, but in her ability to focus, to observe, to understand. When she sets her mind to something, she sticks with it to conclusion, examining things in a deep, layered sense.

I had raised concern about her schooling a few months back. She'd made me understand that *I shouldn't worry*. That she'd *go back to school* and that she'd *catch up*. She'd taken my hand and had led me into the family room. Matt and I had created quite a little library in there. We believed in reading, in the power of books. We had planned to pass this love and lesson on to Alexa. We'd paid a contractor to install wall-to-wall built-in bookshelves, and we never got rid of any book we read.

Matt and I would spend an hour or so together each month choosing specific volumes to add. Shakespeare. Mark Twain. Nietzsche. Plato. If we thought it had something of value to communicate, we bought it and put it on a shelf.

It was part collection, part working library. None of it was vanity. That was our rule: Never buy a book to gain the approval of others.

Matt and I weren't poor, but we weren't rich, either. We weren't going to leave behind a huge material estate. We had hoped to will Alexa the usual things: a house that was paid off, memories of being loved by her parents, maybe some money in the bank. We also wanted to leave her something that would be uniquely us. Something only her parents would leave her, an inheritance of the heart. This library as a legacy, a small sampling of the collected works of man. The dream of this was something Matt and I shared, something we could *do*, rich or not.

Alexa was just starting to get interested in this room before she died. I haven't added anything to it since. I've had dreams of waking up to find it aflame, the books screaming as they burn.

Bonnie had pulled me into this forgotten *(avoided)* place. She'd pulled out a book and had handed it to me. *How to Sketch*, by some unknown but obviously talented author. She'd pointed at herself. It had taken me a moment to understand what she was saying.

'You read this?'

She had smiled and nodded, pleased that I understood. She'd grabbed another, *Basics of Watercolor*. And another, *Art and Landscapes*.

'All of these?' I'd asked.

She'd nodded.

Bonnie had pointed at herself, had mimed being thoughtful, then had indicated the library with a sweep of her hand.

I had stared at her, considering. It came to me. 'You're saying, when you want to know about something you come in here and read a book about it?'

Head nod, big smile.

I have the ability to read and to learn, and the drive to do both, she had been telling me. *Isn't that enough?*

I wasn't sure it *was* enough. There were the three R's, after all. Well, okay, she had 'reading' down, but hey, there were still the other two. And of course, there was the socialization aspect of things, peers and boys and just saying no. The complex dance of learning to share the world with others.

All of this had whirled through my mind. The fact that Bonnie had read books about art and painting and now painted on a regular basis – and painted well – had mollified me to a point, quieting some of my fears and allowing me to rationalize shelving the problem for another day.

'Okay, sweetheart,' I had said. 'For now, okay.'

Her spiritual precociousness was evident in other ways; not just in her paintings, but in her ability to listen with complete attention and tremendous patience, in her over-mature ability to go right to the heart of emotional matters.

She was a child in many ways, it was true, but in some ways she was far more perceptive than I was.

I sigh. 'Today I went and saw a girl named Sarah.'

I tell her an abridged version of Sarah's story. I don't tell her about Sarah being forced to have sex with Michael, or the graphic details of the Kingsleys' deaths. I do tell her the important things; that Sarah is an orphan, that she feels chased by someone she calls The Stranger, that she is a young woman who's reached the zenith of despair and now sits ready to tumble downward, free-fall, into darkness, forever.

Bonnie listens with interest and thoughtful intensity. When I finish, she looks off, deeply contemplative. She turns back to me, points at herself, then at me, and nods. It takes a moment for our telepathic shorthand to kick in.

'She's like us, that's what you're saying.'

She nods, hesitates, then indicates herself with emphasis.

'More like you,' I reply, getting it.

A nod.

I stare at her.

'You mean because she saw the people she cared for getting murdered, sweetheart? The way you saw your mom get killed?'

She nods, then shakes her head. *Yes*, she's saying, *but not just that*. She bites her lower lip, thinking. She looks up at me, indicates herself, and pushes me away.

Now it's my turn to bite my lip. I stare at her – and suddenly I understand.

'She's like you would be without me.'

She nods, her face sad.

'Alone.'

A nod.

Communicating with Bonnie is like reading pictographic writing. Not everything is literal. Symbology plays a part. She's not saying that she and Sarah are one and the same. Sarah is a young

154

girl who has lost everything and everyone she loves and – here is where the semblance ends – who is now alone in the world. Bonnie is saying, *She is what I could be if there was no Smoky, if my life was just foster homes and memories of my mom dying.*

I swallow. 'Yeah, honey. That's a pretty good description.'

Bonnie has her scars. She's mute. She still has nightmares sometimes, nightmares that make her scream in her sleep.

But she's not alone.

She's got me, and I've got her, and that makes all the difference in the world.

I could see Sarah with more depth now: Sarah screamed in the night, but there was no one there to hold her when she woke up. There hadn't been for a very long time.

A life like that might make you surround yourself with the color black, I mused. Why not? Everything was darkness, best to make sure you remember that fact, best not to let yourself indulge in the fantasy of *hope*.

A clink of glasses distracts me from my own musings. Elaina has returned with our drinks.

'Orange juice for the two of you, water for me,' she says, smiling and sitting down.

'Thanks,' I say, and Bonnie nods, and we sip our OJ.

'I heard what you were telling Bonnie,' Elaina says after a moment. 'About the girl, Sarah. Terrible thing.'

'She's in bad shape.'

'What's going to happen to her now?'

'I guess once she's released from the hospital, she'll go into protective custody. After that, it depends. She's sixteen. She'll either go into a group home or foster care until she's an adult or she's emancipated.'

'Will you do me a favor?'

'Of course.'

'Will you talk to me about this? Before she gets released from the hospital?'

I puzzle over this request for a moment, but only a moment.

It's Elaina, after all. Her purposes are pretty easy to divine. Particularly when combined with her earlier revelation to me about being an orphan. 'Elaina, it would not be a good idea for you to take this girl on. In spite of the obvious – that there's a psycho out there who seems to have a fixation on her – she's messed up. She's hurt, that's true, but she has a serious hard side to her. I don't know anything about her background, whether or not she does drugs or steals or . . . anything.'

Elaina gives me one of her tolerant-but-loving smiles. A smile that says: *I love you, but you are being thickheaded.*

'I appreciate the concern, Smoky, but that will be between Alan and me.'

'But –'

A quick shake of the head. 'Promise you'll call me before she's discharged.'

End of conversation, game over, give it up if you know what's good for you – but I love you. I smile, I can't help it. Elaina makes you smile, it's what she was born to do.

'I promise.'

Elaina watches Bonnie during the day (and often the evening) for me. She and Alan have become a part of Bonnie's family. It works. They don't live far, there's no one I trust more, and Bonnie loves them both. I'm fumbling with the problem of Bonnie's muteness and I know – I know – that I have to address her schooling soon. But for now, this works.

They were even happy to bow to my fears, without questioning me or making me feel silly about it. Their house had been alarmed (up-the-wazoo style, same as mine), and Tommy had set up a simple video surveillance system. And of course, there was Alan, a giant with a gun, who slept here as well.

I owe them both.

'I promise,' I say again.

*

Alan had returned. He was busy losing a game of chess to Bonnie. Elaina was in the kitchen making us all a late lunch while I spoke to Callie on the phone.

'Got the pages all printed out, honey-love. What now?'

'Print out another six copies. One for Barry, one for James, one for Alan, one for Assistant Director Jones, one for Dr Child, and one for yourself. Courier Barry, James, Dr Child, and AD Jones their copies at home. I'll call and let them know they're coming. I want everyone to read this. Once we've all gotten through it, we'll compare notes.'

'Fair enough. What about your and Alan's copies?'

I look toward the kitchen and smile.

'Are you hungry?'

'Does the wind blow? Does the moon circle the earth? Is the root of a prime number –'

'Just get over here.'

I am on the phone with Assistant Director Jones. I have called him at home to bring him up to speed on everything. One of the first things you learn in any bureaucracy, never let the boss get blindsided.

'Hold it,' he says, interrupting me. 'What did you say the name of the guy at the second scene was?'

'Jose Vargas.'

He whistles through the phone.

'Better come see me tomorrow, Smoky,' he says.

'Why?'

'Because I can tell you all about Vargas. The trafficking beef? I was on that case.'

'No kidding?'

Barry had said it was a federal case. The fact that AD Jones had been a part of it is unexpected. And maybe a plus.

'For real, as the kids say. Come see me tomorrow.'

'Yes, sir.'

'Good. Have you thought about the other thing we discussed?'

You're kidding, right?

'Some.'

A brief pause. I think he's waiting for me to fill the silence, to expand on that one-word answer. When I don't, he lets it go.

'I want regular briefings. And I want to see that diary.'

'It'll be on its way to you within the hour, sir.'

Callie had shown up not long after I finished the call with AD Jones. Bonnie still played chess with Alan, who was teaching her the finer points of the game. Callie sat down next to Bonnie and the two of them began to play against Alan, who found himself fighting to keep pieces on the board.

It was during a rematch of this doubles tournament that Elaina managed to maneuver me into the kitchen, in her firm but gentle way.

'So,' she said. 'Are we planning to finish what we started on Saturday?'

1forUtwo4me?

I'm putting a cracker into my mouth as she asks me this, and I freeze mid-bite. I finish up and swallow, feeling guilty and evasive without knowing why.

'Smoky,' she chides. She grabs me by the chin and brings my face up. 'It's me.'

I look at her, let a little bit of that patented Elaina-goodness flow into me, womb and warmth. I sigh. 'I know. Sorry.' I shrug. 'Truth? Of course we will. But when?' I shake my head. 'I don't know yet.'

'Fair enough. But you'll let me know?'

'Yeah,' I mumble around my cracker, feeling like a child. 'Of course.'

'You've been doing so well, Smoky, and clearing out that home was a good idea. I want to make sure you finish, that's all.'

Then she smiles, baldness and all, an Elaina-smile that makes further words unnecessary.

*

It's early evening by the time the day winds down and Bonnie's yawning tells me that it's time to go.

I'd stayed here later than I'd planned, but I needed this. Callie's jokes and Alan's mock-anger at being beaten by Bonnie at chess, Elaina's ever-present warmth and Bonnie's full-body grins, had all served to recover some of what this weekend had started out as: a normal life.

Can you give all of this up? Should you? Is Quantico the solution?

Shush, I tell myself.

'I'm going back to the office,' Callie tells me at the door. 'I'm going to dig through Mr Vargas's computer. I'm sure I'll find many distasteful things.'

'Don't stay too late,' I say. 'We're meeting at the office bright and early tomorrow morning.'

Elaina and Alan each get a hug, as does Callie, first from Bonnie, and then from me. I work with my family, my family is my work, that's how my life has worked out.

That's what you get for marrying the gun.

I'm in too good a mood to take my own bait.

17

'I'm going to read this for a little while, sweetheart,' I say to Bonnie. 'I won't keep you up, will I?'

I have asked her this before, many times. The answer is always no. Bonnie could sleep through an air raid, just so long as she doesn't have to sleep alone. She shakes her head, smiles, kisses me on the cheek.

'Good night, honey,' I say, and kiss her back.

One more smile, and she turns away from me, toward the cool shadows. Leaving me in my small pool of light, to think and then to read.

I have my notepad pages from the other night. I add some things we now know.

PERPETRATOR:

Under *Methodology* I add:
Interview with Sarah Langstrom confirms he drugs his victims.
He forced her to disembowel the adult Kingsleys and to cut Michael Kingsley's throat. (His behavior re: her is specific WHY?)

Under *Behaviors* I add:
Disembowelment is a way of revealing the inner 'true nature' of his victims. Continues to support theory of revenge as a motive.

He closes the eyes of female victims pre-mortem but he still disembowels them. They may deserve less but they still, in his mind, *deserve*.

Perpetrator claims earlier victims, including a married poet and a philosophy student.

Artwork with the blood is an oddity. Extraneous and unnecessary. Why do it? Substitution for letting Sarah cut the victims?

Murder gives him an erection, but no visible abuse to the bodies, and none noted in Sarah's account.

Of course, I realize, it could just be that his scalpel is his cock. The cutting could be the sexual act for him.

Religious overtones. Getting orders from God?

Under *Description* I add:

Caucasian or Caucasian appearing.

Approximately six feet tall.

Shaves off all body hair.

Very fit, muscular. 'Perfect body.' Works out (Narcissist).

Key: Tattoo on his right thigh of an angel carrying a flaming sword. He'll have designed this himself.

I add notes regarding the program found on Michael Kingsley's home computer. If put there by the perpetrator, it points to technical expertise, or access to technical expertise.

I consider the angel tattoo. It either represents his actions or it represents himself. He seems lucid enough for it to be the former, but the blood art falls on the crazy side, which is strange and unsettling.

Is he beginning to decompensate?

Decompensation, at its simplest, is the act of something going from a stable state to an unstable one. It's not universal among serial killers, but it's a common phenomenon. Ted Bundy spent years as a careful, clever, charismatic assassin. Toward the end of his 'career' he spun out of control, and this helped lead to his capture.

Dr Child, one of the only profilers I really respect, talked about this subject to me once, and what he said comes to me now.

'I believe,' he said, 'that all violent serial offenders are, to some degree, insane. I'm not referring to the legal definition of insanity. I'm proposing that finding joy in the murder of other human beings would not be the behavior of a sane individual.'

'I can agree with that,' I'd said. 'Guilty *by* reason of insanity, so to speak.'

'Just so. Serial murder is a behavior precipitated by a lifetime of prior stressors. It's an act that generates further stress. It demands paranoia, it's always obsessive, and the most important factor: *It is not under the individual's control.* Regardless of the possible consequences – the probable eventuality of capture – he not only will not stop – he *cannot.* Inability to halt a behavior even when one knows that behavior is destructive to self is a form of psychosis, yes?'

'Sure.'

'This is why, in my opinion, we see decompensation in so many serial offenders, be they organized, disorganized, or in between. The pressures, internal, external, imagined, real – build up and eventually break down the *already damaged mind.*' He'd smiled, but it wasn't a happy smile. 'I think the same raving lunacy sits there in all of them, latent and waiting to bloom. Provide enough stress and you can bring it to life.' He'd sighed. 'The larger point being, Smoky: Beware of trying to put the monsters into easy boxes. There are no rules here, only guidelines.'

The point in the present being: The blood art is not important. Revenge as a motive makes sense, and will help lead us to him. His treatment of the children is important, and will help lead us to him. The tattoo? Pure forensics. I need to concentrate on finding the artist, not figuring out its significance. Whether he feels he's *like* the angel or *is* the angel is, for now, just mental chatter.

I take the page with the notes I'd written about Sarah. I correct her name now.

SARAH LANGSTROM:

Been with the Kingsley family approx. one year

Then I'm stumped.

What else have we really learned about her?

Two things come to me. I write them down because they're true, although neither is particularly significant.

She's a Survivor.
She's losing her mind. She's suicidal.

That's an impetus at least.

More unresolved, but that's okay. Everything is about unceasing forward motion. Look, examine, deduce, posit, evidence, evidence, profile. We have a physical description of the perpetrator and we have a basic understanding of his motive. We have a living witness. We have a footprint. We know this perp keeps videos as trophies and when we catch him those videos will hang him.

We also have Sarah's diary and I need to read it and see where that leads. The victims are the key to him, and from what I can see, she is his favorite. The point of it all.

I set aside the notepad pages and examine what Callie gave me.

The pages are white, blown-up, larger than the originals, easy to read. Sarah's flowing black cursive beckons, and she begins by speaking to me directly.

Dear Smoky Barrett,

I know you.

I guess what I really mean is that I know about you. I've studied you in the way you study a person who could be your last and only hope. I've stared at your photograph until my eyes were bloodshot, memorizing every scar.

I know that you work for the FBI in Los Angeles. I know that you hunt evil men, and that you're good at it. All of that is important, but it's not why you give me hope.

You give me hope because you've been the victim too.

You give me hope because you've been raped, and you've been cut, and you've lost the things you love.

If anyone could believe me, I think – I think – it would be you.

If anyone could make it stop – could want to make it stop – it would be you.

Is that true? Or am I just dreaming when I should be slitting my wrists?

I guess we'll find out. I can always slit my wrists later, after all.

I've called this a diary but that's not what it really is. No.

This is a black flower. This is a book of dreams. This is a path to the watering hole, where the dark things go down to drink.

Like that? What I mean to say is: It's a story. Here on paper, that's where you'll see me run. The only place you'll see me run. Here on the white and crinkly, I can really move. I'm more of a sprinter than a runner, as I think you'll see, but the point is, ask me to explain what I've written out loud and I'll struggle, but give me a pen and a pad or a computer and a keyboard and I'm going to go, go, go.

Part of this, I think, is because of the brightness of my mother's soul. She was an artist and some of it seems to have rubbed off. The rest of it, I think, is because I'm going crazy inside. Loony as a goony. The white and crinkly is where all the crazy comes out, unfiltered and screeching. A big black batch of mind-crows.

I have a rhyme for it (a crazy-rhyme of course): 'A little bit of dark, a little bit of light, a little bit of shimmy-shimmy makes it just right.'

I think about what I feel, in other words, and I write you a path to the watering hole.

I started writing about two years ago, in one of the schools I went to. The English teacher, a very decent man named Mr Perkins (and you'll find out in a minute why I know he was a decent man), read the first story I ever wrote and asked me to stay after class. He told me, when we were alone, that I had a gift. That I might even be a prodigy.

For some reason that praise brought out The Crazy. The Crazy is one of the creatures that drinks down there at the watering hole, dark-skinned and big-eyed and goony. The Crazy is angry. The Crazy is mean. The Crazy is, well, crazy.

So I grabbed Mr Perkins's crotch and said: 'Thanks! Want a blow job, Mr P?'

Just like that.

I'll never forget the two things that happened. His face fell and his cock got hard. Both at the same time. He pulled away and sputtered and walked out of the room. I think he was afraid, and I can't really blame him. I also understand that the first of the two (the falling face, the dismay) was the real Mr P. Like I said, a very decent man.

I walked out of the classroom, fevered and grinning and heart hammering. I walked out of the school and around the back and I pulled out a lighter and lit that story on fire and cried while it burned and blew away in the breeze.

I've written a lot since then, and I've burned it all.

I'm almost sixteen years old now, as I begin writing this, and though I find I kind of want to burn it too, I won't.

Why am I telling you this? For two reasons.

The first one is a broad one, bigger than a breadbox. I want you to know that my sanity has become something I can see inside myself, like a white line or a vibration of light. It used to be strong and constant, but now it's weak and flickers a lot. Dots of darkness fly around it, like a swarm of sluggish death-bees. Someday soon, if things don't change, the dots will overwhelm the light and I'll be a goner. I'll sing forever, and never hear a word.

So if I hiccup sometimes, if my needle jumps the groove, understand: I'm hanging on with my fingernails here. I spend a lot of my time watching that white line of light, because I'm afraid if I look away, I'll look back and it'll be gone, but I won't remember it was ever there.

The Crazy is down at the watering hole, and it's a short walk from that bad water to me saying or acting in ways I shouldn't, okay?

Okay.

The second reason is because of what comes next on the white and crinkly. I could have done a diary, I guess, a nice, dry, factual recounting. But come on – I'm GIFTED. I'm a PRODIGY.

Why not tell a story instead?

So that's what I've done.

Is it all true? That depends on your definition of truth. Could I read my parents' minds? Do I really know what they were thinking when The Stranger came for them? No.

But I knew them. They were my people. It may or may not be what they were thinking, but that doesn't make it untrue because it's the kind of thing they would have thought. That's the point, don't you see?

The truth is that I don't know.

The truth is that I do know.

That's what recorded history is all about: three-parts truth to one-part fiction. The truth is in the time and place and the basic events. The fiction is in the motivations and the thoughts. Since history only exists if we remember it, is it really such a bad thing to fill it out with a little humanity, even if that humanity is imagined?

They were my parents, and I loved them, so I wrote them as characters, and I filled them with thoughts and hopes and feelings and then I read what I wrote and I cried and I said:

Yeah.

That was them.

I dare anyone to tell me otherwise. Actually, I don't, because if they did, The Crazy would come running, you can bet on that. I'd probably slap them till they bled and scream at them until they went deaf and I went hoarse.

And no, they never told me about their sex life, but fuck you, they were people, they were my people, and I want you to feel them living and sweating and laughing so you'll feel it when they're hurting and screaming and dying.

Okay?

Some things I found out about afterward, by asking questions. I asked Cathy, for example, and she was truthful with me. I don't think she'd have a real problem with anything I wrote about her. I hope not.

Some things are me describing how I personally remember feeling or what I remember thinking. Even though I'm filtering the memories of a younger me through the mind of an older me, the spirit of those memories, the good and the bad, is true. I'm able now, at nearly sixteen, to give a voice to things I thought when I was six and nine and so on.

Some parts are things the monster told me.

Who knows what the truth is there?

Okay, okay. I'm stalling, I know.

How should I begin it? Once Upon A Time?

Why not? No reason you can't begin a horror story the same way you begin a fairy tale. We're going to end up at the same place no matter how it begins: down at the watering hole, next to the dark things with too-big eyes and the water *that sounds like a giant smacking his lips as it beats against the shore.*

It'll help, as you read it, to think of it as a dream. That's what I do. A black flower. A book of dreams. A midnight trip to the watering hole. Come and dream with me, have a nightmare with your eyes open and the lights all on.

Once Upon A Time, there was a younger Sarah, a Sarah who didn't watch the white line of light and hadn't yet met The Crazy.

No, no. That's true, but that's not where I want to start.

So: Once Upon A Time, there was an angel, and she was known as my mom.

The first thing I remember about my mom is that she loved life. The second thing I remember is her smile. Mom never stopped smiling.

The last thing I remember is that she wasn't smiling when he killed her.

I remember that most of all.

Sarah's Story

Part One

18

Sam Langstrom shook his head at his wife, bemused.

'Let me get this straight,' he said, forcing back a smile. 'I ask you when we should leave for Sarah's dental appointment. In order to answer, you want to know what time it is *now*?'

Linda frowned at him. 'Yeah, so?'

'Well, babe, see – the appointment? It's already at a set time. Since we know how long it takes to get from here to the dentist's office – how does what time it is right now have anything to do with when we should leave?'

Linda was beginning to get annoyed. She looked into her husband's eyes. She saw the twinkle there that never failed to make her smile. Eyes that said, *I'm amused, but not at your expense. I'm just loving some character quirk of yours right now.*

He loved her eccentric parts, and she knew that she had them, no doubt about that. She was a terrible housekeeper; he was a bit neat. She was a social butterfly; he preferred to stay at home. She was quick to anger; he was more patient. They were opposites in so many ways, but not in the ways that mattered. Their differences complemented each other, as differences in couples had been doing since time began.

In those parts of life where the rubber met the road, they were one person, they had one mind. Love each other until they died.

Loyalty to each other, no matter what. Love Sarah, always, forever, unending.

Their daughter was a representation of their most unifying principle: love and be loved.

Their souls fit together in all the right places, but in other ways, they were worlds apart. As in this moment, where Sam's organized mind met her more Bohemian one and bounced off it with a smile.

'It has to do with checks and balances,' she said, grinning back at him. 'If we should leave at twelve-thirty to get there on time, but it's already twelve-fifteen, and I know it's going to take me twenty minutes to get ready, then . . .' She shrugged. 'We'll leave at twelve thirty-five, but we'll have to drive a little faster.'

He shook his head at her in mock amazement. 'There's something very wrong with you.'

She stepped into him, kissing him on the nose. 'The very thing you love about me, my perfect flaws. So, again? What time is it now?'

He looked at his watch. 'It's twelve-ten.'

'Well, see then, silly? We leave at twelve-thirty. That wasn't so hard now, was it?'

He laughed, he couldn't help himself.

'Fine,' he said, shaking his head. 'I'll let the beasts out and get the munchkin ready.'

The 'beasts' were their two black Labrador retrievers, known affectionately as the 'Black Forces of Destruction,' or, as Sarah often referred to them: 'Puppyheads!' They were two sixty-pound bundles of largely untrained love and loyalty, savages, unfit for civilized company.

Sam opened up the baby-gate that he'd erected as a barrier to keep the beasts out of the rest of the house, and was rewarded with an immediate nose in his butt.

'Thanks, Buster,' he said to the smaller male.

No problem, Buster replied, wagging his tail and smiling an open-mouthed dog-smile.

172

The larger female, Doreen, was circling him like a mentally disturbed person, or maybe a shark, asking the same silent but obvious question, over and over and over.

Is it time yet? Is it time yet? Is it time yet?

'Sorry, Doreen,' he said as she continued to circle him. 'It's going to be a late lunch today. But . . .' He paused, giving her an exaggerated, expectant look. 'If you guys go outside, I might give you a *treat*!'

At the word *treat*, Doreen launched herself into the air like a pogo stick, all four legs off the ground, a spontaneous and full-body expression of ultimate joy.

Hooray! she seemed to be saying. *Hooray, Hooray, Hooray!*

'I know,' Sam said, grinning. 'Dad is good, Dad is great.'

He walked over to the cupboard and fished out a couple of Milk-Bones. Doreen continued to launch herself into the air, now truly overjoyed. Buster was not a jumper, he preferred to comport himself with a little more dignity, but he was looking pretty happy.

'Come on, guys and gals,' Sam said and headed toward the sliding glass door that led into the backyard.

He opened it and stepped through. The beasts followed. He closed the door and stood, a treat in each hand.

'Sit,' he said.

They sat. Their eyes had achieved missile-lock on the treats. 'Sit' was one of the few things they were trained to do. They would only do it if a promise of food was involved.

He lowered his hands so that they were level with the dogs' heads. 'Wait,' he cautioned. If they tried to take the treats before 'wait' was done, he'd make them 'wait' even longer, something that was pretty unpopular. 'Wait,' he said, again. Doreen was quivering and starting to look a little bit crazy-eyed. Sam took mercy on her and issued the word they were waiting for: 'Okay.'

Two muzzles full of teeth leapt toward the treats in his hands, somehow grabbing the Milk-Bones without taking fingers along with them. Sam used this distraction to open the sliding glass door and step back into the house, closing it behind him.

Buster figured it out first. He stopped mid-crunch and looked at Sam through the glass, betrayal in his eyes.

You're abandoning us? he seemed to be asking.

'See you soon, buddy,' Sam murmured, smiling.

Time to look for the other beast that lived in this house. He was pretty sure she was hiding. Sarah wasn't too keen on the dentist. Sam secretly agreed with her on this. He always felt just a little bit guilty when they took her to one of her medical appointments, knowing that it would invariably end in tears. He admired Linda's cool head and practicality in these matters. Pain for the child's greater good, the province of Mom. Not a strength for most fathers.

'Munchkin?' he called out. 'You ready?'

No answer.

Sam moved toward Sarah's room. The door was open. He peeked his head in and saw his daughter sitting on her bed. She was clutching Mr Huggles in her arms.

'Sweetheart?' he asked.

The little girl turned her eyes to him and stole away his heart. *Woe, woe,* those eyes said, expressive as a baby seal's. *Woe to have parents that make you go to the dentist . . .*

Mr Huggles, a monkey made from socks, stared at Sam with accusing eyes.

'I don't want to go to the dennist, Daddy,' Sarah said, mournful.

'Den-*tist*, honey,' he replied. 'And no one likes going.'

'Well then why *do* they?'

The perfect logic of a child, he thought.

'Because if you don't take care of your teeth, you might lose them. Not having any teeth is no fun.'

He watched his child mull this over, really think about it.

'Can Mr Huggles come?' she asked.

'Of course he can.'

Sarah sighed, still not happy, but resigned to her fate. 'Okay, Daddy,' she said.

'Thanks, babe.' He glanced at his watch. Perfect timing to the end of these negotiations. 'Let's you, me, and Mr Huggles go find Mommy.'

In contrast to the drama that preceded it, the visit to the 'dennist's' office had been short and uneventful. Sarah's guarded suspicion had finally given way to smiles under the onslaught of Dr Hamilton's unending joviality. He'd even examined Mr Huggles.

This had led to a celebratory mood for the family, which had led to ice cream and a trip to the beach. It was nearly three in the afternoon by the time they returned home. The beasts forgot to be unhappy about being fed so late because they were just so darn happy about being fed *now*.

There was some obligatory petting, the getting of the mail, the technical brilliance of setting up the shows to record for the evening. Sam called it 'the arrival dance.' It was the checklist you went through each time you left for more than a few hours and came back. The details of living. Some men, he knew, complained about it. He loved it. It was comforting, it was right, it was his.

'You ready for tomorrow, Sarah?' he heard his wife ask.

Tomorrow was Sarah's birthday. The question was rhetorical.

He winced at the squeal that came from his daughter's mouth. An earsplitting, semi-alien screech.

'Presents, party, cake!' she cried, jumping up and down in excitement. It was very reminiscent of Doreen earlier, Sam mused. The dog and his daughter had disturbing similarities at times.

'Don't jump on the couch, munchkin,' he murmured as he looked through the mail.

'Sorry, Daddy.'

A certain *poised* feel to the silence that followed made him glance over at his daughter. He braced himself when he saw the look in her eyes. Exuberant mischief. The promise that a mildly destructive act was about to happen.

'But,' she giggled, a psychotic leprechaun, 'can I *jump on you*?'

She let out a squeal that was the sound of a pig being murdered and launched herself into the air, coming down on him like a pillow filled with goose down and rocks.

He 'ooofed' a little. More than I did a year ago, he thought to himself. Someday soon his days as a human trampoline would be over for good. He'd miss it.

Sarah was still small enough for now. He grinned and wrapped his arms around her.

'Zo . . .' he said, faking an exaggerated German accent and a sinister voice, 'you know vat zis means . . . *yes?*'

He felt her freeze, quivering and giggling in delight and terror. She knew what was coming.

'It means zat ve will haf to resort to . . . *tickle torture!*'

The torture began, and there was more squealing, and Doreen started barking and leaping around while the long-suffering Buster looked on.

Silly humans and a stupid dog, he seemed to be saying.

'Not so loud,' Linda Langstrom warned with a smile, watching as her husband and daughter dissolved into playful chaos. It was half-hearted. *Don't blow, wind*, she might as well be saying.

The truth was that she shared in their delight. Sam was always so peaceful and practical, the calm to her storm. It's not that he was stiff – Sam had a dry humor that never failed to make her laugh, a way of seeing the comedy of life – but he had a certain . . . quietness. A tendency, not to take himself seriously, but to *get* serious. And yet he was always willing to toss that aside for his family.

He sure tossed it aside when he proposed to her.

They were both in college. He was getting a degree in computer science, she in the arts. Some days their schedules conflicted. She'd have a night class that started an hour after his last day class ended, he had a night job – they really had to work to find time together on those days.

Sam had decided he was going to ask her to marry him and that he was going to be wearing a tuxedo when he did. It was one of his quirks: Once he decided to do something at a particular time, in a particular way, that was how it was going to be. It was a quality that could be either endearing or annoying, depending on the circumstances.

It had been one of those 'one-hour-window' days. There was no way he'd be able to get to their apartment (they'd been living together for a year), put on the tuxedo, and get back in time to propose to her before his night job started.

Sam's solution? He'd worn the tuxedo all day long, through all of his classes, through the heat of the day and the jibes of his fellow students.

The one-hour window arrived, and there he was, and he took her breath away. More than a boy, but not fully a man, silly and handsome and down on one knee, and she said yes, of course, and he skipped his job and she skipped her classes and they smoked grass and made love all night while the music played loud. They never managed to get all their clothes off; when she woke up in the morning, the bow tie from the tuxedo was still circling Sam's neck.

They were married a year later. Two years after that they had both graduated from college. Sam got a job right away with a software company, where he excelled. She painted and sculpted and took pictures, waiting with patient certainty to be 'discovered.'

Two years later and still unknown, Linda began to have serious doubts. The total certainty from her early twenties was beginning to wane as she hit twenty-five.

Sam had dismissed her doubts, in an absolute kind of way that she still loved him for.

'You're a great artist, babe,' he'd said, holding her eyes with his. 'It'll work out.'

Three weeks later, he'd come home from work, and had tangoed into her studio – literally tangoed, stepping and twirling toward her with an over-serious look on his face and a phantom rose between his teeth.

'Let's go,' he'd said, holding out a hand.

'Hang on a minute,' she'd said, concentrating on her brushstroke. It was a painting of a baby, alone in a forest, and she *liked* it.

He'd waited, tangoing with himself.

Linda had finished and folded her arms, smiling at Sam as he danced. 'What's up, silly man?'

'I have a surprise,' he'd said. 'Let's go.'

She'd raised an eyebrow. 'A surprise?'

'Yep.'

'What kind of surprise?'

'The kind that surprises you, of course.' He'd tapped his foot, had motioned with his hands toward the door. 'Giddyap. Get a move on. Take the lead out.'

'Hey,' she'd said, feigning indignation. 'I'm not a horse. And I need to change.'

'Nope. Tarzan say Jane go, now.'

She'd giggled (nobody could get her giggling like Sam), and had ended up letting him drag her out of the house and to the car. He'd driven them down the local highway, taking the exit that led to the new mall that had just opened. He'd pulled into the parking lot.

'The surprise is at the mall?'

He'd waggled his eyebrows at her. More giggling ensued.

It was an indoor mall, and Sam had led her inside, through the milling crowds of shoppers, walking, walking, walking – until he stopped.

They were standing in front of a medium-sized empty store.

She frowned. 'I don't understand.'

Sam had indicated the empty space with a sweep of his hand.

'It's yours, babe. This is the space for your store. You can figure out a name, haul in your art and photos, and *make* the public discover you.' He'd reached out a hand, had touched her face. 'You just need to get seen, Linda. Once they see you, they'll know what I know.'

She'd felt like the air had been sucked from her lungs. 'But . . . but . . . isn't this expensive, Sam?'

His smile had been somewhat rueful. 'It's not cheap. I took money from the house, from our home equity line. You can survive for about a year without turning a profit. After that, it'll get a little dicey.'

'Is . . .' She'd turned to him. 'Is this smart?' she'd asked in a whisper. Wanting what he was offering her, but doubting her ability to keep it from hurting them.

Sam had grinned. It was a beautiful grin, filled with happiness and strength. All man, now, no boy at all. 'It's not about smart. It's about us.' The smile had been replaced by seriousness. 'It's a gamble on you, babe, and win or lose, it's something we have to do.'

They'd gambled, and they'd won. The location had been a perfect choice, and while she didn't make them rich, she made a good profit. More important, she was doing what she loved, and her husband had helped make sure of that. It didn't make her love him more, that was impossible. What it did was add a new layer of permanence and certainty. This was the secret to their love: its priority. They kept their love important, above money, pride, or the approval of others.

They continued to love each other, in life and in the bedroom. Two years later, Sarah was born.

Sam liked to joke that Sarah was a 'red-faced, cone-headed beauty.' Linda had watched in wonder as that tiny mouth found her nipple with single-minded certainty. Life had thrilled through Linda, something undefinable but huge, new and ancient at the same time. She'd tried to get that feeling onto canvas with paint. She'd failed each time. Even the failures were magnificent.

Linda watched her husband and her daughter fight their tickle-war as Doreen struggled to be a part of it in her desperate, doggy way.

Sarah was special. The cone-head had gone away within hours, of course, and as the years moved on, Sarah had only grown more beautiful. She seemed to skip caterpillar, going straight to butterfly, hold the cocoon. Linda wasn't sure where it came from.

'Maybe we'll get lucky,' Sam would joke. 'Maybe she'll get ugly when she becomes a teenager and keep me from having to buy a shotgun.'

Linda didn't think so. She was pretty sure that her munchkin was going to be a head-turner.

'I think she's just the best parts of both of us,' Sam had said once.

Linda liked that explanation.

19

Sarah had babbled nonstop through supper about her birthday, all excited eyes and energy. Linda wondered how in the world she was going to get her calm enough to go to sleep. A common parental problem, the 'Christmas Syndrome.'

At least during Christmas, she could tell Sarah that Santa wouldn't come unless she went to sleep. Birthdays were more of a challenge.

'Do you think I'll get a lot of presents, Mommy?'

Sam looked at his daughter, puzzled. 'Presents? Why would you get presents?'

Sarah ignored her father. 'And a big cake, Mommy?'

Sam shook his head, regretful. 'Definitely no cake,' he said. 'Girl's gone wonky in the head. Soft in the noggin.'

'Daddy!' Sarah rebuked.

Linda smiled. 'Plenty of cake and presents, babe. But you're going to have to wait,' she cautioned. 'The party isn't until after lunch, you know that.'

'I know. But I wish it was like Christmas, where you get your presents in the morning!'

Bingo, Linda thought. Sneaky, yet obvious. Why didn't I think of it before?

'I'll tell you what, sweetie,' she said. 'If you go to bed tonight –

on time – and don't give me any hassle about it, I'll let you open a present in the morning. How's that sound?'

'Really?'

'Really. If' – she held up a finger – 'you go to bed on time.'

Sarah nodded her head in that overenthusiastic way of small children, head all the way back, then chin to chest, repeat.

'Then it's a deal.'

Sam was putting his daughter to bed. Buster followed them as always, his routine. Doreen was the kind of dog that loved everybody. She'd probably lead a burglar through the house with her tail wagging, glad for the company, hopeful she'd get a treat for being helpful. Buster loved too, but his love was sparing, his view of the world more suspicious. He picked few people to love, but those people were *his*, and he loved them with his whole self.

He loved Sarah most of all, and slept with her in her bed each night.

Sarah was under the covers. Buster jumped up and nestled beside her, resting his head on her small stomach.

'All set, munchkin?'

'Kiss!' she said, stretching her arms out toward him.

Sam leaned forward, planting a kiss on her forehead, accepting her gossamer hug.

'How about now?' he asked.

Her eyes popped open wide. 'My Little Pony!' she cried.

'My Little Pony' was a child's character, mixing fairy-stuff with pony-stuff, resulting in improbable light blue ponies with manes of pink. Sarah had a doll version that she slept with.

'Hmmm . . .' Sam said, looking around. 'Where is My Little Donkey?'

'Daddy!' Sarah half-yelled, a mix of exasperation and delight.

Fathers tease their daughters in many ways; this was one of Sam's. It had started a year ago, him substituting 'donkey' for 'pony.' At first Sarah's distress had been real, but over time it had become a tradition between them, something he knew they'd laugh about together when she was older.

He found it on the floor next to her bed and deposited it into her waiting hands. She hugged it to her, wiggling farther under the blankets. The movement forced Buster to move his head. He glared and sighed, a deep, doggy-sigh. *The lot of an unappreciated animal*, he seemed to be saying.

'How about now?' Sam asked.

'You need to leave, Daddy,' Sarah admonished. 'I got to go to sleep so I can wake up and open my present.'

'Propen your mesent?' he said, puzzled.

She giggled. Sarah loved when Sam made up spoonerisms – where you reversed the first letters of two words, like the 'the spork and the foon.' She thought that was the mat's ceow.

'Olive juice, munchkin.'

'Olive juice, Daddy.'

Another one of their silly traditions. If you mouthed 'olive juice,' it looked from a distance like you were saying 'I love you.' Sam had demonstrated this to Sarah when she was four. She'd thought it was the most brilliant thing ever, well worth repeating a few thousand times. Now they said it to each other every night.

He had no way of knowing this would be the second-to-last time he'd ever say it.

Sarah squinched her eyes shut, and petted Buster, and tried to make her brain turn off.

Tomorrow was her birthday! She'd be six, almost a grown-up, which was *interesting*, but the presents, *that's* what she was most excited about.

She looked around at her walls, lit by the hallway bulb that came through the half-open doorway to her room. They were covered with paintings her mother had done. Her eyes searched for and found her favorite: the baby, alone in the forest.

Someone hearing about it, not seeing it, might think it was a scary picture. But it wasn't, not at all.

The baby, a girl, was peaceful, lying on a bed of moss, eyes closed. Trees were to the left of her, a brook to the right. The sun was out, the sky had some clouds in it, and if you looked close, you could see a smiling face in those clouds, looking down on the baby girl.

'Is it watching her, Mommy?'

'That's right, honey. Even though she's alone in the forest, she's never *really* alone, because the woman in the clouds is watching over her.'

Sarah had stared at the picture, loving it.

'The baby is me, isn't it, Mommy? And the cloud-lady – that's you.'

Her mother had smiled then, the smile Sarah loved so much. It had no secrets, no hidden meanings. It was just the sun, dazzling and happy and warm on your face.

'That's right, babe. That's what it is, for you and me and anyone else who looks at it.'

Sarah had been puzzled. 'It's you for other people too?'

'No, it's *Mommy* for other people. They could be grown-ups, out in the world, away from their mommies, but they're never alone, because Mommy is always there.' She'd grabbed her daughter, had hugged her in a spontaneous motion that had made Sarah laugh out loud. 'That's what mommies are, and what they do. They watch over you forever.'

The painting had been a gift on her fifth birthday. It hung on the wall that faced the foot of her bed, a talisman.

Her mother never bought her birthday gifts. She made them. Sarah loved them all. She couldn't wait to see what she was going to get tomorrow.

She squinched her eyes shut again, and petted Buster (who licked her hand) and willed her brain to turn off.

She fell asleep once she stopped trying, a smile on her face.

The first thing Sarah realized when she woke up was that Buster wasn't there. This was strange; the dog went to sleep when she did, and got up when she did, every day.

The second thing she noticed was that the sun wasn't shining. This too was strange. It was night when she closed her eyes, morning when she opened them. That's the way it worked.

There was something about this dark. Something heavy and scary. It no longer felt like the dark before her birthday. This felt like the dark of a closet when you got locked in. Stuffy, hot, close.

'Mommy?' she whispered. Part of her wondered why she didn't say it louder. If she really wanted her mother to hear her, why was she whispering?

Her six-year-old mind provided the answer: because she was afraid something *else* would hear too. Whatever it was that was creating this scary dark.

Her heart was beating *so* fast, her breath was coming even faster, she was headed toward full-blown terror, the place of waking up after a nightmare, except that in those times, she always had *Buster*, and now Buster wasn't here –

Look at the picture, stupid, she ordered herself.

She found her mother's painting in the dark. The baby, asleep on the moss, peaceful and safe. She fixed her gaze on the face in the clouds. The face that meant Mommy, that pushed back this scary dark, that said Buster was in the backyard, that he'd used the doggy-door to relieve himself, that she'd just woken up because he was gone, and that soon he'd be back and she'd fall asleep again and wake up in the morning, and it would be her birthday.

Her heart stopped hammering as she thought these things. Her breathing slowed and her fear began to subside. She even started to feel silly.

Almost a grown-up and acting afraid of the dark like a little baby, she chided herself.

Then she heard the voice and she knew it was the voice of a stranger, here in her house, in the dark. The terror returned and her heart skipped. She froze, eyes too wide.

'"I never saw a wild thing sorry for itself,"' the voice intoned, moving toward her door. '"A small bird will drop frozen dead from a bough without ever having felt sorry for itself."'

The voice wasn't deep or high, but somewhere in between.

'Do you hear me, Sarah? A famous poet named D. H. Lawrence wrote those words.'

He was standing outside her door. Her teeth chattered, though she was unaware of it.

This was beyond terror. This was waking up from a nightmare to find that the thing in the nightmare had *followed you out*, was shambling down the hallway toward your room to *hug you*, to hold you tight while it laughed and moaned and you screamed and lost your mind.

'We could learn a lot from the wild things. Pity, for yourself or for others, is useless. Life will go on whether you live or die, whether you're happy or unhappy. Life doesn't care. Ruthlessness, now that's a useful emotion. God is ruthless. That is a part of his beauty and his power. To do what is right, consequences or deaths of innocents be damned.'

He paused. Sarah could almost hear him breathing. She could also hear her own heart, so loud she thought her eardrums were going to burst.

'Buster didn't feel sorry for himself, Sarah. I want you to know that he came right for me. No hesitation. He knew I was here for *you*, and he ran toward me without thinking about it twice. He was going to kill me to save you.'

Another pause. Then a chuckle, low and long.

'I want you to know that so you understand: Buster's dead because he loved you.'

The door flew open wide, and The Stranger was there, and he threw something onto Sarah's bed.

The light from the hallway lit up the object: Buster's severed head, teeth still bared, eyes wide with rage.

Sarah unfroze then. She began to scream.

186

20

'I need you to watch, Sarah, and I need you to listen. This is the start of something.'

They were in the living room. Mommy and Daddy sat on chairs with handcuffs around their wrists and ankles. They were naked. Seeing her father nude embarrassed Sarah and added to her terror. Doreen was lying on the floor, watching them all, unaware that anything was wrong.

Stay stupid, puppyhead, Sarah thought, and maybe he won't kill you like he killed Buster.

Sarah was seated on the couch in her nightgown, handcuffed as well.

The Stranger, as she thought of the man, was standing. He had a gun in his hand. He had panty hose pulled over his head. The panty hose stretched and twisted his features, made it look as though his face had been melted by a blowtorch.

Her fear was still there, still strong, but it had moved away from her. It was a scream in the distance. It was a waiting, a terrible waiting, the executioner's axe frozen at its apex.

Her parents were terrified. Their mouths were covered with tape but their eyes showed their fear. Sarah sensed they were more afraid for her than themselves.

He walked over next to her daddy and leaned forward so that he could look into Sam's eyes.

'I know what you're thinking, Sam. You want to know why. Believe me, I wish that I could tell you. I wish it more than anything. But Sarah's listening, you see, and she might tell others, later. I can't have my story being told until I'm ready.

'I can say two things: It's not your fault, Linda, but your death is my justice. It's not Sarah's fault, but her pain is my justice. I know, you don't understand. That's all right. You don't need to understand, you just need to know that these things are *true.*'

He stood up.

'Let's talk about pain. Pain is a form of energy. It can be created, like electricity. It can flow, like a current. It can be steady or it can pulse. It can be powerful and agonizing, or weak and just annoying. Pain can force a man to talk. What a lot of people don't know is that pain can also force a man to think. It can form a man, mold a man, make him who he is.

'I *know* pain. I *understand* it. It's taught me things. One of the things I've learned is that while people fear pain, they can tolerate much, much more of it than they think. If, for example, I tell you that I'm going to jam a needle into your arm, you'll become fearful. If I actually do it, the pain will seem excruciating. But if I do it again, every hour on the hour, for a year, you'll learn to adjust. You'll never like it, but you'll no longer fear it. And that is what this will be about.'

The Stranger turned his gaze on Sarah.

'I'm going to stick that metaphorical pin into Sarah. Over and over and over, for years and years and years. I'm going to use the pain to sculpt her, like an artist. I'll make her over into my own image, and I will call her what she'll become: *A Ruined Life.*'

'Please don't hurt my mommy and daddy,' Sarah said. She was surprised to hear her own voice. It sounded strange, far away, too calm for what was happening.

The Stranger was surprised as well. He seemed to approve, nodding and smiling with his melted face. 'Good! There it is: love. I want you to remember this moment in the future, Sarah. I want you to think back and mark this as the last time you were without real pain. Trust me, it will sustain you in the coming years.' He paused, examining her face. 'Now, hush, and watch.'

She watched as he turned toward her parents. Things still felt dreamy to her, all hazy and indistinct. Fear was there, horror was there, tears were there, but they were pinpricks in the distance. Things shouting at her from the horizon. She had to strain to hear them, and her reluctance to do so was heavy, crushing, a weight she couldn't lift.

She'd looked into Buster's dead eyes, she'd screamed, and then her heart had gone away. Not for good, and not far, but far enough that she didn't have to listen to it shriek.

Buster . . .

There was anguish waiting in that word, a pain powerful enough to suck a soul under forever. At some level, she knew Buster was only the beginning. The Stranger was more than a black tide, he was an ocean of darkness. A huge, empty *nothing* in human form with a gravitational presence strong enough to bend light waves and laugh sounds and goodness.

The correct instinct of a civilized society is to protect the young from evil, but in doing so, society sometimes loses sight of a basic truth: A child is always ready to believe in the existence of monsters.

Sarah knew The Stranger was a monster. She had accepted this as a totality the moment he'd thrown Buster's severed head onto her bed.

'Sam and Linda Langstrom,' The Stranger spoke, 'please listen carefully. The thing you need to understand is that death's inevitable. I'm going to kill you both. You need to dismiss any hopes you might have that you're going to live. Instead, you need to focus on what you can control: what happens to Sarah.'

Linda Langstrom's heart had sped up when the man said he was going to kill them. She couldn't help it; the desire to live was visceral. But when he told them that Sarah's fate was still unde- cided, her heartbeat had actually slowed. She'd been looking at

Sarah, worrying, only half- listening to the man. Now she turned her eyes to him, forced herself to focus.

The Stranger smiled. 'Yes. There it is. That's one mix of love other than the love of God that comes close to having real power – mother to child. Mothers will kill, torture, and maim to save a child. They'll lie and steal and prostitute themselves to feed a child. There's a certain divinity to it. But nothing is ever as strong as the strength achieved when you give yourself over to God.'

He leaned forward until his eyes were level with Linda's. 'I have that strength. Because of that, I get to kill you. Because of that, I get to do my work with Sarah. Because of that, I never have to apologize. The strong don't have to be sorry. All they have to do is continue to breathe.' He stood back up. 'So, what does that kind of strength do when it's defied by a lesser love? It demonstrates its power by forcing choices. And now I'm going to give you some choices, Linda. Are you ready?'

Linda looked at The Stranger's face, examined the panty-hose-twisted features. She realized that trying to bargain with this man would be like bargaining with a rock, a block of wood, a rattle-snake. She was nothing to him, nothing at all. She answered his question with a nod.

'Good,' he replied.

Was it her imagination, or was he breathing faster now? Getting excited?

'Here is the scenario. Sam, you need to listen to this as well.'

He didn't need to demand Sam's attention; Sam had never taken his eyes off the man. Sam had been staring at The Stranger, his heart filled with a hate so pure it was almost unbearable. His desire to murder this man was excruciating.

Just let me get these cuffs off, he raged inside, and I'll tear you apart. I'll slam your head against the floor until your skull cracks and I see your brain . . .

'Sarah will live. You are both going to die, but she will live. If you've had concerns, that should allay them. I'm not going to kill her.' He paused. 'But I could decide to hurt her.'

He transferred the gun to his left hand, reached into his back pocket with the other and came out holding a lighter. It was flashy; a mix of gold plating and mother-of-pearl, with an inlaid picture of a domino tile on one side, the two-three piece.

He flipped the lighter open, and flicked the wheel with his thumb. A small flame lit, blue at the bottom.

'I could burn her,' The Stranger murmured, looking into the flame. 'I could torch her face. Turn her nose into a lump of melted wax, fry off her eyebrows, blacken her lips.' He smiled, still looking at the flame. 'I could sculpt her literally rather than figuratively, using flame as my knife. Fire is strong and ruthless. Absent of love. A living representation of the power of God.'

He snapped the lighter shut in a sudden motion and returned it to his pocket. He moved the gun back to his right hand.

'I could burn her for days. Please believe me. I know how to do it. How to make it last. She wouldn't die, but she'd beg for death in the first hour, and she would lose her mind long before bedtime.'

His words, and the certainty with which he delivered them, terrified Linda. A raw and ragged terror. She didn't doubt him. Not even a little bit. He'd burn her baby, and he'd smile and whistle as he did it. She realized that she feared this more than dying, and for a moment (*just a moment*) she felt relief. Parents like to think that they'd die for their children – but would they? When a gun came out, would they step between it and their child? Or would something more primal and shameful take over?

I would die for her, Linda realized. In spite of what was happening, this made her proud. It was freeing. It gave her focus. She concentrated on what The Stranger was saying. What did she have to do to keep him from burning her baby?

'You can prevent this,' The Stranger continued. 'All you have to do is strangle your husband.'

Sam was startled from his reverie of rage.

What did he just say?

The Stranger reached into a bag near the couch, pulling out a small video camera and a collapsible tripod. He placed the camera on the tripod and positioned it so that it was pointing at her and Sam. He pushed a button, there was a musical tone, and Linda realized they were now being filmed.

What did he just say?

'I want you to put your hands around his neck, Linda, and I want you to look into his eyes, and I want you to strangle your husband. I want you to watch him die. Do it, and Sarah will not burn. Refuse, and I'll put the flame to her until she smokes.'

The rage had gone away, far, far away. Had it ever really been there? It didn't feel like it to Sam. He was dazed. He felt like someone had just hit him in the face with a hammer.

It was as if his ability to comprehend had been ratcheted up to a superhuman level. He was thinking in fractals, seeing the interconnectedness of everything in strobe flashes. Truths arrived in rifle cracks of illumination.

This leads to this leads to that . . . and the sum is always the same.

He and Linda were going to die. He understood that with a sudden certainty.

Too sudden?

No. This man was implacable. He wasn't testing them. He wasn't pranking them, this wasn't a trick. He was here to kill them. Sam wasn't going to break free and save his family. There wouldn't be any Hollywood-movie moment of sudden redemption. The bad guys were going to win and get away clean.

This leads to this leads to that . . .

Only one outcome wasn't yet decided, the most important one: What was going to happen to Sarah.

He looked at his daughter. Sadness overwhelmed him.

What would happen to Sarah? He realized he'd never really know. His little girl, if she survived this, would go on. Sam would end here. He'd never know if any sacrifice made had saved her or not.

She looked so small. The couch was just a yard away, but it might as well have been a light-year. A new wave of sadness, choking and desperate. He was never going to touch his little girl again! The kiss he'd given her last night, the hug, had been the last of it.

He looked over at Linda. She was listening to The Stranger, her eyes intent. Sam drank in the image of her chestnut hair and her brown eyes, and then he closed his own and *remembered* her so hard that he could almost smell her, a scent of hand soap and woman, as uniquely Linda as her DNA.

He remembered her clothed and classy, and he remembered her naked underneath him, in her studio, covered in paint and sweat.

He remembered his daughter too. He remembered that the surge of love he'd felt when he first heard her cry was so strong it threatened to consume him. It was fierce, and it was huge, and it was larger than he could ever hope to be alone.

He remembered her laughter, and her tears, and her trust.

Last, he remembered them together, the wife and the daughter. Sarah asleep in Linda's arms as a baby, after a long and colicky night.

He remembered and he felt sad and he felt angry and he wanted to fight, but –

The sum is always the same.

He opened his eyes, and he turned to Linda, and this time she was looking back at him. He tried to make his eyes smile, tried to show her the all of everything inside him, and then – he closed his eyes, once, and nodded.

It's okay, babe, he was telling her. *Do it, it's okay.*

Linda knew what her husband was saying. Of course she did – they'd talked without words, plenty of times. *We may be different in some ways*, he was saying, *but in those places where the rubber meets the road, we're one person.*

One tear slid from her right eye.

'I'll remove his gag, and I will uncuff your wrists. You will put your hands around his neck and then you'll squeeze until he's dead. You'll kill him, and Sarah will watch, and it will be terrible for you, I know, but I won't touch Sarah when I'm done with the two of you.'

He cocked his head, seeming to notice for the first time that something had passed between Sam and Linda.

'You've already decided, haven't you? Both of you.' He was quiet for a moment. 'Did you hear that, little one? Mommy is going to kill Daddy to keep me from burning you with fire. Do you know what you should learn from that?'

No reply.

'The same lesson as before. Mommy is going to be ruthless, and it's going to save you. Did you hear me, Sarah? Mommy's ruthlessness is going to save you. Her willingness to feel pain for you is going to save you. Strength, finally, to support that mother-love.'

Sarah was hearing what The Stranger was saying, but they weren't real words to her. She believed in monsters. In the end though, the monsters always lost.

Didn't they?

God made sure that nothing truly bad happened to good people. This wouldn't be any different. It was scary, it was terrifying, it was terrible that Buster had died. But if she could hold it together, The Stranger wouldn't win. Daddy would stop him, or God would stop him, or maybe even Mommy.

She kept herself from believing what he was saying, and concentrated on waiting for the moment that it would all be over, and Mommy and Daddy and Doreen would be okay.

Linda Langstrom listened to The Stranger talking to her daughter. Rage and despair roared up inside her. Who was this man? He'd walked into their home in the middle of the night, without fear or hesitation. He'd entered their bedroom with a gun, had woken them with a whisper. 'Scream and you will die. Do anything other than what I tell you and you will die.'

His control had been absolute from the start. He was both the irresistible force and the immovable object, and now he'd backed them into a corner, with only one way out. She had to kill Sam, or the man would torture Sarah. What choice was left with such inexorable options? The Stranger was manipulating them, she knew this. He might still hurt Sarah. Kill her, even.

But . . . he might not. And that possibility, well . . . what choice was left?

Her rage was impotent, she was aware of that. Her despair was suffocating. Sam would die. She'd die. Sarah *might* live. But who'd raise her? Who'd love her?

Who would watch her baby from the clouds?

'I'm going to take off both of your gags. Sam, you will be allowed two final sentences – one to your wife, onc to your daughter. Linda, you are allowed a single sentence to Sam. Exceed these parameters, and Sarah burns. Do you understand?'

They both nodded.

'Very good.'

He removed Linda's gag first, then Sam's.

'I'll give you a minute. A sentence isn't much, when it's your last chance to speak. Please don't be frivolous.'

Sam looked at his daughter and his wife. He glanced down at Doreen, who wagged her tail at him, stupid, lovable dog.

He wondered at his lack of fear. On one hand, everything was bright and sharp-edged, on the other it was all a floating surreality. Shock? Maybe.

He made himself focus. What were his last words going to be? What should he say to Linda, who was about to be forced to kill him? What did he want his daughter to remember about this moment?

All kinds of things flew into his head, sentences with fifty words, apologies, good-byes. In the end, he let the words come from him without inspection, and hoped they were right.

He looked at his wife. 'You are a work of art,' he told her.

He looked at his daughter. 'Olive juice,' he said, smiling.

Sarah stared at him for a moment, surprised, and then she smiled the smile that had stolen his heart from the beginning. 'Olive juice, Daddy,' she said.

Linda looked at her husband and fought to keep herself from choking with grief. What was she going to say to this man? To her Sam, who'd saved her in so many ways? He'd saved her from her own self-doubt, had saved her from living a life without loving him. A sentence? She could speak for a year without stopping and it still wouldn't be enough.

'I love you, Sam.' She blurted out the words, and at first she wanted to scream, to take them back, they weren't enough, that couldn't be the last thing she ever said to her husband.

But then she saw his eyes and that smile, and she understood that while it wasn't the perfect sentence, it was the only one. She'd married her first love, the love of her youth. She'd loved him through laughter and anger, with kisses and yells. Love is where it started, love is where it was going to end.

She expected The Stranger to say something, to make fun of these last words, but he didn't. He stood and waited, silent. He seemed almost respectful.

'Thank you for complying,' he said. 'I really don't want to have to burn Sarah.' A pause. 'Now we're going to begin the strangling. It's not as easy as you might think, so please listen to what I tell you.'

Linda and Sam listened to the man, but kept their eyes on each other. They talked without words. The Stranger droned on, giving Linda matter-of-fact advice on how to kill her husband.

'I don't need it to be painful, or to last for a specified time. If he goes quickly, that's fine. It just needs to happen. The areas you'll want to concentrate on are here and here.' He touched areas high on each side of Sam's neck, near the jawline. 'The carotid arteries. Cutting off the blood flow in those places will knock him unconscious before the lack of air kills him. Concurrent with that, you'll need to exert pressure forward with both hands in order to cut off the airflow through his windpipe.' The Stranger demonstrated without actually touching Sam's neck. 'Then you hold on till he stops breathing. Simple. I will re-cuff him from behind so he can't reach up to try and tear your hands away.' The Stranger shrugged. 'It happens, even with suicides. One man had pulled a plastic bag over his head, had taped it closed around his neck, and then had handcuffed his own hands behind him. I suppose he changed his mind once it started getting difficult to breathe. He almost tore his thumbs off trying to rip his hands from the cuffs. We don't want any of that here.'

Sam was sure The Stranger was right. He could feel his own fear, far off but persistent. Knocking at his door.

Little pig, little pig, let me in . . .

No. He didn't want to die, that was true. But he was going to. This leads to this leads to that, and the sum is always the same. Save Sarah. You can't always get what you want. Life's a bitch –

– and then you die.

Sam sighed. He took one more look around. First at the room, the kitchen, the shadowy front area beyond that. His home, where he'd loved his wife and raised his child, where he'd fought the good fight. Then at Sarah, the living, breathing result of the love between him and Linda. Finally, he looked into his wife's eyes. A deep, lingering look, and he tried to tell her many things and everything, and he hoped she understood all of it, or some of it, and then he closed his eyes.

Oh, Sam, no . . . Linda understood what he was doing, what he'd just done. He'd said good-bye. He'd closed his eyes, and she knew he didn't plan to open them again. Logic was a big part of who Sam was. It was one of the things she loved about him, it was one of the things about him that drove her crazy. He had this ability, to see things three moves ahead, to arrive at an understanding while she was still puzzling over it.

Sam had probably known they were going to die long before The Stranger ever told them so. He'd examined the situation, had weighed the possibilities of the man's motivations, and had realized the inevitable. Everything since had been him waiting. And feeling.

'You go *fuck* yourself!'

The words came out of her mouth before she could stop them,

driven by emotion, not logic. The Stranger paused, looked at her, cocked his head.

'I'm sorry, what did you say?'

'I told you to go fuck yourself,' she snarled. 'I'm not doing it.'

She looked over at Sam. Why hadn't he opened his eyes?

The Stranger leaned toward her. He gazed at her for a long moment, and she was reminded of a statue. Stone, unfeeling, resolute.

'You're mistaken,' he said.

He put the tape back over her mouth, and then Sam's. He didn't seem angry as he did it. Without speaking, he walked over to Sarah, gagged her, grabbed her handcuffed wrists, and yanked her hands forward. He stuffed his gun in his pants, and reached into his back pocket, pulling out the flashy gold-plated lighter. Linda's heart froze when she heard the 'snick' of it opening. His thumb pumped once on the wheel, and there was fire.

He made sure that Linda was watching as he held Sarah's palm over the flame for three full seconds.

Sarah screamed the whole time; The Stranger did what he had said was the only duty of the strong: He kept on breathing, calm and sure.

21

Sarah couldn't believe how much it hurt. She'd been forced to stop crying so that she could breathe through her nose.

All the far-away things were now close. Her emotions were a blinding sheet of white lightning inside her, terror, grief, horror. The monster was inescapable. She knew that now. This knowledge was destroying her.

Her mother had raged as Sarah had been burnt. Linda had yanked so hard against her handcuffs that she would have torn the flesh on her wrists to the bone, if the insides of the cuffs had not been padded. Mommy was still Mommy, but she crackled with a threatening energy Sarah had never seen.

Even The Stranger was impressed.

'Magnificent,' he'd said. 'You are one of the scariest things I've ever seen.'

Sarah had agreed.

'The problem, Linda, is that I'm scarier.' He'd shaken his head. 'Don't you understand? You can't win. You won't beat me. I am strength. I am certainty. Your choices are unaltered: Do what I say, or watch as I burn Sarah into a semblance of a circus freak.'

Her mother had quieted down then. Sarah had tried to look at her daddy, but his eyes were closed.

'I'm going to give you a few moments to collect yourself. A full minute. After that, you'll either tell me that you're ready, and we will move forward, or I will put the torch to Sarah in *earnest.*'

Sarah quivered in fear at the thought of more fire, more pain. And what did he mean by 'moving forward'? She'd been in her far-away place, waiting for the monsters to go away. He'd talked during that time, said something important. She strained to remember.

Something about Mommy and Daddy . . .

Mommy killing Daddy . . .

She remembered, and her eyes opened wide, and the far-away place beckoned once more.

Linda struggled to get herself under control. She was full of white noise and static, one big short-circuit of the soul. Rage had taken over. She hadn't been able to hold it back. She'd seen red and the anger and futility had marched in, banishing what little equilibrium she'd had left. Her wrists ached, and she felt over-oxygenated and sick to her stomach from the adrenaline rush.

Sam, damn Sam, still had his eyes closed. She knew why, and she hated him for it. Hated him for being right. For knowing it was over, knowing there weren't any other choices, and for accepting that.

No, no, she loved Sam, she didn't hate him. This was him, who he was. His mind was one of the things she loved most about him. His clarity, his brilliance. He was being so courageous right now. He'd said good-bye, closed his eyes, and left his neck exposed, ready for her strangling hands.

WWSD?

The saying had jumped into her mind: What Would Sam Do?

It was a mantra that she used when her emotions battled with her common sense. Sam was calm, Sam was logical, Sam was steady-as-she-goes. Capable of rage when it mattered, but able to let the small things go with a shrug.

When someone cut her off on the freeway and she started swearing out loud at them in front of Sarah, she'd take a breath and ask: WWSD? What Would Sam Do?

It didn't always work, but it had woven itself into the fabric of her, and it appeared now at the time when she most needed it.

Sam would weigh the facts. Linda took a deep breath, closed her eyes.

Fact: We can't escape. He's handcuffed us, the cuffs aren't budging. We're trapped.

Fact: He can't be bargained with.

Fact: He's going to kill us.

These last two facts *were* facts. The Stranger's calm resoluteness, the workmanlike way in which he did everything, including burning Sarah's hand, left no doubt about what he was and what he would do. He'd do what he said.

But will he spare Sarah if we do what he asks?

Fact: We can't know for sure that he will.

Fact: We can't know for sure that he won't.

It all led to what had caused Sam to close his eyes: this leads to this leads to that, and the sum is always the same.

Fact: The possibility that he will spare her is all that's left. The only thing we might still be able to control.

She opened her eyes. The Stranger was watching her.

'Have you made your decision?' he asked.

She blinked once for yes. He removed the tape over her mouth.

'I'll do it,' she said.

That hint of excitement again, a ghost that appeared and disappeared in his eyes.

'Excellent,' he said. 'I'm going to re-cuff Sam's hands behind his back first.'

He did this in quick, practiced motions. Sam kept his eyes closed and didn't resist.

'Now, Linda, I'm going to remove the handcuffs from your wrists. You could decide to have another one of your "moments."' He shook his head. 'Don't. It won't get you anywhere, and I'll burn

Sarah's left hand until it's a melted lump. Do you understand?'

'Yes,' she replied, her voice full of hate.

'Good.'

He removed the cuffs. She did consider attacking him, just for a moment. She fantasized about shooting her hands out, grabbing his neck, and squeezing with all the rage and sorrow in her heart, squeezing until his eyes exploded.

But this, she knew, was pure fantasy. He was an experienced predator, alert to the tricks of his prey.

Her wrists throbbed. It was a dull, deep pain. She welcomed the sensation. It reminded her of Sarah's birth. Beautiful, terrible agony.

'Do it,' The Stranger commanded, his voice flat and taut.

Linda looked at Sam, Sam with his eyes still closed, her beautiful man, her beautiful boy. He was strong in ways that she was weak, he had tenderness, he could be callous and arrogant, he had been responsible for her longest laughs and her strongest grief. He'd looked past her outer beauty to gaze upon the uglier parts of her, and had loved her still. He had never touched her in anger. They'd shared moments of sex as love and tenderness, and they'd fucked outdoors in a rainstorm, shivering as the cold water pelted their naked skin and she screamed above the wind.

Linda realized that she could continue this list forever.

She reached out with her hands. They trembled. When they touched his neck, she choked.

Sense-memory.

The feel of Sam, igniting remembrance of another ten thousand moments. A million tiny paper cuts on her soul, she bled from them all.

He opened his eyes and a million cuts became a single, searing pain.

Of all his physical features, Linda loved Sam's eyes the most. They were gray, intense, surrounded by long eyelashes that any woman would envy. They were capable of such deep expression, of such emotion.

She remembered him looking at her with those eyes over a table on a wedding anniversary. He'd smiled at her.

'Do you know one of the things I love most about you?' he'd asked.

'What?'

'Your beautiful lunacy. The way you can arrange the chaos of a sculpture or a painting, but couldn't arrange an underwear drawer to save your life. The way you fumble through loving me and Sarah with your whole self. The way you never forget a shade of blue, but can never remember to pay the phone bill. You bring a wildness to my life that I'd be lost without.'

Sam was loving her now, she could tell. Those eyes, those intense gray eyes, radiated emotion. Love, sadness, anger, pain, and joy. She fell into them, and she hoped he understood everything that she was feeling right now, every bit of it.

He winked once, and it made her laugh – a strangled laugh, but a laugh nonetheless – and then he closed his eyes again, and she knew he was ready, that she'd never be ready, but that the time was now.

She started to squeeze.

'If you don't grip harder, he'll spend a long time dying,' The Stranger said.

Linda squeezed harder. She could feel Sam's heartbeat beneath her fingers, could feel the *life* of him, and she began to cry. Deep, ropy sobs, wrenched from that undefinable part of her that was capable of hurting the most.

Sam could hear his wife crying. He could feel her hands tightening around his neck. She'd gripped in the right places; the blood flow to his brain was being cut off. It created a huge pressure in his head, along with a lightheadedness and a faint pain in his chest. His lungs were starting to burn.

He kept his eyes closed, looking into the black. He prayed that he'd be able to keep them closed while he died. He didn't want Linda to have to see him, to watch life leave him.

More burning now, panic was starting to come, he could sense it in the distance.

Fight it, Sam, he commanded himself. Hold on, it won't be long now, you'll pass out soon.

He would, he knew. He could feel it, black edges around his consciousness. Sparking. Once he fell into that blackness, that'd be it. That sparking was the last bit of himself. First he'd be enveloped by the black, and then he'd become the black.

Ooops . . .

He'd lost a moment there. Instead of sparks, there had been a flash, not of light, but of darkness. He realized that it wasn't something he was going to be aware of, it was going to sneak up on him. A flash of dark would come and then it would stay, forever.

Another flash, but this one was brilliant, blinding, excruciating in its loveliness. He and Linda, naked in a rainstorm, the raindrops powerful and so *cold*. They shivered and they fucked and she was on top and lightning lit up the sky around her head as he came, so *hard* –

– Sarah wailing in the delivery room and he couldn't breathe and his knees were weak and he was filled with such *triumph* –

– Sarah rushing toward him, hair in the wind, arms wide, laughing at the world, Linda rushing toward him, hair in the wind, arms wide, laughing at the world –

OliveJuiceOliveJuiceOliveJuice –

The last flash, and Sam Langstrom died.

He was smiling.

22

Linda's mind was empty.

Sam slumped forward in the chair. She'd felt his pulse speed up underneath her fingers, then she'd felt it go faint, and then she'd felt it stop altogether.

She felt Sam's blood on her hands. It wasn't really there, but she felt it. One word ran through her mind, over and over and over, a huge black bat that blotted out the stars: Horror, horror, horror, horror . . .

'That was very well done, Linda.'

Why doesn't his voice ever change? she wondered. It always sounds the same. Calm and happy, while terrible, terrible, terrible things . . .

She shuddered once and fought back a sob.

Maybe he's not really there, inside. He's like a golem, clay made to walk without a soul to guide it.

Linda looked over at her daughter. She felt her heart sag inside her. Sarah's eyes were open, but they weren't seeing. They were staring. A 'not there' kind of stare. She was rocking back and forth. Her lips were clenched together so tightly that they'd gone white.

I know how you feel, babe, Linda thought in despair.

'I know that you are hurting,' The Stranger said. His tone

became soothing. 'We're going to end that now, all that terrible, awful pain, forever.'

He looked at Sarah, watched her rock back and forth. A string of drool had collected at one corner of her mouth and was falling, falling, falling.

'I'll keep my word, you know. So long as you do what I ask, and don't deviate, I won't hurt her.'

You've already hurt her forever, Linda thought. But maybe she'd have a chance if she didn't die. You could recover from emotional trauma; there was no coming back from death.

The Stranger walked over behind Sam. He pulled keys from a jacket pocket, knelt down, and removed the cuffs from around Sam's ankles, then he removed the cuffs from around Sam's wrists. Sam toppled forward, thudding to the floor like a bag of sand.

'Here's what's going to happen,' The Stranger said to Linda. 'I'm going to give you these keys.' He did. 'Please remove the cuffs from your ankles.' Linda did so. He reached behind him with his left hand, pulling a weapon from his waistband. 'I'm going to place this handgun on the floor, here.' He did so. He moved behind Sarah and put his own gun to the back of her head.

'In a moment I will begin counting. When I reach five, if you haven't used that gun to blow your own brains out, then I will shoot Sarah in the back of the head. Following that, I'll rape you for hours and torture you for days. Do you understand?'

Linda nodded, listless.

'Good. Now, handguns are powerful things. You could touch that weapon, something could spark, and you might feel that it's transferred its power to you. You might decide to do something brave and insane. Don't. The moment its barrel starts moving toward me, I kill Sarah. The moment that it points away from your head, I kill Sarah. Do you follow?'

Linda stared at him, not speaking.

'Linda,' he said, patient. 'Did you hear what I said?'

She managed a nod. It took all her strength. She was so tired.

Sam I Am is gone, she thought. I feel dead already.

206

She looked down at the weapon on the rug. The one she'd be holding soon. The one that would end this, that would let her join Sam, that would save Sarah *(she hoped)*.

Handgun, handgun, burning bright . . .

'I'm going to give you the same gift that I gave your husband. One sentence only. This is your last chance to say something to Sarah.'

Linda looked at her white-lipped, shivering, oh-so-beautiful daughter.

Will she even remember what I say?

Linda would have to hope so. She'd have to hope that her words would drill down somewhere into Sarah's consciousness, that they'd surface later and be a comfort.

Maybe they'll come to her in her dreams.

'I'm in the clouds watching you, Sarah, always.'

Sarah continued to rock back and forth and drool.

'That was very nice,' The Stranger said. 'Thank you for complying.'

There it was again, that rage. Linda felt white-hot and blue-flame, rolling lava, exploding suns.

'Someday, you'll die,' she whispered, her voice quavering. 'And it'll be a bad death. Because of this. Because of the things you do.'

The Stranger stared at Linda, then smiled.

'Karma. An interesting concept.' He shrugs. 'Perhaps you're right. But if you are are, that will be then. We are in the *now*. In the now, I start counting.' He paused. 'It's going to be a measured count. Slow heartbeats. You have until I get to five.'

'The last thing I'll be thinking of is going to be you. You dying a bad death.'

The words were worthless, they'd change nothing, but they were the last resistance she could offer. The Stranger didn't even appear to have heard her.

'One,' he counted.

Linda forced herself to turn away from her rage. To look at the gun he'd placed on the floor.

So this is it.

Extraneous things began to fade. It was if someone had turned down the volume on life. She could hear the beating of her heart and The Stranger's slow count.

One was over. Then would come Two. Then Three. Then Four. And then . . . ? Should she let herself hear Five? Or should she pull the trigger just before Five?

Why wait, don't hesitate . . .

One was still echoing in her brain as she moved toward the gun. She could hear it vibrating in the air. She found herself in an elongation of time, as if each second was filled with a lifetime of sharp edges and she was rubbing up against all of them at once.

There's more pain in life than pleasure. It was something she knew as an artist, a secret ingredient she added to the potpourri of her paintings or sculptures.

The sharp edges, that's how we know we're still in the game.

She knelt down on the carpet and picked up the weapon. She made sure not to point the barrel at The Stranger.

'Two.'

It shocked her as he said it, like a slap in the face.

The sting passed.

Linda marveled at the coldness of the steel. Its smooth polish. The heavy, brutal promise of the thing.

This end toward enemy, she thought, looking at the barrel.

Someone invented this. They dreamed it, sketched it, tossed and turned about it. *Let's take a hunk of steel and fill it with steel-jacketed birds, and let's send them exploding outward into other human beings.*

'Three.'

Her awareness of the number was more clinical this time.

This weapon had a silencer on it. It was a gun that spoke of assassins and hit men and secret death.

It was just a piece of metal, though. Nothing more, nothing less. It wasn't human. You didn't anthropomorphize a gun; you pointed it and fired.

What was it the marines said? *This is my rifle. There are many like it, but this one is mine . . .*

'Four.'

Time stopped. It didn't just slow – it froze. She was covered in ice. Trapped in amber.

And then, a strobe-flash.

Sam on the floor.

Strobe-flash.

Sam in her arms.

Strobe-flash.

Sam hanging up the phone. His face white. Looking at her. 'My grandfather died.' Tears, and Sam in her arms again.

Strobe-flash.

Sam above her, eyes clouded with a mix of love and lust, face contorted with pleasure. She urged him to hold on, just another second, just another second, just another second . . .

This was that moment, she realized in wonder. That feeling you got as you hung on to the knife-edge precipice of near-orgasm, straining, trying to fend off the beckoning detonation and blinding light. The place where you stopped breathing, where your heart stopped beating, a moment of life and death.

Strobe-flash.

Sarah.

Sarah laughing.

Sarah crying.

Sarah living.

Oh.

God.

Sarah.

Linda realized in a final strobe-flash that she would miss this most of all: loving her daughter. She was pierced by a longing that was the sum of all the longings she'd ever felt or sculpted or painted.

If pain could be rain, this was an ocean of it.

It came out of her in a howl. It wasn't something she could

control. It sprang from her. A scream of agony to stop birds in flight.

Even The Stranger grimaced at the sound of this howl, just a little. It was a physical force.

SarahSamSarahSamSarahSam

Strobe-flash.

The gunshot came and went in the room, a silenced thunderclap.

Sarah stopped rocking for a moment.

The left side of Linda's head exploded.

Linda had been wrong.

Her last thought hadn't been about death.

It had been about love.

Hey, it's me. Modern-day Sarah. I'm going to write about the past and then take a break and come back to the present in places. It's the only way I'll ever get through this.

About my mom – maybe her last thought was about fear, maybe it was about nothing, I don't know. I can't really know. She was there and Daddy was there and I was there and he was there, these things are true. He made her kill them both while I watched, this is true. Is it true that my mom was that noble at the end, alone and suffering inside her head? I don't know.

But then again, neither do you.

I do know that my mom had a lot of love in her. She used to say that her family was a part of her art. She said that without me and Daddy, she'd still paint, but all the colors would be dark ones.

I like to think that she had some certainty, in that last moment, that what she was doing really would save my life, because it did, no matter what else happened later.

I don't know for sure whether her last thought was about love.

But her last action was.

23

I close Sarah's diary with a trembling hand and glance over at my clock. It's three A.M.

I need a break. I'm only just into Sarah's ordeal, and I already feel shaky and restless about it. She wasn't wrong; she has a gift. Her writing is too vivid. The happiness of the way her life used to be contrasts with the bitter humor of her prologue. It makes me feel sad and dirty. Wrung out.

What did she call it? *A trip to the watering hole.*

I can see it in my mind. An obscene full moon in the sky, dark things drinking *bad water* . . .

I shiver because I also feel the *fear* rising inside me. Bad things happening to Sarah, a short step away from bad things happening to Bonnie . . .

I glance over at Bonnie. She is deep in sleep, her face untroubled, one arm thrown across my stomach. I disengage myself from her, lifting her arm away with the same gentle care I'd give to a ladybug I was setting free in the backyard. Her mouth opens, once, and then she curls into herself and continues to sleep.

In the beginning, she'd wake up at the slightest change or motion. The fact that she can now keep sleeping eases some of my concerns about her. She's getting better. She doesn't talk yet, it's true. But she's getting better. Now if I can just keep her alive . . .

I slide out of the bed and tiptoe out of my bedroom, down the stairs, and into the kitchen. I reach into the cabinet above the refrigerator and find my secret vice and small shame. A bottle of tequila. Jose Cuervo, a friend of mine, just like the song.

I look at it and think: I am not an alcoholic.

I have spent time reviewing that statement, along the lines of 'all crazy people say they're not crazy.' I looked without giving myself the benefit of a doubt and arrived at that certainty: I am not an alcoholic. I drink two or three times a month. I never drink two days in a row. I get pleasantly buzzed but I never get truly shit-faced.

There's a truth, though, a big, bellowing elephant in the room: I never drank for comfort until after Matt and Alexa died. Never, not once, no way.

It troubles me.

I had a great-uncle on my father's side who was a drunk. He wasn't the funny, friendly, charming drunk-uncle. He wasn't the artistically inclined, self-tortured, pitiable drunk-uncle either. He was embarrassing and violent and mean. He reeked of booze and sometimes worse. He grabbed me by the arm at a family gathering one time with enough force to leave a bruise, put his boozy mouth about an inch from my terrified face (I was only eight) and proceeded to say something garbled and sly and disgusting that I've never fully deciphered.

The things we see as children make lasting impressions. That's the picture of a drunk that always stuck with me. Anytime I was drinking and found myself heading toward *a little too much*, Great-Uncle Joe's rheumy-eyed, unshaven face would pop into my head. I'd remember the smell of whisky and tooth decay and the cunning look in his eyes. I'd set down whatever I happened to be drinking at the time, and that would be it.

Not long after my family died, I found myself in the liquor section of the supermarket. I realized that I had never bought anything other than a bottle of wine, certainly not at a supermarket, definitely not in the middle of the afternoon. The tequila caught my eye, the song came to mind.

212

Screw it, I'd thought to myself.

I'd grabbed the bottle, paid for it without meeting the checker's eyes, and hustled home.

I spent about ten minutes at home with my chin in my hand, gazing at the bottle, wondering if I was about to become a true cliché. If I was about to become Great-Uncle Joe, a chip off the old block.

Nah, I'd thought. No one pitied Great-Uncle Joe. They'll pity you.

It went down good, it felt good, I liked it.

I didn't get drunk. I got . . . floaty. That's as far as I've ever taken it.

The problem, I think now, as I pour an inch (never more) into a glass, is that I continued this habit even after the agony of losing my family subsided. Now, it helps me with my fear, or in times of great pressure. The danger is in that arena: not drinking because I *want* to, but because I *need* to. I know that means it's not a healthy habit I have here.

'To rationalization,' I murmur, toasting the air.

I down the glass in a single gulp and it feels like I just swallowed paint stripper or fire, but it's a good feeling, putting pressure behind my eyes and delivering an almost instantaneous feeling of contentment. Which is the point. Contentment is so much harder to come by than joy, I've always thought. A single shot of tequila does it, for me.

'Jose Cuervo, da do do do dah dah,' I sing in a whisper-voice.

I consider a second shot, but decide against it. I cap the bottle and replace it in the cabinet. I rinse the glass, taking care to get rid of any lingering smell. More tiny red flags, I know: drinking alone, hiding it. In the end, I have to accept that, rationalized or not, my drinking isn't out of control, and hope that I'll recognize it if it ever becomes so.

I consider the moment. Why is Sarah's tale getting so under my skin? Why the need to run to Mr Cuervo right now? It's a terrible story, but I've heard terrible stories before. Hell, I've *lived* terrible stories. Why is this one hitting me so hard?

Bonnie's already nailed it: because Sarah is Bonnie, and Bonnie is Sarah. Bonnie is a painter, Sarah is a writer, both have lost parents, both are dark and damaged. If Sarah is doomed, does that mean that Bonnie is too? These similarities stoke my fears. Fear is what I struggle with most, these days.

I had played down the actual level of my terrors about Bonnie when I had talked to Elaina. The fear, when it comes, surpasses mere discomfort. I have hyperventilated. I've locked the bathroom door and crouched on the floor, arms around my knees, shaking with panic.

Posttraumatic stress is what a shrink would probably diagnose. I imagine that's accurate. But I'm not interested in talking my way through this. I'm going to suffer my way through it, and hope that I don't screw up Bonnie along the way.

I find what works best is to divert my thoughts in these moments, to think of something, anything else. What flies into my mind this time isn't particularly helpful.

1forUtwo4me, babe.

Why, Matt? I made my peace with Alexa. Why can't I make my peace with you? Why can't I forget about it?

He shakes his head.

Because you're you. You have to know. It's how you're built, how God or whoever made you.

He's right, of course. It's a truth that applies to everything: Sarah's diary, 1forUtwo4me, the future. It's one of the things that drives me forward, that helps me navigate through my fears: the desire to see how the story ends. Bonnie's story, the next victim's story. Whatever.

What about my story?

Quantico. The second elephant in the middle of my personal room. It appears as I think of it, all sad-eyed and wise. I stroke its gray skin and realize what about it bothers me.

That it doesn't bother me enough.

Here I am, I realize, offered a plum because my face won't look right on a poster. Here I am, considering a move that would

214

separate me from the only family I have left, that would end a new and possibility-filled relationship with Tommy, that would pack away this house and all its memories for good – and all I can feel is a sense of opportunity.

Considering leaving my friends and the life I've known should be tearing me apart. Instead, I am ambivalent. Why?

It's not like things haven't been getting better. Packing away Matt and Alexa's things is progress. No more nightmares is progress. Sharing even a small part of myself with a man other than Matt is progress. Why don't I seem to care more?

Enlightenment evades me for now, but I realize here, at last, is the discomfort I'd been looking for. Maybe I've been fooling myself. Maybe what I'd thought was emotional growth was simply me learning to walk in spite of my disabilities.

Maybe the parts of me designed to feel most deeply have been injured beyond repair.

That doesn't explain the booze now, does it?

With that it's time to shove the elephant away. He goes quietly, but stares at me with those wise, sad eyes that say, *It's true, we elephants have* long *memories to go with our* long *trunks, but no tusks here, even though memories can have* long *teeth.*

I lick my own teeth and search for contentment, but I can already tell that both it and sleep will be absent.

Contentment . . .

Wait, elephant, I cry. *Come back.*

He does, because he's my elephant after all. He stares at me with those patient eyes.

I just realized why. It's because for all the progress I've made . . . I'm still not happy. You know?

He touches me with his trunk. Looks at me with those wise, sad eyes. He does know.

I'm not sad or suicidal, but that doesn't mean I'm happy.

Memories, yes, the elephant's wise, sad eyes say, *memories can have long teeth.*

Yes, I think, *and the happy memories have the longest teeth of all.*

That's the problem: I've known true happiness. Real, fulfilling, down-to-the-bone, close-to-the-soul happiness. Feeling 'okay' doesn't cut it anymore. It's as if I was on a drug that made the world glow and now that I'm off it, now that I'm going cold turkey, it's not that the world is *bad*, per se – but it doesn't *glow*, dammit.

I'm not confident that Tommy or Elaina or Callie or the J-O-B or even Bonnie will make me happy in that way again. I cherish them all, but I mistrust their ability to fill the void, to bring back the glow. Ugly and selfish but true.

That's why Quantico appeals to me. A nuclear changeup, a mushroom cloud of 'different,' perhaps that's what I really need. A raw and brutal break to shake the foundation and rattle the rafters of *me*.

The elephant plods off without being asked. I can talk to my metaphors without shame when I swallow tequila, it seems.

Elephant, I think, *thy name is 'Not-Happy.' Or maybe, 'No-Glow.'*
Will Quantico solve that?

Who the fuck knows? I want a cigarette.

I sigh and resign myself to wakefulness. Time to shove aside the personal and drown myself in the professional. It's an old solution, but a faithful one. It doesn't *glow*, exactly, but it's guaranteed to banish the elephants that ail you.

I plod back upstairs and grab my notes and return to the living room. I sit on the couch and try to organize my thoughts.

I take the page titled PERPETRATOR and add to it: PER-PETRATOR AKA 'THE STRANGER.' I think about what I've read so far in the diary. I begin to write, my notes now less structured and more extemporaneous.

He was caused pain = he's causing others pain. Revenge.
    The question remains, though: WHY SARAH?

The logical suspicion would be that he's making Sarah pay for something her parents did. But he told Sam and Linda that they were *not* at fault. *It's not your fault, but your death will be my justice.* Was Sarah simply chosen at random?

I shake my head. No. There is a connection, and it's not imaginary. I feel as though some aspect of it is staring me right in the face. Something about who he was speaking to . . .

I sit up straight, suddenly energized.

If Sarah's account was accurate, The Stranger was speaking to *Linda* when he said, *Your death will be my justice.*

Linda specifically.

A phrase I had heard earlier today comes back to me:

The Father and the daughter . . .

Revenge isn't random and he loves his messages. That wasn't a slip of the tongue.

I write.

What if the object of revenge goes back another generation? He said to Sarah yesterday, while he was flicking blood onto her, 'The Father and the daughter and the Holy Spirit.' He told Linda Langstrom, 'It's not your fault, but your death will be my justice.' Could we be talking about Linda's father? Sarah's grandfather?

I read it back to myself and experience that flush of energy again.

I'm in my home office, faxing the pages containing my notes to James. I didn't call him; James will hear the fax and wake up. He'll be pissed and grumble about it, but he'll read them regardless. I need him to know what I know.

The grandfather.

It feels, if not certain, at least very possible.

The machine beeps to let me know it's done and I go back downstairs. I check the clock. Five A.M. Time marches on.

I want the morning to come, and I want it here now, dammit!

A thought comes to me.

217

Sarah said no one's believed her about The Stranger. Why? From what I've read so far, that makes no sense.

I glance over to the diary pages waiting on the coffee table. I glance at the clock and the hours I have left to burn.

Only one way to find out.

Sarah's Story

Part Two

24

So how do you like the story so far? Not bad for an almost-sixteen-year-old, huh? Like I said, I'm a sprinter more than a runner, and we sure sprinted through that first bit, didn't we? A summary: Happy me, bad man comes, dead Buster, dead Mommy, dead Daddy, unhappy me.

Now we'll take a jump. A leap to the next starting line.

First, some backstory: I was hazy and crazy after everything that happened, and somehow both Doreen and I ended up in the backyard. Doreen, poor dummy, got thirsty or hungry or both and couldn't rouse me (I was too busy lying on the back patio, drooling on the concrete) and she started howling. God, could she howl.

Anyway, so our next-door neighbors, John and Jamie Overman, called the cops because of all the racket and because I guess they peeked over the fence and saw me drooling and thought, Hey that's kinda strange.

Two coppers showed up (cheezit!), a guy named Ricky Santos and a new rookie named Cathy Jones. Cathy becomes what we call an IMPORTANT CHARACTER in my story.

Over the years, unlike most other people, she actually gave a poop-ydoody.

More on her later. That's the thirty-second recap. Now we'll head back into third-person view.

Time for another trip to the watering hole. Ready?

1–2–3: GO!
Once Upon A Time, things were totally, totally screwed . . .

Sarah sipped water through a straw and tried not to feel tired.

A whole week had gone by. A week of floating in marshmallows because of the drugs they gave her. A week of sly voices whispering in her head. A week of pain.

One day she'd woken up and hadn't started to scream right away. That was the end of her visits to Marshmallow Land. She still had dreams, though. In those dreams, her parents were

(nothing they were nothings nothing at all)

And Buster was a

(puppyhead – puppyshead?)

(nothing nothings nothing)

She woke from these dreams shivering and denying, shivering and denying.

Right now she was wide awake, though. A lady-policeman was sitting in a chair next to the bed, asking Sarah questions. The lady's name was Cathy Jones, and she seemed nice, but her questions were puzzling.

'Sarah,' she started, 'do you know why your mommy hurt your daddy?'

Sarah frowned at Cathy.

'Because The Stranger made her,' Sarah answered.

Cathy frowned. 'What Stranger, sweetheart?'

'The Stranger that killed Buster. That burned my hand. He made Mommy hurt Daddy and hurt herself too. He said he would hurt me if they didn't.'

Cathy stared at Sarah, perplexed.

'Are you saying there was someone in your house, honey? Someone that forced your mommy to do the things she did?'

Sarah nodded.

Cathy leaned back, uneasy.

What the hell?

Cathy knew that forensics had been through the Langstroms'

222

home and that they hadn't found anything to point away from a murder-suicide. There was a note from the mother that said: *I'm sorry, take care of Sarah.* There was the fact that Linda's prints were found in a number of damning places, notably the hacksaw that beheaded the dog, her husband's neck, and the gun she'd used to shoot herself.

There was also the matter of the antidepressants the mother appeared to have been taking, no sign of forced entry, Sarah being left alive – if it looked like a dog and barked like a dog . . . Cathy had been asked by the detectives in charge to get a statement from Sarah for corroboration. A loose end, nothing more.

So what do I do here?

Ricky's voice came to her.

Just take the statement. That's what you're here for. Take it, give it to the detectives, and move on. The rest of it is not your problem.

'Tell me everything you remember, Sarah.'

Sarah watched the lady-policeman walk out of her room.

She doesn't believe you.

It was something Sarah had become aware of about halfway through her story. Adults thought kids didn't know anything. They were wrong. Sarah knew when she was being humored. Cathy was nice, but Cathy didn't believe her about The Stranger. Sarah frowned to herself. No, that wasn't quite right. It's that she seemed . . . what? Sarah puzzled over the nuances for a moment.

It's like she doesn't think I'm lying – but she doesn't think that what I'm saying is true.

Like I'm

(crazy).

Sarah leaned back in the hospital bed and closed her eyes. She felt the pain riding in like dark horses. The horses, they'd gallop into her soul and rear and scream, their hoofs sending black sparks flying off her heart.

Sometimes the pain she felt had clarity. It wasn't a dull ache, or a background noise. It was a ragged wound, nerve endings, and fire. It was a blackness that swept over her and made her think about dying. In those moments, she'd lie in her bed in the dark and would try to get her heart to stop beating. Mommy had told her a story about this once. About wise men in ancient China who could dig an open grave, sit next to it, and will themselves to die. Their hearts would stop and they'd topple forward into the waiting dirt.

Sarah tried to do this, but no matter how much she concentrated, how hard she wished, she couldn't die. She kept on breathing and her heart kept on beating and – worst of all – she kept on *hurting*. It was a pain that wouldn't go away, that wouldn't lessen or subside.

She couldn't die, so she'd curl up in her bed and cry without making noise. Cry and cry and cry, for hours. Cry because she understood now, understood that Mommy and Daddy and Buster were gone, and they weren't coming back. Not ever.

After the grief came the anger and shame.

You're six! Stop being such a crybaby!

She didn't have an adult there to tell her that being six meant it was still okay to cry, so she curled up in the dark and tried to die and wept and berated herself for every tear.

Cathy not believing her, Cathy thinking she was a cuckoo-bird, brought a new kind of pain.

It made her sad and angry. Most of all, she felt alone.

Cathy sat in the patrol car and looked out the window. Her partner, Ricky Santos, was downing a milk shake as he gave her the once-over.

'Kid's story bothering you?' he asked.

'Yeah. Any way you slice it, it's bad news. If we're right, she's crazy. If we're wrong, she's in danger.'

Ricky sucked on his straw and contemplated the insides of his sunglasses.

'You gotta let it go, partner. That's how it works for us uniforms. We don't get to follow things through to the end, not very often.

We parachute in, secure things, turn it over to detectives. In, out, clean. You carry things around when you're not in a position to do anything about them, you're gonna go crazy. Why cops end up drunks, or at the wrong end of their revolvers.'

Cathy turned to him.

'So you're saying – what? Don't give a shit?'

Santos smiled at her, a sad smile.

'Care while it's your problem. That's what I'm saying. You're gonna see a hundred Sarahs. Maybe more. Do the right thing for them while it's your job, and then let it go and move on to the next one. It's a war of attrition, Jones. Not a single battle.'

'Maybe,' she said.

But I bet you have a case you could never let go of. I think Sarah's going to be mine.

Saying it to herself made Cathy feel better.

Mine.

'I'll be right back,' Cathy said.

Santos looked at her. He was inscrutable. A sphinx in shades.

'Okay,' he replied, and sucked on his straw.

They had parked at a McDonald's next to the hospital. Cathy exited the patrol car and walked across the street. She entered through the front doors and wound her way down the hallways to Sarah's room.

Sarah was sitting up, looking out the window. The view was of the hospital parking lot.

How depressing. Way to promote healing, guys.

'Hey,' Cathy said.

Sarah turned toward her and smiled. Cathy was struck again by the beauty of the little girl.

She walked over to Sarah's bed.

'I wanted to give you this.'

Cathy held a business card between her fingers.

'That's got my name and number on it. My e-mail address too. If you ever need help with anything, you can get in touch with me.'

Sarah took the card and examined it before looking back up at Cathy.

'Cathy?'

'Yeah, honey?'

'What's going to happen to me?'

The pain that Cathy had been keeping at arm's length tried to crawl right up her throat. She fought it back down with a swallow.

What's going to happen to you, kid?

Cathy knew that Sarah had no living relatives. Unusual, but it happened. It meant she was going to become a ward of the state.

'Someone's going to come take care of you, Sarah.'

Sarah mulled this over.

'Will I like them?'

Cathy grimaced inside.

Maybe not.

'Sure you will. I don't want you to worry, Sarah.'

Man, those eyes. I gotta get out of here.

'Hold on to that card, okay? And call me if you need to. Anytime.'

Sarah nodded. She even managed a smile and now Cathy didn't just want to walk out of the room, she wanted to *run*, because that smile was heartbreaking.

(Gut-wrenching)

'Bye, honey,' she stammered as she turned and walked away.

'Bye, Cathy,' Sarah called after her.

Back in the car, Santos – now shake-less – regarded her.

'That make you feel better?'

'Not really, Ricky.'

He regarded her for another moment. He seemed to be mulling something over.

'You're gonna make a good cop, Cathy.'

He turned the key in the ignition and put the car in reverse as Cathy stared at him in surprise.

'That's the nicest thing anyone's ever said to me, Santos.'

He smiled at her as he put the car in drive and headed out of the parking lot.

'Then you need new friends, Jones. But you're welcome anyway.'

25

Sarah sat in the car and watched the lady change.

Karen Watson had shown up in the hospital room and explained
to Sarah that she was there from Social Services, and that she was
going to take care of her. Karen had seemed really nice and had
smiled a lot. Sarah had felt hopeful.

Once they were out of the hospital, Karen had changed. She'd
begun walking faster, yanking Sarah forward.

'Get in, kid,' she'd said, when they reached the car.

Her voice sounded *mean*.

Sarah puzzled over the change, trying to make sense of it.

'Are you mad at me?' she asked Karen.

Karen looked at her once before starting up the car. Sarah took
in the dull eyes, the carelessly coiffed brown hair, the heavy face.
The woman looked tired. Sarah thought she probably always
looked tired.

'I don't really care about you one way or the other, princess, if
you want to know the truth. My job is to get a roof over your
head, not to love you or be your friend or anything like that.
Understand?'

'Yes,' Sarah replied, her voice small.

They drove off.

*

The Parkers lived in a worn-out house in Canoga Park, which was located in the San Fernando Valley. It resembled its owners: in need of work that would never be done.

Dennis Parker was a mechanic. His father had been a good man, had loved fixing cars, and had taught Dennis the trade. Dennis hated the work – hated all work, really – and he made sure that everyone knew it.

He was a big man, just over six feet tall, with broad shoulders and beefy arms. He had scraggly dark hair, ever-present stubble, and muddy-colored, mean-looking eyes.

Dennis would tell friends that he liked three things above all others: 'Cigarettes, whisky, and pussy.'

Rebecca Parker was a stereotypical California blonde with too many sharp edges to be truly attractive. She'd been beautiful for about four years, from sixteen to twenty. She made up for her deteriorating looks in the bedroom – not that it took much skill to please Dennis. He was usually full of booze by the time he was trying to get into her pants. She had a pair of heavy breasts, a waist that had stayed slim, and what Dennis liked to call 'a tight little panty-hamster.'

(Note from Sarah: This is true. Theresa told me he actually said that once. Charming, yes? Oh, who is Theresa? Read on and find out.)

Rebecca's job was simple: managing the care of three foster children, the maximum number they could legally take in. They were paid for each kid, and it was a fair part of their income.

Rebecca's duties included feeding the kids, telling them to go to school, and making sure that neither she nor Dennis left any visible marks on the kids when they delivered a beating. The trick was to pay just enough attention to the children to keep Social Services from getting pissed off, but not so much that it ate into her own free time or – most important – their bottom line.

Karen knocked on the door of the Parkers' house as Sarah stood next to her. She heard footsteps coming, and then the door opened. Rebecca Parker peered through the screen door. She was wearing a tank top and shorts, and had a cigarette in her hand.

'Hey, Karen,' she said, opening the screen door. 'Come on in.' She smiled. 'You must be Sarah.'

'Hi,' Sarah replied.

Sarah thought that the lady looked and sounded nice, but she was beginning to understand that looks could be deceiving. Plus the lady smoked – yuck!

Karen and Sarah walked inside the Parkers' home. It was clean, sort of. It smelled like stale cigarettes.

'Jesse and Theresa are at school?' Karen asked.

'Yep,' Rebecca replied. She guided them into the living room, and gestured for them to take a seat on the couch.

'How are they doing?' Karen asked.

Rebecca shrugged. 'They're not failing anything. They're eating. Neither of them is doing any drugs.'

'Sounds fine, then.' Karen indicated Sarah with a nod of her head. 'As I told you over the phone, Sarah is six. I need to place her quickly, and I thought of you and Dennis. I know you are looking for a third.'

'Since Angela ran away, yes.'

Angela had been a pretty fourteen-year-old girl whose mother had died of a heroin overdose. She was already a hard case and Karen had placed her with the Parkers because she knew they could deal with her. Angela had run away two months ago. Karen figured she was probably heading down the same path as her whore mother.

'It'll be the usual routine. You need to get her in school, make sure her shots are up to date, and so on.'

'We know.'

Karen nodded in approval. 'Then I'm going to leave her with you. I brought her bag, she has plenty of clothes and underwear and shoes, so you won't have to worry about that.'

'Sounds good.'

Karen stood up, shook Rebecca's hand, and headed toward the front door. Sarah went to follow her.

'You're staying here, kid.' She turned to Rebecca. 'I'll be in touch.'

And then she was gone.

'Let me show you where your room is, honey,' Rebecca said.

Sarah followed the woman in a daze.

What was happening? Why was she staying here? And where was Doreen? What had they done with her puppyhead?

'Here it is.'

Sarah looked through the door into the room. It was small, about ten feet by ten feet. There was a single dresser and two small beds. The walls were bare.

'Why are there two beds?' she asked.

'You're sharing the room with Theresa.' Rebecca pointed toward the dresser. 'You can put your clothes in the bottom drawer. Why don't you go ahead and unpack your stuff, and then come meet me in the kitchen?'

Sarah had managed to cram all of her clothes into the bottom drawer of the small dresser. She'd arranged her shoes under her bed. As she'd unpacked, she'd caught a whiff of a familiar scent, the smell of the fabric softener her mother used. It had caught her by surprise, a punch in the stomach. She'd had to bury her face in a shirt to cover up her crying.

Her tears had subsided by the time she'd finished emptying out the small bag Karen had left. She sat down on the edge of her bed, filled with bewilderment and a dull ache.

Why am I here? Why can't I sleep in my own room?

She didn't understand any of this.

Maybe the Rebecca lady knew.

'There you are,' Rebecca said as Sarah showed up in the kitchen. 'Did you get all your stuff packed away?'

'Yes.'

'Come have a seat at the table. I made you a bologna sandwich, and I got you some milk – you do like milk, right? You're not lactose intolerant or anything?'

'I like milk.' Sarah sat down in the chair and picked up the sandwich. She *was* hungry. 'Thank you,' she said to Rebecca.

'No problem, sweetie.'

Rebecca sat down at the other end of the table and lit up a cigarette. She smoked and watched Sarah as the little girl ate.

Sad and pale and small. That's too bad. But everybody learns the same thing sooner or later: It's a tough old world.

'I'm going to explain some of the rules of the house to you, Sarah. Things you need to know while you're living here with us, okay?'

'Okay.'

'First of all, we're not here to entertain you, understand? We're here to give you a roof over your head, to feed and clothe you, make sure you get to school and all of that – but you're going to have to keep yourself occupied. Dennis and I have our own lives, and our own things to do. We don't have time to be your play-mates. Understand?'

Sarah nodded.

'Okay. Next thing, you'll have chores around the house. Get them done and you won't get in trouble. Don't get them done and you will. Bed time is at ten. No exceptions. That means lights out and under the covers. The last rule is simple, but it's important: Don't talk back. Do what we say. We're the grown-ups, and we know what's best. We're giving you a place to live and we expect to be treated with respect. Understand?'

Another nod.

'Good. Do you have any questions for me?'

Sarah looked down at her plate. 'Why am I living here? Why can't I go back home?'

Rebecca frowned, puzzled.

'Because your mom and dad are *dead,* honey, and there's no

one else that wants you. That's what Dennis and I do. We take in kids that don't have anywhere else to go. Didn't Karen explain that to you?'

Sarah shook her head, still staring at her plate. She looked numb.

'Thank you very much for the sandwich,' she said, her voice small. 'Can I go to my room now?'

'Go ahead, honey,' Rebecca said, stubbing out her cigarette and lighting another. 'You new ones usually cry for the first few days, and that's okay. But you'll need to learn to toughen up fast. Life goes on, you know?'

Sarah stared at Rebecca for a moment, taking this in. The little girl's face crumpled and she fled the table.

Rebecca watched her go. The blonde took a long drag on her cigarette.

Pretty girl. It's a shame what happened to her.

Rebecca waved her hand in dismissal, though she was alone. Her eyes were angry and miserable and surrounded by too much mascara.

Well, that's too bad. It's a tough old world.

Sarah lay on her strange new bed in her strange new house and curled into herself. Tried to make herself small. To make herself

(Go away)

Because maybe if she could

(Go away)

She'd reappear back at home, with Mommy and Daddy. Maybe – and this idea perked her up, filled her with hope – this was all just a long, bad dream. Maybe she'd gone to sleep on the night before her birthday and never really woken up.

Her brow furrowed in thought. If that was true, then all she needed to do was go to sleep in her dream.

'Yes!' she whispered to herself.

That was it! She'd just go to sleep here (in her dream), and then she'd wake up in the real world. Buster would be there, snuggled up next to her, and her mother's painting would be there, hanging on the wall at the foot of her bed. It would be morning. She'd get up and go out and Daddy would tease her about not having any presents or cake, but there *would* be presents and cake . . .

Sarah hugged herself in her excitement. This *had* to be the solution to – she looked around – all this.

Just close your eyes and go to sleep, and when you wake up, everything will be happy again.

Because she was exhausted and only six, Sarah fell asleep without any effort at all.

26

'Wake up.'

Sarah stirred. Someone was shaking her. Someone with a soft female voice.

'Hey, wake up, little girl.'

Sarah's first thought was: It worked! This was Mommy, telling her to get up on her birthday!

'I had a bad dream, Mommy,' she murmured.

A pause.

'I'm not your mommy, little girl. Come on, wake up. It's almost time for dinner.'

Sarah opened her eyes in surprise. It took a moment for her to focus on the girl speaking to her. The girl had spoken the truth: She wasn't Mommy.

It's no dream. It's all real.

Acceptance arrived again, painful and absolute.

Mommy's dead. Daddy's dead. Buster's dead and Doreen's gone, and I'm all alone and no one is ever coming back.

Something of what she was feeling must have showed on her face, because the girl talking to her frowned.

'Hey, are you okay?'

Sarah shook her head. She couldn't talk.

The girl's face softened.

'I understand. Well, anyway, my name is Theresa. I guess we're foster-sisters.' She paused. 'What's your name?'

'Sarah.' Her voice sounded weak, faraway.

'Sarah. That's a pretty name. I'm thirteen – how old are you?'

'Six. I just had a birthday.'

'That's cool.'

Sarah examined this strange but friendly girl. Theresa was pretty. She looked vaguely Latin, with brown eyes and thick, dark hair that ran just past her shoulders. She had a small scar near her hairline. Full, sensual lips softened a serious face. She was pretty, but Sarah thought she looked tired too, like a nice person who'd had a hard day.

'Why are you here, Theresa?'

'My mom died.'

'Oh.' Sarah fell silent, unsure of what to say. 'Mine did too. And my daddy.'

'That sucks.' A long pause. Then, soft and sorrowful: 'I'm really sorry, Sarah.'

Sarah nodded. She felt her face getting hot, her eyes begin to prickle.

Don't be a silly old crybaby!

Theresa didn't seem to notice. 'I was eight when my mom died,' she said, talking while Sarah listened and struggled with her tears. 'A little older than you, but close enough. So I know how you feel and what you can expect. The main thing you have to understand is that for the most part, none of the people you deal with really care about you. You're alone. I know that sucks to hear, but the sooner you realize it, the better off you'll be.' She grimaced. 'You don't belong to any of these people. You're not their blood.'

'But . . . but . . . if they don't care, why do they do it?'

Theresa gave Sarah a worn-out smile. 'Money. They get paid to.'

Sarah stared off, taking this in. A frightening thought occurred to her.

'Are they bad people?'

236

Theresa's expression was grim and sad. 'Sometimes, yeah. Every now and then you'll get a good foster-family, but a lot of the time, it's bad.'

'Is it bad here?'

The thing that flew across Theresa's face was bitter and dark and complex, part blackbird, part teardrops, part dirt.

'Yeah.' She grew silent, looking off. She took a deep breath and smiled. 'Probably not so much for you, though. Rebecca's not the one you have to watch out for. She doesn't drink the way Dennis does. As long as you do what she says and you don't cause any trouble, she'll leave you alone. I don't think they'll hit you much.'

Sarah paled. 'H-hit me?'

Theresa squeezed Sarah's hands. 'Just keep to yourself and you'll be fine. Don't talk to Dennis when he's drunk.'

Sarah listened to all of this with the pragmatism of a child, in spite of her fear. She believed what Theresa said, that these people didn't care about her, that they'd hit her, that she shouldn't talk to Dennis when he was drunk.

The world was becoming more and more terrifying, more and more solitary.

Sarah looked down at her hands. 'You said we're foster-sisters. Does . . . does that mean you're my friend, Theresa?'

It was humble and plaintive and it made Theresa's breath hitch in her chest.

'Sure, Sarah.' She forced conviction into her voice. 'We're sisters, remember? Yeah?'

Sarah managed to smile. 'Yeah.'

'Good girl. Now come on, it's time for dinner.' Theresa's face grew stern. 'Don't ever be late for dinner. It makes Dennis mad.'

Sarah was terrified of Dennis from the moment she laid eyes on him.

He was a simmering volcano, full of heat, ready to erupt. This was something that anyone who met him sensed.

He felt

(dangerous)

And

(mean)

He stared at Sarah as she and Theresa sat down.

'You Sarah?' he asked. His voice rumbled. The question crackled like a threat.

'Y-yes.'

He gazed at her for a long moment before turning his attention to Rebecca.

'Where's Jesse?'

Rebecca shrugged. 'I don't know. He knows better, but he's been getting pretty defiant.'

Sarah was still staring at Dennis, wide-eyed, so she saw the rage that passed over his face at this. It was a snarl of pure hate.

'Well,' he said, 'I'm going to have to do something about that.' His face closed up again. 'Let's eat.'

The meal was meat loaf. Sarah thought it was okay. Not as good as Mommy's, but that kind of felt right, anyway. Dinner passed in silence, punctuated by the clink of silverware and the sounds of chewing. Dennis had a can of beer, and he took large gulps of it between bites of his meat loaf, putting it down and staring around the table. Sarah noticed that he spent a lot of time looking at Theresa, while Theresa was careful never to look at him.

Dennis was on his third beer by the time dinner was over.

'You girls clear the table and do the dishes,' Rebecca said. 'Dennis and I are going to watch TV. When you're done, you can go to your room.'

Theresa nodded and stood up and began gathering the dishes. Sarah helped. The silence continued. Rebecca smoked her cigarette and stared at Dennis with a mix of desperation and resignation, while Dennis simmered and stared at Theresa with an emotion Sarah couldn't define.

Everything about this was alien to her. Dinner at home had always been full of conversation and stories, laughter and dogs.

238

Daddy teased her, Mommy would watch and smile. Buster and Doreen would sit at attention, hoping beyond hope for table scraps that (almost) never came.

There, Sarah was special, and things were light and fun.

Here, things were heavy. Things were dangerous. She wasn't special, not a bit.

She followed Theresa into the kitchen and over to the sink.

'I'll rinse the dishes off,' Theresa said, 'and you put them in the dishwasher. Do you know how to do that?'

Sarah nodded. 'I used to help Mommy do it.'

Theresa smiled at her. She started the process, and they fell into a comfortable rhythm. Things almost seemed normal.

'Who's Jesse?' Sarah asked.

'He's the other one of us living here. A boy, sixteen.' Theresa shrugged. 'He's nice enough, but he's started defying Dennis. I don't think he's going to be here much longer.'

Sarah placed a handful of forks into the cutlery basket. 'Why?' she asked. 'What's going to happen to him?'

'He's going to piss Dennis off, and Dennis is going to beat him up, and this time I think Jesse's going to fight back. Even that bitch Karen Watson won't be able to ignore that.'

Sarah took a plate that Rebecca handed her. 'Is Ms Watson mean?'

Theresa looked at her, surprised. 'Mean? Rebecca and Dennis are bad, but Karen Watson? She's pure evil.'

Sarah considered this concept. Pure evil.

They finished rinsing the dishes. Theresa put dish detergent into the dishwasher and turned it on. Sarah listened to the muffled 'thunka-thunka' sounds coming from the dishwasher and was comforted by them. They sounded no different from the ones at home.

'Now we go to our room,' Theresa said. 'Straight there. Dennis will be really drunk by now.'

Sarah sensed danger again. She was starting to understand that this was life here. You walked across a minefield of eggshells at

239

night, while the enemy listened with bat ears for the sound of a single crack. The air in this home was heavy with tension and caution and (she sensed) real danger.

Sarah followed Theresa as they left the kitchen. She glanced toward the couch as they passed the living room. What she saw happening there made her blink in shock. Rebecca and Dennis were kissing – that was no big deal, she'd seen Mommy and Daddy kiss plenty of times – but Rebecca didn't have her shirt on, and her boobies were showing!

Something twisted in Sarah's belly at the sight. She knew, at some visceral level, that she wasn't supposed to be seeing this kind of thing. Kissing was fine, boobies were fine (she was a girl, after all) but boobies mixed with kissing . . . her face burned and she felt queasy.

They entered the bedroom and Theresa closed the door, taking great care to make no noise.

(Eggshells and tension, eggshells and tension)

Sarah sat on her bed. She felt faint.

'Sorry you had to see that, Sarah,' Theresa muttered, angry. 'They're not supposed to do that where people can see them – especially kids.'

'I don't like it here,' Sarah said in a small voice.

'Me neither, Sarah. Me neither.' Theresa fell silent. 'I'm going to tell you something else. You won't understand it now, but you will in the future. Don't trust men. They only want one thing – what you saw on the couch. Some of them don't care how old you are, either. Some of them like it *better* that way.'

There was a bitterness to Theresa's voice as she spoke that made Sarah turn to her. The thirteen-year-old was crying, silent, angry tears that were meant to be felt but not heard.

Sarah jumped off her bed and went over to sit by Theresa. She put her small arms around the older girl and hugged her. She did this without thinking, as much a reflex as a plant turning toward the sun.

'Shhh . . . don't cry, Theresa. It'll be okay. Don't cry.'

The older girl wept for a few more moments before wiping away her tears and forcing a shaky smile.

'Look at me, being a big old crybaby.'

'It's okay,' Sarah said. 'We're sisters. Sisters can cry in front of each other, right?'

Theresa looked stricken, filled with a commingling of old wounds and old happiness. They ran together through her spirit, a muddy flood, few whites, many grays.

In later years, Sarah would remember this moment, convinced that it led Theresa to do the things she did.

'Yeah,' Theresa replied, her voice shaky. 'We're sisters.' She grabbed Sarah and hugged her. Sarah closed her eyes and hugged back and inhaled. She thought Theresa smelled like flowers in summer.

For a moment – just a moment – Sarah felt safe.

'So,' Theresa said, breaking the hug with a smile, 'do you want to play a game? All we have is Go Fish.'

'I like Go Fish.'

They grinned at each other and sat on the bed and played, ignoring the grunts and moans from other parts of the house, safe on their island in a sea of eggshells.

27

Theresa and Sarah had played for an hour and a half, and then had talked for another two. The room was a like a sanctuary from the truths that had brought them here. Theresa had talked about her mother, and had shown Sarah a single picture.

'She's beautiful,' Sarah had said, awed.

It was true. The woman in the photograph was in her mid-twenties, a mix of Latin and something else that came together to produce laughing eyes, exotic features, and a mane of chestnut hair.

Theresa had glanced at the photo one more time before putting it back under her mattress with a smile.

'Yeah, she was. She was really *funny* too, you know? Always laughing about something.' The smile had disappeared. Theresa's face had grown colder, her eyes more distant. 'She got raped – sorry, she got killed by some stranger. A man that liked to hurt women.'

'My mommy got killed by a bad man too.'

'Really?'

The six-year-old had nodded, somber. 'Yes. But no one believes me.'

'Why?'

Sarah had related the story of The Stranger. Of what he'd made her parents do. When she'd finished, Theresa hadn't said anything for a moment or two.

'That's some story,' she'd finally replied.

Sarah had looked up at her new sister, hopeful. 'You believe me?'

'Of course I do.'

The love that Sarah had felt for Theresa at that moment had been fierce.

She'd wonder, years later, if Theresa really had believed her. She'd wonder and shrug it off. The truth was unimportant. Theresa had given her a feeling of safety and hope when she needed it most. Sarah loved her for it forever.

Rebecca had knocked on their door just before ten o'clock.

'Time for bed,' she'd said.

Now they lay in the darkness, staring at the ceiling.

Sarah was allowing herself to feel some relief. Things had been bad. So bad. And most things still were. She knew that this wasn't a good place to stay. She didn't know what her future held. But she wasn't alone anymore, and that, well, that was *everything* right now.

'Theresa?' she whispered.

'Yeah?'

'I'm glad you're my foster-sister.'

A pause.

'Me too, Sarah. Now go to sleep.'

Sarah was sleeping her first dreamless sleep in many days when the sounds woke her up.

A man was there, covered in shadows, crouched over Theresa's bed.

The Stranger!

She began to whimper.

The sounds stopped. A thick stillness hovered in the air.

'Who's that? Sarah? You awake?'

She realized the voice belonged to Dennis. Terror became puzzle-
ment, followed by a creeping unease.

Why is he here?

'Answer me, girl,' he hissed. 'You awake?'

His voice sounded so *mean*. She whimpered again and nodded.

He can't see you, silly!

'Y-yes,' she stammered.

Silence. She could hear Dennis breathing.

'Go back to sleep. Or keep quiet. Whichever.'

'It's okay, Sarah,' Theresa said, her voice faint in the darkness.
'Just close your eyes and cover your ears.'

Sarah closed her eyes and pulled the covers up over her head,
trembling. She kept her ears uncovered, listening hard.

'Go on, put it in your mouth,' she heard Dennis whisper.

'I – I don't want to. Please, Dennis, just leave me alone.' Theresa's
voice was filled with misery.

A quick sound, followed by a gasp from Theresa that made
Sarah shiver.

'Put it in your mouth, or I'll put it somewhere else. Somewhere
that'll hurt. You understand?'

The silence that followed seemed unending. Then, wet noises.

'That's it. Good girl.' Sarah didn't know what his 'good girl'
really meant, but she knew it was something bad.

(*Very bad*)

That was what she felt in this room right now, the presence of
something very, very *bad*. Something ugly. Something that made
her feel dirty and ashamed without knowing why.

The noises changed, got faster, and then they stopped and
Dennis groaned, a heavy, horrible groan that made Sarah tremble.

Another long silence. The sounds of motion, moving sheets.
The floor creaked. Footsteps. She heard them coming near her
bed.

(*Monsters*)

They stopped and she knew Dennis was there. Standing over
her. She tried not to move, not to breathe. Tried to

(Be nothing)

She could smell him. Smoke and alcohol, mixed with a musky sweat, all of which made her want to scream and gag at the same time.

'You're pretty, Sarah,' he whispered. 'You're going to grow up to be a nice-looking young lady. Maybe I'll come pay you a visit in a couple of years.'

(Be nothing Be nothing Be nothing)

Sarah was so terrified that she began to get nauseous.

She felt him move away. Heard his footsteps padding toward the door and out the room.

They were alone now. Sarah could hear her own heartbeat, fast like a hummingbird, loud like a drum.

This died down enough for her to become aware of Theresa crying. It was a faint, deep sound.

Talk to her, dummy.

I'm scared. I don't want to come out from under the covers. Please don't make me, I'm only six, I don't want to do this anymore no more –

Shut up! She's your SISTER, you big fraidy-cat!

Sarah squeezed her eyes shut tight one last time before opening them. She took a deep breath and mustered all the courage her child heart could deliver. She pulled down the covers.

'Theresa?' she whispered. 'Are you okay?'

Sniffling sounds.

'I'm fine, Sarah. Go to sleep.'

She didn't sound fine, not at all.

'Do you want me to come hug you and sleep with you?'

A pause.

'Don't come over here. Not in . . . *this* bed. I'll come there.'

Sarah watched Theresa's shadow rise and move toward her. The bedsprings squeaked as the older girl climbed into bed with her.

Sarah reached out with her hands. They met Theresa's shoulders and she realized that the older girl was sobbing, face pressed against the pillow to mask the sound.

Sarah pulled on Theresa's shoulders with her small hands, urging the older girl toward her.

'Shhh . . . it's okay, Theresa. It's okay.'

Theresa came into the small girl's arms without resistance. Her head found Sarah's chest and she sobbed and sobbed and sobbed. Sarah hugged Theresa's neck and petted her hair and cried a little herself.

What happened? A few hours ago we were playing Go Fish and felt happy, then Dennis comes and does these bad bad bad bad bad things.

A new fear thrilled through Sarah.

Maybe this is how everything's going to be now!

She set her mouth and shook her head.

No. God wouldn't let life be like that.

She thought these things as Theresa wept. The sobs turned into quieter tears, which turned into sniffles, which turned into nothing. Theresa kept her head on Sarah's chest. Sarah kept stroking her hair. Mommy used to do that for her when she was upset, and it always helped.

Maybe all mommies do that. Maybe Theresa's mommy did it too.

'Men are bad, Sarah,' Theresa whispered, breaking the silence.

'My daddy wasn't,' Sarah replied, regretting the words as they came out of her mouth.

She was only six, but she knew that Theresa wasn't really talking about men like Sarah's daddy. She was talking about men like Dennis. Although he was the first such man Sarah had ever met, she knew that Theresa was one hundred percent right about him.

All Theresa said was 'I know,' and she didn't sound mad.

'Theresa?'

'Yeah?'

'What did he mean when he said he'd come visit me in a few years?'

Another long silence, this one filled with things Sarah couldn't identify at all.

246

'Don't you worry about that, little girl,' Theresa said. The tenderness in her voice brought an unexpected prickle of tears to Sarah's eyes. The older girl's hand came up to her cheek and touched it, once. 'I won't let him get you. Not ever.'

Sarah fell asleep believing this.

28

'What color, honey?'

It was Sunday and Sarah was with her mother in her studio. She liked to do this sometimes, just sit down and watch Mommy paint or sculpt, or whatever. Her mother looked most beautiful when she was being an artist.

This painting was a landscape. Mountains in the background, preceded by a large open meadow dotted with lushly leafed trees. The colors were vibrant and unreal: a purplish sky, butter-yellow grass, the sun an impossible orange. Sarah thought it was amazing. Her mother was asking her what color she thought the leaves on the trees should be.

Sarah frowned. She didn't have words to explain why she liked the painting. Mommy had told her in the past that that was okay, that what you felt was more important than what you thought. What she felt about this painting was 'pretty' and 'joyful.'

'The real colors, Mommy. But shinier.'

Sarah didn't have the vocabulary, but Linda knew her meaning was exact. Sarah was seeing something in her mind and trying to describe it. It was up to Linda to figure out what.

'Shinier . . . you mean brighter? Like a lightbulb gives more light or less light?'

Sarah nodded.

'Okay, honey.'

Linda began mixing oranges and reds, bemused.

Maybe she's got some artist in her.

Sarah was saying that the leaves should be the correct colors of autumn leaves, but brighter, in fitting with the rest of the painting.

She glanced at her daughter.

'Do you like this painting, babe?'

'I love it, Mommy. It makes me want to go and play and jump and stuff.'

Mission accomplished, Linda thought, happy and satisfied.

She turned back to the painting and began coloring the leaves, over-bright.

Sarah watched her mother. She was aware of a deep feeling of happiness. She was a child, she lived in the now, and the now was very, very good.

Her mother stopped painting and went rigid. Her back was to Sarah. She stood there, unmoving, frozen in place.

'What's the matter, Mommy?'

Linda jerked at the sound of her daughter's voice and began to turn around in slow motion. Taffy-time. When her face became visible, Sarah jerked back in horror.

Her mother was screaming a soundless scream, eyes wide, mouth open, teeth apart.

'M-m-mommy . . . ?'

Linda's hands flew up to the sides of her head. The paintbrush flew, speckling Sarah with blood as it spun through the air.

Sarah could see the painting behind her mother. The leaves on the trees were burning.

The scream stopped being silent, a terrible sound, like someone had torn the roof off hell. It played in stereo, full of echoes and reverb and rage.

'What did you do! What did you do! What did you –'

Sarah woke up.

'What did you do!'

The scream was real. It was here, now, in this house.

The Stranger?

The door to the bedroom was open.

'Dennis! Oh God! What did you do, Theresa?'

Sarah realized that Rebecca was the one screaming.

Get out of bed, fraidy-cat. Theresa might need your help!

Sarah whimpered in terror, frustration, anger.

I don't want to have to be brave anymore.

Silence.

Too bad, fraidy-cat. That's the way it is now.

Sarah was weeping and shaking in fear, but she made herself get out of bed. Her legs belonged to someone else, they wobbled and shook.

She moved toward the door, but when she got to it, she froze.

What if there are more

(nothings)

Out there?

What if Theresa's become a

(nothing)

(puppyshead)

?

Move it, fraidy-cat. You're six. Stop acting like a baby.

Sarah made herself move forward, out of the room, into the hall. Her fear was so strong now that she began to sob.

'What did you do?' Rebecca continued to shriek.

Sarah's sobbing grew stronger as she forced herself to keep walking toward the sound of Rebecca's screams. Her nose began to run and the world blurred.

Don't want to go look! Don't want to!

The other voice was gentler now.

I know you're afraid. But you have to. For Theresa. She's your sister.

Sarah bawled, but nodded her head in response, and forced her feet to keep moving.

A moment later and she was in the doorway of Dennis and Rebecca's room. Theresa was there, sitting on the floor, her head down. She had a knife in her lap. It was coated with blood. Rebecca was naked on the bed, hysterical, her hands moving over Dennis in frantic motions. She was covered in blood too.

Dennis was still. His eyes were open.

Sarah realized in a flash that Dennis was

(*nothing*)

A

(*puppyshead*)

now.

'What did you *do*?'

Sarah gasped.

Oh no. Theresa did this.

She ran over to the older girl, crouched down on her knees, and shook her.

'Theresa! What happened?'

The older girl's face was slack and pale, her eyes listless.

'Hey, little girl,' she whispered. 'Like I told you. He'll never bother you at night. Ever.'

Sarah recoiled in horror.

'Go call the police, Sarah.'

Theresa bowed her head and began rocking back and forth.

Sarah watched her, confused and frantic.

What do I do?

The card. From the lady-policeman.

'What did you d-d-dooooooooooo?'

Call her, now.

As she ran from the room, she realized at some level that the eggshells and the danger were gone from this house. She wondered how this could be.

Many years later, she understood how that could be. By then, she had stopped believing in God.

29

Cathy Jones sat with Sarah. They were in Cathy's personal car –
Cathy wasn't on duty, but the girl had called her, so she'd come
after calling it in to the station.

This is just fucking horrible, she thought to herself.

She looked at Sarah. The girl's cheeks and eyes were red from
crying.

Who can blame her? She checks in to a new home, and the
foster-father gets murdered by one of the other kids the first night.
Jesus.

'Sarah? What happened?'

The six-year-old sighed. It was a heavy sigh, filled with a worldly
weight that dismayed the young policewoman.

'Dennis came to visit Theresa in her bed. He did bad things.
He said he'd come see me in my bed in a few years too.' Sarah's
face crumpled. 'Theresa said that she'd never let him do that.
That's why she killed Dennis. Because of me!'

Sarah threw herself into Cathy's arms and began to sob.

Cathy froze. She was unmarried, she had no kids, she'd been
an only child with an undemonstrative father. She gave herself an
F in intimacy.

Hug her, dummy.

She wrapped her arms around the six-year-old. Sarah started crying harder.

Now say something to her.

'Shh. It's okay, Sarah. It'll be okay.'

It occurred to her that maybe Dad had had it right, being sparse with words of praise and comfort. Because she didn't think what she was saying was true, not at all, no, sir. She didn't think it was going to be okay. Not ever.

'The girl said that?'

Sarah's crying had died down to sniffles, and Cathy had left her alone while she went over to talk to the detective on the scene, Nick Rollins.

'Yes, sir. She said that this guy Dennis – the foster-father who got killed – came to visit the other girl in bed.'

'Fuck me,' Rollins said, shaking his head. 'Well, if it bears out, that might change the outcome for the doer. If he was raping her, and threatening to do the same to your girl . . .' He shrugged, sad. 'It'll keep her from going down for murder.'

They both looked up as female officers led Theresa from the house in handcuffs. The girl kept her eyes on the ground and shuffled like a chained ghost.

'What do you want me to do?' she asked Rollins.

'Sit tight with the girl. Someone from Social Services is on the way over.'

'Yes, sir.'

Cathy watched as Theresa was helped into the backseat of a police car. The policewoman glanced over at her own vehicle. Sarah was staring through the windshield, watching the darkness, seeing nothing.

Cathy was back with Sarah, sitting in her car while they waited for the woman from Social Services. Rollins had gotten a statement from Sarah. He'd been very good with the little girl; Cathy was grateful.

'Cathy?' Sarah asked, breaking the silence.

'Yeah?'

'You didn't believe me when I told you about the man at my house, did you?'

Cathy shifted in her seat, uncomfortable.

How do I deal with this one?

'I wasn't sure if I should believe you or not, Sarah. You were . . . pretty upset.'

Sarah scrutinized Cathy. 'Did you tell the other policepeople, though? What I said?'

'Yes. Of course.'

'They didn't believe me, did they?'

Cathy shifted again, sighed. 'No, Sarah. They didn't.'

'Why not? Do they think I was lying?'

'No, no. Nothing like that. It's . . . there's nothing that shows anyone else was there. And sometimes, when bad things happen, people . . . get confused. Not just kids. Grown-ups too. That's what they think. Not that you're lying. That you were confused.'

Sarah turned back to the windshield.

'I wasn't. Confused. It doesn't matter. The mean lady is here.'

Cathy saw a worn-looking middle-ager moving toward them.

'Mean, huh?'

Sarah nodded. 'Theresa said she was pure evil.'

Cathy stared at the little girl. She might have dismissed a statement like this yesterday. But now? The girl who'd killed a child molester to save Sarah had said the woman was 'pure evil.'

'Sarah. Look at me.'

The little girl turned to the policewoman.

'You hold on to my card. And you call me if you need me.' She indicated Karen Watson with a nod. 'Understand?'

'Okay.'

That's it, huh? That's all you're going to do for her?

The inevitable reply came, the one that Cathy pulled out in any situation that demanded more intimacy than she was willing to give:

254

It's all I've got right now.

She was an old hand at ignoring the feeling of shame. She wasn't in quite enough denial to blame it all on dear old Dad, though.

Karen had helped Sarah pack her clothes and shoes. She had been acting really nice again. Sarah had understood: There were other people watching. Once they were alone, she'd known that Karen would turn mean again.

They were driving now, and sure enough, Karen was giving her angry looks. Sarah didn't care. She was too tired.

'Messed up a good thing,' Karen muttered. 'Not like you have many options. Well, now you'll see what happens when you can't get along.'

Sarah had no idea what Karen was talking about. Something bad. She was too sad to be afraid.

Theresa, Theresa, why why why? You should have talked with me. We were sisters. Now I'm all alone again.

They had pulled up to a large one-story building, made of gray concrete and surrounded by fences.

'Here we go, princess,' Karen said. 'This is a group home – you'll be staying here until I feel like giving you another chance with a foster home.'

They got out of the car. Sarah followed Karen to and through the front door of the home. They walked down a hall until they got to a reception desk. A tired-looking woman in her forties stood up. She had brown hair and was the skinniest person Sarah had ever seen. Karen handed a form to the woman.

'Sarah Langstrom.'

The woman read over the form, glanced at Sarah. She nodded at Karen.

'Okay.'

'See you later, princess,' Karen said. She turned around and walked away.

'Hi, Sarah,' the woman said. 'My name is Janet. I'm going to get you settled into bed for now, and then I'll show you around in the morning, okay?'

Sarah nodded.

Don't care, she thought. Don't care about anything. Just want to go sleep.

'This way,' Janet said.

Sarah followed Janet down the hallway, through one set of locked doors, then another. The walls were painted institution green. The floors were worn linoleum. The home looked like every other heavily used but grossly underfunded government building in the country.

The hallway they were in now was lined with doors. Janet stopped in front of one and opened it, taking pains to be quiet.

'Shhh,' she said, putting a finger to her lips. 'Everyone's asleep.'

Janet kept the door open a crack so they could use the light from the hallway. Sarah saw that she was in a large room, fairly clean, filled with six sets of two-tier metal bunk beds. Girls of various ages were sleeping in each.

'Over here,' Janet whispered, indicating one of the sets of beds. 'The bottom bunk will be yours. The restroom is down the hall. Do you need to go?'

Sarah shook her head. 'No, thank you. I'm tired.'

'Go to sleep, then. I'll see you in the morning.'

She waited until Sarah had crawled under the covers before leaving. The door clicked shut and now it was dark. Sarah wasn't afraid of this dark, because she was in that place again, where she wanted to

(Be nothing)

She didn't want to think about Theresa or Dennis or blood or strangers or being alone. She just wanted to close her eyes and see the color black everywhere.

She had started to fall into an exhausted sleep when she was woken up by a hand at her throat. It was choking her. Her eyes flew open.

'Quiet,' a voice whispered.

The voice belonged to a girl – a strong girl. The hand around Sarah's neck was viselike.

'My name is Kirsten,' the voice said. 'I run this room. What I say goes, period. You got it?'

She loosened her grip on Sarah's neck. Sarah coughed.

'Why?' she asked once she'd caught her breath.

'Why what?'

'Why do I have to do what you say?'

A hand came out of the dark. The slap rocked Sarah's head, and the pain was shocking.

'Because I'm the strongest. I'll see you in the morning.'

The shadow was gone. Sarah's cheek ached. She felt more alone than ever.

Yeah, but you know what?

What?

At least you're not being a crybaby.

She realized that this was true. What she was feeling wasn't grief.

It was anger.

As she began to fall asleep again, the words Kirsten had said came back to her.

I'm the strongest.

A final flare of anger.

Not forever.

She fell into the blessed black.

Hey, there. Me again, back in the here and now.

Looking back at it, Kirsten wasn't completely wrong, you know. That's the truth of the group home: The strongest ones rule over the weaker ones. She taught me that, although I wasn't thankful then. Hell, I was only six. Now I'm older, and I know the truth.

Someone had to do it.

I learned that lesson good.

*

I put the diary down again as the rising sun greets me through the windows. There's no way I can finish this before I have to go in to work, but at least I have my answer: No one believed her because he covered his tracks when he killed the Langstroms. No one was after Sarah, they'd probably thought, she was just having a run of really bad luck. This was borne out by the events that followed with her first foster-family.

That being the case, a new question arises: Why had The Stranger decided to come out into the open now?

I ignore all of the other questions, the ones about Sarah and the landscape of her soul; those edges are far too sharp for such a beautiful sunrise.

Book Two

Men Who Eat Children

30

I curse the rain and ready myself for the run to the front steps of the Los Angeles FBI building.

Southern California had very little rain and a whole lot of sun for nearly a decade. Mother Nature is making up for lost time with a heavy rainstorm every three days or so. It started in February and it's been going on for two months now. It's wearing thin.

Nobody carries an umbrella in Los Angeles, even if they should. I'm no exception. I stuff the copy of Sarah's diary into my jacket to protect it, grab my purse, and poise my thumb so I can hit the lock button of my key fob on the run.

I open the door and sprint, cursing, cursing, cursing. I'm drenched by the time I arrive.

'Rain got you good, Smoky,' Mitch remarks as I pass through security.

No response beyond a smile or a grimace is expected. Mitch is the head of security for the building, a grizzled ex-military man; fifty-five or so, fit, with hawk eyes and a certain coldness to him.

I drip-dry on the elevator as I head up to the floor my office is on. Other agents ride up with me, looking just as bedraggled. Everyone got drenched; each region has its own piece of stubbornness. This is ours.

The current incarnation of my position is known as NCAVC

Coordinator. NCAVC stands for 'National Center for the Analysis of Violent Crime' and it is headquartered in DC. Every bureau office has someone in charge of being the local 'rep' for the NCAVC, a kind of Amway network of death. In sleepier, slower places, one agent covers multiple areas of responsibility, NCAVC Coord being just one of many hungry mouths he or she has to feed.

We're special here. We get some of the best psychos around, in a volume that justifies a full-time Coordinator In-Charge (me) and a multi-agent team. I have been in charge of my team for almost a decade. I hand-selected everyone; they are the absolute best around, in my not-so-humble opinion.

The FBI is a bureaucracy, so there are always rumbles and rumors about changing the name or the composition of my squad. For now, we are here, and we are generally more than busy.

I head down the hallways, turning right and then left as I continue to drip on the thin, tight-woven gray carpet until I get to the NCAVC Coord offices, known within the building as 'Death Central.' I enter and my nose twitches at the smell of coffee.

'Good grief, you're drenched.'

I give Callie a baleful look. She, of course, is dry and perfect and beautiful. Well, not perfect, maybe. Her eyes are tired. A mix of pain and painkillers? Or just a lack of sleep?

'Coffee ready?' I mumble.

The need for caffeine is great.

'Of course,' Callie says, pretending to be offended. 'You're not dealing with an amateur here.' She indicates the pot. 'Freshly brewed. Hand-ground this morning by yours truly.'

I go over and pour myself a cup. I take a sip and shiver in mock-delight.

'You're my favorite person ever, Callie.'

'Of course I am.'

Alan comes ambling in from the back part of the offices, cup in hand.

'Thought I was your favorite person,' he rumbles.

'You are.'

'You can't have more than one favorite person,' Callie complains.

I toast her with my cup and smile. 'I'm the boss. I can have as many favorite people as I want. I can even have rotating favorite people. Alan on Monday, you on Tuesday, James . . . okay, James is a stretch. But you get the idea.'

'True enough,' Alan says, toasting me back and returning the smile.

We all share a comfortable silence and sip Callie's divine coffee. Letting the morning creep through us at a decent pace. It's not always like this – in fact, it's rarely so. Many, many mornings the coffee comes in Styrofoam, is far from divine, and is drunk on the run.

'Did everyone get here before me?' I ask. 'Geez. I thought I was being an early bird. The conscientious boss and all that.'

'James isn't here yet,' Alan offers. 'I couldn't sleep last night. Started reading that diary.' He gives me another toast with his cup, a bit sarcastic this time. 'Thanks for that.'

'Likewise,' Callie says.

'Then we're a club,' I reply. I rub my eyes with one hand. 'How far did you guys get?'

'I got to the arrival at her second foster home,' Alan says.

'I'm not there, yet,' I say. 'Callie?'

'I finished it,' she says.

The door opens and James enters. I nurse a secret satisfaction that he's as soaked as I am. Later in arriving too. Ha ha.

He doesn't say anything to anyone. Just marches past us toward his desk.

'Good morning,' Callie calls after him.

'I finished the diary last night,' he calls back.

That's all he says. No 'hello' or 'good morning.' James is all business.

'That's our cue,' I say. 'Let's get to work.'

I'm facing everyone. They're seated, I'm standing.

'Let's begin with the diary.' I tell them where I've gotten to.

'James, you finished it. Fill me in. Anything immediately probative past what I've already read?'

He considers this. 'Yes and no. She goes into another foster home, and that doesn't end up well. She has some bad experiences in the group home. Oh, she intimates at one point to having been sexually abused.'

'Great,' I mutter.

'From a purely investigatory standpoint,' James continues, 'there are three areas of immediate follow-up based on what she wrote. There's the original crime scene – the murder of her parents. There's the cop who took an interest in her. Cathy Jones. Jones disappears later, and Sarah doesn't know why.'

'Interesting,' Alan notes. 'And there is his mention to her of prior victims. The poet, the philosophy student.'

'Okay, that's good,' I say. 'Now let's talk about motive,' I begin. 'Revenge. Does anyone disagree?'

'Makes sense,' Alan says. '"Pain," "justice," all that. The question is, revenge for what? And why is Sarah in the mix?'

'Sins of the father,' I say.

They all look puzzled. I fill them in on my deductions from last night.

'Interesting,' Callie murmurs. 'Something the grandfather did. It's possible.'

'Let's examine the overall picture. He stated to Sarah that he is "making her over in his own image." He calls her his sculpture and gives that sculpture a title: *A Ruined Life*. What does that tell us?'

'If he's making her into him, that he thinks *his* life was ruined,' Alan replies.

'Right. So he devises a long-term plan, not to kill her, but to destroy her emotionally. That's pretty severe pathology. It tells us he wasn't just ignored by Mommy. Something was done that requires devastation of a girl's life as a response. What are some possibilities?'

'Going off the "own image" concept,' Alan says, 'he orphaned her. So he was probably orphaned at an early age himself.'

'Good. What else?'

'I think he was raised in an unsupportive environment,' James says. 'He destroyed anyone or anything that vaguely promised to become a support system for Sarah. He isolated her completely.'

'Okay.'

'Additionally,' James continues, 'we can surmise that he was the recipient of sexual abuse.'

'Based on?'

'It's inductive. Orphaned, a lack of emotional support – he fell into the wrong hands. Statistically, that means he was sexually abused. It fits with the sheer ambition of his plan for Sarah. Fits with the need for a plan at all.'

'Callie? Anything to add?' I ask.

Her smile is cryptic. 'Yes, but for now I'll just say I agree. Let's get to me last.'

I frown at her, she sips her coffee and smiles, unfazed.

'So he was orphaned and abused,' I continue. 'The question: Which does he want revenge for, one or both? And why multiple victims?'

'I don't follow,' Alan says.

'We have Sarah as a living victim, a kind of symbolic recipient of revenge. Fine. If we follow that line of thought, the Kingsleys become incidental. Collateral damage, their bad luck to have fostered Sarah. But we *also* have, from Sarah's accounts, the poet and the philosophy student. Why were they in the line of fire? And why the difference in MO between them and Vargas?'

Alan shakes his head. 'You've lost me.'

'Vargas got the same treatment as the Kingsleys,' James explains. 'His throat was cut, he was disemboweled. Terrible enough, I guess, but not the most painful way to go. When he talks about the poet and the philosophy student, it's different. Sounds like their deaths were no fun at all. The same goes for Sam and Linda Langstrom. Nothing quick or painless about that.'

'You're saying he changes his MO based on what he considers to be the severity of their crime?' Callie asks.

'I'm saying he feels like he's handing out justice. Within that paradigm, not every offense merits the same punishment.'

Alan nods. 'I'll buy that. Let's call them primary and secondary victims. Vargas and the Kingsleys would be secondary victims. Sarah and her parents, the poet and the philosopher, they'd be primary victims, deserving the worst he can dish out.'

'Yes,' James replies.

'Except we're theorizing that Sam and Linda are secondary, in their own way,' Alan muses. 'Descended from the *actual* bad guy.'

'Not secondary to *him*, though. It still fits the construct. If Grandfather Langstrom did something to affect The Stranger as a child, and he's no longer available for justice, then his progeny deserve to suffer by proxy,' James says.

'It would also mean that The Stranger views Granddad's crimes as particularly bad,' I say.

'You're basing that on what he's done with Sarah?' James asks.

'Of course.'

'How do you know the poet and the philosophy student, who-ever they are, didn't have children as well? How do you know there aren't other Sarahs out there?' he asks.

I pause, considering this pretty unsavory, pretty *terrible* thought. 'I guess I don't. Okay, so we theorize he was orphaned, fell into the wrong hands, and suffered abuse. The scars on his feet support that. Anything else?'

Silence.

'My turn,' Callie says. 'I spent a good part of my evening digging through Mr Vargas's computer. It's infested with pornography of every kind, including hardcore kiddie porn. He's indiscriminate in his perversion. In addition to the kiddie porn I saw scat, besti-ality.' She makes a face. 'Vomit eating.'

'Okay, we get the idea,' Alan says, looking distressed.

'Sorry. All of that, however, seemed to have been for personal consumption. It supports what we already know: Mr Vargas was an unpleasant individual. His e-mail wasn't revelatory either. The video clip, however, was.'

'Video? Of what?' I ask.

She indicates her monitor. 'Crowd around and I'll show you.'

We form a semicircle. The media player has already been invoked. 'Ready?' she asks.

'Go ahead,' I reply.

She hits play. A moment of blackness. An ugly rug comes into view.

'I recognize that,' I murmur. 'The carpet in Vargas's apartment.'

The camera jitters and the shot moves up, rolling around like a drunk as the camera is wrestled onto a tripod. It settles down to auto-focus on the same sad bed, the one I'd found Vargas and the girl dead on. A nude girl clambers onto the mattress. She's too young, only just pubescent. She takes a moment to arrange herself. Gets on her hands and knees. Her wrists are in handcuffs.

'That's the girl from last night,' I say.

A voice outside the shot murmurs something. I can't make out the words, but she turns her head up and looks right into the camera lens. Her living face is placid, almost docile. It's not all that different from her dead face. She has beautiful blue eyes, but they're as hollow as a drum. Full of nothing.

Jose Vargas comes into view. He's dressed, wearing blue jeans and a dirty white T-shirt. He looks his age. His back is slightly stooped. He's unshaven. His face is tired, but his eyes, they're bright. He's looking forward to whatever it is he's about to do.

'Is that a switch in his hand?' Alan asks.

'Yes it is,' Callie replies.

The switch is a thin branch that's been stripped from a tree. I can see a hint of its green core at one end. Vargas has prepared for corporal punishment the old-fashioned way.

He moves behind the girl. Leans forward, seems to be checking the camera. Nods to himself. He gives the girl a critical eye.

'Ass higher in the air, fucking *puta*,' he barks.

The girl hardly blinks. She wiggles a little, forcing her posterior higher.

'That's better.' Checks the room again, the camera, again. 'That's good.' A last nod to himself and Vargas gives the camera his full attention. He smiles and it's an ugly smile, full of brown teeth or the spaces where teeth should be.

'Man needs a dentist,' Alan mutters.

'So, Mr You Know Who,' Vargas begins. 'Hello. *Buenos dias*. It's your old friend, Jose.' Vargas gestures at the girl. 'Some things, I guess, never change.' He spreads his hands to indicate the room. Shrugs. 'Other things, they change a lot. Money is not so good these days. All that time in prison, it left me with not many – what do they say? – *job skills*.' Another gap-toothed smile. 'But I have skills, yes? You know this. I remember them, the things you taught me when I was younger, in those times that were better. I'll show you how *much* I remember. Yes?'

Vargas holds up the switch. Smiles.

'Teach the property. But never leave marks that make the property less valuable. Jose remembers.'

Vargas pulls his arm back. His mouth falls open. It's almost cavernous. An indescribably hungry look comes over him. I doubt he's aware of it. The switch pauses at the top of the arc, trembles in his excited hand, and then comes whistling down. The impact on her feet is barely audible, but the girl's response is extreme. Her eyes bug out, her mouth opens in a wide O. A moment later, silent tears begin to fall. She clenches her teeth, trying to ride the pain.

'Say the words, *puta*!' Vargas barks.

'Y-you are the God,' the girl stammers. 'So I t-thank you the God.'

'Accent sounds Russian,' James notes.

Vargas comes down with the switch again. His eyes are brighter, his mouth wider. He drools a little. Madness.

This time, the girl arches her whole body, and cries out.

'The words!' Vargas shouts, grinning now.

It goes on like this a few more times. When it's over, Vargas is panting and sweating and his eyes are fluttering. I can see a bulge in his jeans. The girl sobs openly.

Vargas stumbles a little, seems to remember his original purpose. He brushes a lock of greasy hair from his eyes, gives the camera another sly and dirty smile.

'You see? I remember *everything*.' The girl sobs louder. 'Shut up, fucking *puta*!' Vargas snarls at her, incensed by the interruption. She puts her hands to her mouth to stifle the noise.

'I think, Mr You Know Who, that you will give Jose money for what he remembers.' Another grotesque smile. 'You go now, watch this again. I know you will, anyway, yes? Jose remembers that about you. You enjoy these things. You watch this again and you think about what you are going to say to Jose when you talk to him. *Adios*.'

Vargas glances at the sobbing girl, rubs his crotch, and smiles at the camera.

Blackness.

'Wow,' I say. I feel ill.

'Mr You Know Who. That's original. So we have Vargas blackmailing someone who's familiar with this whole practice of caning feet,' Alan says.

'Behavior modification,' James opines. 'Torture combined with forced, repetitive usage of a degrading phrase that admits subservience.'

'Beats the feet so as not to mark up other parts of the body and reduce value,' Alan adds.

'It continues to fit,' I say. 'The Stranger has the same marks. That's no coincidence. Vargas's attempt at blackmail confirms the involvement of others and it points toward the sexual abuse, as well.'

'You know,' Alan says, shaking his head, 'if he'd stuck with Vargas and his kind, I might not have much of a problem with our perp.' His face is grim. 'Man that would do that to a child? That's a man that deserves to die.'

No one argues this point.

'I did a thorough search of his hard drive,' Callie says. 'I was hopeful. Vargas encoded the video for some reason, I thought he might have uploaded it to a server somewhere or the like.' She shakes her head. 'No such luck. I suppose he encoded it and then he burned it to disc and sent it to whomever he was black-mailing.'

'This seems to lead back to the human-trafficking angle,' I say. 'Barry says that was handled at our level. Here in California, actually. It's a key point of follow-up.' I rub my face, move back to the front of the office. 'Okay, what else?'

'Key change in his behavior,' James says. 'When he murdered the Langstroms, he took steps to conceal himself. Now he's stepped out into the open. Why?'

'All kinds of reasons that could be,' Alan rumbles. 'Maybe he's sick, dying, running out of time. Maybe it's taken him a while to figure out the identities of the guys he thinks need killing. The interesting confluence is that it's all happening at the same time that Vargas is getting his blackmail scheme going. Looks like some things that were buried dug themselves up.'

'It points to an endgame,' I say. 'He knows that we'll be after him. Hell, he's invited it. He sees things coming to a conclusion.'

'So where do we go from here, honey-love?'

I consider this question. We have many different directions we could go in. Which are the most likely to bear fruit?

'Time to divide and conquer. Alan, I want you to take the Langstroms. Gather up all the information you can get on them, their deaths, their background. No stone unturned. Find out who the grandfather is. If my hunch is right, he's important. Call Barry if you need someone to run local interference.'

'Got it.'

'James, I want you to work on two things. I want a VICAP search on the murders of our poet and philosophy student. Let's see if we can find out who they were.'

VICAP stands for Violent Criminal Apprehension Program. Its purpose is to create a collated database of violent crimes that allows for a nationwide cross-referencing of violent acts.

'Fine. The second thing?'

I fill him in on the computer program found on Michael Kingsley's computer. 'Check the progress with that, see if they need assistance with resources. And I'm going to want to have a talk in my office shortly.'

'Very well.'

He doesn't ask what I mean when I say we need to 'talk.' He knows I want us to have a closer mental look at The Stranger together, the only 'meeting of the minds' he and I are capable of.

'And me?' Callie asks.

'Call Barry and see where things stand on the sketch artist for the tattoo. Also, see if he's made any progress on identifying the Russian girl.'

'Anything else?'

'Not for now. Okay, that's it.'

Everyone gets rolling. I go into my own office and close the door. I need to go see AD Jones, to find out what he knows about Vargas, but in light of everything I read last night, there's something else that needs doing first. I dial Tommy's number. He answers on the second ring.

'Hey.'

'Hey,' I reply, smiling to myself. 'I need a professional favor from you.'

'Name it.'

'I need a bodyguard.'

'For you?'

'No. For the victim I told you about. Sixteen-year-old girl named Sarah Langstrom.'

Tommy is all business. 'Do we know who's after her?'

'Not by sight.'

'Do we know when he's going to do it?'

'No. And there's a twist. She's probably only the target by proxy; it's the people close to her that end up dead.'

He pauses. 'I can't do it myself. You know I would if I could, but I'm in the middle of something.'

'I know.' I don't press him on what his 'middle of something' is. Tommy's use of the understatement is an art form. For all I know, he's talking to me on the phone while his car is surrounded by gunmen.

'Don't you have people for this?' he asks.

'For general surveillance, but I want a full-time professional bodyguard. I'll sell it to the boss and the Bureau will pay the bills.'

'Gotcha. Well, I have someone. A woman. She's good.'

I sense hesitation in his voice.

'What?' I ask.

'Just rumors.'

'About her?'

'Yeah.'

'Like?'

'That she spent some time killing people.'

I pause.

'What kind of people?' I ask.

'The kind of people the United States government needs dead.' He pauses. 'Allegedly. If you believe in stuff like that.'

I digest this.

'What do you think about her, Tommy?'

'She's loyal and she's lethal. You can trust her.'

I rub my eyes, thinking. I sigh. 'Fine. Give her my number.'

'Will do.'

'You know some interesting people, Tommy.'

'Like you.'

I smile, again. 'Yeah. Like me.'

'I have to go.'

'I know, I know. You're in the middle of something. I'll call you later.'

He hangs up. I sit for a moment, wondering what someone described as 'loyal and lethal' will be like. A knock on the door interrupts this train of thought.

James pokes his head in.

'Are you ready?' he asks.

I glance at the clock on my wall. AD Jones can wait a little while longer, I suppose.

'Yeah. Let's talk about our psycho.'

31

James and I are in my office, behind closed doors.

Just thee and me, my disagreeable friend.

James, misanthropic James, has the same gift I do. His lack of tact, his rudeness – the man is a consummate asshole, it's true – none of that matters when we sit down to commiserate on evil. He sees it like I do. He hears and feels and understands.

'You have an edge on me, James. You finished the diary. Did you read the notes I faxed you?'

'Yes.'

'Tell me what you think.'

He stares at a space on the wall above my head.

'I believe the revenge motive is correct. The video with Vargas, the messages on the wall – the references to justice in particular – it all fits. The thing that I felt reading the diary, however, is that he's begun to mix his paradigms.'

'English, James.'

'Look, the original purpose is a pure one, within its own framework. Revenge. He was the recipient of bad acts. He's visiting bad acts on those directly responsible – or in Sarah's case, we're theorizing – the descendants of those directly responsible. That's the path we're following, and I believe it will bear fruit.' He leans back in his chair. 'But let's examine the way in which he dispenses justice.'

'Pain.'

James smiles, a rare thing. 'That's right. The endgame is murder, sure. But how quickly you arrive at dead ... well, that depends on how much pain he thinks you deserve. He's obsessed with the subject. I think he's crossed the line from dispensing justice with clarity to a true enjoyment of inflicting pain.'

I consider this. The behavior James is describing is common, too common. The abused becomes the abuser. Molest a child, and he often grows up to become the molester. Violence is contagious.

I imagine The Stranger, on his knees like that poor blond girl in the video, while some drooling stranger whips his feet, again and again.

Pain.

He grows up, chock-full of rage, and he decides it's time for payback. He gets going on his plan, and everything is moving along, but then somewhere along the way, a switch flips. The rage he's attempting to expiate mutates into a twisted type of *joy*.

So much better to be the one holding the whip than the one being struck. So much better, in fact, that it begins to feel good. Hell, it begins to feel *great*. Once an individual falls down that rabbit hole, the white lines blur into gray and a journey back is pretty much impossible. It would explain the contradictions at the scenes. The blood-painting and erection versus the calm, cool, and collected of a man-with-a-plan.

'So he likes it now,' I say.

'I think he *needs* it,' James replies. 'And the best thing is, he's got the perfect rationalization in place. That old standby: The end justifies the means. He's owed, the guilty will be punished. If innocents suffer along the way, that's unfortunate.'

'Not really unfortunate, though, you're saying.'

'Correct. Look at Sarah. He's loving what he's done to her. It moves him.' James shrugs. 'He's hooked. I bet his creativity extends further, to other victims. If we scratch the surface, I think we're going to find imaginative, colorful deaths, all of them variations on a quintessence of pain.'

Everything he's saying is unproven and for now, unprovable. But it *feels right*. It shifts something inside me, lets it slide into an oily waiting place. He's not delusional. He knows what he's doing and why, and his victims aren't just of a type – they're directly involved with his past. *But* – and it's a big *but* – he's hooked on death now. Murder isn't just a resolution to injustice anymore. It's become a sexual act.

'Let's talk about two specific things,' I say. 'The change in his behavior and his plan for how to end things for Sarah.'

James shakes his head. 'I'm concerned about the first. I can understand him going public with his actions and the reasons for that. It goes hand and hand with revenge as a motive. You don't just want them to experience justice, you want the world to know why.'

'Sure.'

'But he's become aware of changes, in himself. I think his original plan might have involved him getting caught, going out in a blaze of glory that would highlight his story for the world. But now he's discovered that he really *enjoys* killing people. If he dies, he can't do that anymore. That's a strong addiction to turn away from.'

'If he doesn't want to get caught, he's had plenty of time to plan for an escape route.'

'Exactly. I believe that the original *intent* of the plan remains the mandate. He wants everything to come out, wants the sinners and their sins revealed. But he'd prefer to walk away from that. Probably with the rationalization of continuing his "work." Lots of other sinners out there, after all.'

'We need to be careful,' I murmur. 'At some point he's going to try and lead us by the nose. We need to watch out for that, challenge our conclusions.'

'Yes.'

I sigh. 'Fine. What about Sarah? Does he end this by killing her? Or does she get to live?'

James ponders this, staring up at the ceiling. 'I think,' he says, 'that it all depends on how successful he is in his goal to make her over in his own image, and then, how much he identifies with her as a result. Is she really him? If so, does he let her live, suffering, or does he perform a mercy killing? I'm not sure.'

'I'm arranging for her to be protected.'

'Advisable.'

I tap my fingers on the desk. 'Based on the Vargas video, the motive, the scars on his feet, I'm going with the following: He was a victim of commercial-level child trafficking, resulting in heavy physical and sexual abuse. This occurred over a long period, and now that he's grown up, he's pissed and he's working to make things right. So to speak.'

James shrugs. 'It's plausible. At least some aspects of it, I think, are true. It's a shame, really.'

'What's that?'

'You saw the Russian girl. She was broken. Nothing substantial left inside. Our perpetrator, though – he's not broken, not at all. It means he started out strong. The basic building blocks were tough ones.'

'In the biggest picture, he's broken too. But I understand what you're saying. Anything else you can think to add?'

'Just one thing. You asked me if there was anything probative about the diary. Obviously, most of it's true, or her version or view of the truth, but –'

'Wait. Tell me why you think that. Why you believe it.'

'Simple logic. We're accepting as a known that Sarah Langstrom is not the doer in the Kingsley murders. Fine. This girl spends the last few months writing about a lunatic who kills the people around her *and then it actually happens*? The odds of that being a coincidence are beyond astronomical. In light of the Kingsley killings, Sarah's story only makes sense if at least some part of it is true – unless she can see the future.'

I blink. 'Right. Makes sense. You were saying?'

'I was saying that while I believe in most of her story, there's something missing. I can't quite put my finger on it, but something, some aspect of her story, is bothering me.'

'You think she's lying about something?'

He sighs, frustrated. 'I can't say that. It's just a feeling. I'm going to be rereading it. If I figure it out, I'll let you know.'

'You should trust that feeling,' I say.

He gets up to leave. He stops at the door. Turns to me.

'Have you figured out what Sarah is for us?'

I frown. 'What do you mean?'

'What Sarah represents to us. We know how The Stranger sees her, she's his sculpture. A creation made of pain for the purpose of vengeance. But she's something for us too. I realized it last night. I was wondering if you had.'

I stare at him, searching for an answer.

'Sorry,' I say. 'I don't know what you're talking about.'

'She's *Every Victim*, Smoky. You read her story and that's what you get: She's every victim we've ever failed to save. I think he knows that. That's why he's dangling her in front of us. He's holding her just out of reach and making us watch her scream.'

He exits, leaving me dumbfounded.

He's right, I see that. It fits with my own sense of things.

I'm just surprised that James cares enough to see it himself.

Then I remember James's sister, and I wonder about what he said, and about the depth of feeling required to come to that conclusion. Rosa was a victim he failed to save.

Is that the real reason James is always so disagreeable? Because he couldn't stop caring about the death of his sister?

Maybe.

Regardless, he was right, and his observation dictated even more caution from us.

Sarah wasn't just The Stranger's revenge – she was his bait.

32

'I'm going to see AD Jones,' I tell Callie as I exit my office. 'Come with me.'

'Why?'

'The trafficking case? It turns out he was involved.'

'You don't say?'

'Cross my heart and you know the rest.'

I am back in that windowless office, seated with Callie in front of the gray megalith AD Jones calls a desk.

'Tell me about the case,' AD Jones says without preamble. 'In particular, talk to me about Jose Vargas.'

I launch into a recap of everything that's happened up to this point. When I'm done, AD Jones leans back, staring at me while he taps his fingers on the arm of his chair.

'You think this perp – The Stranger – is an abused kid from Vargas's past?'

'It's the current working theory,' I say.

'It's a good theory. The scarring on the feet of the perp and the Russian girl? I've seen that before.'

'You said you were involved in the trafficking case that Vargas was suspected of participating in.'

'Yep. I was on the task force in 1979, directly under the agent-in-charge, Daniel Haliburton.' He shakes his head. 'Haliburton was a fixture here, a dinosaur, but a great investigator. Tough. I was new, just two years out of the academy. It was a messy case. Real bad stuff. I was excited anyway. You know how it is.'

'Yes, sir.'

'LAPD Vice had experienced a spike in child hookers and kiddie porn. It was always an ongoing problem, but this was different. They noticed a lot of these kids shared commonalities.'

'Let me guess,' Callie says. 'Scarring on the feet.'

'That was one of them. The other was that none of them came from the US. They were predominately South American, some were European. We guessed the Europeans were being routed through South America and then up here into the States.'

He pauses, looking off into the past.

'Most of the victims were girls, but there were some boys too. They ranged in age from seven to thirteen, none older. All of them were in bad shape. Many of them were suffering from multiple STDs, unhealed vaginal and anal tearing . . .' He waves a hand. 'You get the idea. Suffice to say, it was the kind of case that makes an impression on people.'

'The only good thing about pedophiles,' I say, 'is that they're universally hated.'

'Yeah. So the LAPD called us in. No one cared about credit or PR or politics. It was refreshing. We formed a task force, they did the same, and it was a full-court press.' A faint smile. 'That meant different things back then than it does now. Ethical debate in law enforcement was a little more . . . fluid.'

'I take it you mean – hypothetically speaking, of course – that suspects were questioned in an overly aggressive manner.'

His smile is grim. 'That's one way to put it. "Patient presented with unexplained bruising." Like that. Not my thing, but' – he shrugs, pained – 'Haliburton and his buddies came from a different time.

'The traffickers were smart. One point of contact. Money

changed hands then the child changed hands. No further concourse between the buyer and the seller after that.'

'How many children are we talking about?' I ask.

'Five. Three girls, two boys. That number dropped to two girls and one boy not long after we had them in protective custody.'

'Why?'

'One of the boys and one of the girls had had enough. Committed suicide. So we had the children,' he continues, rolling over this tragedy, wanting to get past it, 'and we had the dirt who bought them. One of the girls and one of the boys were owned by a pimp, a real scumbag by the name of Leroy Perkins. That guy had a soul like a block of dry ice. He wasn't even personally into kids, he just liked the money they could bring in.'

'That seems worse, somehow,' I say.

'The other girl was owned by a pervert who *did* like kids. He generated some cash on the side by filming himself having sex with them and then selling the movies to like-minded baby-rapers. His name was Tommy O'Dell.

'Hypothetically, a certain segment of cops and agents leaned on Leroy and Tommy very, very hard. They wouldn't talk. We threatened to put them into the prison general population and to leak who and what they were to the other cons. No go. I thought Tommy O'Dell would crack, I really did. He was a worm. He didn't. Leroy never came close. He told Haliburton at one point, "I talk to you, it'll take weeks for me to die. Then they'll kill my sister, my mom – hell, they'll even kill my houseplants. I'll take my chances inside."'

'It sounds like he was convinced that he was dealing with some very scary people,' Callie says.

'Scarier than us, that's for sure. We tried longer than we should have and got nowhere. That left us with the kids. It took some time and coaxing, but we got a couple of them to talk about what they'd gone through.' AD Jones grimaces. 'Bad, bad stuff. Conditioning – the caning of the feet – combined with verbal degradation and rape. A lot of the time they were hooded or blindfolded, and they were kept very isolated, from one another as well as from the traffickers. Even so, one of the kids had seen Vargas, and had heard his name. He was able to describe him. We gathered Vargas up.' The look in his eyes is chilling. 'We were committed to doing just about anything to get him to talk, and this time – hypothetically – I was ready to lend a fist.'

He pauses then. It's a long, thoughtful pause, layered through with regret.

'The boy's name was Juan. He was nine. Cute kid, smart kid, talked a lot once he got going, even though he had a slight stutter. He was from Argentina. I admired him, we all did. He'd been through hell but was still fighting to keep his head above water, and trying to do it with dignity.' AD Jones gives me a look that's about a million years old. 'Dignity. And he was nine.'

'What happened?' I ask.

'We had the kids stashed at a safe house. The night before Juan was going to officially lay things out on tape for us, someone hit it. They killed a cop, an agent, and took all three kids.'

'Took them?'

'Yes. Back to hell, would be my guess.'

I can't speak for a moment, I'm so appalled by this thought. Those children had been rescued from the monsters. They should have been safe.

'Didn't that point to –'

'An inside job?' He nods. 'Of course. Things got turned upside down, here and at the LAPD. Everyone on the task force was put under a microscope and got a metaphorical rectal exam. Nothing was ever found. The best part? We had no physical evidence to tie Vargas to the children. All we had was the word of a long-gone witness. Vargas walked, O'Dell and Perkins went away. Perkins survived. O'Dell got shanked. No more kids with scarred feet showed up. We never found Juan or the other two girls, but we heard from an informant that some children matching their description had crossed back into Mexico and then been shot.' He shrugs, frustrated even now. 'Every other lead dead-ended, from

Immigration to Vice to Organized Crime. We cast our nets wider. Let other cities know what to watch out for. Nothing. The task force was disbanded.'

'It sounds like whoever was behind this then is still around now,' I say. 'Vargas made that video for blackmail purposes.'

'Doesn't that seem odd to you?' Callie asks.

'What's that?'

'The bad guys were scary in 1979. Vargas didn't strike me as a particularly heroic individual.'

'Get the case files, Smoky. If you need questions answered by someone who was there, let me know.' His smile is humorless. 'That was the one for me. Up to that point, I figured we'd always get the bad guy. Justice would prevail and all that. That's the case where I realized there were going to be plenty of times the bad guys got away. It's also where I realized that there were' – he hesitates – 'men who eat children.' A pause. 'Metaphorically speaking, I mean.'

Except it's not really a metaphor is it, sir? That's why you paused. They do eat them, raw and weeping and warm. They swallow them whole.

I'm back at Death Central. Callie is getting the administrative wheels in motion that will deliver the files on the human-trafficking case to us. My cell rings.

'Something I wanted to let you know about right away,' Alan says.

'What?'

'In the process of digging into the Kingsleys, I decided to check in with Cathy Jones. The cop from the diary?'

'Good thinking.' It's a good idea. She was a trained observer who was there, and she also knew Sarah in the years following. 'What did you find?'

'What I found was bad and weird. A lot bad. Well, a lot weird too. Jones made detective two years ago. A month after that, she was off the force for good.'

'Why?'

'She was attacked in her home. She was beaten into a three-day coma. And it gets worse.'

'Worse how?'

'He beat her head with a pipe. Various injuries resulted, but the most severe was permanent damage to her optic nerves. She's legally blind, Smoky.'

I'm silent, taking this in. Failing to some degree.

'But that's not all.'

'What else?'

'The attacker whipped her. On the bottoms of her feet. Bad enough to leave scars.'

'What?!' I almost shout, I'm so surprised.

'No kidding. I had the same reaction. So that's bad, but –'

'I already know what's weird – that he let her live.'

'Exactly. He's killed everyone else we know about so far, except for Sarah. Why not Jones?'

'Have you talked to her?'

'That's why I'm calling. I got an address on her, but I'm in the middle here . . .'

'Give it to me. Callie and I will go see –' I stumble over the word *see* for a moment. 'We'll go talk to her.'

33

Cathy Jones lives in a condo in Tarzana, her neighborhood yet another example of a suburb tucked away amidst the urban sprawl of greater Los Angeles. It's a nice enough building, kept up, but perhaps a little worn around the edges.

The rain has stopped for now, but the sky is gray and the clouds still look angry. Callie and I spent almost an hour navigating our way here. LA hates the rain and it shows; we'd passed two accidents on the freeway.

We'd called ahead, but had gotten only her voice mail.

'Ready?' I ask Callie, as we stand in front of the door.

'No. But knock anyway.'

I do.

A moment passes. I hear the sound of footsteps on a hardwood floor, and then a voice, clear but uncertain.

'Who's there?'

'Cathy Jones?' I ask.

A pause. Then a dry reply:

'No, *I'm* Cathy Jones.'

Callie looks at me with an eyebrow raised.

'Ms Jones, this is Special Agent Smoky Barrett, of the FBI. I'm here with another agent, Callie Thorne. We'd like to speak with you.'

The silence is heavy.

'About what?'

I could reply, 'Your attack.' I decide to take a different approach.

'Sarah Langstrom.'

'What's happened?'

I hear raw alarm in the question, mixed with perhaps a hint of resignation.

'Can we come in, Ms Jones?'

Another pause, followed by a sigh.

'I guess you'll have to. I don't go outside anymore.'

I hear the sound of a dead bolt being turned, and the door opens.

Cathy is wearing a pair of sunglasses. I see small scars at her hairline and temples. She's a short woman, slender but compact. Athletic. She's wearing slacks and a sleeveless blouse; I can see the wiry muscle in her arms.

'Come in,' she says.

We enter. The condo is dark.

'Feel free to turn on some lights. I don't need them. Obviously. So make sure you turn them off before you leave.'

She leads us into the living room, sure-footed. The interior of the condo is newer than the outside facade. The carpet is a muted beige, the walls an off-white. The furniture is clean and tasteful.

'You have a very nice home,' I offer.

She sits down in an easy chair, indicating the couch to us with a sweep of her hand.

'I hired a decorator six months ago.'

We sit.

'Ms Jones –'

'Cathy.'

'Cathy,' I correct. 'We're here because of Sarah Langstrom.'

'You said that already. Cut to the chase or hit the road.'

'Blind *and* disagreeable,' Callie says.

I shoot a furious look at Callie, aghast. I should have known better; Callie is the undisputed master of incisive ice-breaking.

She'd assessed Cathy Jones and had understood sooner than I had: Cathy wanted to be treated like a normal person more than anything else. She knew she was being an ass; she wanted to see if we were going to coddle her or call her on it.

Cathy grins at Callie. 'Sorry. I get tired of being treated like a cripple, even when it's a little bit true. I found that pissing people off tends to even the playing field the fastest.' The smile disappears. 'Tell me, please. About Sarah.'

I relate the story of the Kingsleys, of Sarah's diary. I talk about The Stranger, and recount our analysis of him. She sits and listens, her ears turned toward my voice.

When I finish, she sits back. Her head turns toward the window in the kitchen. I wonder if this is an unconscious mannerism, something she did when she still had her sight.

'So he's finally shown his face,' she murmurs. 'So to speak.'

'It appears that way,' Callie replies.

'Well, that's a first,' Cathy says, shaking her head. 'He never did when I was around. Not with the Langstroms, not later with the others. Not even with me.'

I frown. 'I don't understand. He did this to you – how do you figure he wasn't revealing himself?'

Cathy's smile is humorless and bitter. 'Because he made sure that I'd keep my mouth shut. That's the same as staying hidden, isn't it?'

'How did he do that?'

'The way he does everything. He uses the things you care for. For me, it was Sarah. He said, quote, "to take my lumps and keep my mouth shut" or he'd do to Sarah what he was going to do to me.' She grimaces, a haunted mix of anger and fear and remembered pain. 'Then he did what he did. I knew I could never let him do that to her. So I kept my mouth shut. That and . . .' She pauses, miserable.

'What?' I prod.

'It's one of the reasons you're here, right? You want to know why he kept me alive. Why he didn't kill me. Well, that's one of

286

the reasons I kept my mouth shut. Because I lived. Because I was afraid. Not for her. For me. He told me if I didn't do what he said, he'd come back for me.' Her lips tremble as she says this.

'I understand, Cathy. Truly, I do.'

Cathy nods. Her mouth twists and she puts her head in her hands. Her shoulders tremble some, though not much, and not for long. It's a quiet cry, a summer thunderstorm, there and then gone.

'I'm sorry,' she says, raising her head. 'I don't know why I bother. I can't actually cry anymore. My tear ducts were damaged along with everything else.'

'Tears aren't the important part,' I say, the phrase seeming lame even as it comes out of my mouth.

Who are you, Dr Phil?

She fixes her sightless gaze on me. I can't see her eyes through the black lenses of the sunglasses, but I can feel them. 'I know you,' she says. 'About you, I mean. You're the one who lost her family. Who got raped and got her face cut up.'

'That's me.'

Even blind, the gaze is piercing.

'There is a reason.'

'I'm sorry?'

'That he didn't kill me. There is a reason. But let's get to that last. Tell me what else you want to know.'

I want to press her, but discard the idea. We need to know everything. Impatience with the sequences of it all would just be counterproductive.

We cover the Langstrom murders, according to what we read in Sarah's diary.

'Very accurate,' she confirms. 'I'm surprised she remembers so many details. But I guess she's had a lot of time to think about it.'

'So that we're clear,' I say. 'You were one of the responding officers? You were there, you saw the bodies and Sarah?'

'Yes.'

'In Sarah's diary, she says that no one believed that her parents had been forced to do what they did. Is that true?'

'It was true then, it's still true now. Go and pull the case file. You're going to find that it's never been ruled as anything other than a murder-suicide, case closed.'

I'm skeptical. 'Come on. You're saying there was nothing there, forensically?'

Cathy holds up a finger. 'No. That's not what I'm saying. I'm saying that no one took a hard, close look because he'd set up the scene so well. You get a sense, sometimes, when a scene has been staged. You know?'

'Yeah.'

'Right. Well, you didn't get that sense here. You had a suicide note, held down by a glass of water with Mrs Langstrom's fingerprints and saliva on it. You had her fingerprints on the gun, as well as blowback of both gunshot residue and blood consistent with what you'd expect from a suicide. You had her fingerprints around her husband's neck. Her fingerprints on the hacksaw used to decapitate the dog. She was taking antidepressants on the sly. What would you have thought?'

I sigh. 'Point taken.'

Hearing the story from the lips of another professional puts it into a different light for me. I see it as Cathy saw it, as the homicide detectives would have seen it, without the benefit of a Kingsley crime scene or Sarah's diary.

'You hinted that there *was* something there to find,' Callie murmurs.

'Two things. Small, but there. The autopsy report on Mrs Langstrom noted some bruising around both her wrists. It wasn't considered probative because we weren't looking for anything. But if you do have a reason to look . . .'

'Then you think about handcuffs and Sarah's story,' I say. 'You think about Mrs Langstrom getting angry and yanking on those padded cuffs as hard as she could and bruising up her wrists.'

'That's right.'

'What was the other thing?'

'In the accepted scenario she shot the dog and she shot herself. No one reported hearing gunshots, and we're not talking about a twenty-two popgun. Which makes you start thinking about a silencer, even though no silencer was on the gun at the scene.'

'What made *you* start looking?' Callie asks.

Cathy is quiet for a moment, thinking.

'It was Sarah. It took a while, but as time went on, and I got to know her, I began to wonder. She's an honest girl. And the story was so damn *dark* for a girl her age. People kept dying or getting hurt around her. Once you give in to the possibility, you start seeing clues everywhere.' She leans forward. 'His real brilliance has always been in his subtlety, his understanding of how we think, and in his choice of victim. He doesn't overdo his staging, so it looks natural. He leads us to a conclusion, but not with so many bread crumbs that we'd get suspicious. He knows we're trained to reverse-engineer in the direction of simplicity rather than complexity. And he chose a victim in Sarah with no relatives, so there's no one that's going to hang around and demand that we take a closer look, no one that's going to worry at it.'

'But there was, wasn't there?' I say in a quiet voice. 'There was you.'

Cathy does that looking-toward-the-window thing again. 'That's right.'

'Is that why he did this to you?'

Cathy swallows. 'Maybe that was part of it, but I don't think it was the big reason. Doing what he did to me was useful to him.' She seems to be breathing a little faster.

'Is there anything about what he did to you – about what happened to you – that would be helpful?' I ask, prodding. 'I know it's difficult.'

She turns to me. 'This guy is – or has been – a ghost. I think anything that puts a face on him is going to help, don't you?'

I don't reply; it's a rhetorical question.

Cathy sighs, a ragged sigh. Her hands tremble and the quickened breathing continues.

'Funny. I've been wanting to tell the real story for almost two years. Now that I can, I feel like I want to jump out of my skin.'

I take a gamble. I reach over and grab one of her hands. It's clammy with sweat and it shakes. She doesn't pull it away.

'I used to pass out,' I tell her. 'After it happened. For no reason at all.'

'Really?'

'Don't pass it around,' I say, smiling, 'but yes. Really.'

'Truth, honey-love,' Callie says, her voice soft.

Cathy pulls her hand away from mine. I take this as a struggle for strength on her part.

'I'm sorry,' she says. 'I've been taking pills for anxiety since it happened, until about two weeks ago. I decided I wanted to wean myself off them. They turned me into a zombie, and it's time to get strong again. I still think I made the right decision, but' – she waggles her hand – 'it makes things harder, sometimes.'

'Do you have coffee?' Callie chirps.

Cathy frowns. 'Sorry?'

'Coffee. Caffeine. Nectar of the gods. If we're going to sit and listen to something horrible, I think coffee is sensible and recommended.'

Cathy gives her a faint, grateful smile.

'That's a great idea.'

The normality of a cup of coffee seems to calm Cathy. She holds on to the cup as she speaks, stopping to take a sip when things get too rough.

'I'd been poking around in the case files for years, trying to find something that would convince a senior detective to take another look. You have to understand, while I was considered a decent cop, I was still just a uniform. It's a whole different social strata, the plain-clothes and the unies. The guys in Homicide are driven by statistics. Solve rates, murder rates per capita, all that stuff. If you want them to add an unsolved to the pile – particularly if it means taking it out of the solved column – you'd better have something compelling. I didn't.'

'The wrist-bruising wasn't enough?' I ask.

'No. And let's be honest, I don't know if it would be enough for me, if the situations were reversed. The bruising was noted, but according to the ME's notes, it could have come from any number of things. Her husband grabbing her wrists too hard, for one. Remember, she's supposed to have strangled him.'

'That's true.'

'Yeah. Anyway, I'd been chasing this for a few years, on my own time, and getting nowhere.' She pauses, looking uncomfortable and ashamed. 'To be honest, I wasn't always pushing on it the way I should have. Sometimes, I doubted the whole scenario. I'd lie in bed at night, thinking, and I'd decide I *didn't* believe her, that she was just a messed-up kid who'd cooked up a story to explain the otherwise senseless deaths of her parents. I'd generally come back to my senses, but . . .' She shrugs. 'I could have done more. I always knew that, in the back of my mind. Life just kept moving forward. I can't really explain it.' She sighs. 'In the meantime, I did my job and got my promotions. And then, I went for detective.' She smiles at the memory. She's probably unaware that she's doing it. 'Passed the test with flying colors. It was cool. A big deal. Even my dad would have approved.'

I note the use of the past tense regarding her father, but I don't press her on it.

'I wanted Homicide, but I was assigned to Vice.' She shrugs. 'I was a woman, and not bad looking, but I was tough. They needed someone to play hooker. I was disappointed at first, but then I started to enjoy it. I was good at it. I had a knack.'

More of that unconscious smiling. Her face is animated.

'I kept in touch with Sarah. She was getting harder and colder every year. I think I was the only thing keeping her in touch with herself, in a way. I was the only person who'd known her the whole time that really cared.' She turns her sightless eyes to the kitchen window, contemplative. 'I think that's why he came after me when he did. Not because I'd become a detective. Not because I was poking around. Because he knew I cared. He knew he could count on me to pass on his message if I thought it might help Sarah.'

'What message?' Callie asks.

'I'll get to that. The other thing . . . I think it was *time* to take me away from her.' She turns her head to me. 'You understand?'

'I think so. You're talking about his overall plan for Sarah.'

'Yes. I was the last one left who knew who Sarah was, inside. The last person she could be sure of. I don't know why he let it go on as long as he did. Maybe to give her hope.'

'So he could snatch it away,' I say.

She nods. 'Yep.'

'Tell us about that day.' Callie's voice is soothing, a gentle push.

Cathy's hand grips the coffee cup in a reflexive motion, a brief spasm of emotion.

'It was just like any other day. That's the thing, I think, that throws me the most. Nothing special had happened on the job, or personally. The date wasn't significant, and the weather was as usual as it comes. The only difference between that day and another is that *he* decided it was the day.' She sips from her cup. 'I'd finished up a late shift. It was past midnight when I got home. Dark. Quiet. I was tired. I let myself in and went straight for the shower. I always did that. It was symbolic for me – do a dirty job, come home and shower it off, you know.'

'Sure,' I reply.

'I got undressed, I took my shower. I put on a bathrobe and grabbed a book I was reading – something trivial and silly but entertaining – and then I poured myself a cup of coffee and took a seat right here.' She pats the arm of the easy chair with one hand. 'Different chair, same location. I remember putting my coffee cup down on the table' – she goes through the motion, caught up in the memory – 'and the next thing I knew, there was a rope around my neck, pulling me back, so fast, so strong. I tried to think, to do something, to get my hands up between the rope and my neck, but he was too fast. Too strong.'

'We call that a blitz attack,' Callie says, her voice kind. 'In the case of a strong attacker, it's successful most of the time. There probably wasn't much you could have done.'

'I tell myself that too. I usually believe it.' She sips from her cup. It's her lip that trembles, this time. 'He knew what he was doing. He yanked back and up' – she grabs her own throat, demonstrating – 'and I was out within seconds.' She shakes her head. 'Seconds. Can you believe that? He could have killed me right then. I would never have woken up. I'd have died. But . . .' Her voice trails off. 'But I did wake up. Over and over. He had the rope twisted around me, John Wayne Gacy–style. He'd tighten it up, cut off the blood to my brain, I'd go out. He'd loosen it and I'd come around. Then he'd tighten it up again. I woke up once and my bathrobe was gone. I was naked. I woke up again, and my hands were cuffed behind my back, my mouth was gagged. It was like drowning over and over again, and waking up in a new part of the nightmare every time. The thing that was worst of all, for some reason, was that he didn't *speak*.'

I can hear the stress in her voice, the anxiety at this particular part of the memory.

'I remember thinking I just wanted him to say something, to explain, to make it make sense. But nothing.' Her hands are still shaking and restless. She clasps them in her lap, she rubs her arms with them. She is a portrait of unconscious, continuous, nervous motion.

'I don't know how long it went on.' She manages a somewhat wry, somewhat sickly grin. 'Too long.' The sunglasses again, looking at me. 'You know.'

'I know,' I agree.

'Then I woke up and he let me stay that way. I was on my bed, hands and ankles cuffed. It took me a little bit of time to really come around. I remember wondering if he'd raped me, that if he had, I wouldn't know for sure.'

'Did he?' I ask.

'No. No, he didn't.'

Still no sexual pathology with females, I think to myself.

'Go on,' I say.

'He started talking. He said, "I want you to know, Cathy, that there's nothing personal in this. You have a part to play, that's all. Something you have to do for Sarah."' Her lower lip trembles. 'That's when I knew. Who he was. I don't know why it hadn't occurred to me before that, but it hadn't. "Here's what's going to happen," he said. "I'm going to beat your body and you'll probably never be a cop again, Cathy Jones. When it's done, you'll tell them you have no idea who could have done this to you, or why. If you do otherwise, I'll destroy Sarah's face and dig out her eyes with a spoon."'

Cathy's voice continues, hushed.

'It didn't register, what he was saying, but also, in a way, it did. So I did what any self-respecting detective would do. I begged. I begged like a baby. I – I wet myself.'

I hear the shame in her voice and I recognize it.

'He wants you to feel bad about that,' I say. 'To be ashamed of your fear, like it means something.'

Her mouth twists. 'I know. Most of the time I get that. It's hard sometimes.'

'Yeah.'

This seems to calm her a little. She continues.

'Then he showed me something. He told me he was putting it in the drawer of my nightstand. "A few years from now, someone is going to come knocking, asking questions. When they do you can tell them your story and give them what's in the drawer. Give it to them and tell them: 'Symbols are only symbols.'"'

I struggle with my impatience. What? What's in the drawer? And what the hell is that supposed to mean, 'Symbols are only symbols'?

'I don't remember most of it. I get flashes, sometimes, big and bright, almost unreal. Like a painting with too much white in it.

I remember the sounds more than the pain. Thudding noises, deep vibrations inside my skull. I guess that was him beating on my head with the pipe. I remember tasting blood, and thinking that something really bad was happening, but I wasn't sure what. He whipped my feet so bad I couldn't use them for a month.' Gaze back to the kitchen window. 'The last thing I remember seeing, ever, was his face. Too much light on it, too bright, that God damn panty-hose stocking mask. Looking down at me and smiling. The next thing I remember is waking up in the hospital and wondering why I couldn't open my eyes.'

She goes quiet. We wait her out.

'I came around after a while. Remembered. Realized I was blind.' She stops, remembering. 'You know what it was that convinced me he meant what he said? About going after Sarah? About going after me?'

'What?' Callie asks.

'The way he'd told me "it wasn't personal." I remembered him saying it, and how he looked and sounded when he did. Matter of fact. Not angry, not rushed, not crazy-looking or rage-filled, or *anything*. Normal, even smiling, like someone talking about a good book they'd just read.' She reaches for her coffee cup, finds it, takes a sip. 'So I did what he said. I kept my mouth shut.'

'For what it's worth, I think that was a wise call,' I say. 'The picture we're getting of this guy is of someone who doesn't bluff. If you'd spoken up, he probably would have hurt Sarah, or you, or both.'

'I tell myself that a lot,' she replies, trying to smile. 'Anyway.' Another sip from the cup. 'He messed me up good. Fractured my skull, including shattering a line of it so bad they had to carve some of the bone away. He broke my arms and my legs with that pipe, and knocked out most of my teeth. These are implant-retained dentures. What else? Oh yeah – to this day I can't step outside without having a full-blown panic attack.'

She stops speaking, waiting for a response. I remember the aftermath of my own attack, and recall how much I hated the aphorisms people trotted out, stock phrases they used because, really, words hadn't been invented that were adequate.

'I don't know what to say,' I tell her.

Her smile, this time, is warm and genuine. It catches me off guard.

'Thanks.'

She understands that I understand.

'Now, Cathy – what did he give you?'

She points toward the back of the condo. 'Bedroom is on the right. It's in the top drawer.'

Callie nods to me and gets up, heading to the bedroom.

A moment later she returns. Her face is troubled. She sits down and opens her hand, revealing what she has clasped inside.

The shiny gold glints in the light. A detective's shield.

'It's mine,' Cathy offers. 'My shield.'

I stare at it.

Symbols are only symbols.

I'm one hundred percent stumped. I look at Callie, raise an eyebrow in query. She shrugs.

'Do you have any idea why he put special significance on this?' I ask Cathy.

'No. I wish I did, but I don't. Believe me, I've spent a lot of time thinking about it.'

My frustration rises. Not at Cathy. I'd come here hoping for answers, excited at that possibility. All I had was another puzzle.

'Can you tell me something?' Cathy asks.

'Of course.'

'Are you good?' she asks me. 'Will you get him?'

This is the voice of the victim, breathy, a little hungry, filled with doubt and hope. I'm unable to decipher the emotions running across her features. Joy, anger, grief, hope, rage, more. A rainbow of light and dark.

I stare at her, taking in the scars at her hairline, my own face in the lenses of the sunglasses, seeing the ugliness he created, but also seeing some of the beauty that he couldn't destroy. A terrible feeling comes over me. Pain and rage and an almost unbearable desire to kill something evil.

Callie answers for me.

'We're the best, honey-love. The very best.'

Cathy stares at us, and I feel 'seen,' blind or not.

'Okay,' she whispers. Nods. 'Okay.'

'Cathy, do you want protection?' I ask.

She frowns. 'Why?'

'I . . . we're after this guy. At some point, he's bound to know it. Maybe he even wants us to be after him. It might reopen his interest in the past.'

'In me, you mean.'

'It's possible. I know he promised if you did what he said he'd leave you alone, but he's really not to be trusted.'

She pauses, thinking, for the longest time. The moment seems to hang forever. She ends it with a shake of her head.

'No thanks. I sleep with my gun under my pillow. I have a hell of an alarm system.' Her grin is humorless. 'And I kind of hope he does decide to come pay me a visit. I'd be happy to blow his ass away.'

'Are you sure?'

'I'm sure.'

I glance at Callie, and the unspoken goes between us: *We'll get a car parked in front whether she wants it or not.*

She takes another sip of coffee. Lukewarm by now, I'm sure. 'Do me one favor?'

'Anything,' I say, meaning it.

'When this is over, let me know.'

I reach over, grip her hand.

'When this is over, I'll have Sarah let you know.'

A pause, and then she squeezes my hand, once.

'Okay,' she says again.

She pulls her hand away, reaching for strength.

34

I'm gazing out the passenger-side window; I'd asked Callie to drive so that I could think. We'd discussed the visit with Cathy, tried to pick apart the mystery of the shield and his stupid word game. We'd gotten nowhere.

I feel exhilarated and disconnected and let down, a cocktail of excitement and unreality. I am exhilarated because we are in motion. We're on the hunt, and we know things we didn't know before. I'm let down by the questions that continue to stack up without answers to go along with them.

The unreality hit me on the way to the car. Last night, while reading Sarah's diary, I met Cathy Jones for the first time. She was a new cop, healthy, dedicated, flawed, more good than bad. Human. Meeting her today at her home, seeing her as she's become – it's like knowing the end of a story you haven't read all the way through yet. Like traveling in a time machine.

My phone rings, startling me from my reverie. I glance at the caller ID, see it's Alan.

'What's up?' I answer.

'Something interesting,' he rumbles. 'Something maybe good for us.'

I sit up straighter. 'What?'

'Well, I'm standing in front of the Langstrom house. And you know what? It's still the Langstrom house.'

I frown, perplexed. 'I don't get it.'

'I got together with Barry. We were going over the case file – and I have some thoughts on it, by the way – and I just wasn't feeling it. I decided I needed to see the scene. Even if it is ten years later.'

'Sure.'

'Barry has a lady friend in the Hall of Records and also knows some woman in the phone company.' I can almost hear Alan rolling his eyes. 'To make a long story short, we find out that the house is currently owned by – get this – The Sarah Langstrom Trust.'

'What?' The surprise in my voice is sharp. Callie shoots me a look.

'That's what I said. I figured, okay, maybe the parents were a lot better off than we thought. Maybe there's a future happy ending here, Sarah's going to come into a lot of money. Turns out that one is true, but the other isn't. The Langstroms did okay, definitely in the higher percentile of upper-middle-class. But they weren't *rich* rich, you know?'

'So?' I ask, waiting for the explanation-as-punch-line.

'So, it turns out that the trust was set up by an anonymous donor *after* the Langstroms were murdered. Someone who was supposedly a big fan of the late Mrs Langstrom's work.'

'Wow,' I say, meaning it.

'Yeah. The trust doesn't have any physical location, just a lawyer named Gibbs who administers it. He won't give up the name of the donor right now, but he's not being an asshole. Just abiding by the rules of the bar.'

'We'll have to get a subpoena,' I say, still excited. 'An art fan? That hits pretty close to home.'

'That's what I thought. Anyway, Gibbs kept on proving he's not an asshole. He said that as long as we got something in writing from Sarah saying it was okay, and he could verify it with her on the phone, he'd let us into the house. We drove over to the hospital and saw her.'

'How is she doing? How did she react to the news?'

An uncomfortable silence that communicates an uncomfortable shrug. 'She was pretty shook up about it. She wants to see the house. I had to promise her we'd take her soon to get her to stay in bed.'

I sigh. 'Of course we'll take her.'

'Good. So, we got her okay, got her on the phone with Gibbs, and then the lawyer brought us over here. Guess what?' He pauses for emphasis. 'The place hasn't been entered since the Crime Scene Unit released it ten years ago.'

'Are you kidding me?' I can't keep the disbelief out of my voice. Callie gives me another look.

'Nope. The only stuff missing are some things from what was Sarah's room. Maybe the perp came back and took some souvenirs.'

'Give me the address,' I say without hesitating.

I get it and hang up, excited.

'Tell me,' Callie says, 'or I'll sing the national anthem, here and now, with gusto.'

This is a threat. Many things about Callie are beautiful. Her singing voice isn't one of them.

Malibu, I've always thought, is a mix of the rich and the lucky. The rich are the ones who can afford to buy homes in this desirable, not-far-from-the-ocean community today. The lucky are the ones who bought before prices put most homes out of reach of the average bear.

'Beautiful,' Callie observes as we roll down the Pacific Coast Highway.

'Sure is,' I reply.

It's just after lunch, and the sun has decided to make an appearance. The ocean is to our left, broad, blue, the world's immovable object and unstoppable force all rolled into one. You can love the ocean, and many do, but don't expect it to love you back. It's too forever.

On the right the hills are crisscrossed by the snaky, windy streets that lead to various Malibu homes and neighborhoods. Lots of green as a result of the rains, I note. Not good news for the upcoming fire season.

We find our turnoff and after ten minutes and a few false starts, pull up to the given address. Alan and Barry have remained outside, Alan standing and listening as Barry leans up against Alan's car and smokes and talks. They see us and approach as we climb out.

'Nice,' I remark, looking at the house.

'It's a four-bedroom,' Barry says, consulting a notepad, his own Ned. 'Three-thousand-plus square feet, three full baths. Bought twenty years ago for about three hundred thou, worth about a mil and a half now, and fully paid off by the mystery benefactor.'

The home is a slice of America sans California. A large, white-fenced front yard, the requisite tree made for climbing, a hand-laid flagstone path to the front door, and a general sense of comfort-ableness to it. The home itself is painted in off-whites and beige, and appears kept up.

'I guess there's a management service?' I ask Alan.

He nods. 'Yeah. Gardeners come out once a week, brush clearing done before fire season, new coat of paint every two years or so.'

'Two?' Barry says. 'I do mine every five.'

'Salt air,' Alan explains.

'Where's the lawyer?' I ask.

'He got a call from a client and had to go.'

'Do we have the key?' I ask.

'We do.' Alan smiles, opening a huge hand to reveal a ring with two keys on it.

'Then let's go inside.'

When I enter the home, that sense of disconnectedness rushes over me again. I'm back in the time machine.

The problem, I think, is that Sarah's story was too vivid. She gathered up everything she could still feel and used it to bring her story to life, to take us down to the watering hole.

I half expect Buster and Doreen to come running, and I feel a twinge of sadness when they don't.

The home is unlit. The sunlight creeping through plantation shutters provides a dusky illumination. I move to just inside the doorway, and my shoes touch a floor of rich cherry hardwood, layered with a patina of dust. The wood continues forward into the kitchen on the right. I make out granite countertops, well-matched cabinets, and dusty stainless steel. The left is dominated by a large open room – not a living room per se, but a place to entertain. Ten people could mill around in it comfortably, twenty if they don't mind brushing up against each other. The hardwood continues there.

Past this room is more open space, edged on the right by the kitchen, leading to the living room proper, which is where the carpet begins. It's bold, a dark brown. I move forward for a better look and smile a sad smile. The brown is matched by the rest of the living room, from paint to furniture. Decorated by a dead artist with an instinctive understanding of color.

A hallway heads off to the left from the living room, leading to the rest of the house. On the right, past a large and very comfortable-looking couch, are a series of sliding glass doors, thick-glassed, leading into what looks like a large backyard.

The house is silent, almost oppressive.

'Feels like a tomb,' Barry mutters, an echo of my own thoughts.

'It is,' I say. I turn to Alan. 'Let's go through this step-by-step.'

He flips open the case file – which I note is pretty thin – and consults it.

'No sign of forced entry,' he begins. 'Perp probably got a copy of the keys. Responding officers Santos and Jones entered through the sliding glass doors from the backyard. The bodies of Mr and Mrs Langstrom were found just inside.' He nods his head toward the spot.

We walk over and look.

'You weren't kidding about nobody being here since CSU,' I mutter.

A square of the brown carpeting is missing, cut away by the Crime Scene Unit for the blood evidence it contained. They only took what they thought they'd need; dark splotches are still visible elsewhere, including spots on the wall and couch. Gunshots to the head are messy.

'Mr Langstrom was handcuffed nude – they both were. Position of his body was facedown. Mrs Langstrom ended up on her back, with her head resting right about where that missing piece of carpet is.'

I gaze down, envisioning the tableau.

'The ME notes on-site that Mr Langstrom's eyes show petechial hemorrhaging, and that bruising around the neck is consistent with strangulation. Autopsy confirmed.'

'Did Mrs Langstrom get an autopsy?' I ask.

As a suicide, she might not have.

'Yeah.'

'Go on.'

'Lividity confirmed that they hadn't been moved postmortem. They died as and where they were found. Liver temps put time of death at roughly five A.M.'

'That's the first thing that reads weird to me,' Barry says.

I look at him. 'What's that?'

'TOD is five in the morning. The cops were called hours later. What kind of gun did she use?'

Alan doesn't have to consult the file. He's already considered the question Barry is posing. 'Nine mil.'

'Loud,' Barry opines. 'Noisy. She shot the dog and she shot herself. Why didn't anyone hear anything?'

'Cathy Jones asked the same question,' Callie replies.

'Sloppy,' Alan says in disgust, shaking his head.

He's talking about the inductive police-work. Alan spent ten years in Los Angeles Homicide before coming to the FBI, and he was known for his attention to detail and his refusal to take shortcuts. He would have thought about the sound of the gunshot if he'd been the one investigating ten years ago.

'Go on,' I tell him.

'Sarah was found outside, in a near catatonic state. No mention of a burn on her hand anywhere in the file.' The look he gives me is significant. 'So when we went to see her in the hospital, I checked. She's got a small scar there.' He frowns, more disgust. 'Sloppy again. They didn't check shit, just ate what they were spoon-fed.'

I point out what's important. 'Bad then,' I say, 'but good for us now. They weren't looking, which means that there could still be something here that will lead us to him.'

'What about the gun?' Callie asks, thoughtful.

Alan gives her a quizzical look. 'What about it?'

'Did they look into it? Did the Langstroms even own a gun?'

Alan flips through the file, nodding as he finds something. 'It was unregistered. Serial number filed off. Says here they figured she'd bought it on the street.' His voice becomes sarcastic. 'Yeah, because Linda Langstrom would know exactly where to go to buy a hot gun. Why would she even bother? If she planned to kill herself, she wouldn't have been worried about it being traced.'

I look at Barry. 'Would the gun still be in evidence?'

'I'm guessing yes. Evidence destruction is a hassle. It takes about an hour to fill out the paperwork, and from what I've seen so far, the guys on this case didn't seem inclined to go the extra mile.'

'Then let's get it, Alan. Have Ballistics check out the gun.'

'Might have a history,' he says, nodding.

'What next?' I ask.

'Bullet was a hollow point, so there was maximum destruction on exit.' He flips a page. 'Linda Langstrom's fingerprints were found on her husband's neck. Consistent with her being the doer. There was the note, and the antidepressants.'

'What about that?' I query, interested.

'Nada,' he replies. 'Just a note that she had them. No follow-up.'

'Other physical evidence?'

He shakes his head. 'CSU only fine-toothed in here, and even that was pretty perfunctory. They left the rest of the house untouched.'

'They weren't looking for evidence to break a case,' Callie muses. 'They were collecting evidence to confirm what they already knew.'

'*Thought* they knew,' Alan clarifies.

'Where was the dog killed?' I ask.

Alan consults the file again. 'Near the entryway.' He frowns. 'Take a look at this.'

He hands me a photograph. I peer at it and grimace. In it, Buster the faithful dog is headless, lying on the hardwood floor near the entryway. I take a closer look and my eyes narrow.

'Interesting, huh?' Alan asks.

'Sure is,' I reply.

The photograph shows Buster lying on his side. His head – or where his head would be – is pointed toward the front of the house. A bloody hacksaw lies a short distance away.

'If Linda Langstrom was the killer,' I say, 'why was the dog in the entryway? And why was he facing toward the door? It's suggestive of him responding to someone entering the house, not someone already here.'

'There's more,' Alan says. 'Blood evidence found in Sarah's bedroom. Testing showed that it was nonhuman. That backs up her story about the dog's head being tossed on her bed. It doesn't fit. Linda cutting the dog's head off is already a stretch. Tossing it into Sarah's room? No fucking way.' I can see anger building in Alan. I don't respond, letting him run his course. 'You know, it's not that this guy was that fucking smart. The cops on this case were lazy. Sloppy. Didn't give a shit. I would have caught the discrepancies with the gun, and I sure as hell would have thought long and hard about the damn dog. Once I heard Sarah's story, and I confirmed that her hand was burned, I would have been all over this house. Fuck.' He boils for another few seconds and then he puffs out his cheeks and exhales, a long sigh. 'Sorry. I'm a little pissed. Could be that none of this had to happen.'

'Maybe not,' I acknowledge. 'It's also possible you would have processed the house and found nothing, and ended up ruling it a suicide too.' I pause as a thought comes to me. 'You know what the really terrible thing is? That it wouldn't have mattered. Sarah had no family. If he didn't leave any forensic evidence – and I'm betting he didn't – then the outcome for Sarah would have been the same even *if* they believed her.'

'Foster care and all the bad it brought her,' Alan says.

'That's right. Now we have the benefit of hindsight and new information. Let's concentrate on rectifying things.' I turn to Callie. 'I want you to get together with Gene, and then I want you to turn this house inside out. Let's see if we can find something, now that someone's actually looking.'

'My pleasure.'

'In fact,' I say, deciding, 'get on that now. You can take the car, I'll catch a ride with Alan.'

She nods, not responding with words. I sense a brief struggle in her and watch as a hand strays to her jacket pocket.

Pain, I realize. It just hit her hard. Out of nowhere.

I can tell from her eyes that she knows I know. I also get the message in bright flashing neon: *Move on, let it go, privacy is the altar I worship at.*

'What do you want me to do?' Barry asks, breaking the moment. 'Not that I don't have plenty to keep me busy. Lots of other dead people out there, and this isn't exactly my jurisdiction. Thankfully, I know a lady detective who works the Malibu precinct.'

'I appreciate that you came when I asked, Barry. Really.'

His smile is faint. He shrugs. 'You never cry wolf, Smoky. So I always come. What else do you need from me?'

'The evidence, all of it. Especially the gun.'

'Will do. You'll have it today.'

'And something else that you might not like.'

'What?'

'I want you to look into the detectives that ran this case back then, discreetly.'

A long pause as he considers what I'm asking, why I'm asking.

'You thinking one of them could be the doer?'

'The work was sloppy. I've seen worse, and I understand why they came to the conclusions they did, but I don't understand why there was never any real follow-up with Sarah. I see notes from Cathy Jones, who was a rookie. I don't see any interview of Sarah by the detectives assigned. I want to know why. If I poke around, it will send up alarms.'

Barry sighs and shakes his head. 'Fuck. Yeah. I'll look into it.'

'Thanks.'

I look at the room, thinking. Taking in the tomb that used to be a home. I nod, satisfied that we can leave, for now.

'Let's go,' I say to Alan.

'Where to?'

'Gibbs. I want to meet this lawyer.'

'If his lips are moving, he's lying, honey-love,' Callie says.

We all head out the door.

'What are you doing when your lips are moving, Red?' Barry asks.

She smiles. 'Enlightening the world, of course.'

This is Callie, I think. This will always be Callie, pain or pills or not, a wisecracking, taco-loving, donut-dunking friend.

We all climb into our respective vehicles and head off in different directions.

'How long will it take us to get there?' I ask.

He checks the clock on the car dash. 'About forty minutes would be my guess.'

'I'm going to spend the time reading.'

I pull the diary pages from my purse.

She is him, I think, and he is her.

Sarah is a microcosm. The Stranger is showing her to us to approximate the story of his own life. Understanding what Sarah went through is the closest I'll come, right now, to understanding what he went through.

I settle back. The clouds start crying again.

Sarah's Story

Part Three

35

Let's take an honesty break.

It occurs to me that writing this as a story is about more than just being a good writer. It's about distance. As long as I write about these things in third person, it's almost like it's happening to someone else, a fictional character or something. Isn't denial great?

If you really want to get deep and start lobbing metaphors, then we can talk about how similar this is to a seriously fucked-up fairy tale. Gretel with no Hansel, and the witch is way too smart. She got me in the oven and she's roasting me slowly. Red Riding Hood, but the wolf caught me and instead of swallowing me whole, he's taking the time to chew his food.

So, where were we? Oh yeah: the group home.

The group home was an arena and we were its gladiators.

The group home was where I learned how to fight. I learned the difference between a warning and an attack. I learned that you didn't have to be afraid to hurt someone, and that size wasn't the only thing that mattered.

I learned to be violent, in a way that I'd never even thought of before. Was that a part of his plan?

I wondered. I wonder. It doesn't matter. It's not really me, anyway, right?

'I said, give me the pillow.'

Sarah set her mouth and forced herself not to look away from Kirsten.

'No.'

The older girl was incredulous.

'What did you say?'

Sarah trembled inside, just a little.

Stand up to her. No more fraidy-cat, remember?

It was easier to say or think than do, that was for sure. Kirsten wasn't just three years older, she was a big girl. She had broader shoulders than most of the other girls in her age group, she had big hands, and she was strong. She liked violence. A lot.

Doesn't matter. You're eight now. Stand up to her.

'I said no, Kirsten. I'm not letting you boss me around anymore.'

An ugly smile curled the bigger girl's lips.

'We'll see about that.'

Sarah had been living at the Burbank Group Home for two years. It was a *Lord of the Flies* environment, where might made right, and adult supervision was based on punishment, not prevention. It was an atmosphere that nourished the angers and brutality of someone like Kirsten.

Sarah had no friends here. She'd kept her head down and her eyes open. She'd acquiesced to Kirsten's demands to hand over desserts and better bedding and the thousand other small tortures the older girl devised.

But Sarah had recently seen the future, and it had changed her view of things. She'd found out what happened in the dorms of the older girls. Here, she was being asked to hand over a pillow. There, she might be asked to hand over herself.

The idea of this tapped into something in Sarah, something unyielding and angry and stubborn.

Sarah had spent a lot of time observing Kirsten. She realized that the older girl relied entirely on her size and strength. There was nothing skillful about her attacks. She always – *always* – went for the slap first. Sarah had received enough of them.

Teeth-rattling, bone-jarring, raising bruises that could last a week.

Now was no different. Kirsten stepped forward, cocked her arm back, and sent her hand whistling through the air toward Sarah's cheek.

It was the kind of attack that only worked on opponents who were too afraid to fight back. Sarah did what anyone would do if they weren't afraid – she ducked.

Kirsten's hand passed through the air above her head. A look of pure surprise crossed the older girl's face.

Now, while she's off balance!

Sarah's life was simple. Wake up, shower, eat, school, and then back to the dorms or common areas. It gave her plenty of time to think about things when she needed to. Consideration had revealed to her that a closed fist was superior to an open hand.

She stood up, cocked her arm back, made a fist, and punched Kirsten in the nose as hard as she could, her whole body behind it. The impact shocked her.

That hurt!

It hurt Kirsten too. Blood burst from both nostrils and the bully stumbled back, falling, landing on her butt.

Now, finish her. Don't let her get up!

Sarah had seen girls oppose Kirsten's reign of terror twice before. She'd noticed in those instances that Kirsten wasn't satisfied with a slap or two. One of the girls had been kicked unconscious, and then Kirsten had shaved her head. The second girl had her arm bent behind her back until it broke with a horrible, audible crack. Kirsten had stripped her naked while the girl screamed, and then had locked her out in the hallway.

Sarah knew that this defeat would have to be just as decisive.

Kirsten was already struggling to get back up. Sarah kicked her in the face. Her foot caught Kirsten in the mouth, causing her lower lip to split open. Kirsten's eyes bugged out, she screeched in pain, and there was blood everywhere.

A dark and savage joy began rising in Sarah. This wasn't waiting for something bad to happen. This wasn't waking up from one nightmare to find yourself living another. This was

(better)

This was under her control.

She kicked Kirsten again, this time catching her in the nose. The older girl's head snapped back, and the blood sprayed, a brief but satisfying fountain. Kirsten looked up at Sarah in terror.

Sarah's nostrils flared at the sight of it.

More. Don't stop.

She jumped onto Kirsten, pushing the girl onto her back, and she began to punch her, over and over and over, until her fists went numb, and then she stood up and kicked Kirsten in the stomach, arms, chest, legs. The older girl curled into herself, trying to protect her face.

Sarah didn't feel out of control. Just the opposite. She felt detached. Joyous, but detached. Like she was eating a particularly delicious piece of cake in a dream.

She stopped when Kirsten began to sob.

Sarah stood over her for a moment, catching her breath. Kirsten was sobbing, her arms curled around her head. Sarah caught glimpses of bleeding lips, a crooked nose, an eye that had begun to swell shut.

You'll live.

She got down on her knees and put her lips up to Kirsten's ear.

'If you ever try to hurt me again, I'll kill you. Do you hear me?'

'Y-y-yes!'

A thunderclap inside her, and the anger was gone. Just like that. Something her mother had once said came to her.

'If you can turn your enemies into friends, then you'll live a better life, babe.'

She hadn't known what it meant at the time. She thought she might, now.

She stuck her hand out.

'Come on. I'll help you get cleaned up.'

Kirsten peeked an eye out, still fearful. She gave Sarah's hand a distrustful look.

'Why would you help me?'

'I don't want to be your boss, Kirsten. I just want you to leave me alone.' She leaned forward, wiggled her hand. 'Come on.'

After a few more seconds of disbelief, Kirsten uncurled. She sat up, eyeing Sarah with a mixture of fear and interest. Her hand was shaking as she reached out to take Sarah's. She winced as she stood up.

Kirsten's face was a mess.

'I think I broke your nose.'

'Yeah.'

Sarah shrugged. 'Sorry. Do you want me to help you clean your face in the bathroom?'

Kirsten regarded the smaller girl for a moment. 'Nah. I'll go myself, and then I'll go see the nurse.' Kirsten tried to smile, failed, and shrugged instead. 'I'll tell her I slipped and fell on my face.'

Sarah watched as the older girl limped off. Once she was gone, Sarah sat down on her bunk and put her head in her hands. Her adrenaline rush was over. She felt shaky and a little sick to her stomach.

She lay back and looked up at the bottom of the bed above her.

Maybe things are going to get better now.

It had been two years. Two years since her parents died and Theresa killed Dennis and she came here to this violent, friendless place. The Stranger still visited her dreams sometimes, but less and less.

She was only eight, but she wasn't an innocent anymore. She knew about death and blood and violence. She understood that the strong survived better than the weak. She knew what sex was, in all its guises, though she had (thankfully) not yet experienced it firsthand.

She'd also learned to hide her emotions, or evidence of them. She had three objects, three talismans, whose meanings she kept hidden from the other girls. There was Mr Huggles. There was a family picture of her, Mommy, Daddy, Buster, and Doreen. And there was the photo of Theresa's mother.

She'd grabbed it from its hiding place underneath Theresa's mattress. She intended to return it to Theresa someday.

She thought about her sister a lot, sometimes. She knew she'd always consider Theresa a sister, that she'd always remember that one safe night of Go Fish and laughter. She knew she'd never forget why Theresa had done what she did. Sarah understood all of that, now.

She reached into her back pocket and pulled out the picture of the beautiful young mother. Sarah ran her fingers over it, smiling at the laughing eyes and chestnut hair.

She knew that Theresa was in juvenile detention until she was eighteen. Cathy Jones had told her.

Three more years, and she'll be free.

She put the photo back, and laced her fingers behind her head. She'd tried writing Theresa once. Just a short, silly little letter. Sarah had gotten a two-sentence response back:

Don't write me while I'm in here. I love you.

Sarah understood. She fantasized sometimes about Theresa turning eighteen and coming to adopt her. Silly dreams, she knew. She couldn't help it.

Cathy Jones came to see her every three or four months. Sarah welcomed her visits, though she was curious about the woman's reasons. Cathy was very hard to read.

Whatever. Just don't lose her card.

Sarah had begun to think like a survivor. To classify things as assets or liabilities. Assets were important. Cathy was an asset. Cathy could find out about important things, like Theresa, or the fact that Doreen had been adopted by John and Jamie Overman. Things like that.

Other than Cathy, Karen Watson had been her only contact with the outside world. Sarah grimaced. She understood what Theresa had meant by 'pure evil' now. Karen Watson wasn't just

316

uncaring – she despised the children she was responsible for. She was one of the few people Sarah really hated.

A knock at the door startled her from her reverie. She sat up. Janet poked her head into the room.

'Sarah? Karen's here to see you.'

'Okay, Janet.'

The skinny woman smiled and left. Sarah frowned.

What could that witch want?

Karen was seated at a table in the common area. Sarah walked over and sat down facing her. Karen studied the young girl.

'How are you doing, princess?'

'Fine.'

What Sarah really wanted to say was 'What do you care?' but she knew better. The strong did better than the weak, and in this relationship, Karen was the strong one.

'Do you think you've learned your lesson now? About getting along in a foster environment?'

The first time Karen had asked Sarah this question was a year ago. Sarah had just had a birthday without a cake, and was feeling sad and angry. She'd screamed at Karen, and then had run off. She'd had a year to think about it, and this time, she was ready.

'I think so, Ms Watson. I really do.'

Sarah wanted out of this place. Karen Watson was the key. Assets and liabilities.

Karen smiled at this capitulation. 'Well, good. I'm glad to hear that, Sarah, because I have a family I can place you with. Not a rich couple by any means, but you'd be the only one there.'

Sarah bowed her head, demure. 'I'd like that, Ms Watson.'

Karen gave her an approving nod. 'Yes. I think you've learned your lesson.' She stood up. 'Pack your things tonight. I'll take you there tomorrow.'

Sarah watched her go. She smiled to herself.

Fuck you, you old bitch.

*

Sarah was back in her room, staring up at the mattress above her again, when Kirsten returned. Both of the bigger girl's eyes were blackened. Her nose had been splinted, and her lips had been stitched. She limped. She winced when she breathed. She went over to her own bunk, which was out of Sarah's line of sight. Sarah heard the bunk creaking as Kirsten climbed into it, and then there was silence. They were alone.

'Cracked some of my ribs when you kicked them, Langstrom.'

She didn't sound angry.

'Sorry,' Sarah ventured, though she knew she didn't really sound that sorry.

'You did what you had to.'

Another long silence ensued.

'Why'd you pack your bag?'

'I'm going to a foster home tomorrow.'

Another silence.

'Well . . . good luck, Langstrom. No hard feelings.'

'Thanks.'

Sarah was shocked when a few tears spilled from her eyes. This offering from her enemy had affected her in a way she couldn't understand. But she knew who to be grateful to.

'Thanks, Mommy,' she whispered to herself.

She wiped away the tears.

Assets and liabilities. Tears were a liability.

36

'Hi, Ms Watson; welcome, Sarah. Come in, please.'

The woman's name was Desiree Smith, and Sarah wanted to like her on sight. Desiree was in her early thirties and she had the look of a friendly soul – happy eyes, smiling lips, an open book. She was short and dirty-blonde. Her frame was thick without being heavy, and she was pretty without being beautiful. Desiree had an uncomplicated worldview, a genuine and simple warmth.

Sarah examined her surroundings once they were inside the house. It was clean and unostentatious, filled with a happy clutter but not messy.

Desiree brought them into the living room.

'Please sit down,' she said, indicating the couch. 'Can I get you anything, Ms Watson? Sarah? Water? Coffee?'

'No thank you, Desiree,' Ms Watson said.

Sarah shook her head. She knew better than to ask for something if Witch Watson hadn't.

'I got everything done based on the legal requirements you went over with me, Ms Watson. Sarah has her own room, with a brand-new bed. I stocked the fridge with some basics. I have the emergency numbers listed next to the phone – oh – and I got the paperwork needed to enroll her in school.'

Ms Watson smiled and nodded in approval.

Go on, pretend to care, Sarah thought. So long as you leave when you're done.

'Good, Desiree, that's very good.' Ms Watson reached into her battered leather carryall and pulled out a folder, handing it over to Desiree. 'Her immunization records are there, as well as her school records. You'll need to get her enrolled immediately.'

'I will. First thing Monday.'

'Excellent. Where's Ned, by the way?'

Desiree looked worried. Sarah noticed that the woman had started to wring her hands, but had forced herself to stop.

'He got called last minute to do a long-haul. It was a lot of money – we couldn't turn it down. He really wanted to be here. That's not a problem, is it?'

Ms Watson shook her head, waved her hand. 'No, no. I've met him before, and you've both passed your background checks.'

Desiree's relief was obvious. 'That's good.' She looked at Sarah. 'Ned's my husband, honey. He's a truck driver. He really wanted to be here to meet you, but he'll be back next Wednesday.'

Sarah smiled at the nervous woman. 'That's okay.'

Don't worry. Witch Watson just wants to get in, leave me, and get out.

'Any last questions for me, Desiree?'

'No, Ms Watson. I don't think so.'

The social worker nodded, and stood up. 'Then I'll be going. I'll check in on you in a month.' She turned to Sarah. 'Be good, Sarah. Do what Mrs Smith tells you.'

'Yes, Ms Watson,' Sarah replied, demure again.

Go away, Witch, she thought.

Sarah waited on the couch while Desiree led Karen to the door and said her good-byes. The door closed, and Desiree came back over and flopped down on the couch.

'Whew! I'm glad that's over with! I was so nervous.'

Sarah gave her a curious look.

'Why?'

'We've never taken in a child before, Sarah, and we really wanted to. Ms Watson bringing you over and taking a look around was the last hurdle.'

'Why is it so important to you?'

'Well, honey, sometimes Ned is gone a lot. He's here a lot too, but sometimes on a long-haul he'll be gone for two weeks. I do some work from home as a travel agent, but it gets lonely. We both like children, and it just seemed to make sense, you know?'

Sarah nodded. She pointed toward one of the photographs on the wall. 'Is that Ned?'

Desiree smiled. 'That's him. You'll like him, Sarah, I promise. He's a beautiful man. He doesn't have a mean bone in his body.'

So you say.

She pointed to a photo she'd noticed earlier of Ned and Desiree with a baby. 'Who's that?'

Desiree's smile changed. It became a sad smile that spoke of a hurt that was ever-present but no longer crippling. Some event had colored her soul without breaking her.

'That was our daughter, Diana. She died five years ago, when she was just a year old.'

'How did she die?'

'She was born with a bad heart.'

Sarah studied the photograph, thinking.

Can you trust this one? She seems nice. She seems really nice. But maybe it's a trick.

Sarah was only eight, but her experience at the Parkers', followed by two years in the group home, had taught her an important lesson: Trust no one. She liked to think of herself as hard, cold, a prisoner with a sneer on her face.

The truth was that she was only eight, and what she really wanted was for the warmth in this woman to be real. She wanted it with a deep-down desperation that made her heart tremble.

'Do you miss her?' Sarah asked.

Desiree nodded. 'Every day. Every minute.'

Sarah watched the woman's eyes as she said these things, looking for lies. All she saw was a river of sorrow, tempered by acceptance of the possibility of hope.

'My parents died,' she blurted out without meaning to.

The river of sorrow turned into compassion. 'I know, honey. And I know about what happened at the Parkers' too.' Desiree looked down, seemed to be searching for the words she wanted. 'I want you to know something, Sarah. It'll seem sometimes to you like I don't understand the bad things that can happen in this world. Even with everything I've experienced, like losing Diana, I'm an optimist. I try to find the good side of things. But that doesn't mean I'm an idiot. I know evil exists. I know you've seen too much of it. I guess what I'm saying is that I've got your back.'

Hope welled up in Sarah's heart. It was crushed by a wave of cynicism.

'Prove it,' she said.

Desiree's eyes widened in surprise. 'Oh, well . . .' She nodded. 'Fair enough.' She smiled. 'How about this? I know that Karen Watson isn't a very nice person.'

It was Sarah's turn to be surprised. 'You do?'

'Yep. She puts on an act, but I was watching. I saw the way she looked at you. She doesn't really care about you, does she?'

Sarah scowled. 'She doesn't care about anyone but herself. You know what I call her?'

'What?'

'Witch Watson.'

Desiree's mouth twitched and then she laughed. 'Witch Watson. I like that.'

Sarah smiled back. She couldn't help herself.

'So,' Desiree said. 'Okay?'

'Okay,' Sarah replied.

Maybe, she thought.

'Good. Now that that's settled, I want to introduce you to someone. I kept him in the backyard while Ms – sorry – *Witch* Watson was here, but now I want you to meet him. I think you'll like him.'

Sarah was puzzled. Was Desiree crazy after all? It sounded like she was talking about keeping someone in the backyard.

'Uh, okay.'

'His name's Pumpkin. Don't be afraid of him – he's friendly.'

Desiree walked over to the sliding glass door that led into the backyard and opened it up. She whistled.

'Come on, Pumpkin. You can come inside now.'

There was a ferocious-sounding 'woof.'

A dog!

Happiness shot through Sarah's soul like an arrow.

Pumpkin appeared at the door, and Sarah understood the reason for the name immediately. The dog's head was huge. Crazy-huge – like a pumpkin.

He was a coffee-colored pit bull, and he looked both ridiculous and terrifying, with his jowls flopping and his tongue lolling and his oversized skull. He raced up to Desiree, looked up at her and spoke: 'Woof!'

Desiree smiled and leaned over to pet the pit bull. 'Hey, Pumpkin. We have a visitor. A girl. She's going to be staying with us, and her name's Sarah.'

The dog cocked its head, aware that its owner was talking to him, but unable to understand any of it.

Sarah got up off the couch. Pumpkin turned at the sound.

'Woof!'

The dog came bounding over. Sarah would have been terrified if not for the fact that Pumpkin was wagging his tail in the universal sign of dog happiness. He bumped into her with his massive head and proceeded to lick her offered hand, coating it with slobber.

Sarah grinned. 'Yuck!' She petted the pit bull, who sat back on his haunches and grinned. 'You sure are a goofy-looking dog, Pumpkin.'

'I rescued him from a bar eight years ago,' Desiree said. She smiled. 'It was in my younger days, and I wasn't always that smart. I noticed a group of bikers over by a pool table laughing and making noise, and when I went over to see what they were doing, there was Pumpkin. He was just a puppy, but they had him up on the pool table, and they were shooting pool balls at him. He was scared, and whining.'

'How mean!'

'Yeah, I thought so too. I yelled at them all, and I might have tried to start a fight – which would have been really stupid on my part – but my girlfriend grabbed my arm and dragged me away. I was still very upset about it, so I kept drinking and – I don't remember how it happened – when I woke up the next morning Pumpkin was lying next to me in my bed.'

Sarah continued to pet the dog, bemused by this strange woman and her tale of drunken dog-rescuing. Something hitched in her chest. She was mortified to find that tears were running down her face.

'What's the matter, Sarah?'

Desiree was empathetic. She didn't move closer or try to hug Sarah.

Sarah wiped her face with a small, angry hand.

'Just ... we had dogs, and my mom would have liked the story about Pumpkin, and –' She sat back down on the couch, miserable. 'Sorry. I'm not a crybaby.'

Pumpkin put his head in her lap and looked up at her, as if to say: *I'm sorry you feel bad, but can you keep doing the petting thing?*

'There's nothing wrong with crying when you're sad, Sarah.'

Sarah looked up at Desiree. 'What if you're always sad? You'd never stop crying.'

She thought for a moment that she'd said something wrong because of the pain that twisted Desiree's face. Then, understanding:

She's feeling that way for me.

No matter how precocious, no matter how hardened, an eight-year-old only has so much complexity to draw on. Sarah's interior walls had developed cracks, which had become fissures, and while the dam had not burst, the tears wouldn't stop. She put her hands to her face and cried.

Desiree sat down next to her on the couch but was careful not to do anything else. Sarah was grateful. She wasn't ready for that yet, to surrender herself to the arms of an adult again. It was nice to have Desiree there, though. Pumpkin displayed his own empathy; he'd stopped demanding to be petted and was licking Sarah's knee.

Desiree didn't speak until Sarah was done crying.

'So,' she said, 'you met Pumpkin. Do you want to see your room?'

Sarah nodded and managed a smile. 'Yes, please. I'm tired.'

You know one of the things I've realized? I've realized that a dog really is man's (or woman's) best friend.

As long as you feed them and love them, dogs love you back. They won't steal from you or beat you or betray you. They're honest. What you see on the surface is what you get underneath.

Not like people.

'We're here,' Alan says, pulling me away from my reading.

I fold the pages in half and replace them in my purse with great reluctance.

Sarah's experiences had awakened in her a taste for violence. But she was still guilty of hope.

Was that how it had been for him? A slow erosion of the soul? At what point did the taste become a hunger?

Did any part of him still hope?

37

Terry Gibbs, the lawyer, has an office in Moorpark. I am familiar with Moorpark by accident; Callie's daughter and grandson live here.

The secret of Callie's daughter had haunted her for years. A killer had discovered this, and had attempted to exploit this knowledge to his advantage. The result? Callie and I, breaking the sound barrier, pounding on her daughter's door with our guns drawn, expecting the worst.

Marilyn was fine, the killer is dead, and Callie now has a relationship instead of a regret. This satisfies both my sense of justice and my sense of irony, a self-satisfaction that's probably as ugly as it is gratifying. I feel the killer's death deserves my gloating more than my guilt.

Moorpark is an up-and-comer, located in Ventura County, west of Los Angeles. In many ways it's California of old; if you drive down the 118 freeway to get there, you pass through miles of unpopulated hills and mini-mountains. Sometimes there are even cows.

Moorpark used to be a rural town. Now it is a growing suburban hub, middle to upper-middle class, with some of the fastest-appreciating homes in Southern California.

'Give it twenty years and it'll be an urban-sprawl shit hole,' Alan comments, gazing out the window, providing a cynical future-echo to my thoughts.

'Maybe not,' I offer. 'Simi Valley, the town next door, is still very nice.'

Alan shrugs, not believing a word of it. We turn off the 118 freeway onto Los Angeles Avenue.

'Up here on the right,' Alan says. 'In the business park.'

We exit the street into a large collection of four- to five-story office buildings, as new as the rest of Moorpark with glass that gleams in the sunshine.

'Pull up over there.' Alan points.

As we park the car, my cell phone rings.

'Is that Smoky Barrett?' a perky female voice asks.

'Yes. Who's this?'

'This is Kirby. Kirby Mitchell.'

'Sorry – do I know you?'

'Tommy must not have told you my name. Silly guy. You asked for a referral from him? For personal protection? That's me.'

I realize that the cheerful voice belongs to my 'loyal and lethal' bodyguard and possible ex-assassin.

'Oh, right. Sorry,' I fumble. 'Tommy didn't give me your name.'

Kirby chuckles. It's a chuckle that matches the rest of her voice: light, a little melodic. The sound of someone without a care in the world, someone who'd been happy to wake up that morning, who hadn't needed any coffee when she woke up, who probably went on a five-mile jog straight out of bed, smiling the whole way.

I'm considering not liking her, but that's the problem with cheerful people. You feel obligated to give them a chance. I'm also intrigued. The idea of a Pollyanna-assassin appeals to the perverse side of my nature.

'Well,' she says, a juggernaut of good cheer, 'no harm done. Tommy's great, but he's a guy, and guys forget the details sometimes, it's a man thing, I think. Tommy's better than most, and a hunk to boot, so let's forgive him, okay?'

'Sure,' I reply, bemused.

'So, when and where would you like to meet?'

I glance at my watch, thinking. 'Can you meet me in the reception of the FBI building at five-thirty?'

'FBI building, huh? Coolness. I guess I'd better leave all my guns in the car.' A melodious laugh, somehow amusing and disturbing at the same time, given the context. 'I'll see you at five-thirty, then. Bye!'

'Bye,' I murmur. She hangs up.

'Who was that?' Alan asks.

I stare at him for a moment. Shrug. 'Possible bodyguard for Sarah. I think she's going to be a hoot.'

Coolness.

Terry Gibbs ushers us into his office with a smile. It's a small office, with his desk in the front, and file cabinets along a far wall. Everything has a used but sturdy look to it.

I take stock of the lawyer as he motions for us to sit down in the two padded chairs facing his desk.

Gibbs is an interesting mix of a person. It's as though he couldn't decide who he wanted to be. He's a tall man. He's bald, but he has a moustache and a beard. He has the broad shoulders and athletic moves of a fit man, but he smells of cigarettes. He wears glasses with thick lenses, which highlight intense, almost beautiful blue eyes. He's wearing a suit without a tie, and the suit looks expensive and tailored, a mismatch with the office furniture.

'I can see what you're thinking in your eyes, Agent Barrett,' he says, smiling. He has a nice voice, smooth and flowing, not too deep or too high. The perfect voice for a lawyer. 'You're trying to match up the thousand-dollar suit and the crappy office.'

'Maybe,' I admit.

He smiles. 'I'm a one-man band. I don't make the big bucks, but I do okay. It forces compromise: flashy office or flashy suit? I decided on the flashy suit. A client can forgive a messy office. They'll never forgive a lawyer in a cheap suit.'

'Kind of like us,' Alan says. 'You can show them the badge, but all they really want to know is if you got the gun.'

Gibbs nods, appreciative. 'Exactly.' He leans forward, resting his arms on the desk, hands clasped, serious. 'I want you to know, Agent Barrett, I'm not being intentionally uncooperative on the Langstrom trust. I'm bound, ethically and legally, by the rules of the bar.'

I nod. 'I understand, Mr Gibbs. I assume that you have no problem with us getting a subpoena?'

'None whatsoever so long as it legally sets aside my obligations to comply with the rules of privilege.'

'What can you tell us?'

He leans back in the chair, looking off at a space over our heads, thinking.

'The client approached me approximately ten years ago, wanting to set up a trust to benefit Sarah Langstrom.'

'Man or woman?' I ask.

'I'm sorry. I can't say.'

I frown. 'Why?'

'Confidentiality. The client demanded absolute confidentiality in every way. Everything is in my name for that reason. I have power of attorney, I administer the trust, and my retainer is paid from the trust.'

'Did you consider that someone wanting that much confidentiality might not be up to anything good?' Alan asks.

Gibbs gives Alan a sharp look. 'Of course I did. I made some inquiries. At the other end of those inquiries I found a child orphaned by a murder-suicide. If Sarah Langstrom's parents had been killed by an unknown intruder, I would have refused to take on the client. As it was, with the mother ruled the murderer, I couldn't think of a reason to refuse.'

'We're looking into the possibility that it wasn't a murder-suicide,' I say, watching his reaction. 'It may have been staged to appear that way.'

Gibbs closes his eyes for a moment and rubs his forehead. He seems distressed. 'That's terrible, if true.' He sighs and opens his eyes. 'Unfortunately, I'm still bound by attorney-client privilege.'

'What else can you tell us without violating that?' Alan asks.

'The trust is a fund, designed to keep up the family home, and to provide Sarah Langstrom with means. It's to be released to her control on her eighteenth birthday.'

'How much?' I ask.

'I can't give you an exact amount. I can say that it will let her live comfortably for many years.'

'Do you report to your client?'

'Actually, no. I assume there's some form of supervision in place – a way for the client to keep an eye on me, to make sure I'm not emptying out the cookie jar. But I haven't had contact with the client since the formation of the trust.'

'Isn't that unusual?' Alan asks.

Gibbs nods. 'Very.'

'I noticed that the exterior of the home is well kept up. Why not inside? It's a dust farm,' I say.

'One of the conditions of the trust. No one was to enter the home without Sarah's permission.'

'Strange.'

He shrugs. 'I've dealt with stranger.' He stops speaking for a moment. A pained, almost delicate look comes across his face. 'Agent Barrett, I want you to know, I'd never have knowingly participated in anything that would bring harm to a child. Never. I lost a sister when I was younger. My little sister. The kind big brothers are supposed to protect. You understand?' He looks miserable. 'Children are sacred.'

I recognize the guilt I see rising in his eyes. It's the kind of guilt that comes with feeling responsible for something you couldn't have done anything about anyway. The kind that appears when fate is at fault but you're the one left holding the bag.

'I understand, Mr Gibbs.'

*

330

We'd spent an hour fencing with the lawyer, trying to extract more information from him without any luck. We're back in the car, and I'm trying to decide on my next move.

'I got the idea that he wanted to tell us more,' Alan says.

'Me too. I agree with your original assessment. I don't think he's trying to be a jerk. His hands are tied.'

'Subpoena time,' Alan says.

'Yes. Let's head back to the office and get in-house counsel on it.'

My phone rings.

'An update on other fronts,' Callie says.

'Go ahead.'

'As it turns out, the files on the Vargas case – both ours and the ones at the LAPD – are missing.'

My heart sinks.

'Oh, come on. Are you kidding?'

'I wish I was. The best guess is lost over time, although I suppose we could theorize that they'd been stolen, all things considered.'

'Whichever one it was, we don't have the files.' I rub my forehead. 'Fine. I know you're working on processing the Langstrom home – but do me a favor. Call AD Jones and see if he can give you a list of names of the agents and officers who worked the case.'

'Will do.'

I hang up.

'Bad news?' Alan asks.

'You could say that.' I relate the substance of the call to him.

'Which do you think? Lost or stolen?'

'My vote is on stolen. He's been planning for years, and he's been manipulating things to allow discovery at his pace. That makes this too much of a coincidence.'

'Probably right. Where to now?'

I'm prepared to answer when my phone rings again.

'Barrett,' I answer.

'Hey, Smoky. It's Barry. Are you still in Moorpark?'

'We're just leaving.'

'That's good. I did some checking into the detectives originally assigned to the Langstrom case. Get this: One's dead. He ate his gun five years ago. Not particularly probative, to be honest – the guy had been on the ragged edge for years, apparently – but what is interesting is that his partner retired two years later. Just quit, four years short of his thirty.'

'That is interesting.'

'Yeah. It gets better. I got ahold of this guy. His name's Nicholson. Dave Nicholson. I told him what was up and get this: He wants to see you. Now.'

Excitement thrills through me. 'Where does he live?' I ask.

'That's why I asked if you were still in Moorpark. He's close. He retired to Simi Valley, just up the road.'

38

David Nicholson, Barry had filled me in, had been a good cop. He came from a family of cops, starting on the East Coast in New York with his grandfather, migrating westward in the sixties with his father. His dad had been killed in the line of duty when David was twelve.

Nicholson had made detective in record time, apparently deserved. He was known to have a sharp mind and a meticulous nature. He was given to flashes of insight and was a feared interrogator. He sounds like Alan's long-lost white brother.

None of which reconciles with the loose ends left in the Langstrom case. This fact, and the fact that he wants to see me – *now* – fills me with hope.

'This is the place,' Alan says as we pull up to the curb.

The home is on the outer edges of Simi Valley, on the LA side, where many of the older homes lie. Not a house on the block has more than one story. They're all ranch-home layouts, built in the unimaginative style of so many homes of the sixties. The yard is well kept up, with a plain concrete path leading to the front door. I see a curtain in a window to the right of the door move aside and catch a glimpse of a face, peering out.

'He knows we're here,' I say to Alan.

We get out and walk toward the house. Before we get there, the door opens and a man comes out, standing on the concrete block that forms the porch. He's barefoot, wearing jeans and a T-shirt. He's a tall, big man, about six foot three. He has broad shoulders and a big chest. His hair is dark and thick, he has a square-jawed, handsome face, and he seems younger than his fifty-five years. His eyes, however, lack vitality. They are dark and empty, full of echoes and open spaces.

'Mr Nicholson?' I ask.

'That's me. Can I see some ID?'

Alan and I pull out our respective badges. He inspects them and inspects us in turn. His gaze lingers on my scars, but not overlong.

'Come in,' he says.

The interior of the home is a throwback to the late sixties/early seventies. There's wood-paneling on the walls, a flagstone fireplace. The one nod to the present is the dark hardwood flooring that runs through the home.

We follow him into the living room. He indicates a plush-looking blue couch and we sit.

'Get you anything?' he asks.

'No, sir.'

He turns away from us and stares out the sliding glass doors that lead into his backyard. It's a small yard, longer than it is wide, more dirt than grass. A wooden fence encloses it. I don't see any trees at all.

Moments pass. Nicholson continues to stare, frozen in place.

'Sir?'

He starts.

'Sorry.' He comes over and seats himself in an armchair that's been placed kitty-corner to the couch. The chair is an ugly green, but it looks comfortable and weathered and well-used. Faithful furniture, quietly loved. It faces a twenty-inch television. A foldable dinner-tray stands next to it.

I can imagine Dave Nicholson sitting here at night, watching television, a microwave meal placed on the dinner-tray in front of him. Normal enough, but for some reason, in this place, it's a sad picture. An undercurrent of waiting and depression layers everything. It's as though the furniture should all be draped with sheets, and the house should have a wind blowing through it.

'So listen,' he says, before I can ask him any questions. 'I'm going to tell you something I'm supposed to tell you, and then I'm going to tell you something I'm not supposed to tell you. Then I'm going to do what I was supposed to do.'

'Sir –'

He waves me off. 'Here's what I'm supposed to tell you: "It's the man behind the symbol, not the symbol, that's important." Got that?' His voice is monotonous and matches the hollowness in his eyes.

'Yes, but –'

'Here's the next thing. I threw things off on the Langstrom investigation, steered the conclusions. He told me that the evidence would point to a murder-suicide, as long as I didn't look too hard. All I had to do was accept what was on the surface. So I did.' He sighs. He seems ashamed. 'He needed the Langstrom girl – Sarah – to be left alone. Said he had plans for her. I shouldn't have done it, I know that, but you have to understand – I did it because he has my daughter.'

I freeze, shocked. 'Your daughter?'

Nicholson stares at something above my head, talking almost to himself. 'Her name's Jessica. He took her away from me ten years ago. He made me helpless and he told me what to do, yes he did. He told me that someone would come asking questions, years down the line, and that I was to give them the message I just gave you. If I did all that, and one final thing, he said he'd let her go.' His eyes plead with me. 'You get it, right? I was a good cop, but this was my *daughter*.'

'Are you saying he took her hostage?'

He points a thick finger at me. 'You make sure she's okay. You make sure he keeps his end of the bargain. I think he will.' He licks his lips, nods too fast. 'I think he will.'

'David. You need to slow down.'

'Nope. I've said enough already. I need to finish up now. One last thing.'

He reaches a hand behind his back. It comes out holding a large revolver. I jump up, followed by Alan. I reach for my weapon, it finds my hand, but I'm not the one Nicholson wants to kill. The barrel finds his own mouth, a brutal thrust, it angles up. I reach toward him.

'No!' I yell.

He closes his eyes and pulls the trigger, and his head explodes in a 'bang' and I am showered in his blood.

I stand there, gaping, as he topples forward from the armchair.

'Jesus!' Alan yells, rushing toward Nicholson.

I stand there and watch, dazed. Outside, the clouds open and the rain begins to fall again.

39

Alan and I are inside Nicholson's home. The local cops are here, wanting to take charge, but I ignore them in my fury.

A man – a cop – is dead, and I know his death is much more than a suicide. I want to know why.

I had washed my hands and gloved them, and I can still feel the spots where I scrubbed his blood from my face.

I stalk through the living room, down the hallway, into Nicholson's bedroom. Alan follows.

'What are we looking for, Smoky?' he asks, his voice cautious.

'A God damn explanation,' I snap, my voice hard and furious and cracking around the edges.

The suddenness of it, the awfulness of it, had shocked me like a backhand across the face. My stomach was queasy from the rush of adrenaline. I couldn't get my mind around the death yet, not fully. I only knew that I was enraged. *He* had done this. It was *his* fault.

The Stranger. I'm sick of his games and his puzzles and everything else.

I want to fucking kill him.

Nicholson's bedroom is like the rest of his house, careless and Spartan. Things are clean enough, but the home has no soul. The walls are bare, the window coverings are cheap and mismatched.

He slept here, he ate here, it kept the rain off his head. That was all.

I spot a photograph in a frame, on a table next to the bed. Nicholson is in it, smiling, his eyes alive. He has his arms around a young girl, who looks to be about sixteen. She has her father's thick, dark hair. The eyes belong to someone else. A mother's ghost?

Alan looks at the photo as well.

'Looks like a father/daughter picture to me,' he says.

I nod, still not speaking.

Alan opens the walk-in closet and begins to rummage around on the shelves. He pauses, a lack of motion, silence.

'Wow,' he says. 'Check this out.'

He walks out of the closet. He has a shoebox in his hands, the top off. I catch a glimpse of Polaroid photographs. Lots of them. Alan takes one out and hands it to me.

The girl is pale and she is nude. In this photograph she appears to be in her early twenties. The photo was taken full-frontal. She stands with her hands clasped behind her, her feet slightly turned in, her gaze averted and despondent. She has large breasts and an unshaven pubic area. She looks exposed and emotionally numb.

I compare this photograph to the one in the frame.

'It's definitely the same girl,' I say.

'This box is full of them.' Alan speaks as he rummages. 'Looks like they're in chronological order. Always nude. Different ages.' He rummages some more. 'Jesus. Based on changes in her face and body, these go back a lot of years.'

'Over ten, I imagine.' I feel deflated. My rage has dissipated, leaving emptiness behind.

Alan stares at me, taking this in. He taps a foot and jiggles the shoebox in one giant hand. 'Okay. Okay. Makes sense. He takes Nicholson's daughter hostage. But Nicholson's not just a dad, he's a cop. The perp needs a way to keep Nicholson on a leash, so he provides him with regular proof of life.' Taps his foot harder.

338

'God damn. Why didn't Nicholson go to the FBI? Why leave his daughter in this guy's hands for that long without doing *something*?'

'Because he believed him, Alan. He believed that The Stranger would do what he said. If Nicholson deviated from the plan, The Stranger would kill the daughter. If Nicholson stuck to the plan, he'd keep her alive. And he sent Nicholson regular proof that he was keeping his word.'

'I get that, but still – would you have done what Nicholson did? For as long as he did?'

The answer is instantaneous. I don't have to give it much thought. The possibility of Alexa, alive, or the current reality of her death?

'Probably, yes. If he was convincing enough. Yes.' I look at him. 'What if it was Elaina?'

His foot stops tapping. 'Point taken.'

I stare at the photograph. 'Why? Why Nicholson?'

'Thought we knew that. He needed Nicholson to steer the Langstrom investigation.'

I shake my head. 'Bullshit. I mean, yes, he used him for that purpose – but why take the risk? Why bother? He could have covered his tracks better – hell, he covered them pretty well as it is. Involving Nicholson increased his exposure. Why was The Stranger willing to take that chance?' I run a hand through my hair. 'We need to dig through Nicholson's past.' I pace. 'It's all about the past in this case, we just haven't found the connections yet. Who did I give the job of finding out about Sarah's grandfather to?'

'That'd be me. I haven't gotten to it yet. There was the lead with the Langstrom home, the trust.' He gestures, a way of indicating where we are now and why. 'Nicholson. Things have been moving pretty fast.'

'I know, and I understand, but it's important.'

'Got it.'

I stare down at the sad girl in the sad Polaroid. It's representative of this case, something going on forever, something terrible, something that can be traced to the past. Nicholson, Sarah's grandfather, a case from the seventies.

Where did they all come together?

I'm talking to Christopher Shreveport, the head of CMU. CMU is the Crisis Management Unit. They deal with response to critical incidents, such as kidnappings and the like.

'She's a hostage?' he asks me.

'Yes. Unless she's dead already.'

Silence. Shreveport isn't cursing, but I can *feel* him wanting to.

'I'm going to send an agent over there by the name of Mason Dickson.'

'Is that a joke, Chris?'

'Just the one his parents played on him when they named him. He's trained with CMU at Quantico and he's our local go-to guy for kidnappings in your area. He'll do what he can. I wouldn't hold your breath. Something tells me Mason isn't going to be able to do much until you crack the case.'

'Maybe he'll just keep his word and let her go.'

'Everyone should have a dream, Smoky. That one can be yours.'

40

It's now late afternoon. The rain has stopped again, but the gray clouds won't disperse. The sun is fighting to shine, a losing battle. Everything feels stark and wet and barren. This type of weather emphasizes the concrete nature of Los Angeles in an unflattering way. It matches my mood.

Agent Mason Dickson had shown up approximately fifty minutes after I finished talking to Shreveport. He was a redhead with a baby face sitting on a six-six lanky frame. He was improbable, but he seemed competent enough. We'd briefed him, handed him the shoebox of Polaroids, and left, feeling impotent about it all.

Alan gets a call on his cell as we pull into the FBI building parking lot. He murmurs a few times.

'Thanks,' he says, and then hangs up. 'Sarah Langstrom is getting released tomorrow,' he tells me.

I tap my purse with a finger, thinking, uneasy.

'Elaina talked to me yesterday,' I say. 'I think she wants Sarah to come live with you guys.'

A sad smile crosses his lips. The shrug is infinitesimal.

'Yeah. She talked to me about it. I exploded, said no way. Really put my foot down.'

'And?'

'And we'll be taking Sarah.' He looks out the windshield, his eyes finding the gray clouds that just won't go away. 'I can't say no to her, Smoky. I was never very good at it. Post-cancer, I can't seem to do it at all.'

'Can I ask you something, Alan?'

'Always.'

'Did you ever decide? About whether you're going to leave the job, I mean.'

He doesn't answer right away. Keeps gazing out the windshield, gathering his words carefully, like a wheat farmer gathering his bushels by hand.

'You ever watch any of those cold case real crime shows?'

'Sure. Of course.'

'Me too. You know what always strikes me about those shows? That so many of the cops they interview about old cases are young and retired. I mean, it's rare to see a really old guy who's still on the job.'

'I hadn't thought about it until now.' And I hadn't. But as I do, I realize he's right.

He turns to me. 'You know why? Because working homicides is dangerous, Smoky. I'm not talking about physical danger. I'm talking about spiritual danger.' Waves a hand. 'Mental danger if you don't believe in the soul. Whatever. The point is, you look in that direction too long, you run a risk of never recovering from what you see.' He hits a fist into his palm, lightly. 'I mean, *ever*. I've seen some shit, Smoky . . .' He shakes his head. 'Saw a half-eaten baby, once. Mommy took a bad hit of acid and got hungry. That's the case that made me an alcoholic.'

I start at this. 'I didn't know,' I say.

He shrugs. 'Before my Bureau days. You know what got me to quit drinking?' He looks away. 'Elaina. I got soused one night and came home at three A.M. She told me I needed to stop. I –' He grimaces. Sighs. 'I grabbed her by the arm, told her to mind her own business, and then I passed out on the couch. Woke up the next morning to the smell of bacon. Elaina was cooking breakfast, taking care of me like she always did, as though nothing had happened. But something *had* happened. She was wearing this sleeveless comfort-shirt she liked, and she had a bunch of bruises on her arm. Bruises from where I'd grabbed her.' He rests for a moment, gathering another few bushels. I wait, mesmerized. 'That mom who ate her baby came around, of course. When she realized what she'd done, she . . . shrieked. I'm talking about a sound a human being shouldn't be able to make, Smoky. Like a monkey that'd been set on fire. She shrieked and once she started, she never stopped. Well, that's how I felt when I saw those bruises on that lovely woman's arm. I felt like shrieking. You understand?'

'Yes.'

He turns to look at me.

'I quit the booze and I bounced back. Because of Elaina. There have been some other bad times, and I've always bounced back. Because of Elaina, always because of Elaina. She's . . . she's my most precious thing.' He coughs once, a little self-conscious. 'When she got sick last year, and that psycho targeted her, I was afraid, Smoky. Afraid of getting to a place where I needed her but she was gone. If that happened, I'd never make it back. It's all a balancing act, you know? Knowing how far I can go out, how much I can see, and still make it back to her. One day I'm going to say it's enough, and I hope I know when it's right.' He smiles at me. It's a real smile, but it's too complex to be called 'happy.' 'The answer to your question is that for now I'm here, but one day I won't be and I don't know when that day will come.'

We pass through security, and are moving through reception when a fit, vibrant, thirtyish-looking blond woman with a bright smile places herself in front of us. She holds out a hand for me to shake. She almost crackles with confidence and energy.

'Agent Barrett? Kirby Mitchell.'

I start, and then realize that it must be past five-thirty by now. I had forgotten.

Ah, yes, the killer, I want to say. *Pleased to meet you – but should I end that with a question mark? Time will tell, I guess.*

Instead, I smile and shake her hand and give her a once-over.

Kirby in person is a match for her phone voice. She's attractive and slender, perhaps five foot seven, with blond hair that may or may not belong to her, twinkling blue eyes, and a perpetual smile composed of over-bright teeth. She has the look of someone who spent her early twenties as a fun-loving beach bunny, hanging out with surfers, drinking beer next to bonfires, sleeping with guys as blond as she is and who smelled of seawater and surf wax and maybe a little bit of the Mary Jane. The kind of girl who was always ready to slip on a cocktail dress at five on a Friday. It would have been black and short and she would have danced till the place closed down. I had had friends like her, wildness in a bottle.

Except that she's a bodyguard, and according to Tommy, an ex-killer. The disparity of these things both intrigues and concerns me.

'Pleased to meet you,' I manage.

I introduce her to Alan.

She grins and punches him on the arm, playful. 'Big guy! Do you find that a help or a hindrance? Doing your job, I mean?'

'Help, mostly,' he replies, bemused. He rubs his arm where she hit him, a look of surprise on his face. 'Hey, that hurt.'

'Don't be a baby,' Kirby says. She winks at me.

'We're heading to our offices,' I say.

'Lead the way, FBI people.'

The offices are empty. Everyone is occupied, doing the things I sent them off to do. Callie is processing the Langstrom home. James is probably dealing with Michael Kingsley's computer. It's been a day of sprinting, and it's not over yet.

Kirby continues to jabber away, and I watch her as we go through the offices. I realize that as she speaks, her eyes are roaming. Taking in the surroundings. They pause the longest on the whiteboard, and then move on, missing nothing.

I've seen eyes like hers before, on leopards or lions or the human versions thereof. They flicker like candles, seeming casual but seeing everything.

We all go into my office and sit down.

'So now that we're all friends,' Kirby says, still perky, 'let's talk about how I work. I'm very good, you should know that. I've never lost a client, and I don't plan to – knock on wood!' She raps my desk with a knuckle, grins. 'I'm trained in surveillance, hand-to-hand combat, and I can use, gosh, just about anything when it comes to weapons.'

She counts off on her fingers. 'Knives, handguns, most automatic weapons. I'm okay as a sniper as long as it's not past four hundred yards. The usual.' Another one of those twinkle-eyed smiles. '"Mess with the best, die like the rest," silly, I know, but I just love that saying, don't you?'

'Uh, sure,' I reply.

'I have one rule.' She waggles a finger at me, a good-natured warning. 'No leaving me out of the loop. I have to know everything to do my job. If you fudge on that, and I find out, then I'll have to quit. I'm not trying to be a meanie-beanie, that's just the way it has to be.'

'I understand,' I say.

Meanie-beanie?

'Okay.' She continues talking, a juggernaut of words. Kirby is like a freight train. Hop on board or get rolled over, the choice is yours. 'Now, I know you're probably looking at me and thinking, "Who is this airhead?" Tommy's an honest kind of guy – cute too' – she winks at me, conspiratorial – 'so I'm sure he felt he just *had* to mention that I *maybe, allegedly, might have* killed some people in the past for the military-industrial complex. And you're looking at *that*, and then you're looking at *this*.' She indicates the whole of herself with a sweeping gesture. 'And you're thinking, maybe she's a wack-a-doodle, am I right?'

'Maybe a little,' I admit.

She smiles. 'Well, this is just who I am. I'm a California girl, always have been, always will be. I like my hair blond, I like two-piece bikinis, and I love the smell of the ocean.' She shimmies in her chair. 'And I love to dance!' Another multi-kilowatt smile. 'I have what they called on my psych eval "an overdeveloped ability to assign certain human beings to the category of *other*." The average person isn't built to kill, you see. It's not a part of the makeup. But we *have* to kill, all the time. Soldiers have to. SWAT snipers have to.' She nods once, toward me. 'You have to. So what to do, what to do, problems, problems. The answer is: We decide that they are *other*. They aren't like us, maybe they aren't really human, whatever. Once that's done – and this is something the psychological and military communities have known for a long time – they're a lot easier to kill, let me tell you.' Another perky smile, but this time she doesn't let it reach her eyes. I think she's doing this on purpose, to show me the killer she keeps inside. 'I'm not a psycho. I don't get all jolly about blowing people away, I'm not into all that "guts to grease the treads of our tanks" stuff.' She laughs as though this idea is the silliest thing ever, *ho ho ho*. 'Nope, it's just really easy for me to decide who the enemy is, and hey, once that's done, they're not a member of my club anymore, you know?'

'Yes,' I reply. 'I do.'

'Coolness.' The Kirby-train rushes on. She talks in waves, in a way that makes it impossible to get a word in without interrupting her. 'Now, as far as the résumé goes, I have a degree in abnormal psych, and I speak fluent Spanish. I was in the CIA for five years, and the NSA for six. I spent a lot of time in Central and South America doing, ummmmm, odd jobs.' Another conspiratorial wink, which gives me a little bit of a chill. 'Got bored and quit – and gosh, was that hard. I could tell you some stories. Those intel agency guys really take themselves seriously. They didn't want to let me go.' She smiles and again it doesn't quite bleed into her eyes. 'I convinced 'em.'

Alan raises a single eyebrow, but says nothing.

'So – where was I? Oh yeah: I got out and spent a few months wrapping up some old business. A couple of really icky guys from Central America were bugging me. They thought I was still working for the NSA.' She rolls her eyes good-naturedly. 'Some men never learn the meaning of the word *no*. It was almost enough to make me swear off Latin men – but not quite!' She laughs, and I find myself smiling against my will at this dangerous pixie of a woman. 'I spent about six months beaching-out, got even more bored, and decided it might be fun to go into the private sector. It pays a lot better, let me tell you. I still get to shoot people every now and then, and I can make it to the beach in between jobs.' She spreads her arms in a 'ta-dah' gesture. 'And that's the story of little old me.' She leans forward. 'Now let's hear about the client and the cuckoo-bird that's after her.'

With a last glance at Alan, who sends me a subtle shrug, I launch into the story of Sarah Langstrom and The Stranger. Kirby focuses on me with those leopard eyes, listening with intensity, nodding to let me know that she's hearing what I'm saying.

I finish and she sits back, thinking, tapping her fingers on the chair. She smiles.

'Okay, I think I have the picture.' She turns to Alan. 'So, how are you going to feel about having me at your home, big man?' Another playful punch to the arm. 'More important, how is your wife going to feel?'

Alan doesn't answer right away. He fixes his gaze on Kirby, thoughtful. She bears this scrutiny without a seeming care in the world.

'You'll protect my wife and the girl?'

'With my life. Though geez, let's hope it doesn't come to that, huh?'

'And you're good?'

'Not the best there is, but darn close.' Unending cheerfulness, the optimistic assassin.

Alan nods. 'Then I'm glad to have you. And Elaina will be too.'

'Coolness.' She turns to me with the snapping-fingers look of someone remembering something they'd almost forgot. 'Oh hey.

I need to ask. If the cuckoo-bird does come calling – do you need him alive or dead?'

The smile doesn't falter. I look at this very dangerous woman and consider my answer. If I ask her, Kirby Mitchell will consign The Stranger to the category of 'other.' If he shows his face, she'll kill him with a smile and head off to the beach for a bonfire and some beer. I only hesitate because I understand; this is not a theoretical question she's posed.

Want me to kill him? Hey, no problem. I'll do that, and then we'll hit a club, drink some margaritas. Coolness.

'I'd prefer him alive,' I say. 'But keeping Elaina and Sarah safe is the priority.'

It's a shitty, evasive answer. She takes it in stride.

'Gotcha. Now that that's settled, I'm going to head over to the hospital. I'll be there until tomorrow, and then we'll move her over to your place, big guy.' She stands up. 'Can one of you escort me out of here? And hey, can you believe all this rain?'

'I'll take you,' Alan says.

She whirls out of the office, leaving me feeling like I've just been run over, but, somehow, in a *good* way.

I look at my watch. It's after six o'clock. Ellen, our in-house counsel, might still be here. I pick up the phone and dial her extension.

'Ellen Gardner,' she answers. She sounds calm, unruffled. Ellen always sounds this way. It's just a little bit inhuman.

'Hi, Ellen, it's Smoky. I need a subpoena.'

'Hold that thought,' she answers without hesitation. 'Let me get a notepad.'

I picture Ellen, sitting behind her cherrywood lawyer's desk. She's an angular woman, made of up lines that are not so much severe as they are businesslike. She's in her mid-fifties, with brown hair that she keeps cut short (and dyed, I suppose – I've never seen a gray), and a tall, thin, almost boyish frame. Ellen is crisp and precise and all business – a lawyer, in other words. I heard

348

her laugh, once. It was a merry, unfettered sound that reminded me not to hold to stereotypes.

'Go ahead,' she says.

I tell her everything, the big picture as well as the specifics of the Langstrom trust.

'So the lawyer says we need a subpoena to compel him,' I finish. 'He says he'll cooperate as long as it "legally sets aside his obligations to comply with the rules of privilege."'

'Right,' she replies. 'That's where you have a problem.'

'What?'

'There's no legal grounds for a subpoena to compel yet.'

'You're kidding, right?'

'No. At this moment, all you have is a closed case. A murder-suicide. Following that, you have an anonymous philanthropist who decides to set up a trust to care for the home and for Sarah. But there's no crime established yet, right?'

'Not officially,' I admit.

'Okay. Next question: Is there any way to establish that the trust itself is an ongoing criminal enterprise? Does its existence assist, or was it set up to assist, in the commission of a crime or fraud?'

'That might be more difficult.'

'Then you have a problem.'

I chew my lip, thinking. 'Ellen, the only information we really need is the name of the client. We need to know who he is. Does that help?'

'Gibbs is claiming privilege on that because the client requested confidentiality of identity?'

'That's right.'

'That won't hold up. If you can prove it's probable the client has information vital to an ongoing investigation, I can get you that name.'

'I gotcha.'

'It has to be real, though. Start by finding something that changes the Langstroms' murder-suicide to good old-fashioned double murder. Once you have that, the trust becomes a logical avenue of investigation, and we can compel Gibbs to reveal the identity of his client.' The tone of her voice changes, friendlier, less crisp. 'I'm giving it to you straight, Smoky. Gibbs might have seemed helpful, but that little phrase he dropped on you about "legally setting aside his rules to comply with privilege"? It's a bear.'

I want to argue, but I know it's a waste of time. Ellen is a solver. She thinks in the direction of *how could we,* not *you can't because.* If she's saying it, she's saying it because it's so. I sigh, resigned.

'Gotcha. I'll get back to you.'

I hang up and dial Callie.

'Overworked Incorporated,' she answers. 'How can I help you?'

I smile.

'How is it going there?'

'Nothing to brag about yet, but we're taking it slow. We're still processing the front of the house.'

I fill her in on the day from where our paths diverged. I begin with Gibbs, continue with Nicholson, and end with Ellen. She's quiet for a moment after I finish, digesting this.

'This has been quite the forty-eight hours, even for you.'

'You can say that again.'

'Well, call it quits then. Gene and I are here. James is off being disagreeable somewhere. Bonnie is waiting at Alan and Elaina's. If you're not going to listen to me and get a dog, honey-love, then at least go home and see your daughter.'

I smile again. Callie is Callie – she can almost always make me smile.

'Fine,' I say. 'But call me if you find anything.'

'I kind of promise to maybe do that,' she quips. 'Now go away.'

I hang up and sit back, closing my eyes for a moment. Callie's right. It's been an insane few days. Singing, blood-covered sixteen-year-olds. The terrible diary.

And the one that hits home, suddenly. My hands tremble against each other. I bite my lower lip, using the pain to fight back tears.

A man killed himself in front of me today, Matt. Looked at me, spoke to me, and then put a gun in his mouth and pulled the trigger. His blood was on my face.

I didn't know Dave Nicholson. It didn't matter. He wasn't in that category that Kirby had talked about. He wasn't 'other.' He was one of us, all human, and I can't help mourning him.

I hear footsteps on the carpet, and I swipe my hand across my eyes. A knock, and Alan pokes his head in.

'I got your friendly neighborhood killer off to her car.'

'How does home sound? At least for a little while?'

He thinks about it. Sighs.

'For a little while, yeah. That's a great idea.'

41

I told Alan I'd meet him at his house; I have one other stop to make.

I drive to the hospital through more rain, and that's fine, because I'm raining inside. It's nothing heavy, just a light but continuous drizzle. This is a part of the job, I reflect. The internal weather. Home and family is sunshine, most of the time. Work is almost always rain. Sometimes it's thunder and lightning, sometimes it's just a drizzle, but it's always rain.

I realized some time ago that I don't love my job. It's not that I dislike it – far from it. But it's not something to love. It's something to do because you have to. Because it's in your blood. Good, bad, or indifferent, you do it because you don't have a choice.

Except now you do have a choice, don't you? Maybe there's more sunshine to be found at Quantico, yes?

Even so.

I reach the hospital parking lot and park and resolve, as I race through the rain to the front doors, to be quick. It's almost seven o'clock, and I feel the need for a heavy dose of Elaina and Bonnie. Some sunshine.

When I get to the room, Kirby is there, sitting in a chair outside the door, reading one of those trashy gossip tabloids. She looks up at the sound of my footsteps. Those leopard eyes flash for a moment before she hides them behind a twinkle and a smile.

'Hey, boss-woman,' she says.

'Hi, Kirby. How is she?'

'I introduced myself. I had to do some talking, let me tell you. She wanted to be sure I could kill things. I had to convince her, or she wanted me gone. I convinced her.'

'Okay.'

'Good' or 'Great' doesn't seem appropriate.

'That's a fucked-up child, Smoky Barrett,' Kirby says. Her voice is soft, cozened perhaps by a hint of regret. It's a new sound, and it makes me consider her in a new light.

Kirby seems to sense this. She smiles and shrugs. 'I like her.' She turns back to her paper. 'Go on in. I need to find out what's happening with Prince William. I'd jump his royal bones in a heartbeat.'

This yanks a grin from me. I open the door and enter the room. Sarah's lying in bed, looking through the window. I don't see evidence of any books, and the TV's off. I wonder if this is all she does all day, if she just lies here and stares out at the parking lot. She turns to see me as I come in.

'Hi,' she says, and smiles.

'Hi yourself,' I reply, smiling back.

Sarah has a good smile. It's not pure like it should be – she's been through too much – but it gives me hope. It shows that she's still herself inside.

I pull up a chair next to her bed and sit down.

'So what do you think about Kirby?' I ask.

'She's . . . different.'

I grin at this. It's a concise and perfect description.

'Do you like her?'

'Sure, I guess. I like that she's not afraid of anything, and that she chooses to do this kind of thing. You know – dangerous stuff. She told me not to feel guilty if she gets killed.'

This is enough to get rid of my grin.

'Yeah. Well, she'll protect you, Sarah. And she'll protect the people who live in the home you're going to tomorrow too.'

She frowns. 'No foster home. I need to go to the group home. He doesn't kill people there.'

That's true, I think. 'Do you know why that is, Sarah?'

'Maybe. I think it's because I don't care about anyone at the group home. And I think it's because he knows just living there is bad. I mean, it is – the group home sucks. Girls have been beaten and molested and . . .' She waves a hand. 'You get the idea. I think it's enough for him that he knows I'm there *because* of him.'

'I see.'

I sit back for a moment, considering. I'm trying to choose my words, which is hard, because I'm really only realizing how I feel about this right now, myself. I love Elaina. And there is Bonnie, who stays at Alan and Elaina's while I am at work. A not-small, very selfish part of me wants to say: *Yes! I agree! You need to go to a group home. People die around you!*

But then I feel a great stubbornness rise up in me at that. The same stubbornness that kept me from moving out of the home I'd been raped in, that my family had died in.

'You can't give in to fear,' I say to her. 'And you're going to have to accept help from others. This is different than all the other times, Sarah. We know what he is. We believe he exists. And we're taking steps to protect ourselves and you from him. The man and woman you're going to live with know what we're dealing with, and have chosen to take you in anyway. And you're going to have Kirby to watch over you, don't forget that.'

Her eyes are downcast. She's struggling with this.

'I don't know.'

'You don't have to know, Sarah,' I say, my voice soft. 'You're a child. You came to me and asked for my help. Now you're getting it.'

She sighs, a long, ragged sigh. Her eyes come back up to meet mine and they look grateful.

'Okay. Are you sure they'll be safe?'

I shake my head. 'No. I'm not sure. There's no way to be one hundred percent certain. I thought my family was safe, but they died anyway. The point isn't to have a guarantee. It's to do everything you can, and not let fear run your life.' I point toward the door. 'I have a pretty lethal bodyguard out there, and she's going to go everywhere you do. And I have a team of the best – the absolute best – hunting for The Stranger. That's all I can offer you.'

'So you know, then? For sure, that he's real?'

'Yes. One hundred percent.'

The relief runs through her in a full-body shudder, startling me. It resembles the body language of disbelief. I realize there might be some of that mixed in there.

She puts a hand against her forehead. 'Wow.' She touches her cheeks with the palms of both hands, like someone trying to hold themselves together. 'Wow. Sorry. It's hard to come to terms with after all this time.'

'I understand.'

She turns to me. 'Did you go inside my house?'

'Yes.'

'Did you –' Her face crumples. 'Did you see what he *did*?'

She starts to cry. I go over and take her in my arms.

'Did you see what he *did*?'

'I saw,' I say, and stroke her hair.

42

Elaina had cooked dinner, and Bonnie and I stayed to eat. Elaina worked her usual magic, turning the dining room into a place of merriment. Alan and I had been somber upon arrival; by the time dessert arrived, we'd laughed more than once and I felt loosened up and happy.

Alan had opted for a final try at chess with Bonnie. I was pretty sure it was going to be a fruitless endeavor. Elaina and I left them to it and worked together in the kitchen, a slow and amiable rinsing of dishes and filling of the dishwasher.

Elaina poured us both a glass of red wine and we sat at the island in the kitchen together and didn't say anything for a little bit. I heard Alan grumble, and imagined Bonnie smiling in reply.

'Let's talk about Bonnie's schooling,' Elaina says, out of the blue. 'I have a suggestion.'

'Uh, sure. Go ahead.'

She swirls the wine around in her glass. 'I've been thinking about this for a while. Bonnie has to go back to school, Smoky.'

'I know.' I sound, and feel, a little defensive.

'I'm not criticizing. I'm aware of all the circumstances. Bonnie needed time to arrive, to grieve, to normalize a little. You too. I think that time has come and gone, though, and my concern now is that your fear is the real barrier.'

My first instinct is to get angry and deny, deny, deny. But Elaina's right. It's been six months. I've been a mother before, I know the drill, and yet, in that time, I haven't gotten immunization records for Bonnie, or found her a dentist, or sent her to school. When I step back from the day-to-day and view it as a whole, I'm dismayed.

I've spun a cocoon for Bonnie and me. It's spacious, it is lit by love, but it has a fatal flaw: Its architecture was inspired by fear. I put a hand to my forehead.

'God. How could I have let this go on so long?'

Elaina shakes her head. 'No, no, no. No blame, no shame. We review our faults, we accept the fact of them, we change for the better. That's called responsibility, and it's a lot more valuable than beating yourself up. Responsibility is active, it improves things. Blame just makes you feel bad.'

I stare at my friend, dumbfounded as always by her ability to put words to the simple and the true.

'All right,' I manage. 'But I have to say, Elaina, I am afraid. God, the thought of her out there in the world . . .'

She interrupts me. 'I'm thinking homeschooling. And I'm thinking that's something I'd really enjoy doing.'

I stare at her, dumbfounded again. Homeschooling had occurred to me, of course, but I had dismissed it as I had no way to implement it. But Elaina-as-teacher . . . I realize it's a perfect solution. It deals with, well, *everything*. Bonnie the inquisitive and Bonnie the mute, equally.

Don't forget Smoky the fearful and Smoky the neglectful.

'Really? You'd want to do that?'

She smiles. 'No, I'd love to do that. I researched it on the Web, and it's not that hard.' She shrugs. 'I love her like I love you, Smoky. You're both family. Alan and I aren't going to have children of our own, and that's okay. It just means I have to find other ways to have children in my life. This is one of those ways.'

'And Sarah?' I ask.

She nods. 'And Sarah. This is one of the things I'm good at,

Smoky. Dealing with children, with people, who have been hurt. So I want to do that. The same way you want to chase after killers, and probably for the same reasons: because you need to. Because you're good at it.'

I ponder the echo she gives to my earlier thoughts, and smile at her.

'I think it's a great idea.'

'Well, good.' She gives me a kind look. 'I'm pushing you on this because I know you. As long as you're not hiding from the truth of things, you won't let Bonnie down. It's just not who you are.'

'Thank you.'

It's all I can think of to say, but I can tell from her smile that she gets it as I meant it.

What about the deception, here? If you go to Quantico, if they aren't enough to give you the 'happiness' you think you need (and how selfish and ungrateful is that, anyway?), then you'll be taking a child away from Elaina. Elaina, who's never gotten to be a mom even though you and I both know she'd be better at it than anyone we know, present company included.

Even so, I think, and for now, the voice goes quiet.

We sip our wine and smile as we listen to Alan's grumbling about being beaten at chess by a girl.

It's nine-thirty and Bonnie and I are back home, foraging through the kitchen together in search of munchies. She's let me know that she wants to watch some television, and made it clear that she understands I want to continue reading Sarah's diary.

I find a jar of olives and Bonnie grabs a bag of Cheetos. We head into the living room and curl into our respective, well-worn spots on the couch. I pop the cap of the olive jar and bite into an olive, feeling the salty taste of it burst into my mouth.

'Did Elaina talk to you?' I ask her, talking around the olive. 'About homeschooling?'

She nods. *Yep.*

'What do you think about that?'

She smiles and nods.

I think it's just fine, she's saying. I smile.

'Cool. Did she tell you about Sarah too?'

Another nod, more somber this time, layered with meaning. I understand.

'Yeah,' I reply, nodding myself. 'She's in bad shape. How are you with that?'

She waves her hand, a dismissive gesture.

So not a problem it's not worth asking about, that wave says.

I'm not selfish, that wave says.

'Okay,' I say, smiling, hoping the smile shows her that I love her.

My phone rings. I check the caller ID and answer.

'Hello, James.'

'VICAP requests are in. Nothing yet, but maybe by the morning. The program on Michael Kingsley's computer continues to defy all attempts to unlock it. I'm home, going to reread the diary.'

I fill him in on the day. He's silent afterward. Thinking.

'You're right,' he says. 'It's all connected somehow. We need to get the information on the grandfather, that case from the seventies, Nicholson.'

'No kidding.'

I look at my trusty notes, reviewing what I've written.

I grab the PERPETRATOR AKA 'THE STRANGER' page.

Methodology:

I add:

Continues to communicate to us. Communication is in puzzles. Why? Why not just say what he wants to say?

I consider this.

Because he doesn't want us to understand immediately? To buy time?

> Attacked Cathy Jones, but let her live so she could deliver a
> message.
>   Took David Nicholson's daughter hostage for two reasons:
> so that Nicholson would steer the Langstrom investigation, and
> so that Nicholson could deliver another message. Risky.
>   Message from Jones — her badge and the phrase: 'Symbols
> are only symbols.'
>   Message from Nicholson — 'It's the man behind the symbol,
> not the symbol, that's important,' followed by his suicide.
>   Why did Nicholson have to die? Answer: because his
> connection goes deeper than the Langstrom investigation.
> Vengeance.

I reread what I've just written.

I'm just spinning my wheels here.

I put the pages aside. They're not going to help me anymore tonight. I grab the diary pages and get comfortable.

I think, as I start reading, that I'm beginning to understand how Sarah's story fits into the bigger picture, not for The Stranger, but for her.

She's telling us what happened to her. That is a microcosm, a way of understanding the story of all those who've been ruined and harmed by The Stranger's actions. If we understand her pain, her story says, then we understand the Russian girl, Cathy Jones, the Nicholsons.

If we cry for her, then we cry for them. And we remember.

I turn the page and continue reading.

Sarah's Story

Part Four

43

Some people are just good. Do you know what I mean? Maybe they don't have special or exciting jobs. Maybe they're not the most beautiful or the most handsome, but they're just, well, good.

Desiree and Ned were like that.

They were good.

'Stop it, Pumpkin,' Sarah scolded.

The dog was trying to stick his head in between her lap and the table, hoping to catch falling crumbs or *(hallelujah!)* actual pieces of food. Sarah shoved the dog's monstrous noggin away.

'I don't think he's going to listen. That dog loves cake, don't ask me why,' Ned said. 'Come on, Pumpkin.'

The pit bull left with great reluctance, stealing glances back at the cake on the table as he was ordered into the backyard. Ned returned and resumed punching candles through the frosting.

Sarah had come to love Ned, just as Desiree had promised. He was a tall, lanky man, a little on the quiet side, but with eyes full of smiles. He always wore the same clothes: button-up flannel shirt, blue jeans, hiking boots. He kept his hair a little longer than was in vogue, he was inclined to meander, and had a slight scruffiness that was endearing; it spoke of a vague absent-mindedness when it came to caring for his own appearance. Sarah had seen him get angry, both at her and at Desiree, but she had never felt endangered. She knew that Ned would cut off his own hands before he would ever hit either of them.

'Nine candles, gee-whiz,' he said, rueful. 'Better start checking for gray hairs.'

Sarah smiled. 'You're such a dork, Ned.'

'So I've heard.'

The last candle was placed just as Desiree came through the front door. Sarah noticed that she was flushed, excited.

She's really happy about something.

Desiree was carrying a wrapped present, a large rectangular something, and she bustled into the kitchen, leaning the present up against the wall.

'Is that it?' Ned asked, nodding toward the present.

Desiree smiled and glowed. 'Yep. I wasn't sure I was going to be able to get it. I can't wait until you see it, Sarah.'

Sarah was mystified, in that good, birthday kind of way.

'Cake's all ready?' Desiree asked.

'I just put the last candle on.'

'Well, let me wash my face and cool down and we'll have a birthday!'

Sarah smiled, nodded, watched Desiree hurry off, towing Ned behind her.

She closed her eyes. It had been a good year. Ned and Desiree were great. They adored her from the start, and after a month or two of this as a constant, Sarah tossed away the last of her distrust and adored them back. Ned was away a lot, as Desiree had first told her, but he made up for it when he was home, always kind, always attentive. Desiree herself was . . . well . . . in Sarah's secret place, in the most guarded part of her heart, Sarah realized that she was beginning to love her foster-mother.

She opened her eyes, looked at the cake, at the presents on the table and the one against the wall.

I could be happy here. Am happy here.

Not everything was perfect. Sarah still had nightmares every now and then. She'd wake up some mornings weighed down with a sadness that had come out of nowhere. And although she liked her school, she'd rebuffed offers of friendship, not by refusing them outright, but by simply never following up on them. She wasn't ready for that, not yet.

Witch Watson had shown up a lot at first, but only once in the last nine months, which suited Sarah just fine. Cathy Jones had stopped by a few times, and seemed to be truly gratified that Sarah was doing well.

Sarah had long ago accepted a place in Desiree's arms when comfort was needed. The one thing she still hadn't shared was her story about The Stranger. She didn't think Desiree would believe her. Sometimes, she wasn't sure she believed it herself. Maybe Cathy had been right. Maybe she had been confused.

She shook these thoughts from her head. Today was her birthday, and she planned to enjoy it.

Ned and Desiree came back.

'Ready for candles?' Desiree asked Sarah.

Sarah grinned. 'Yeah!'

Ned had a lighter, and he lit each candle. They sang a raucous, somewhat off-key 'Happy Birthday.'

'Make a wish, honey, and blow!' Desiree cried.

Sarah closed her eyes.

I wish . . . I could stay here for good.

She took a deep breath, opened her eyes, and blew out every flame.

Ned and Desiree clapped.

'I always knew you were full of hot air,' Ned joked.

'So, do you want to eat cake first, or open your presents?'

Sarah could tell that Desiree was bursting for her to open the mystery present.

'Presents first.'

Desiree snatched the rectangle from its place against the wall and handed it to Sarah.

Sarah hefted it. It was big, but it was light. A painting, or maybe a photograph. She began to tear the paper away. When she saw the top edge of the frame, her heart jumped.

Could it . . . ?

She tore the rest of the paper off as fast as her hands would allow. She saw what it was, and stopped breathing. Her chest hurt.

It was the painting her mother had done for her. The baby in the woods, the face in the clouds. Sarah looked up at Desiree, wordless.

'I could tell how much you loved that painting when you told me about it, honey. And you know what? It turns out that Cathy Jones packed away some of the stuff in your bedroom after they . . . well, after the police were done with things. Just some photos and toys and some other stuff. She kept it in storage for you so it wouldn't get lost. That is the one, right?'

Sarah nodded, still wordless. Her heart was thudding in her chest. Her eyes burned.

'Oh my God,' she finally said. 'Thank you so so so so much. I —' She looked at Desiree, who smiled, at Ned, whose eyes softened. 'I don't know what to say.'

Desiree's hand touched Sarah's hair, moved a lock of it back behind the young girl's ear. 'You're welcome, honey.' Desiree was beaming.

Ned coughed, and held out an envelope. 'This is the other part of that present, Sarah. It's a . . . well, a kind of gift certificate.'

Sarah wiped the tears from her cheeks and took the envelope. She still felt overwhelmed, a little bit giddy, and her hands trembled as she opened it. Inside was a simple white card that said *Happy Birthday* on the front. She flipped the card open and read the inside.

Redeemable by Sarah, it said, *for one adoption.*

Sarah's mouth fell open in shock. Her head snapped up and she saw that while Desiree and Ned were smiling, they looked nervous too. Almost scared.

'You don't have to, if you don't want to,' Ned said, his voice soft. 'But if you do, Desiree and I would like to adopt you permanently.'

366

What's happening to me? Why can't I talk?

She felt as if she was being rolled by an ocean wave. She was a boat hitting the top of a swell and then sliding back down the trough, only to be picked back up again.

What's wrong?

It came to her, a sudden clarity. This was the part of her that she'd kept buried, hidden, locked in a vault. A place filled with *Nothings* and *Puppysheads*. Frozen agony, thawed in an instant. It was crashing through her inner barriers and it was filled with thunder and thorns.

She couldn't speak, but she managed to nod at them, and then she began to wail. It was a wordless, terrible sound. It caused Ned's eyes to shine and Desiree's arms to open. Sarah fled into them and wept three years of tears.

44

Sarah and Desiree were lounging on the couch while Ned muttered in the home office as he paid the bills. Cake had been eaten. Even Pumpkin had gotten a lick of frosting that Sarah had snuck to him. He was curled up on the floor, his feet twitching as he dreamed a doggy dream.

'I'm so happy that you want to stay with us, Sarah,' Desiree said.

Sarah looked at her foster-mother. Desiree *looked* happy. The happiest that Sarah had ever seen her. This filled her heart with joy. Sarah was wanted. No, more than that – she was *needed*. Ned and Desiree needed *her* to make their life complete.

The fact of this filled a void inside her that had seemed bottomless. A soul cavern stuffed with darkness and pain.

'It was my wish,' Sarah said.

'What do you mean?'

'My birthday wish. What I wished for before I blew out the candles on my cake.'

Desiree raised her eyebrows in surprise. 'Wow. Is that spooky, or what?'

Sarah smiled. 'I think it's kind of magic.'

'Magic.' Desiree nodded. 'I like that.'

'Desirce?' Sarah watched the floor, struggling with something.

'What is it, honey?'

'I – is it weird that this makes me miss my mom and dad? I mean – I'm so happy about this. Why would it make me sad?'

Desiree sighed and touched Sarah's cheek. 'Oh, honey. I think . . .' She paused, contemplative. 'I think it's because we're not them. I mean, we love you, and you've made us feel whole, like a family again, but we're not a replacement for your mom and dad. We're a new thing in your heart, not a substitute for them. Does that make sense?'

'I guess so.' She gave Desiree a probing look. 'So does it make you sad too? About your baby, I mean.'

'A little. Mostly it makes me happy.'

Sarah thought about this.

'It mostly makes me happy too.'

She moved over so she could be cuddled by her new mother. They turned on the television, and Ned came in not long after and they all laughed together even though the shows weren't that funny. Sarah recognized the easy, comfortable rhythm.

This is home.

'Here?' Ned asked.

Sarah nodded. 'Right there.'

Ned pounded the nail into the wall, and hung the painting. He stood back, giving it a critical eye. 'Looks straight.'

The painting faced the foot of her bed, just as it had in her old bedroom. Sarah couldn't take her eyes off it.

'Your mother was talented, Sarah. It's really beautiful.'

'She used to make something for me every year, for my birthday. This one was my favorite.' She turned her head to Ned. 'Thank you for helping bring it back to me.'

Ned smiled and averted his eyes. He was shy about praise. Sarah could tell he was happy.

'You're welcome. You should really thank Cathy.' He frowned, coughed once. 'And, uh, thanks for . . . you know. Letting us adopt you.' His eyes came up to meet hers. 'I want you to know that it's something we both wanted. It means as much to me as it does to Desiree.'

Sarah studied the scruffy, kindhearted truck driver. She knew he'd always be awkward about expressing his love, but she also knew that it was something she could be certain of.

'I'm glad,' she said. 'Because I feel the same way. I love Desiree, Ned. But I love you too.'

A spark jumped in his gray eyes at her words. He looked both wounded and joyful.

'You miss your baby more than Desiree does, don't you?'

Ned stared at her. Blinked once and looked away. His eyes found the painting. He continued to look at it as he spoke.

'After Diana died, I almost quit living. I couldn't move. Couldn't think. Couldn't work. I felt like the world had ended for me.' He frowned. 'My dad was a drunk, and I promised myself that I'd never touch the stuff. But after a month of trying to stop hurting, I went out and bought a bottle of scotch.' He looked at Sarah, smiled one of his gentle smiles. 'It was Desiree that came to the rescue. Grabbed the bottle, broke it in the sink, and then pushed me and yelled at me until I broke down and did what I needed to do all along.'

'She made you cry,' Sarah said.

'That's right. And I did. I cried and I cried, and then I cried some more. And the next morning, I started living again.' He spread his hands. 'Desiree loved me enough to save me even when she was hurting too. So the answer to your question is no. Desiree misses Diana more than I do, not less. Because she's got more ability to love than anyone I've ever known.' He looked uncomfortable and awkward again. 'Anyway, I guess it's time for you to go to bed.'

'Ned?'

'What is it, honey?'

'Do you love me back?'

The moment hung in silence. Ned smiled, a beautiful, brilliant smile that swept his awkwardness away.

That's Mommy's smile, Sarah marveled. Sun on the roses.

He walked over and gave Sarah a fierce hug, filled with his strength and his softness and a father's roaring promise to protect.

'You *bet* I do.'

A loud 'woof' broke the hug. Sarah looked down and laughed. Pumpkin was there, staring up at them.

'Yeah, it's bedtime, puppyhead,' she said.

Ned gave the dog a faux-scowl. 'Still a traitor, I see,' he said.

Pumpkin used to sleep in Ned and Desiree's room. He'd slept in Sarah's bed from the first night.

Sarah helped the dog up onto her bed. She climbed under the covers. Ned gazed down at her.

'Want me to get Desiree to tuck you in?' he asked.

'No, that's okay. You can do it.'

Sarah knew that Ned would like these words. She liked meaning them. She loved him, he loved her back. Him tucking her in was just fine. At home, it had usually been Daddy who'd said good night. She missed this ritual.

'Door open a crack?' he asked.

'Yes, please.'

'Good night, Sarah.'

'Good night, Ned.'

He took one last look at the painting he'd hung for her, and shook his head.

'That's really something.'

Sarah was dreaming of her father. There were no words in the dream, just him, her, and smiles. The dream was filled with a simple happiness. The air trembled, filled by a perfect note stroked from a handmade violin.

The note was an impossibility of perfection, a dead-on expression of all the things the heart could contain, and it could only be heard in a dream. Sarah didn't know who it was that played it, and she didn't care. She looked into her father's eyes and smiled, and he looked back and smiled and the note became the wind and the sun and the rain.

The music ended when her father spoke. You couldn't speak and hear the note. It had to stand alone.

'Did you hear that?' he asked.

'What, Daddy?'

'Sounds like . . . growling.'

Sarah frowned. 'Growling?' She cocked her head and strained to hear, and yes, she could hear it now, a low rumble, like a muscle car idling at a stoplight. 'What do you think it is?'

But he was gone, along with the wind and the sun and the rain. No more smiles, now. This was dark clouds and thunder. She looked up at the sky in her dream and the clouds growled, louder this time, so loud they shook her bones and –

Sarah woke up to Pumpkin, who stared at the door of her room and growled. Sarah stroked the dog's head.

'What is it, Pumpkin?'

The dog's ears twitched at the sound of her voice, but its eyes remained focused on the door. The rumble was becoming louder, a roar in the making.

The next sound Sarah heard sent the cold of space spiking through her, a cold that froze on touch, that took the warmth at her core and turned it into a glacier.

'"I never saw a wild thing sorry for itself . . ."' the voice said.

And the door to her room flew open.

And Pumpkin roared.

'Happy birthday, Sarah.'

I made myself tell it all when it came to my mom and dad. They deserved that. It's where things began, after all.

I can't do it with Desiree and Ned. I can't. Not even in third person. I think it's enough that you know who they were, the kind of people they were, the goodness in them.

He killed them, that's all you need to know. He shot Ned dead and he beat Desiree to death in front of me and he did it all because I loved them and they loved me back and because my pain is his justice, whatever that means.

If you really want to know what it looked like, what it felt like, then do this: Think of something ugly, the ugliest thing you can think of – like roasting a baby on an open fire – and then chuckle about it. Then realize what you're chuckling at, and what that means, and you've taken a turn into what I felt like then.

He did it to open up a big blackness inside of me, to kill hope and to show me how dangerous it is for me to love someone. It worked. For a minute, while I was with Desiree and Ned, I thought I might get to be part of a family. I've never felt that way again.

But God . . . Desiree fought him. She fought him for me, for all the good it did her.

God . . .

I really need to stop saying that. I mean, come on, that's one thing I learned for sure, that night.

There is no God.

He killed them and I watched and I died with them, but I didn't really die, I lived and wished that I'd died, but life went on and I did the only thing left to do.

I called Cathy Jones.

I called her and she came. She was the only one who always came. She also believed me after that night, and she was the only one who ever did that too.

I love Cathy, by the way. I always will. She did the best she could.

45

'You're bad luck, princess,' Karen Watson said as they drove away from Ned and Desiree's. 'Some people just *have* bad luck. Yours rubs off on the people around you.'

Sarah sneered. 'Maybe I'll get really lucky someday, and my bad luck will rub off on you, Ms Watson.'

Karen glanced over at Sarah. Her eyes narrowed. 'Keep talking like that and it'll be a long time before I let you back into any foster home.'

Sarah turned back to the side window. 'I don't care.'

'Really? Fine. Then you can stay in a group home till you're eighteen.'

'I said I don't care.'

Sarah kept her gaze fixed on the scenery rolling by. Karen felt dismissed. This made her angry.

Who the hell did this kid think she was? Didn't she understand what a burden she was?

Screw it. She'd dismiss Sarah right back.

'You can rot in there then, for all I care.'

Sarah didn't reply. Karen Watson had gotten under her skin, as always, but only for a moment. The numbness had settled back in, bringing that thousand-pound weight along with it.

Sarah had been taken to an emergency room and examined.

She had a mild concussion (whatever that was), which meant she wasn't supposed to go to sleep. Everything else was bruised and hurt, but no major damage had been done. Not on the outside, at least.

Ned, Desiree, Pumpkin. Mommy, Daddy, Buster.

Your love is death.

She was starting to believe that this was true. Everyone she'd ever loved was gone forever.

A twinge of uncertainty.

Except for Cathy. And Theresa. And maybe Doreen, if she was still alive.

Sarah sighed.

Theresa was in jail. Surely that was enough for The Stranger, for now. She could decide what to do about her foster-sister when she got out. As for Cathy, she was a policewoman, she should be able to keep herself safe, right? Right?

She'd have to worry about that later. She had other things to concentrate on, for now.

Sarah had learned the lessons of the group home from her last stay there. She had no intention of starting out at the bottom of the food chain again.

Janet was still skinny, and still running things at the home. She remained oblivious to the perils of the place. Janet was the worst kind of do-gooder: one who was incapable of recognizing evil. She gave Sarah a sympathetic nod.

'Hi, Sarah.'

'Hi.'

'I know what happened. Are you in a lot of pain?'

The answer was yes, but Sarah shook her head.

'I'm okay. I'd just like to lie down.'

Janet nodded. 'You can't go to sleep, though. You know that?'

'Yeah.'

'Do you need help with your bag?'

'No, thanks.'

Janet led her down the familiar hallways. Nothing had changed in a year.

Probably nothing has changed in the last ten years.

'Here you go. Only two doors down from your old room.'

'Thanks, Janet.'

'Sure.' The skinny woman turned to walk away.

'Janet? Is Kirsten still here?'

Janet stopped and looked back at Sarah. 'Kirsten was killed by another girl three months ago. They got into a fight and things got out of hand.'

Sarah stared at Janet and swallowed once.

'Oh,' she managed. 'Okay.'

The skinny woman looked worried. 'Are you going to be all right?'

Sarah had a hundred pounds of iron sitting on the top of her head.

Numbness. Hug it tight.

'I'm fine.'

Sarah had unpacked her things and settled into her bunk to wait. She'd arrived in the late afternoon; the dorm would remain pretty much empty until early evening. That's when she knew she'd have to make her move.

Her head still ached, but at least she wasn't nauseous anymore. Sarah hated barfing.

Nobody likes it, dummy.

Someone who'd had a more normal life might worry about talking to themselves so much. The thought never occurred to Sarah; when you were alone as much as she was, you talked to yourself to keep from *going* crazy, not because you were.

Numbness cloaked her, soaked her, bonded with her DNA. Sarah felt that she'd crossed a threshold of pain. Sadness, grief – these emotions had to be suppressed. They'd grown too large to let roam free. They'd eat her up if she let them out of their cages.

Other emotions were allowed. Like anger. Like rage. She could feel them building inside her. A well had been dug in her soul and it was filling up with darkish, violent things. A beast of a dog lapped at the well and wouldn't stop growling. She wondered how long she could keep it leashed, or if she could at all.

With all of it had come a tectonic shift in pragmatism. Survival was her god. All else was illusion.

I'm changing. Just like he wanted me to.

How?

I think I could kill someone now if I had to. I couldn't have done that when I was six.

Happy birthday.

She twirled a strand of hair in her fingers and smiled an empty smile.

I broke a girl's finger and I took her bunk, and that was that. I was top dog of the room again, queen of all I surveyed.

Hey, don't make that face.

I'm not proud of what I did, but I did what I had to.

Besides, I have a lot more in common with that 'me' at nine than I do with the 'me' at six. The 'me' at six is long gone and buried deep.

46

When I look back and write this, I think Cathy becomes my mirror. A way to look at how I was through someone else's eyes.

I wonder: Did she think these things? Or am I putting my own words in her mouth? Maybe a little bit of both? Maybe Cathy was Cathy, but in these pages, Cathy is also the me-now looking back at the me-then.

Hea-vy, man . . .

Cathy was dismayed by what she saw happening with Sarah. But what else was new?

It was Sarah's eleventh birthday. Cathy had come by with a simple offering – a cupcake and a single candle. Sarah had smiled at this, but Cathy could tell she was being polite.

What bothered Cathy the most was Sarah's eyes. They weren't open and expressive they way they'd once been. They were full of walls and blank spaces and watchfulness. The eyes of a poker player, or a prisoner.

Cathy was familiar with eyes like this; she saw them on hardened street-hookers and career criminals. They said: *I know how things work, I'm watching you,* and *Don't even think about taking what's mine.*

Cathy had recognized other changes over the last two years. She knew that Sarah was the 'head girl' of her dorm and she had a pretty good guess as to how that had come about. The other girls deferred to Sarah. Sarah's attitude toward them was dismissive. It was prison mentality, the rule of power and violence. Sarah seemed to have learned it well.

Why are you surprised? This place is might-makes-right in spades.

Cathy was frustrated by her own inability to provide hope. She hadn't been able to convince anyone else of her belief in Sarah's story of The Stranger. Truth be told, lying in bed at night, she wasn't sure she'd completely convinced herself. She'd tried, she'd failed, and while Sarah had told her it was no big deal, Cathy knew this was a bald-faced lie. It mattered.

Cathy had been doing what she could. She'd gotten copies of the case files on the deaths of Sarah's parents, and the murders of Ned and Desiree. She'd spent many nights after work poring over them, looking for hints and inconsistencies. She'd even found some. In this way, at least, she and Sarah still connected. Life came into those hard eyes when they discussed the cases. The fact that Cathy believed her was important to Sarah. It mattered.

But we're losing you, aren't we, Sarah? This place and your life are killing you off. Right in front of my eyes.

'I have some news about Theresa,' Cathy said.

A spark of interest.

'What?'

'She's getting paroled in three weeks.'

Sarah looked away. 'That's nice.' Her voice sounded faint.

'She wants to see you.'

'No!' The word snapped out with a vehemence that startled the cop.

Cathy waited, chewed her lip.

'Do you mind if I ask why?'

All the blankness and hardness and distance vanished, replaced by a naked desperation that made Cathy's heart ache.

'Because of *him*,' Sarah whispered, her voice urgent. 'The Stranger. If he knows I love her, then he'll kill her.'

'Sarah, I –'

Sarah reached across the table, grabbing Cathy's hands with her own. 'Promise me, Cathy. Promise me that you'll make her stay away.'

The cop stared at the eleven-year-old for a long moment before nodding. 'Okay, Sarah,' she said in a quiet voice. 'Okay. What do you want me to tell her?'

'Tell her I don't want to see her while I'm in here. She'll understand.'

'You're sure?'

Sarah smiled, a tired smile. 'I'm sure.' She bit her lower lip. 'But tell her . . . it won't be long. When I get out of this place, I'll find a way to get in touch with her. A way we can be safe.'

The smile and the spark and the urgency all vanished. The blankness was back. Sarah stood up, grabbing the cupcake. 'I have to go,' she said.

'You don't want to light the candle?'

'Nope.'

Cathy watched Sarah walk away. The young girl walked straight and tall, a walk that said she was sure of herself without having to double check. She looked small to Cathy. The swagger only emphasized it.

Sarah lay back on her bunk, bit into the cupcake, and eyed the envelope. It was addressed to her, care of the group home. There was no return address, just a stamp and postmark.

It was the first piece of mail she'd ever gotten, and she didn't like it.

Just open it.

Okay. Maybe it's from Theresa.

She thought about Theresa almost every day. Sometimes she dreamed about her foster-sister, fantasy dreams where they sailed or flew away together. The places they came to were *never* dark and *always* had signs posted that proclaimed: *No Sorrow Or Monsters Allowed.*

Those dreams left Sarah wishing she could sleep forever. Theresa was the hub around which Sarah's only wheel of hope spun.

She ripped the envelope open. It contained a simple white card. On the front it said, *Thinking of you on your birthday*. She frowned and flipped up the front. Inside was drawn a picture of a domino, next to it the words *Be A Wild Thing*.

The frosting from the cupcake went sour in her mouth. A chill ran through her body from head to toe.

This is from him.

She knew it to be true. It didn't matter that he'd never sent her anything before this. It didn't need any explanation at all. It just was.

She stared at the card for a moment longer before putting it back in the envelope. She placed it under her pillow and resumed eating the cupcake.

I am turning into a Wild Thing.

Come and see me again and I'll prove it to you.

Her smile was joyless.

One nice thing, she thought, it can't get any worse. That's something.

I know what a silly thing that was to think now. Of course it could be worse. A lot worse. And it was.

Karen Watson ended up in jail. I don't really know why, but I'm not surprised. She was evil. She hated kids and she liked being able to fuck up kids' lives. She was a big old vampire, but instead of sucking blood, she sucked souls, and someone finally caught her doing it.

She made sure all the other homes I went to were bad ones. Bad people. In some places they hit me. In a few places, they touched me, and that was bad, real bad, but we won't talk about that, no way, uh-uh. I guess Theresa tried.

Even so, nothing was ever quite as bad as when Desiree and Ned died. I've thought about it a lot, and that was really the beginning of the end for me. It started with Mom and Dad and Buster, and it ended with Desiree and Ned and Pumpkin. Everything since then, good or bad, has just been me walking through a dream.

Cathy offered to adopt me once, but I didn't let her.

I was afraid, you know? That if Cathy took me in, that would be the end of her.

But Cathy disappeared later anyway. They told me she'd gotten hurt, but they wouldn't tell me how, or who'd done it. She didn't answer her phone when I called, and she never called me back.

I let that drop into the big black pool, like everything else.

That's what I call it – the big black pool. It's what's inside me. It started to fill up the day after Desiree and Ned died. It's thick and stinky and it feels like oil. But it's kind of cool too, because you can drop things that hurt into it, and they sink and disappear forever.

Cathy not calling hurt, so I dropped that into the big black pool. Bye-bye.

One thing I didn't drop into the pool was what happened to Karen Watson, when that cunt went to jail. I know, I know, cunt is the worst word ever, especially for a girl to say, but I can't help it. Karen Watson was a cunt. I mean, come on, the word was practically invented for her! I hated her, and I hoped she'd die in jail. Sometimes I dreamed about someone sticking a knife in her and cutting her stomach open, like a fish. She flopped around and screamed and bled. I always woke up smiling after I had that dream.

One day, she actually did die. Someone slit her throat, from ear to ear. I smiled till I thought my cheeks would split open. Then I cried, and The Crazy blinked a few times and it cried too. Black, watering-hole tears.

Bad water, baby, it's all bad water now.

As for me, I'd always end up back in the group home. I had a rep from before, so not too many girls tried to mess with me. I kept to myself.

Which is for the best, because I'm pretty much over, you know? I get this feeling sometimes, like I'm sitting naked at the north pole, but I'm not cold, because I can't feel anything anyway. And I'm looking down at the big black pool, watching it bubble. Every now and then, hands shoot up out of it, and sometimes I recognize them.

The Stranger left me alone for a few years. I don't know, I guess he was keeping an eye on me. So long as the homes were bad, I guess he was fine.

I got another card on my fourteenth birthday. It said, I'll be seeing you. That's all. I woke up that night screaming and I couldn't stop. I just screamed and screamed and screamed. They had to drag me off and strap me down to a bed and give me some drugs. That time I was the one that got dropped into the big black pool. Blurp. Bye-bye.

The Kingsleys decided to foster me, and I'm not sure why I didn't fight it. I'm finding it hard, these days, to feel like fighting anything. Mostly I float. I float and I shake sometimes and every now and then I talk to myself, then I go back to floating. Oh yeah – and dropping things into the big black pool. I've been spending a lot of time, lately, dropping things into it. I think I've just about got everything now. I want to be an empty room, with white walls. I'm almost there. The black death-bees have almost become the light.

I'm writing this story because it might be the last chance I have to get this all down before I drop myself into the big black pool, forever. I don't really want to go there, but it's harder and harder to keep moving every day, and The Crazy, it seems to want to come up from the watering hole a lot more often. There's something, though, a small, stubborn part of me that still remembers being six. It talks to me less and less, but when it does, it tells me to write things down, and to find a way to give it to you.

*I don't think you're going to be able to save me, Smoky Barrett. I'm afraid I've spent too much time at the watering hole, too much time writing stories I set on fire. But maybe, just maybe – you can get **him**.*

And drop him into the real big black pool.

That's about it. The last sprint on the white and crinkly.

A Ruined Life?

Pretty close, I guess.

I don't dream of my mom and dad anymore. I did have a dream about Buster the other night. It caught me by surprise. I woke up and I almost thought I could feel where his head had been, lying on my tummy.

But Buster's dead, along with the rest of them.

The biggest change is the deepest change:
I don't hope anymore.
THE END?

I finish this last line of Sarah's diary, and I put a hand to my eyes and this time I find my tears. Bonnie comes over to me and takes my other hand in hers and rubs it, offering comfort. I wipe my eyes after a moment.

'Sorry, babe,' I say. 'I read something that made me sad. Sorry.'

She gives me one of those smiles that says, *It's okay, we're alive, I'm just happy you're here with me.*

'Okay,' I say, forcing a smile. I still feel pretty bleak.

Bonnie catches my eye again. She taps her head. This one I know without having to think about it.

'You had an idea?'

She nods. Points to the wall, where a picture of Alexa hangs. Points at the ceiling above our heads. It takes me a moment.

'You had an idea about what to do with Alexa's room?'

She smiles, nods. *Yes.*

'Tell me, sweetheart.'

She indicates herself, mimes sleeping, shakes her head.

'You don't want to sleep there.'

Quick nod. *Right.*

She mimes holding something, moving it up and down in brushing motions, and, as sometimes happens, I get her full meaning in a flood and a flash.

When Bonnie had first made it clear to me that she wanted some watercolors, I was overjoyed. The therapeutic possibilities were obvious; Bonnie was mute, but perhaps she'd speak through her brush.

She painted scenes bright and scenes dark, beautiful moonlit nights, days washed through with rain and grays. There was no trend in her imagery beyond the fact that all were *vivid*, regardless of subject. My favorite, a depiction of the desert under a blazing sun, was a mix of stark beauty. There was hot, bright, yellow sand.

There was blue, forever, cloudless sky. There was a single cactus, standing alone in all that emptiness, straight and strong and tall. It didn't seem to need comfort or company. It was a confident, aloof cactus. It could take the sun and the heat and lack of water and it was fine, thank you very much, just fine. I had to wonder if it represented Bonnie.

She'd since graduated from watercolors to oils and acrylics. She spent a day each week painting, intense, her concentration almost furious. I had watched her without her knowing it, and I'd been struck by her total immersion. I could tell that the world disappeared when she painted. Her focus narrowed to the canvas in front of her, the shouting in her mind, the motion of her hand. She generally painted without stopping, a continuous dead run.

Maybe it was the act that was therapeutic. Perhaps the paintings were secondary. Maybe it was just the *doing* that was important.

Whatever the truth, the paintings were good. Bonnie was no Rembrandt, but she had talent. Her work had a vitality, a boldness that suffused each painting with agelessness.

'You want to turn Alexa's room into a studio?'

Bonnie has been painting in the library, and it's beginning to overflow with paper and canvas and mess.

She nods, happy but cautious. She reaches over to me, takes my hand, gives me a look of concern. Again, understanding, that flash and flood.

'But only if it's okay with me, huh?'

Her smile is soft. I give her one in return, touch her cheek.

'I think it's a great idea.'

She lets the caution drop away from her smile. The shine of it starts to work its way into my darker recesses.

She indicates the TV and gives me an inquisitive look. She's been watching the cartoon channel.

Want to watch with me? she's asking.

That sounds about right.

'You bet.'

I open up my arms so she can snuggle into me, and we watch together, and I try to let her sunshine banish all that internal rain. Be the cactus, I think. We got sun. To hell with the sand.

47

It's morning and I'm trying to calm Sarah down.

She'd met Elaina, and a new look of horror and terror had crossed her face. She'd started to back away, toward the door.

'No,' she says, her eyes wide, shining with unspent tears. 'No way. Not here.'

I understand what's happening. She's recognized the goodness of Elaina, understood it in a flash, and she sees Desiree and her mother and deaths yet to come.

'Sarah. Honey. Look at me,' I say, my voice soothing.

She continues to stare at Elaina.

'No way. Not her. I can't be responsible for that.'

Elaina steps forward, brushing me aside. The look on her face is a mix of compassion and pain. Her voice, when she speaks, is gentle, so gentle.

'Sarah. I want you here. Are you listening to me? I know the risks, and I want you here.'

Sarah continues to stare at Elaina, no longer speaking, but shaking her head, back and forth, back and forth.

Elaina points at her own baldness.

'See that? That was cancer. I *beat* cancer. And you know what else? Six months ago a man came and he grabbed me and Bonnie and he meant to kill us. We beat him too.' She indicates the group that's here, me, Alan, Bonnie, herself. 'We beat him together.'

'No,' Sarah moans.

Now it is Bonnie who strides forward. She looks up at me, she points to herself. I frown at her, puzzled, trying to understand. She points at herself again, and then points at Sarah. Everyone watches, transfixed. It takes me a moment, and then I get it.

'You want me to tell her about you?'

A nod.

'You sure?'

A nod.

I face Sarah. 'Bonnie's mother, Annie, was my best friend. A man – the same one who later tried to kill Elaina and Bonnie – killed Annie, right in front of Bonnie. Then he tied Bonnie to her mother's dead body. She was like that for three days. Until I found her.'

Sarah's stare is now reserved for Bonnie.

'And you know where he is now?' Alan says. 'He's dead. We're still here. We've all been through stuff, Sarah. You don't have to worry about us – let us worry about us. Let us worry about you. This is my home, and I want you here too.'

I can sense her not so much faltering as yearning. Bonnie is the one who bridges the gulf. She walks over to Sarah and takes her hand. The moment hangs and we wait it out.

Sarah's shoulders sag.

Sarah doesn't speak. She just nods. I am reminded of Bonnie, and as I think it, my foster-daughter catches my eye and gives me a sad smile.

'Let's not forget me,' Kirby says, unable to remain silent any longer. 'I'm here, and I'm loaded for bear. Giant, mutant bear.' She grins, showing all those white teeth and lets those leopard eyes flicker. 'If the cuckoo-bird shows up here, he's cuckoo for sure.'

*

There's no freshly ground coffee this morning, but at least it's stopped raining.

Everyone is here in the outer office again, facing me. No one looks as fresh as they did yesterday. Not even Callie. She's immaculate, as always, but her eyes are red-rimmed with exhaustion.

Assistant Director Jones comes through the door, his own cup of coffee in his hands. He doesn't apologize for holding us up, and none of us expect him to. He's the boss. Being late is his prerogative.

'Go ahead,' he says.

'Right,' I say. 'Let's start with you, Alan.'

I knew that Alan had come back over late last night to dig through the Langstroms' lives.

'First things first, Grandpa Langstrom. Well, he was Linda's father, so he was actually Grandpa Walker. Tobias Walker.'

'Hold it,' AD Jones says, putting down his cup of coffee. 'Did you really just say Tobias Walker?'

'Yes, sir.'

'Holy shit.'

Everyone turns to look at him. His face is grim.

'I gave you that list this morning, Agent Thorne. The police and agents who were assigned to the trafficking task force. Take a look.'

Callie scans the page in front of her. Stops.

'Tobias Walker was on the LAPD side of the task force.'

The sensation I feel running through me is overwhelming. Unreality mixed with electric excitement.

'Another name you'll recognize,' she says. 'Dave Nicholson.'

'Nicholson?' AD Jones asks, frowning. 'LAPD, big guy. Good cop. What about him?'

I give him the abridged version of yesterday's events. His shock is acute.

'Suicide?! And his daughter was taken hostage?' He goes to grab his coffee, thinks better of it, runs a hand through his hair. I can't tell if he's dismayed or enraged. Probably both.

An idea is coming toward me, running to me, big enough to blacken my mental horizon. A rising sun of realization.

'What if . . . ?'

Everyone looks at me, questioning. Everyone, I notice, but James. He's staring off, transfixed.

Seeing the same thing?

Maybe. Probably.

'Just listen,' I say. I can hear the excitement in my own voice. 'We have a task force that failed, probably due to internal corruption. We have a motive of revenge. We have some key messages. The one to Cathy Jones, along with her gold shield: *Symbols are only symbols*. The one to Nicholson: *It's the man behind the symbol, not the symbol, that's important*. Combine that with what we know – what does it tell us?'

None of them are fast enough for James. He's there, he's caught up with me. Boats and water, rivers and rain.

'He's referencing the corruption. Just because someone wears a badge, it doesn't mean they're not a bad guy. Symbols are just symbols.'

Understanding lights up Alan's eyes. 'Right, right. We missed the boat. Revenge was the motive. But it wasn't the traffickers he wanted to punish the most. That's why Vargas got off easy. He wanted the task-force members. Whoever it was that sold out that safe house and those kids.'

Silence. Everyone taking this in, everyone nodding at different times. The ring of truth.

'Sir,' I ask AD Jones, 'what do you remember about Tobias Walker?'

The Assistant Director rubs his face. 'Rumors, that's what I remember. He was even more of a dinosaur than Haliburton. Nasty guy. Racist. Carried a blackjack, that kind of thing. Really liked his phone books and rubber hoses. He was the one they looked at the hardest after the attack on the safe house.'

'Why?'

'He'd been investigated for suspected graft three times prior by

LAPD Internal Affairs. Beat it every time, but the rumors persisted, including a rumor that he was in the pockets of organized crime. Nothing anyone could ever prove. He died of lung cancer in 1983.'

'Obviously, our perp is convinced that they were more than just rumors,' James notes.

'Who else?' I say. 'What happened to Haliburton, sir?'

The Assistant Director's face goes ashen. 'In the past, I would have said he killed himself and his wife, but under the circumstances . . .'

'Do you know the details?'

'It happened in 1998. He'd been retired for quite a while. He was in his late sixties, kept himself busy doing whatever it is you do when you're retired. Probably continued dabbling with his poetry.'

'Poetry?' I interrupt.

'It was the thing that made Haliburton human. His contradiction. He was a very conservative guy. Fire-and-brimstone churchgoer, didn't trust anyone with hair past their ears, bought all his suits at Sears. That kind of thing. He was harsh and he was judgmental. Never cracked a joke. But he wrote poetry. And he didn't mind sharing it. Some of it was pretty good.'

I tell him about The Stranger's tale of an amateur poet and his wife.

'Oh man,' he says, shaking his head in disbelief. 'This just keeps getting better and better. Haliburton shot his wife and then shot himself. At least that's what we always thought.'

'What about a "student of philosophy"? Is there anyone on either of the task forces that might fit that description?'

'It doesn't ring any bells.'

'Any other untimely deaths?'

'There were three of us here. Haliburton, myself, and Jacob Stern. Stern retired to Israel in . . . sometime in the late eighties. He was another old-timer. I never heard anything about him after that. The LAPD had Walker, Nicholson, and a guy from Vice by the name of Roberto Gonzalez. We know about Walker and Nicholson – but I don't have any information on Gonzalez. He was a young cop, bilingual. From what I remember, he was decent enough.'

'We're going to have to follow up on him and Stern,' I say.

'The big question now,' Alan observes, 'is the same question as before, but we've just narrowed the playing field: Who is The Stranger, and why does he have such a hard-on for the task-force members?'

'I have another,' Callie says. She glances at AD Jones. 'No offense, sir, but why did you get to live?'

'I think the fact that you're an Assistant Director is the answer,' James says. 'I don't know that it made him cross you off his list, but it might make him save you for last. Killing an AD – that would draw a lot of attention. He might not be ready for that much scrutiny.'

'Comforting,' AD Jones replies.

'Back to Alan's question,' I say. 'Logic dictates he'd be a child who was victimized by the trafficking ring. He can't be a relative.'

'Why?' Alan asks, and then answers his own question. 'Because of the scarring on the feet.'

'Correct.'

I consider this. 'Callie, did you find anything going through the Langstrom house that might be helpful?'

'I spent a very long day and night there with Gene. We found lots of dust, but nothing forensically probative. The antidepressants Linda Langstrom had weren't prescribed by the family physician, but by a physician located on the other side of town.'

'She went out of her way to hide them,' I note.

'Yes. But she never took any of them.'

I frown. 'Does that mean anything to anyone?'

No one replies.

'James? News about the boy's computer?'

'No.'

I think, trying to come up with some magic. Nothing.

'Our most potent avenue of inquiry, then, is the trust.' I relate my conversation with Ellen. 'We need that subpoena. Today.'

'Cathy Jones can do that for you,' AD Jones says. 'She should be able to testify that the Langstroms were probably murdered by a third party. That's a priority.' He tosses his cup in the trash can and heads toward the door. 'Keep me apprised.' He stops, looks back. 'Oh and, Smoky? Catch this guy, will you? I prefer to stay breathing.'

'You heard the man,' I say. 'Callie and Alan, that goes to you guys. James, I want you to find out what, if anything, has happened to the two other names on that list. Stern and Gonzalez.'

Everyone gets into motion, hunters with the scent.

48

'Roberto Gonzalez was murdered in his home in 1997,' James intones. 'He was tortured, castrated, and his genitals were placed in his mouth.'

'Sounds like the description he gave of the "student of philosophy,"' I murmur. 'What else?'

'Stern appears to be alive and well. I alerted the Crisis Management Unit, they're going to get in touch with the Israeli authorities and put him under guard.'

'I agree with your theory about AD Jones – but why Stern? Why'd he get to live?'

James shrugs. 'It could be purely geographic. Too far away, so get to him last.'

'Maybe.' I chew on my lower lip. 'You know,' I say, 'there's another avenue we haven't even looked at.'

'What's that?'

'"Mr You Know Who." The guy Vargas mentioned in his video clip. I'm assuming he's supposed to be the man-in-charge. Wouldn't he be a prime target for The Stranger?'

'We should leave that alone for now.'

'Why?'

'Because it's a question that may never get answered. They didn't find him in 1979 with a task force. Why should we think that we'll find him today?'

'For one thing, we're not corrupt.'

He shakes his head. 'That's beside the point. Yes, I think he was tipped off back then, and yes, I believe someone protected him, or at least his interests. But I don't think it was a big conspiracy, not at the law-enforcement level. It's hard enough to corrupt a cop, no matter what the public at large thinks. It's even harder to get a cop, or an agent, to get into bed with a child trafficker. No. This was the work of one person on that task force, two at the most.'

'Walker?'

'He's the likely suspect. The thing that bothers me, though, is the fact that the whole network just seemed to disappear. It's as if it rolled itself up overnight. No more kids with scars on their feet. That bothers me.'

'Why? The bad guys were being cautious.'

'No. Cautious is what they were *already* doing. Having someone on the inside. Cautious would be finding a new pipeline and a new market. Closing shop altogether? Criminals get smarter, they don't just give up on their business.'

'That's not our concern. For all we know, they never stopped. Maybe they just got smarter, or moved their business elsewhere. Hell, sexual tourism has been growing for years – maybe they set up shop in their home country and got rid of the risk altogether.'

James shrugs, but I know this doesn't satisfy him. He's a puzzle-solver. He doesn't like unanswered questions, whether they're relevant to our investigation or not.

'He's not a sibling, you know,' James says.

The Stranger, he means.

'I know. It's all too personal for that. He experienced something bad, he didn't just observe it happening to a relative.'

'Something still bothers me about the diary, as well,' he says.

I study him. 'Any insight?'

'Not yet.'

My cell rings.

'We have a written statement from Cathy Jones,' Callie tells me. 'We're on our way back.'

'Great work, Callie.'

She sniffs. 'Did you expect any less?'

I smile. 'Bring it to me and then we're going to shoot it straight to Ellen.'

'We'll see you in twenty minutes.'

A rush of adrenaline shoots through me, strong and sudden. It leaves me feeling energized and a little bit shaky, as though everything is outlined in a bright nimbus of light.

Here it is, I realize.

'We're going to be getting our subpoena,' I tell James.

'Remember what we talked about.'

'I haven't forgotten.'

I know what James is saying. Examine every conclusion. We're still walking on the path he laid for us.

49

Everyone is going. Alan, Callie, James, me. We have the subpoena and we're on our way to see Gibbs.

There's an excitement, a kind of electricity in the air. We've been forced, to a great degree, to sit back and suck it up. The whole story, mile after mile of it, a horror show. We've watched Sarah and others suffer in our mind's eye.

Now we could be an hour away from finding out who he is. It doesn't matter, at this moment, that he's led us here. We want to see his face.

We exit the elevator into the lobby and I see Tommy standing at reception, a phone in his hand. He sees me and waves.

'Give me a sec,' I tell the others.

'Hurry up,' James retorts.

'Hey,' Tommy says as I approach. 'I wanted to make sure you got hooked up with Kirby. Find out if that worked.'

I grin at him. 'She's interesting for sure. I –'

I hear a clicking metallic sound that I can't place. I want to dismiss it but something starts shouting inside my head and tells me I'd better not, better not, better not –

I turn, alarmed, and my eyes find a grim-looking, hard-faced Hispanic man standing just inside the lobby. He looks at me, I'm sure he sees me, he turns away –

'Tommy,' I murmur, my hand going toward my gun.

No questions, Tommy's way, he just follows my line of sight and his hand moves toward the inside of his jacket.

What's that?

The hard-faced man throws his hands out before him, and they open, and two things tumble through the air. They are arcing, two perfect lobs –

'Fuck!' Tommy screams.

Tommy is pushing me back, shoving me away, and I'm falling backward, and I realize what's happening in a flash like a rifle-crack.

'Grenades!' I scream, too late.

The explosion inside the lobby area is huge and deafening. I feel a shock wave and heat and something grazes my face and then the air is sucked away, just for a moment, and I'm falling, feeling my head crack against the marble floor and everything goes very, very gray . . .

The puffy clouds in my head are replaced by the smell of smoke and the sound of gunfire.

Automatic weapon, I think, fuzzy.

I come back to myself in a flash, instantly alert. I'm lying on my back. I struggle to a sitting position, and then scrabble to the left, frantic, as something whines off the marble next to me.

God, my head hurts.

My ears are ringing. I look around, see Callie behind a marble pillar, her face smudged and grim as she fires her weapon. I see James struggling to get up, blood running down his face. Alan starts yelling at him.

'Stay down, you moron!'

The automatic keeps firing, not letting up, spraying the lobby with bullets.

The hard-faced man means business, yes indeed, I think, and almost giggle, except that I don't because that'd just be *crazy*.

Gotta clear my head . . .

I hear the return roar of handguns and pull my own, wobbly-bobbly, operating on instinct.

My gun slips into my palm and whispers to me in tones of hushed joy, ready.

I'm in the hallway where Tommy pushed me, and then I remember and then *(Oh God Oh Shit Oh Fuck)* terror thrills through me and I search for him, look for the bloody body that I'm sure, that I'm afraid, that I don't want –

'Over here,' Tommy whispers.

I whip around. Somehow, someway *(Thank God Thank God Thank God)* he's behind me. He's sitting with his back to the wall. His face is gray. He's bleeding from the shoulder.

'You're hit,' I cry.

'No kidding,' he mutters, trying to smile. 'Hurts too. But I'm good. Shrapnel in the shoulder, no vital organs hit. Bleeding's under control.'

I stare at him, trying to take this in.

'I'm okay, Smoky. Go kill that idiot, will you?'

Yes, let's, my gun whispers, and this time I snarl back, filled with a clarity of purpose.

I just need to see him. If I can see him, I won't miss.

I move forward, staying down, my weapon at the ready. The gunfire from the auto continues, an insanity of lead and steel. I can smell the metal, and it cracks and whines and ricochets off every surface.

'Callie!' I yell.

She looks over at me and I point at my eyes.

How many?

She holds up a single finger.

One.

I nod and indicate that I want her and Alan to provide covering fire.

She nods back and I watch as she conveys the plan to Alan. James has managed to move behind the pillar where Callie is. Blood flows from a cut on his forehead. He looks dazed and out of it.

399

Callie gives me a thumbs-up.

I glance back at Tommy once. I grip my gun and crouch, waiting for the lull that has to come.

Everybody has to reload sometime.

The automatic weapon fire seems to go on forever. I know that this is an illusion; time elongates in battle, or becomes meaningless altogether. Sweat pours down my forehead. My head is throbbing, and the cordite in the air is starting to give me a metallic taste in my mouth.

The silence is shocking when it comes. Its absence, after all that roaring, is almost a sound of its own.

I see Callie whip around the pillar, gun ready, and I'm rising as well, looking across the lobby now, searching for the hard-faced man —

I stop. My gun screeches in rage.

The front of the lobby is empty.

50

I run toward the entrance, fly through the metal detectors, they squeal in protest. I register the unmoving body of a security guard. I can't tell if he's alive or dead.

I hit the doors with my shoulder and burst out onto the steps, breathing too hard, my gun in a two-handed grip.

Nothing!

I race down the steps and out into the parking lot. I whip my head left and right, trying to spot him. I hear the doors open and Callie arrives next to me, followed not long after by Alan.

'Where is he?' Callie snarls. 'He just left!'

We hear the growl of a powerful car engine and the squeal of tires and I run toward the sound. I see a black Mustang racing away, lift my gun to fire . . . and then I realize: I can't be *sure* it's actually him.

'Fuck!' I scream.

'You got that right,' Alan mutters.

I bolt back up the steps, taking them three at a time, through the doors again. Callie and Alan are on my heels.

The lobby is a picture of carnage. I see three bodies down and being attended to by other agents. At least four others have their guns out, while Mitch, the head of security, is talking on his walkie, his face grim.

I wipe the sweat off my forehead with a trembling hand, and try to still my internal stress-and-battle voice. I'm still thinking in flashes. I need to move fast, but slow down inside.

'Check on James,' I tell Callie.

I go over to Tommy. He looks a little better. His face isn't as white, though he's obviously in a lot of pain. I crouch down next to him, grip his hand with one of mine.

'You saved my life,' I say, my voice shaky. 'Stupid, heroic dingle-berry.'

'I –' He winces. 'I bet you say that to all the guys who push you away from flying grenades.'

I look for my own witty comeback and find that I can't speak for a moment. I don't love Tommy, not yet, but he matters more than any other man in my life since Matt. We're *together*.

'Jesus, Tommy,' I whisper. 'I thought you were d-d-dead.' My tongue feels Novocain-numb and my stomach is fluttery and queasy.

He stops trying to smile. He pins me with his eyes. 'Well, I'm not. Okay?'

I don't trust my voice right now. I manage a nod.

'James is fine,' Callie calls over, startling me, 'but he'll need some stitches.'

I look at Tommy. He smiles.

'I'm fine. Go.'

I squeeze his hand a last time and stand on legs that I'm grateful to find steady. The elevator doors open up and AD Jones strides out, his weapon at the ready, a phalanx of armed agents at his back.

'What the *fuck* happened?' he barks, a near-yell.

'An intruder came in and tossed two grenades into the lobby,' I say. 'Then he opened up with an automatic weapon. He escaped out the front.'

'Casualties?' he asks.

'I don't know yet.'

'Do we know who the intruder was?'

'No, sir.'

He turns to one of the agents who had come down with him on the elevator.

'I want agents guarding the front door. No one in or out other than medical personnel unless I personally authorize it. Get paramedics here fast, and in the meantime, triage the wounded. I want the agents that are most confident about their first-aid skills to get cracking.'

'Yes, sir,' the agent replies, and gets into action.

AD Jones watches as the agents begin to move, as chaos starts to resolve under the dual dictates of training and command.

'You okay?' he asks me, giving me a critical eye. 'You look a little gray.'

'Stress,' I reply. I reach back and feel my head where it had hit the marble floor. I'm relieved to feel just a bump and not blood. My headache is lessening, so I'm not worried about a concussion.

'We need to find out who this was, and what just happened,' he mutters.

'Yes, sir,' I reply.

He sighs in frustration and fury. 'You saw the guy?'

'Yes, sir.'

'Was he Middle Eastern?'

'No, sir. Hispanic. Late thirties, early forties, maybe.'

AD Jones curses at this.

'How the fuck did he get past security?'

'He didn't. He came through the front doors, lobbed some grenades, opened fire, and left.'

He shakes his head. 'How am I supposed to protect my people from that kind of threat?'

I don't reply. He's not really speaking to me.

'What do you want us to do, sir? Me and my team?'

He runs a hand through his hair, surveys the scene.

'Give me Alan,' he decides. 'Take Callie and follow the line on the subpoena.'

In light of the moment, I'm dumbfounded.

'But, sir . . .' I wipe my forehead again. 'Look, if you need us here, we're here.'

'No. We're not stopping what we do because of this. Screw that. We'll have video of the perp from the security cameras in the next half hour. Between the agents in the building and the team Quantico's sure to be sending, manpower is going to be the least of my worries.'

I don't reply. He scowls at me.

'I'm not asking, Smoky.'

I sigh. He's right, he's the boss, and he's pissed, an unbeatable trio.

'Yes, sir.'

'Get to it.'

I move to Callie. James is standing now, but his gaze is unfocused. He's holding a handkerchief to the wound on his head. Blood has run down his face and neck and soaked his shirt.

'It looks like someone buried a hatchet in your skull,' I say to him.

He smiles, a real smile, and now I know that he's out of it.

'Just a scalp laceration,' he says, still smiling. His voice has a floaty sound to it. 'They bleed a lot.'

I look at Callie, my eyebrows raised. She shrugs.

'I tried to get him to stay seated.' She gives James a critical look. 'I have to say, I like him much better this way.'

'You know what, Red?' James says, overloud, teetering a little as he leans into Callie. 'I need you like . . . like . . . I need a hole in my head.' He cackles at this and then weaves on his feet, unsteady. Callie and I each grab an arm.

'Hey, you know what?' he says in that floaty voice, looking at me now.

'What?' I say.

'I don't feel so good.'

His legs turn into noodles and Callie and I struggle to lower him to a sitting position. He doesn't try to get back up again. His face is pale and greasy with sweat.

404

'He needs a doc,' I say, concerned. 'I'm guessing a bad concussion.'

On cue, the doors open, and the paramedics come rushing in, flanked by agents with their weapons out.

'Ask and ye shall receive,' Callie remarks. She leans down, pats James on the arm. 'They're coming to take you away, honey-love.'

He looks up at her, bleary-eyed. He seems more there, now, more focused. He swallows and winces.

'Good' is all he says, and he sits so that he can put his head between his knees.

'So what's the plan?' Alan asks, coming up next to us.

I give him a once-over. He appears to be uninjured. There's blood on his hands, though, up to the wrists. He notices me looking.

'Young kid,' he says, his voice toneless. 'He was bleeding out from an open stomach wound. I had to reach in and pinch off the bleeder with my hands. He died.' Silence. 'So again, what's the plan?'

I find my voice. 'You're staying here at the request of AD Jones. Callie and I are going to take the subpoena and go see Gibbs.'

'Okay.'

Alan's voice sounds dull, but I realize, looking into his eyes, that he's anything but numb.

'You know,' he says, rubbing his bloody hands on his shirt, 'I can handle what we do. It's tough sometimes, especially when the victims are kids, but I can generally handle it.' He surveys the lobby, shaking his head. 'What I can't handle is this random shit.'

I touch his arm, a brief touch.

'Go,' he says. He looks down at James. 'I'll keep an eye on him.'

He doesn't want to talk anymore right now. I understand.

I turn away, looking, as he had, over the destruction in the lobby. It's become a beehive of activity. I realize in surprise that I'm still holding my gun. I glance at a clock on the wall, hanging cockeyed now but still running.

Nine minutes have passed since we exited the elevator doors.

I holster my gun. One last look toward Tommy, who's being administered to by the paramedics.

'Let's go,' I say to Callie.

I call Elaina first, as we rocket down the freeway. I know that what happened will be on the news soon; I'd seen the vans and choppers moving in as Callie and I drove off.

'Alan's fine, I'm fine, Callie's fine, and James is fine,' I finish. 'Maybe a little bruised, but we're fine.'

She lets her breath out, a sound of relief.

'Thank God,' she says. 'Do you want me to tell Bonnie?'

'Please.'

'Thank you for calling me, Smoky. If I'd seen it on the TV and hadn't heard from you first . . . well, that's why you called, I guess.'

'I knew Alan would be caught up in what's happening there. I didn't want you to worry. Thanks for telling Bonnie. Now I need to talk to Kirby.'

A moment later my killer for hire is on the phone. 'What's up, boss?' she says.

I explain.

'I want you to move them, Kirby. Get them away from Elaina's. Do you have a safe place you can put them?'

'Sure thing. I have some spots set aside for rainy days. Are we expecting rain?'

'I don't think so. Just being careful.'

'I'll call you when we're there.'

She hangs up. No questions, right into action. Tommy was right: Kirby was a good choice.

I have no reason to think that what just happened in the lobby is related to Sarah or The Stranger, no reason at all. But I have no reason not to think it, and these days, my terror tells me, that's a reason all its own.

Callie is silent, watching the road with an unsettling intensity. Her right cheek is smudged. I see what looks like a spot of dried blood on her neck.

406

'It feels strange,' she says, as though she feels me watching her. 'To be leaving while everyone else is back there.'

'I know. They have it covered, though. We need to be doing what we're doing.'

'It still bothers me.'

'Me too,' I admit.

We make very good time getting to Moorpark, and not long after exiting the freeway, we walk into Gibbs's office. His eyes widen and his mouth falls open.

'What the hell happened to you two?' he asks.

'You'll see it on the news,' I say, and hold out the subpoena. 'Here you go.'

His eyes linger on us for a moment. He opens up the writ and reviews it.

'This only compels identity,' he notes.

'That's all we need.'

'Well, that's good,' he says. He seems relieved.

He opens up a desk drawer and pulls out a thin file. He drops it on the desk.

'It's a copy of the signed contract between us and a copy of his driver's license.' He smiles. 'You got good legal advice. I would have fought you on the trust, but identity?' He shrugs. 'It's been ruled on too many times.'

My smile back is perfunctory. I drag the file over and open it. The first page is a contract, typed. It details fees and services, agreements to pay, liability. I skim this, going to the bottom to find what I really want.

'Gustavo Cabrera,' I say out loud.

A name, finally, to put to The Stranger?

Maybe.

I flip the page over. What I see shocks me and yet doesn't – an unsettling combination. Gooseflesh runs across my body.

'Smoky?'

I point to it. Callie looks. Her eyes narrow.

The color photocopy of Cabrera's driver's license is clear and sharp and we recognize him right away.

The hard-faced man from the lobby.

'Son of a bitch,' I murmur.

Are you really that surprised?

No. No, not really.

I fight the urge to leave the office at a dead run. Everything in me screams for motion, but the conversation between James and me comes to me now.

This is the most dangerous part, I realize. We've arrived, he knows we've arrived, and he wanted us here. If we take the steps he's expecting us to take, what are the consequences? He's made his intent clear already, with bullets and grenades. His desire means a conflagration, an Armageddon he plans to grin and groan through.

How do we keep from giving it to him?

And what about the other? The thing that's been trying to swim up through my subconscious, the thing that nagged at James as well?

'Thanks,' I say to Gibbs. 'We have to go.'

'You'll let me know?' he says. 'In case the outcome affects the trust?'

'We will.'

'Who is he?' I'm on the phone with Barry.

'Gustavo Cabrera. Thirty-eight years old. Came to the US from Central America in 1991. Naturalized citizen as of 1997. That's all pretty uninteresting. What is interesting is that he's got himself a huge house on a lot of property with no evidence of holding a steady job, and there's some unsubstantiated chatter about him stockpiling weapons.'

'What – like militia?'

'Or maybe just a gun-nut. Nothing ever came of it. The inform-ant that tip came from was generally considered unreliable and has since died of a drug overdose. Two other pieces of information.

Both are supposed to be confidential – personal medical information – but someone found out and made a note of both. First one: Cabrera is HIV positive.'

'Really?'

'Yep.'

'And the second?'

'Doctor noted at some point Cabrera had been a victim of torture. What appeared to be whip-scars on his lower back and – get this – scars on the soles of his feet.'

'Holy shit. Anything else?'

'That's it.'

'I'll let you know what happens.'

I hang up still feeling troubled and distracted.

There's a missing, a nothing, a something-that-should-be-there.

Cabrera. He seemed to come from the right place, geographically. He's got the scars. Was he The Stranger? Why was I so reluctant to just say yes?

Sarah's diary. What did she leave out?

'What's the problem, Smoky?' Callie asks me, her voice soft. 'What's troubling you so?'

'It's too easy,' I say. 'It's too pat. Something about it doesn't fit him. It doesn't fit who he is.'

'Why? How?'

I shake my head, frustrated. 'I don't know, exactly. I just don't think it should be this simple. Why would he lead us right to him?'

'Maybe he's *crazy*, Smoky.'

'No. He knows exactly what he's doing. He wanted us to get a subpoena, and he wanted us to see that file. He stirred the FBI like a beehive by doing his *Terminator* number in the lobby. He's shot himself to the top of the Most Wanted list and let us see his face after staying hidden for so long. Why?'

'You're the one who can think the way they do,' she prods. Expectant. Confident that I'll provide a revelation.

'I can't see it. I know it's there to see, but I can't see it. Something about Sarah's diary. Something missing from it.'

I can feel it now, on the edge of my vision. I can see it out of the corners of my eyes, but if I turn to view it head-on, it disappears.

Something not there that should be there.

Something, something, some –

I stiffen and my eyes go wide as understanding rushes in.

This is how it happens. This is the end result of drinking down the ocean of information, evidence, considerations, conclusions, possibilities, and feelings. It's like filtering a mountain through a sieve to obtain a grain of sand but, oh, how vital that grain can be.

Oh my God.

Not something.

Someone.

'You've figured it out, haven't you?' Callie murmurs.

I manage a nod.

Not everything, I think, I haven't figured out everything. But this . . . I think so, yeah.

Some things have just become clearer, clearer and more terrible.

51

'Are you sure about this, Smoky?' AD Jones asks me.

'Yes, sir.'

'I don't like it. Too many variables. Someone could end up dead.'

'If we don't do it my way, sir, we could lose hostages that might still be alive. I don't see an alternative.'

A long pause, followed by a deep sigh. 'Set things up at your end. Let me know when you want us to move.'

'Thank you, sir.' I hang up and look at Callie. 'It's a go.'

'I'm still having trouble believing it.'

'I know. Let's go nail down the last facts we need.'

The safe house Kirby had moved Elaina, Bonnie, and Sarah to looks *unsafe*. It's a house in Hollywood, old, beaten-down, ramshackle. I guess that's the point. Kirby opens the door as we approach and ushers us in. She has a grin on her face and a handgun tucked into the front of her jeans. She looks like a deranged blond pirate.

'The gang's all here,' she exclaims. She's stopped trying to cover up her killer's eyes. They roam over the outside and her fingers tap the butt of her gun. She closes the door.

'Hey, Red Sonja,' she says, grinning. She sticks out a hand.

'You must be Callie. I'm Kirby, the bodyguard. What do you do, exactly?'

Callie takes Kirby's hand, flashes her a smile. 'I brighten the world with my presence.'

Kirby nods, not missing a beat. 'Hey, me too. Coolness.' She turns toward the back of the house. 'Olly olly oxen free. Come on out.'

Sarah, Bonnie, and Elaina appear. Bonnie comes to me, hugs me around the waist.

'Hi, munchkin.' I smile.

She looks at me, at Callie. Her eyes fill up with concern.

Callie gets the message. 'We're fine, just some dirty smoke. Nothing a little soap and makeup won't handle.'

'Tommy got hit by some shrapnel in the shoulder, babe,' I tell Bonnie. 'But he's going to be fine. It's not serious.'

She searches my face for the truth. Takes a moment to gauge the state of me. Gives me another hug.

Elaina is worried, but I can tell she's being strong for the girls. Or perhaps they're just letting her think so.

'I'm glad everyone is okay,' Elaina says, her worry appearing in the form of brief hand-wringing. 'But – why did we have to come here?'

'It was a precaution. It could have been a random act of terror. The FBI certainly has plenty of enemies. But the profile we've been considering suggested it's also the kind of thing that The Stranger might try. Turns out we were right.'

Sarah steps forward. Her face is calmer than it should be as she speaks.

'Who is he?'

'His name is Gustavo Cabrera. He's thirty-eight years old and he came from Central America. We don't know much more about him.'

Sarah looks down at the floor. 'So what happens now?'

I sneak a glance at Kirby and Callie. Both of them know. Elaina does not.

412

'Now,' I answer, 'you and I need to talk. Alone.'

Her head shoots up. Her look at me is wary. She shrugs, trying for indifference, but I can see the tension in her shoulders.

'Okay,' she answers.

I raise my eyebrows at Kirby.

'Two bedrooms in the back,' she chirps. 'The rest of us girls will stay right here and talk guns and makeup.'

I walk over to Sarah, touch her lightly on the shoulder. She looks at me and something deep and terrible and haunted stirs in those beautiful eyes.

Does she know? I wonder.

Not for sure, I think. But she *fears*.

I take her back to the bedroom and shut the door and we sit on the bed. I prepare myself to ask the question.

The hardest evidence to see isn't the evidence that's there. It's the evidence that should be there, but isn't. We miss omission because, by its nature, it is absent. This absence is what had troubled first James, and then me, after reading Sarah's diary.

Once we realized what was missing, and coupled it with what we knew of The Stranger, things became clear. It was only a suspicion not yet proved, true, but our confidence was high.

We'd felt him against our skin, James and I.

This made sense.

This made sense.

I ask her the question.

52

'Sarah, where's Theresa?'

The change in her is a lightning strike. Horror fills her face and eyes and she shakes her head, back and forth.

'No, no, no, no, no,' she whispers. 'Please. She's –' Her face twists, her whole face.

Like a towel being wrung tight.

'– she's *all* I have *left* . . . If I lose *her* . . . it's all *gone* . . . gone . . . *gone* . . . gone . . .'

She hunches into herself on the bed, hugging her knees, her head down. She begins to rock back and forth. She's still shaking her head.

'He has her, doesn't he?' I ask.

The thing that had bothered James and me was a complicated amalgam of half-seens and missing grains of sand. The feel of The Stranger. Sarah's love of Theresa. The taking of a hostage. The path we'd been led down.

But most of all, the absolute absence of Theresa from the rest of Sarah's story.

Theresa had been told not to contact Sarah while she was at the group home. Fine.

But then what had happened? She loved Theresa, and she told us what happened to everyone else she loved. What about her Theresa?

414

'Sarah, tell me.'

She keeps her face down, her forehead resting against the tops of her knees, and she begins to talk. Begins to run, even though these words aren't on paper. One more trip to the watering hole.

Sarah's Story

The Real Ending

53

Sarah had turned fourteen as she slept and she hadn't cared. She woke up realizing she was another year older, and she didn't care.

Caring wasn't something she did much, anymore. Caring was dangerous. Caring could mean pain, and pain wasn't something she could deal with.

Sarah walked a tightrope these days. She had been for the last few years. The bad experiences had piled up and her soul had reached a tipping point. She'd realized that she was just a step away from going bonkers. One feather touch was all it would take to send her flying. It wasn't long from flying to falling.

She'd realized this one morning at the group home. She was sitting outside, looking at nothing, thinking of nothing. She was scratching an itch on her arm. She blinked, once, and an hour had passed. Her arm hurt. She'd looked down and found that she'd scratched herself until she bled.

The moment had pierced her numbness. It had terrified her. She didn't want to lose her mind.

Sometimes too, she'd get the shakes. She tried to make sure she was alone when it happened. She didn't want to show her weakness to the other girls. She could tell when it was about to happen: She'd get a queasy feeling in her stomach and the edges of her vision would get dark. She'd go lie in her bed or sit in a toilet stall and wrap her arms around herself and shake. Time had no meaning when this happened.

The moment would pass.

So she was afraid, and she had reason to be. Staying sane was work now. Something she had to *make* happen, not take for granted.

But most of the time, she just didn't care about anything. The big black pool was inside her, bubbling and oily, always hungry. She fed it her memories and lost a little more of herself every year.

She was fourteen now. She felt like she'd lived forever. She felt old.

She got out of bed and got dressed and went outside. She hadn't heard from Cathy, and she was getting ready to drop Cathy into the big black pool, but she figured she could sit outside and wait one more time before doing that. Maybe Cathy would show up. Maybe she'd bring Sarah a cupcake. Cathy did her best, Sarah knew that. Sarah understood the war that went on inside of Cathy's heart, the struggle with closeness. She didn't begrudge the cop for it.

It was a nice day. The sun was out, but there was a cool breeze, so it wasn't too hot. She closed her eyes and leaned her head back, let herself enjoy it for a moment.

A car honked, loud, startling her from her reverie. It honked again, insistent, and she frowned, looking toward the street. She was seated near the fence that surrounded the property, away from other people. A residential street was to the right of her, and the car was there, by the curb. Some shitty blue American car, looked like a real beater. Someone was at the passenger-side window.

It honked again, and now she was pretty sure it was honking at her, and she wondered for a moment if it might be Cathy, but no – Cathy drove a Toyota. She stood up and went to the fence. She peered at the car, her eyes focusing on the face at the dirty passenger-side window.

She could almost make it out, it was a young woman . . .

The face was slammed against the window, and Sarah saw it clearly, and her blood turned to slush in her veins.

Theresa!

Sarah stood, transfixed. She couldn't move. The wind ruffled her hair.

Theresa was older –

(she'd be twenty-one now, yep)

– but it was Theresa

(no bout adout it, take a picture it'll last longer)

– and she was terrified and sorrowful and weeping.

Sarah could make out a shadow behind Theresa. The shadow moved and Sarah saw a face, a face that looked melted by the panty hose that covered it. It grinned.

Sarah stood on the precipice and felt her arms pinwheeling as she tried to keep her balance, and something bubbled up from the big black pool, it was

(Buster's head, Buster's dead, Mommy hugged the gun)

and she was still pinwheeling but –

(Whoopsie . . .)

She turned her face to the perfect sky and she screamed and she screamed and she screamed.

Time passed, probably.

Sarah woke up and marveled that she wasn't crazy. It occurred to her that maybe it wasn't such a good thing. Maybe sanity was overrated.

Her wrists were strapped to the bed. So were her feet. The bed looked medical, the way, well, medical beds look.

She grinned at this.

Drugs, they've given me drugs. Good ones. I feel happy and like I want to kill myself at the same time. Yep, definitely drugs.

Sarah had woken up in this place once before, after a vivid dream that – golly – she just couldn't get out of her head.

Sarah giggled once and passed back out.

Sarah sat on the edge of the bed and tried to plan how she'd do it.

They'd released her from her restraints two days ago. She was in a locked ward, but they didn't keep a real close eye on her. Just gave her meds that she faked taking and left her alone, which was fine by her. It gave her time to plan her suicide.

How do I kill thee? Let me count the ways.

Something they couldn't bring her back from.

She gave it a lot of thought. In the end, she realized she'd have to get out of this place first. They'd never let her die here. Annoying, but true.

She'd have to convince them she was back in control, ready to head back to the

(roll your eyes, party people)

healthy environment of the group home.

No big deal. It wasn't going to be that hard. They didn't care enough here to look at you real close.

Sarah arrived back at the home a week later. Skinny Janet seemed happy to see her, and smiled. Sarah thought about Janet coming upon Sarah hanging by a rope from a rafter, and smiled back.

She arrived in her dorm to find a new girl in her bunk. Sarah explained how things were to her. She explained by breaking the girl's index finger and tossing her and her shit into the middle of the dorm. Sarah wasn't mad – the girl was new. She didn't know what everyone else did: Don't mess with Sarah.

She glanced at the girl, who was holding her finger and howling, and thought, Now you know.

She rolled into her bunk and tuned the girl out. Sarah had more important things to think about. Like dying.

She was still thinking about this a few hours later, when one of the girls came in and walked over to Sarah's bunk. She looked nervous, deferential.

'What?' Sarah asked.

'Mail.' The girl was really nervous.

Sarah frowned. 'For me?'

'Uh-huh.'

'Well, hand it over.'

The girl gave Sarah a white envelope and fled.

Sarah stared at it, and recognized the false banality of the white paper for what it was.

This is from him.

She thought about throwing it away. About not opening it at all.

Right.

She cursed herself and opened it up. Inside was a single sheet of white paper. It was a letter, typed on a word processor and printed out on an ink-jet printer. Faceless, like him. Menacing, like him.

Happy Belated Birthday Sarah,

Do you remember my first lesson about choices? If you do (and I'm sure you do) then you will remember the promise I made to your mother, and you know that I kept that promise. Think of that, as you read the next.

Theresa is fine. I won't say she's well – she's a little under the weather, to be honest – but she is healthy. We've been together now for some three years.

She wants to see you again, and I would like to make that happen. But she won't see you while you're in that place.

Let us know once you are settled into a foster home, and we will be in touch.

There was no signature.

He'd written it so that if someone else read it, they'd find it curious but innocuous. Sarah understood its full meaning, as he'd known she would.

Theresa is alive. She'll stay alive as long as I do what he says. He wants me to go into a foster home again and wait.

Sarah had been resistant to being fostered of late. But she knew all she had to do was let Janet know she was interested and smile when prospective parents came by. She was pretty, she was a girl, couples always wanted to foster her in the hopes of an actual adoption.

The thought came to her, unwanted.

What will happen to them? Whoever it is that takes me in?

She felt the darkness edge her vision and the queasiness rise in her belly. She turned toward the wall, hugged herself, and shook.

An hour later, she destroyed the note and went to see Janet.

54

He visited her one day at the Kingsleys', about a year later, when the house was empty except for her. The family had gone out, she hadn't felt well (so she'd said – she just didn't feel like socializing with people who might be dead before too long).

Michael had already begun abusing her. She was afraid, at first, of how she'd respond. She had to stay here, for Theresa's sake. She had to wait. But what if he touched her and she just ... went insane?

It wasn't that bad. She hated Michael, it was true, but it made a difference that he wasn't an adult. She didn't know why, but it did. It also made a difference that The Stranger would probably kill Michael. This made her smile. One time, she was smiling after they'd had sex, and Michael had noticed.

'What's so funny?'

Just thinking about you dying, she'd thought.

'Nothing,' she'd said.

She didn't think about Dean and Laurel if she could help it. Laurel wasn't exactly an awesome mom, she was no Desiree as a foster-mother, but she wasn't bad. There were moments of genuine care, times when Sarah could feel Laurel's interest in her well-being. So Sarah kept to herself as much as she could.

She was in her room, on her computer, when he appeared. It

was early afternoon. He had the stocking over his face. He was smiling. Always smiling.

'Hello, Little Pain.'

She said nothing. Just waited. That's what she did, these days. She said little, felt less, and waited.

He'd come over and sat down on the bed.

'You got my note, and you believed me. That's very good, Sarah, because I told the truth. Theresa is alive, and you've kept her that way.'

She found her voice. 'Did you hurt her?'

'Yes. And when we're done here, I'm going to go home and hurt her some more. But as long as you do what I tell you, I won't kill her.'

Sarah felt something new clambering through the wreckage inside her. It took her a moment to identify it, and then she did.

Hate. She felt hate.

'I hate you,' she told him. Her voice didn't sound angry to her ears. It sounded normal. It sounded like someone speaking the truth.

'I know,' he acknowledged. 'Now listen to me. I'm going to tell you what to do. When I am done, you'll give me your answer.'

426

55

Sarah has lifted her face from her knees and is now looking at me. I see an exhaustion that dismays me. This is the face of someone who's already given up.

'What did he tell you?' I ask. I'm careful to keep my voice free of anything – anything – that she might misconstrue as judgment.

She looks away from me.

'He told me he needed the password from Michael's computer. He told me that he was going to lead the cops to the wrong man, and that I was going to help him. By writing my diary. By asking for you.'

'He wanted you to ask for me specifically?'

Her voice is toneless. 'Yes.'

'What did he mean by the wrong man?'

'He told me that he had more work to do. I don't know what he meant by that. He said that at one point he was planning to give himself up, but then he changed his mind.'

I digest this. Two thoughts:

One: James was right about him.

Two: It's not Cabrera.

Then, a question:

Why is Cabrera involved?

'Did he tell you anything else?'

She looks at me now, and the look is speculative, calculating. Someone with a huge truth to tell, but someone weighing the risks of telling that truth.

'Sarah. I understand what he did here. He did the same thing to you that he did to your mom, to Cathy Jones, to all the others. He took someone you loved, and used them to force you to do things, to agree to things.' I catch her eyes. 'It's not your fault. I don't blame you. You need to look at me, listen to me, and believe that.'

Her face begins to redden. Whether with grief or anger, I don't know.

'But – but, I *knew*! I knew he would come do things to Dean and Laurel and Michael. And' – she takes in a huge breath, a whoop – 'when he made me slit Michael's throat, all I could think of was how I'd smiled when I thought about him d-d-d-d-dying, and then you, lying to you, and – and – and the man blowing up things at your building today, people got *hurt*, people got *killed* and' – her face goes white now – 'I could have led him here. He could have hurt Bonnie and Elaina. I *knew*.'

'He wanted you to know, Sarah,' I say.

She stands up and walks, back and forth, back and forth, tears running down her face.

'It's more, though, Smoky. He told me if I did what he said, he'd let them go.'

'Who?'

'Theresa and another girl, he said her name was Jessica.'

I sag, angered and dismayed at the same time. He'd made Sarah responsible for the lives of many, given her an impossible burden and a sack of impossible choices to go with it.

I think of the footprints found at the Kingsley scene and of my earlier question about Cabrera. Perhaps he was involved because he had scars on his feet too. Maybe he had his own score to settle?

'Was the other man there, Sarah? At Dean and Laurel's?'

'Not that I saw.'

Maybe Cabrera was there but you just never saw him. Maybe he only had one job – to stand barefoot on the tile.

'Is there anything else, Sarah? Anything you think I need to know?'

Again, that look. Calculating.

'He wanted me to do one more thing, after you killed the wrong guy. One last thing and then he'd let her go.'

'What?'

'He wanted me to fuck him.'

I stare at her, unable to speak for a moment. Here it is, I think. The cherry on the top of his pain-is-pleasure sundae.

A new look, now, on that young-but-old face. It's a look of determination, mixed with a coldness that it takes me a moment to place.

Kirby.

That's what Kirby looks like when she doesn't hide her real eyes.

'He said whatever was going to happen was going to happen in a week or so. I was going to do what he wanted, make sure Theresa was safe, and then I was going to kill him and then kill myself.'

She says it with such certainty that I can't doubt her.

'Theresa has to live, Smoky.' She sits on the bed again, puts her forehead back down on her knees. 'I'm sorry. For what I did. It's my fault that Dean and Laurel and Michael are dead. It's my fault about your building. I'm bad. I'm a bad person.'

She begins to rock now, back and forth, back and forth. The door opens. Elaina.

'I was listening,' she says to me, unapologetic. She walks over to Sarah, who tries to back away from her. Elaina ignores this, and grabs on to Sarah, hugging as best she can while the girl fights her. 'You listen to me,' Elaina says, her voice fierce. 'You're not bad. You're not evil. And whatever happens – *whatever happens* – you've got me. Understand? You've got me.'

Elaina isn't trying to tell her that things aren't bad. She's just telling her she's not alone.

Sarah doesn't hug Elaina back, but she stops fighting. She keeps her head down and shakes as Elaina strokes her hair.

I sit at the old-fashioned Formica-top kitchen table with Kirby and Callie. AD Jones and Alan are on my cell, and the speaker-phone is on. I have filled everyone in on my conversation with Sarah.

'We have a serious problem, sir,' I say. 'Well, a number, actually, but one in particular. Even if we can figure out a way to take down Cabrera without killing him – we don't have a shred of evidence against The Stranger. We don't know who he is. He's never shown Sarah his face. And I'm guessing the footprints at the Kingsley scene belong to Cabrera, not The Stranger.'

'Cabrera might know who he is,' Alan observes.

'True,' I reply. 'But if not, we're in trouble.'

'Deal with what's in front of you,' AD Jones replies.

'Yes, sir.'

'So . . . what? Cabrera is supposed to be the fall guy?'

'Not just the fall guy. The dead fall guy. I'm pretty certain he's supposed to commit suicide-by-cop. Probably at his house. I'm sure if we kill him we'll find all kinds of evidence that shows us he's our perp.'

'And the cuckoo-bird goes free,' Kirby chimes in.

Phone silence as AD Jones ponders this. 'So what's the plan?'

I tell him. He peppers me with questions, ponders it some more, and asks even more questions.

'Approved,' he says, finally. 'But be careful. And Smoky? He killed three agents. Safety of my agents comes first, his safety comes last. You understand what I'm telling you?'

'Yes, sir.'

Of course I do. He's telling me to kill Cabrera if it will save Bureau lives.

'I'll get SWAT together. You get your ass over here and let's get this op on the road.'

'You're fine with Kirby, then, sir?'

'I'm not sure that "fine" is the right word, but I agree with the plan.'

Kirby is smart enough to keep her mouth shut, but she gives me a big grin and a thumbs-up. She's happy, a child getting the birthday gift she'd asked for.

'See you shortly.' I hang up.

'Since I'm staying here on bodyguard duty,' Callie says, her voice dry, 'I only have one question.'

'What's that, Cal?' Kirby asks.

'Where's the coffeepot?'

Kirby shrugs. 'Bad news on that one, Cal. No coffee here. Besides, it's bad for you. All kinds of chemicals in coffee. Yuck.'

Callie fixes her with an incredulous look. 'How dare you criticize my religious beliefs?'

Joking, as always, but to me her voice sounds strained. I look, really look, and I see that she's gone a little pale. For the first time I think I understand how constant this battle is for her. The pain never ends, and she's fighting it, but it's taking its toll.

It's funny, of all the recent terrible things I've seen or read, this is the one that sucker punches me: the idea of Callie being worn down by something.

I walk into the bedroom. Sarah's stopped shaking, but she looks terrible. Whatever she's used to hold herself together over the years has unraveled. She's falling apart. Elaina strokes her hair while Bonnie holds her hand.

I tell them what we're doing. Sarah's eyes come alive.

Well, more alive.

'Will it work?' she asks.

'I think so.'

She looks at me then, really looks at me.

'Smoky . . .' Her voice trails off for a moment. 'Whatever happens, don't let him hurt you or anyone else. Even if it means' – her voice cracks – 'that it doesn't all work out the way I want it to. I can't be responsible for this anymore. No more. No more.'

431

'You're not responsible, Sarah. Let it go. It's up to us now.'

She looks away, and that's all she's going to say for now. Bonnie catches my eye and gives me a look.

Be careful, she's saying.

I smile.

'Always.'

Elaina nods at me, bald and wonderful, and turns her inner beauty back to Sarah. If anyone can revive that girl's soul, Elaina can.

Kirby appears at the door. 'Ready to rock?' she asks, ever perky.

Not really, I think, but let's go.

56

Every FBI field office has its own swat team. Like police SWAT, they spend every working hour training, unless they're handling an actual situation. They keep themselves on the knife-edge and they look it.

The team leader is an agent named Brady. I don't know Brady's first name. I only know him as Brady. He's in his mid-forties. He keeps his dark hair short and tight, military-style. He's tall, very tall, probably six foot four, with an all-business amiableness to him that is neither friendly nor unfriendly. Shaking hands with him is like shaking hands with a rock.

'This is your show, Agent Barrett,' he says. 'Just tell us what you need.'

We're in the conference room on the floor below my offices. Everyone's present and looking grim. Except for Kirby. She's gazing at the six members of the SWAT team in a hungry way, like they're a bunch of yummy, overly fit hot fudge sundaes.

'Gustavo Cabrera,' I begin, dropping an eight-by-ten photo we'd printed out of him. 'Thirty-eight years old. He lives in a house in the Hollywood Hills. Big place, old place, sitting on four acres of land.'

One of the SWAT members whistles. 'That'll be worth some dough.'

'We have maps of the location, as well as plans for the house.' I drop them onto the table. 'Here's the thing: We need him alive. But we're pretty sure that he's been told to get himself killed. He's probably got a decent arsenal, and I imagine he's supposed to make it look authentic.'

'Swell,' Brady says in a dry voice.

'On top of that, we need it to look authentic too. We don't want to kill Cabrera. But we want The Stranger to think we did.'

'How are we going to do that, exactly? Without getting ourselves shot to hell, I mean?'

'Diversion, boys,' Kirby says, stepping forward. 'Diversion.'

'Who the hell are you?' Brady asks.

'Just a blonde with a gun,' she drawls, in a fair imitation of him.

'No offense, ma'am,' one of the younger members of the SWAT team says, 'but you look about as dangerous as my girlfriend's poodle.'

Kirby grins at the young SWAT officer, and winks. 'Is that right?'

She walks over to him. His nametag says *Boone*. He's stocky, muscular, and very sure of himself. Classic type-A.

'Check it out, Boone,' she says to him.

It happens in a blur. She slams a fist into Boone's solar plexus. His eyes bug out as he falls to his knees, gasping for air. In the instant it takes the other SWAT team members to react, she's pulled her gun and pointed it quickly at each one, saying: 'Bang, bang, bang, bang –'

'Bang,' Brady says, in time with her. He'd managed to whip out his weapon and point it at Kirby before she'd pointed hers at him.

She holds the pose for a moment, considering. Then grins and holsters her weapon. She ignores Boone, who's breathing again and is taking in huge, whooping gasps of air.

'Pretty good, old dude,' she says. 'Guess that's why you're the boss-man, huh?'

He grins back at her. It's like watching two wolves get along.

'Get up, Boone,' he barks. 'And let it go.'

The young SWAT officer struggles to his feet. He shoots Kirby a dark look. She waggles a finger at him.

'Are we done with the testosterone display?' AD Jones asks. 'Both the male and the female version?'

'He started it,' Kirby observes. 'If he'd been nicer, I would have touched him somewhere else.'

Everyone chuckles. Even Boone smiles, against his will. I see Brady appraising Kirby, realizing the same thing I have. Kirby isn't just a good operative. She's command material. In her own haphazard way she's managed to relieve the tension in the room, lighten the mood, and get the guys to like and respect her at the same time. It's impressive.

'So what's your name?' Brady asks.

'Kirby. But you can call me "Killer," if you want.' She flashes him a smile. 'All my friends do.'

'You have many friends?'

'Nope.'

He nods. 'Me neither. So explain what you meant by "diversion."'

'Sure thing. You and your macho killer commando squad hit the front, by the book. Bullhorns and "Give up! Give up!" and all that stuff. While you're doing that, and he's distracted, Smoky and I will go in through the back.'

'Quiet, you mean?'

'Smooth as my inner thigh. And that's smoooooth, Mr Brady, sir.'

'Uh-huh. And you don't think he'll be watching the back?'

'Maybe. But that's why you'll have to blow some stuff up.'

Brady raises an eyebrow. 'Come again?'

'Blow some stuff up. You know – "kaboom."'

'How do you propose we do that?'

'Can't you drop a bomb on his lawn or something?'

Brady looks at Kirby, thinking. He nods his head.

'Okay, youngster. The concept's sound. But I think we can execute a little better and not have to – how'd you put it? – "blow some stuff up"?'

Kirby shrugs. 'Whatever. I thought you guys liked blowing stuff up.'

'Oh, we do,' he assures her. 'We just try to avoid it unless we have to. Makes the neighbors nervous.' He leans forward and spreads out the map of the estate. 'Here's what I propose. We're going to have a problem anyway with the size of the grounds if we come on foot. He'll see us from a mile away. Shit, he could have the place mined for all we know. We'll go in from the air, instead.'

'Chopper?' Alan asks.

'Yep.' He points to a position in front of the house. 'We'll hover up and at an angle. Makes it harder for him to get a shot. We'll have to hope he doesn't have a bazooka or some such nonsense. We'll lay out a field of fire. Real serious shit – I think I can get our hands on some fifty cals – along with some smoke grenades. Get his attention, make it sound like World War Three out front.'

'Okay,' Kirby says.

'Yeah. While all that's happening, you two will make your way to the back. Then on your mark, we'll fill the place with tear gas. You infiltrate and . . .' He spreads his hands.

'And hopefully we don't have to kill the poor guy,' Kirby finishes for him.

Brady looks at me. 'How's that sound?'

'Like a really bad idea,' I say, 'but the best under the circumstances.' I check my watch. 'It's four o'clock now. How soon can you be ready?'

'We can be airborne in a half hour. What about you? You'll need vests and masks.'

'No vest for me,' Kirby pipes up. 'Just slows me down. I'll take a mask, though.'

'Your funeral.' Brady shrugs.

She punches him on the arm. 'You don't know how many times I've heard that before.'

Just like Alan had a day earlier, Brady looks surprised and rubs his arm where she'd punched him. 'Ow.'

436

'That's what they all say,' she quips. 'So can we go shoot some stuff now?' She holds up the weapon she'd drawn earlier. 'New gun,' she explains. 'I need to break it in.'

57

Unlike Kirby, I wanted a vest. I understand why she doesn't like them, but I lack her predator's edge. Kirby was born to do this, to kick in back doors and enter houses filled with tear gas and flying bullets. Kirby doesn't have a Bonnie waiting for her. I do.

'This damn mask is going to give me the hat-hair from hell,' she observes, examining the thing.

We're crouched against the wall that surrounds the back of the estate. It's a privacy wall, about six feet high. We're not scaling it in any dramatic fashion. We each have a four-foot-high stepladder.

We'd both been offered MP5 machine guns, and we'd both declined. 'Stick with what you know' is an old adage of the tactical situation. I know my handgun, my sleek black Beretta, as well as I know the color of my own eyes. Kirby had wisecracked about the MP5 clashing with her outfit, but I knew her reasons were the same: Travel light with the weapon of your choosing. Hers was a handgun as well.

'Ready to kick ass, over,' Kirby subvocalizes into her throat mike.

'Roger that,' Brady replies after a moment. 'Armageddon will commence in two minutes from my mark. One, two, three – mark.'

'Ooohh, synchronized watches,' Kirby whispers.

'Countdown's commenced, Kirby,' Brady says. 'You get that?'

'Yes, boss.' She looks at me and grins. 'Hey, Boone. Still think I'm not dangerous?'

'Negative on that, BB.' Boone's voice comes through, amused. BB stood for 'Beach Bunny.' 'You're bad news in a pretty package, that's the truth.'

Kirby checks her weapon as she continues the banter. I'm not interested in joining in. My stomach is fluttering and I'm so charged up I feel like I should be throwing off sparks.

At least your hands are dry, I think.

This has always been the case. No matter what the stakes, no matter how dangerous the scene, my hands never sweat in a gun-fight, and they are always steady.

'Forty-five seconds until the nasty,' Brady says, sounding bored.

I think about Gustavo Cabrera, inside that house. I wonder if he's clutching a weapon as he stares through his windows. Are his hands steady or shaking? What's he thinking of?

'Thirty seconds,' Brady says.

'How are you over there?' Kirby asks me. Her voice is light, but her eyes are assessing me. Taking stock. *Asset or liability?* they ask.

I hold out a hand for her. Show her its rock-steadiness.

She nods. 'Coolness.'

'Fifteen seconds to D-day.'

Kirby checks her own handgun again, humming. It takes me a moment to place the tune. 'Yankee Doodle Dandy.' She catches me staring at her.

'I like the classics.' She shrugs.

'Ten seconds. Get ready.'

We position ourselves at the base of our respective ladders.

My endorphin buddies are back and they've brought their friends.

(Fear and euphoria, euphoria and fear)

'Five seconds. Get ready to open the gates of hell.'

'Bring it on, daddy-o,' Kirby says, full of good cheer even as her killer's eyes blaze.

The machine-gun fire, when it starts, is incredibly loud, even at this distance.

'That's our cue!' Kirby yells.

We clamber up the ladders, reach the top of the wall, and lift ourselves over. We turn around and go into a hanging position, like someone doing a chin-up, before dropping to the ground on the other side. No jumps and rolls in the real world; it's too easy to twist an ankle.

The gunfire continues, and I see flashes as well, over the top of the house. I can hear the helicopter rotors and a series of loud noises that I assume to be flash-bangs going off. As I run, I hear another noise as well. It takes me a moment to place it. Return fire, from an automatic weapon.

Kirby and I race toward the back of the house at a dead run. She's moving faster than I am by a body-length or two, unencumbered by a flak vest or my extra years.

The house is smaller than I would have expected for the land it's on. According to the blueprints, it's just under 3200 square feet, all of which is laid out in a single story. There's a back door that leads through a small hall into the kitchen. We arrive at the door. I'm breathing hard and deep. Kirby appears unruffled.

'We're in place, Mr Boss-man sir,' she says to Brady.

'Roger that. Cutting loose.'

'Cutting loose' means that they're going to start chewing up the front lawn with machine-gun fire like there's no tomorrow, followed by tossing out flash-bang grenades as they fire tear gas canisters in through the front windows.

'Time for some hat-hair,' Kirby says, giving me a wink.

We slip on the masks. They're SWAT issue, with a wide line-of-sight and plenty of peripheral vision, but they're still gas masks. My forehead starts to sweat right away.

'Commencing,' Brady says.

I thought it had been noisy before. That was nothing compared to the sound assault that signals Brady's team is indeed 'cutting loose.'

The sound of two fifty-caliber machine guns fills the air with thunder. Not long after that, the flash-bangs begin to roar, one after the other, not stopping. We hear the crash of shattering glass.

Kirby kicks the door open and we're inside. I can't smell anything but the rubber of my mask, but the house is full of smoke and vapor. Cabrera is firing away with an automatic weapon and the roar of it is immense inside the home. There's no way he could hear anything above that.

Kirby moves forward, her gun out now. I follow, weapon ready as well. We creep toward the sound of his gunfire. The flash-bangs continue to explode. We move through the kitchen and reach the doorway that leads to the living room and the front of the house. We each take a side of the doorway and peer around.

Will you look at that? I think. Pure carnage.

Cabrera is outlined in light. He's crouched and firing up at an angle, toward the chopper, I know. His back is to us and his body shakes every now and then when he fires his weapon – an M16, I now see. He's surrounded by broken glass from the windows.

The plan at this point had been unelegant but simple. As Kirby had put it: 'Try and tackle that sucker.'

I look at Kirby, and she looks back at me. I see her eyes squint in a smile and I nod.

We don't have much time. It won't take long for Cabrera to wonder why Brady's team are such bad shots. He'll smell a trap.

Kirby bolts out, running toward Cabrera. I breathe deep, once, inside my mask, and follow.

Cabrera's instincts kick in and he whips around with the M16, eyes wide, mouth grim. Kirby doesn't slow, moving into him rather than away, forcing the weapon up as it discharges, tracing bulletholes in the ceiling. I have my gun up and am moving back and forth, looking for a shot as the two of them struggle with each other.

'Goddammit, Kirby,' I shout, 'get out of my line of fire!'

My voice is muffled by the mask, drowned out by all the man-made thunder.

Kirby's other hand brings up her gun. Cabrera abandons the M16 and chops one hand down on her wrist, while the other goes for her throat. She blocks the throat blow, but loses her weapon. Cabrera's eyes are red-rimmed by the tear gas, and he's coughing, but he continues to fight.

'Fuck,' I mutter, then 'Fuck!' I shout, bobbing and weaving, my heart pounding, my head pounding, my hands still dry.

Kirby goes for his balls with a swift kick. He turns his leg in, taking it on the thigh, and manages to slam the butt of his palm into her cheek. She stumbles backward as her face whips to the side.

Time freezes.

Finally!

The stumble has given me a clear shot, so I shoot him in the shoulder.

He grunts and drops to a knee. Kirby moves in and slams him in the face with her fist once, twice, three times, and then she's behind him as he struggles to stay on his feet, and she's got him in a choke hold.

He scrabbles at her arms. It's too late. His eyes roll up in his head. She lets go, pushing him forward so that he falls onto his stomach. She whips out a set of zip-ties and secures his wrists.

And just like that, it's over.

'Ceasefire, boys,' Kirby says, the mask giving her voice an echoey sound. 'He's down.'

My hands begin to sweat.

58

Gustavo Cabrera is sitting on a chair, gazing at us. His shoulder has been tended to. His hands are secured in his lap now, rather than behind him. He should be more worried. Instead, he looks like a man at peace. His eyes have been treated for the gas and they're staring at Alan. Assessing.

Alan takes this amiably. Cool as a cucumber, but it's deceptive, because when it comes to interrogations, Alan is a shark. All lion, hold the lamb. He cocks his head, assessing Cabrera right back. Waiting.

'I will confess,' Cabrera says. 'I will tell you everything. I will gratefully tell you where the hostages can be found.'

His voice is soft, lyrical, and vaguely reverent.

Alan taps a finger to his lips, thinking. He stands in a sudden motion. He leans forward and points a huge finger at Cabrera. When he speaks, his voice is large and loud and accusative.

'Mr Cabrera, we know you're not the man we're after!'

The happiness in Cabrera's eyes is replaced with alarm. His mouth opens in surprise, closes, opens again. It takes him a moment to get himself under control. His lips compress into a determined line. His eyes are sad. Still peaceful, though.

'I am sorry. I do not know what you mean.'

Alan barks out a laugh. It sounds vaguely insane and definitely menacing. Scary. I'd be worried if I didn't know it was all an act. He sits back down as suddenly as he'd stood and hunches forward. Relaxed now, just two guys having a talk. He smiles and wags a finger at Cabrera in a 'you old dog' kind of way. A 'don't kid a kidder' kind of way. 'Now, sir. I have a witness. We know it's not you. There's no question about this. The only question is: Why are you really working with this man?' Alan's voice is low and smooth, steady as syrup going onto pancakes. Then: 'Hey! I'm talking to you!' Loud again, a shout.

Cabrera jumps. Looks away. Alan's seesaw between extremes is unsettling him. He's developed a twitch in his cheek.

'He's been a victim of torture,' Alan had told me prior to beginning Cabrera's interview. 'Torture is basically about reward and punishment and establishment of intimacy. The torturer will scream at you and call you hateful things and burn you with cigarettes, then he'll personally apply the ointment to the burns and become all solicitous and soothing. The victim ends up wanting one thing more than anything else.'

'The guy with the ointment and the nice voice.'

'Right. We're not going to burn Cabrera with cigarettes, but moving back and forth between rage and kindness should be enough to rattle him pretty good.'

Roger that, I think. Cabrera was starting to sweat.

'Mr Cabrera. We know you were supposed to die here. What if I were to tell you that we'd be willing to fake your death? To make the rest of the world think you were shot while we were attempting to apprehend you?' Alan is continuing with his normal voice now. He's established dominance and instilled fear.

Cabrera is looking back at him, a hopeful, speculative, complicated look.

'If you help us,' Alan continues, 'we'll carry you out of here in a body bag.' He leans back. 'If you don't cooperate, and let us help you, then I'll march you out of here in front of the cameras, and he'll know that you're still alive.'

No reply. But I can see the conflict in him.

444

He stares at Alan for a moment, searching. He drops his gaze to the floor between us. His whole body slumps. The twitch in his cheek disappears.

'I don't care about myself. Can you understand that?'

His voice is humble, calm. It's difficult to reconcile the gentleness in front of me with the hardness I saw as he burst into the FBI lobby, guns blazing. Which one is his true face?

Both, perhaps.

'I understand the concept,' Alan says. 'I don't understand it as it applies to you. Enlighten me.'

Another searching look. Longer, this time.

'I am going to die, eventually. This is my fault, no one else's. A weakness for women, an unwillingness to be safe.' A shrug. 'I get what I deserve with the HIV. But I tell myself, at times, perhaps it was not entirely my own fault. I was . . . harmed when I was a young boy.'

'Harmed how, sir?'

'For a brief and very terrible time, I became the property of evil men. They . . .' He averts his gaze. 'They had their way with me. When I was eight. These men, they had kidnapped me, while I was getting water for the home. They took me and in the first day, they raped me and they beat me. They whipped my feet until the blood ran like little rivers.'

His voice is slight now, almost dreamy.

'They made a demand, when they beat me. Words to say. "You are the God. I thank you the God." The harder we wept, the more they beat us. Never anywhere else but on the feet.

'I was taken with other children, both boys and girls, to Mexico City. It was a long journey, and we were kept quiet with threats.' His gaze comes back to me, and it looks like it should bleed. 'I prayed, sometimes, for death. I hurt, not just in my body.' He taps his head. 'In my mind.' Taps his chest. 'In my heart.'

'I understand,' Alan tells him.

'Perhaps. Perhaps you do. But this was a special hell.' He continues. 'In Mexico City we heard the guards speaking at times,

445

and from their words we came to understand that we would go to America in the coming months. That our training would be complete and that we would be sold to bad men for great sums of money.'

The trafficking ring, I think. And the circle closes.

'I was in a deep place with no light. I had been raised very religious, you understand. To believe in God, in Jesus Christ, in the Mother Mary. But to my eyes, I had prayed to them each, with all my might, and still the men came to hurt me.' He winces. 'I didn't understand then. The fullness of God's plan. In that dark place, when my despair was greatest, God was going to send me an angel.'

He smiles as he says these words, and a kind of light fills his eyes. His voice finds a rhythm, like a wave that's always coming but never reaches the shore.

'He was special, the boy. He had to be. He was younger than me, smaller than me, but somehow, he did not lose his soul.' His gaze on me is intent. 'Let me help you understand the significance of that. The boy was only six years old, and he was beautiful. So beautiful that the men liked using him best of all. Every day, sometimes twice a day. And he angered them as well. *Because he would not cry.* They wanted his tears, and he refused them. They would beat him to make him weep.' He shakes his head, sad. 'Of course, he always wept, eventually. But still . . . he did not lose his soul. Only an angel could have resisted them in that most important way.'

Gustavo closes his eyes, opens them.

'I was not an angel. I was losing my soul, falling deeper and deeper into despair. Turning away from the face of God. In my despair I thought about killing myself. I think he sensed it. He started coming over to me at night, whispering to me in the dark while his hands touched my face. My beautiful white angel.

'"God will save you," he told me. "You must believe in him. You must continue to have faith."

'He was only six, or perhaps seven, but he spoke with older

words and those words rescued me. I came to know his story, that he had been called by God when he was only four years old, that he had resolved to enter the seminary at the earliest possible age, to devote his life to the Holy Trinity. Then one night, the men came, and stole him from his family.

'"Even so," he would say to me, "you cannot lose faith. We are being tested by God." He would smile at me, and it was a smile of such pureness, of such bliss and belief, that it would pull me away from the despair that wished to drown me.'

Cabrera's eyes are closed in reverential remembrance.

'He did this for a year. He suffered every day, we all did. At night, he spoke to us all and made us pray and kept us from wanting death more than life.' Cabrera pauses, looking off. 'One day, that fateful day, he saved my body as well as my soul.

'It was only the two of us. We were being transported by a guard to the home of a wealthy man, a man for whom just one boy was not enough. I was shaking in fear, but the boy, the angel, as always, remained calm. He touched my hand, he smiled at me, he prayed, but as we drove on, he became concerned when he saw that his prayers were not reaching my heart. I was afraid this time in spite of his words. My fear only grew as we approached, until I was trembling uncontrollably. We arrived at the house, and without warning, he reached over and took my face in his hands. He kissed my forehead, and he told me to be ready.

'"Be not afraid, but trust in God," he said.

'We left the car and the guard fell in behind us. The boy turned without warning and he punched the guard in the groin. The guards were used to our obedience, and so this one was caught by surprise. He doubled over in pain and screamed in rage.

'"Run!" the boy told me.

'I stood there, trembling. Unsure. Ever the victim.

'"Run!" he said again, only this time it was a roar, the voice of an angel, and he fell upon the guard, biting and kicking.

'His words reached me.

'I ran.'

Cabrera rubs his forearm with one hand. I can see him there in the moment, but I can see it mixing with the present as well. The fear of indecision, the joy of making an escape from hell. The guilt of taking what the boy had offered, and of leaving him behind.

'I do not need to tell you the story of every moment, month, or year after that. I did escape, from that hell on earth. I came home to my family. I lived for many years after that as a troubled boy, and later as a troubled man. I was not a saint, I was often a sinner, but – and this is the most important thing of all – I had lived. I had not committed suicide. *I had not damned my immortal soul.* Do you understand? He had saved me from the worst fate of all. Because of what he did for me, I will not be barred from heaven.'

I do not share Cabrera's beliefs. But I can feel the strength of his faith, the succor it provides him, and it moves me.

'I came to America,' he continues. 'I believed in God, but I was troubled, always troubled. I'm ashamed to say that I did drugs at times. That I saw prostitutes. I contracted the virus.' He shakes his head. 'Once again, the despair. Once again, the idea that death might be better than life. It was then, at that moment, that I realized: The virus was a message from God. He had sent me an angel, once, and that angel had saved me. I should have been thankful. Instead, I had wasted many years embroiled in my own sorrows and rage.

'I listened to God's warning. I changed my ways, became a celibate. Grew closer to God. And then, one day eleven years ago, my angel returned.'

Cabrera's eyes now grow mournful.

'Still an angel, but no longer one of light. He was a dark angel. An angel made for the purpose of vengeance.'

The tattoo, I think.

'He told me that he had gone through terrible, terrible things as a result of helping me escape. I cannot tell you the things he told me. They are too evil. He told me that at times, for moments only, he would doubt God's love. But then he would remember

448

me, and he would pray, and he was certain again. God was testing him. God would lead him from that place.' Cabrera grimaces. 'One day, God did. One day, all of the boy's faith, all of his prayers, his sacrifice for me, all these things were rewarded. He and the other children, in America now, were rescued by the police, by your FBI.

'He described it as a glorious moment. It was, to him, as though God had kissed him. His faith and his suffering had been justified.'

Cabrera goes silent now. A long silence. I have a very bad feeling building inside of me. Something that tells me I know what's coming.

'One night, he said, God returned them to hell. Men came to where they were sleeping, and murdered the police that guarded them. Men came and took them away and returned them to slavery. Terrible,' Cabrera whispers. 'Can you imagine? To be safe, and then to be snatched away from hope again? And for him, it was the worst of all. They knew that he had been helping, that he had told the police the name of a guard. They didn't kill him, but they punished him in ways that made his prior existence in hell seem like heaven.'

I knew it already, someplace inside me, but now it is confirmed.

I move so I'm standing next to Alan. 'The boy's name was Juan, wasn't it?' I ask Cabrera.

He nods. 'Yes. An angel named Juan.'

I don't know if his picture of Juan as a young saint is the truth, or the overidealized memories of a once terrified and abused child who found a very good friend when he needed one most. What I do know is that this is a story I've heard before. It's a story where no one wins, not even us.

Killers are killers, and what they do is unforgivable, but there's a certain tragedy in the ones that were made. You see it in their rage. Their actions are less about joy and more about screaming. Screaming at the father who abused them, the mother who beat them, the brother who burned them with cigarettes. They begin with helplessness and end with death. You capture them and put them away because it must be done, but there's no savage satisfaction to it.

'Please go on,' Alan says. His voice is gentle now.

'He told me that he had come to realize God had another plan for him. That he had sinned in thinking himself saintly, in comparing his sufferings to those of Christ. His duty, he now knew, was not to heal, but to avenge.' Cabrera shifts in his chair, uneasy. 'His eyes were terrible to see when he spoke these words. Such rage and horror. They did not look like the eyes of someone touched by God. But who was I to say?' He sighs. 'He had escaped from his captors. He told me about returning in later nights to visit blood and vengeance on the men who had tortured him. It's how he came to understand that it had been two men, an FBI agent and a policeman, who had betrayed him and the other children. These men, he told me, were the most evil of all, the men wearing masks, hiding behind symbols.

'He had a plan, a long design, and he asked me to help. He couldn't be captured once everything had been done, because God had revealed to him that his work extended beyond vengeance for just his own suffering. He needed me to become him, in *your* eyes. I agreed.'

'Sir,' Alan says to him, 'do you know where we can find Juan?'

He nods. 'Of course. But I will not tell you.'

'Why?' Alan asks him. 'You have to know that he's not doing God's will, Gustavo. You *know* that. He's murdered innocent people. He's ruined a young girl's life.' Alan locks eyes with him. '"Thou shalt not kill," Gustavo. You've killed for him. Innocent young men in that FBI lobby died, good men who never hurt a child or did anything less than their job.'

Pain fills his face. 'I know this. I do. And I will pray to God for forgiveness. But you must understand – you must! He saved me. I cannot betray him. I cannot. I am not doing this for what he is now. I'm doing this for what he once was.'

It should be melodramatic; his total sincerity just makes it agonizing.

Alan goes at him again and again, retrieves the sweat and the cheek-twitch, but it's like running into a wall.

Cabrera had been saved from a fate that some would argue was a lot worse than death. Juan had helped him to escape, not just his physical prison, but his despair. Cabrera's own life had been ruined, to some degree, by the evil done to him, but his faith still promised an ultimate salvation, a door Juan had left open for him.

As for Juan . . . well. That was a horror story that I just couldn't take in. The most terrible, terrible, terrible thing was that we had helped create this monster. Someone corrupt had sold him down the river and had ruined the gentle boy with the unshakable faith. Juan had fallen, but not without the help of those he trusted most.

Everything here was about either the absolute worst or the absolute best in people, and I didn't see Cabrera budging.

'There is one good thing I am allowed to do,' he says.

'What's that?'

He inclines his head toward the left side of the home. 'In the den, on the computer. You'll find the location of the girls. Jessica and Theresa. They are alive.' He sighs again, sadder this time 'Placed in hell by an angel. They have had a difficult time.'

'Where are they?'

I'm asking this of Alan. He's already told me, but it's not sinking in.

'North Dakota,' Alan says. 'In what used to be a missile silo. Ten thousand square feet, all of it underground, and the ground it's under is in the middle of nowhere. The government cleaned out a number of silos and underground bases over the years. They sold them, most often to real estate companies who fixed them up and resold the properties to individuals.'

'And that's legal?' I ask, dumbfounded.

Alan shrugs. 'Sure.'

As Cabrera had promised, we'd found the location where Theresa and Jessica were being held on the personal computer in the den, along with grainy photos of what I assumed to be the girls themselves. They were nude and they looked drawn and unhappy, but otherwise unharmed.

'Get in touch with the field office up there. Let's get the girls out and bring them here. Do we know how to enter the place?'

'An electronic combination lock with a thirty-digit code. I'll make sure they have it.'

He heads toward the front door of the house. The air outside is filled with the sound of TV news helicopters. Just them, so far; it was one of the nice things about the home being on land behind gates and walls. Brady has men guarding the entrance to the estate until the local cops take over. No one in, period. Boone and one other member of the SWAT team are in a coroner's wagon, escorting Cabrera's 'body,' ostensibly to the morgue. In reality, Cabrera will never make it to the morgue. He'll be held under guard at a safe house.

I take a moment to look around.

He came here, but he didn't live here.

I hit a number on my speed dial and put the phone to my ear.

'What?' James asks, preamble-less as usual.

'Where are you?'

'Signing myself out. These morons want me to stay here. I'm going home.'

'Not nice, James. The "morons" you're speaking about patched you up.'

'That part wasn't stupid. Keeping me here is.'

I let it go. 'I need another viewpoint.'

'Go ahead,' he says without hesitation.

This is what keeps the rest of us from strangling James. He is always ready to work. Always.

I fill him in on everything that's occurred.

'Cabrera says he knows the identity of The Stranger. He's not going to reveal it.'

James is silent, thinking.

'I'm not coming up with anything.'

'Me neither. Listen, I know you said you were going home, but

452

I need you to get back to Michael Kingsley's computer. He wouldn't have made it unsolvable. He wants us to crack it.'

'Dakota is on it,' Alan says, startling me from my thoughts. 'They're sending agents and a SWAT team. Local bomb squad too, just in case The Stranger decided to be cute.'

'Where's Kirby?'

'Gone. She said she was going back to the safe house.'

'We have a problem, Alan. We have no evidence. Not a shred of forensic data that we can hold up. Even if we *knew* who he was, everything is circumstantial. At best.'

He spreads his hands. 'Only one thing to do, then.'

'What's that?'

'Work the scene. Get Callie and Gene and whoever over here and let them go to town. I've been through this before. So have you. Sometimes there's no substitute for down and dirty police work.'

'I know that. The problem I have with it is conceptual. When I look at this case, do you know what I see? That none of the breaks have been forensic. They've all been about outthinking him. About understanding him. He doesn't leave things behind.'

'But he does leave things out. Like with Theresa. He couldn't control that, and he missed the fact that Sarah omitted it.' Alan shrugs. 'He's smart. He's not superhuman.'

I know that Alan is right. I know it in all the deep-down places inside of me. It still chafes me. To feel so close and realize that, really, we're no closer than we were before.

'Fine,' I say, giving in to the truth. 'Let's get Callie and Gene here.'

'You got it.'

I wander into the den, trying to walk off my frustration, as Alan alerts Callie to her coming task. Like the rest of the home, the den is all about dark wood, dark carpet, brown walls. Old-fashioned and trying for sumptuous; to me it's just ugly.

The desk, I notice, is immaculate and ordered. Too ordered. I move closer and nod to myself. Cabrera has some obsessive-compulsive going on. There are three fountain pens on the left side of the desk. Each one is aligned perfectly straight in relation to the other and with the right angles of the desktop itself. Three more pens are on the right side of the desk and a cursory glance confirms that they align not just with each other but with the pens on the left. A letter opener lies horizontally at the top of the desk near the computer screen. Its placement is equidistant between the two arrangements of fountain pens. Curious, I open the middle desk drawer. I see exact arrangements of tacks, paper clips, and rubber bands. I'm not going to count them, but I'm guessing the quantity of each matches the other.

Interesting, but unhelpful. I grimace, still frustrated.

I stare at the computer screen. One of the icons catches my eyes: *Address Book*.

I bend over and use the mouse to double-click it. A list of phone numbers and addresses opens up. There aren't many of them, and they are a mix of business and personal. I scroll through.

Something flickers in my head. I frown.

I scroll through the names again. Another flicker.

Omissions . . .

Something is missing. What?

I scroll through the list five times before I see it.

'Son of a bitch,' I say, standing up straight, shocked. I cover my eyes with my hand, dismayed at my own stupidity. 'You moron,' I mutter, chastising myself.

It's not the evidence that points to him, but the lack of it.

'Alan!' I bark.

He ambles in, eyebrow raised in question.

'I know who The Stranger is.'

59

'They got the girls out,' Alan says to me. He's just finished a conversation on his cell phone. 'Jessica and Theresa. They're physically healthy, but we're not sure of anything else yet.' He grimaces. 'Jessica's been inside that place for the last ten plus years. Theresa for five. He gave them ten thousand square feet of room, he fed them – hell, he even gave them satellite TV and music. But they were never allowed outside. And they weren't allowed to wear any clothes. He told them . . .' Alan pauses, sighs. 'He told them if they tried anything – like escape or suicide – that he'd kill someone they loved. They're both pretty withdrawn and uncommunicative. He might have beaten them.'

'He probably did,' I say. I'm glad the girls are alive, but the thought of their ordeal, like everything else about this case, makes me feel tired and angry.

We'd been in the car, waiting for Callie, when the call came in. A thought occurs to me.

'Call them back,' I tell him. 'Have the agent in charge ask the girls if they ever saw his face.'

Alan dials, waits. 'Johnson?' he asks. 'It's Alan Washington. Need you to ask the girls something for me.'

We wait.

'Yeah?' Alan shakes his head at me. They hadn't seen his face.

Damn.

Alan frowns. 'Sorry – can you repeat that?' His expression sobers.

'Oh. Tell her Sarah's fine. And, Johnson? I need you to break some news to Jessica Nicholson.' He explains, then hangs up. 'Theresa asked about Sarah.'

I don't reply. What am I supposed to say?

Callie and Gene are here. Callie hops out and strides over, smiling. She's cleaned herself up and looks perfect again, of course. She nods toward the front of the house, taking in the broken windows, the burnt, bullet-chewed lawn.

'I like what you've done with the place.'

'Hey, Smoky,' Gene says. He doesn't look perfect. He looks tired.

'Hi, Gene.'

I'm about to fill them in when I see another car coming toward the house. Brady appears from nowhere as it approaches.

'AD Jones,' he says.

'Hail, hail, the gang's all here,' Callie murmurs. 'By the way, Smoky, Kirby seemed to be disappointed that she didn't get to shoot anyone.'

'She did good,' Brady says, giving Callie a thoughtful once-over.

I watch Callie return the gaze, recognize the semi-lustful spark in her eyes. She holds out a hand.

'I don't think we've met,' she purrs.

'Brady,' the SWAT commander says, taking her hand and shaking it. 'And you are?'

'Callie Thorne. But you can call me Beautiful.'

'Not a stretch.'

Callie grins at me. 'I like him.'

The car arrives next to us, cutting the banter short. AD Jones gets out. He reminds me of both Callie and Brady, tireless and energized, his suit un-rumpled, not a hair out of place.

'Brief me,' he says without preamble.

I fill him in on the assault, and on the subsequent interview with Cabrera. About the girls in North Dakota.

'Any recent update on the girls?' he asks Alan.

'No, sir. But soon.'

I tell him about Juan. Watch as his eyes go wide, then sad. His face falls. He looks off. His mouth moves.

'Christ,' he says. 'We did this.'

I wait, let him gather himself.

'So,' he continues, 'we know who he was. Do we know who he is? Do we have a name?'

I tell him. Alan knew already. This is the first time Callie's heard this, and her look of shock matches AD Jones's.

'Gibbs?' AD Jones asks. 'The trust lawyer? Are you fucking kidding me?'

'I wish I was, sir. It makes sense, and we should have considered it before. It's a huge misstep on my part. He's right there. I just didn't see it until I was going through the contact list on Cabrera's computer. It wasn't what was there, but what was missing.'

He stares at me, frowning. His face clears as he gets it. 'Gibbs wasn't on the list. Jesus Christ.'

'That's right. A quick search through the office didn't turn up anything relating to Gibbs or the trust. Nothing. But Cabrera isn't just meticulous – he's obsessive-compulsive. His contact list wasn't huge, but what was there was very complete. He had numbers for everyone from the woman who cut his hair to the trash company. Home phones, cell phones, e-mail addresses, fax numbers, alternate numbers – but not his *lawyer*? No way he'd leave that out by accident. That, combined with something else Cabrera mentioned while he was talking.' I squint at AD Jones. 'Juan was fair-skinned, wasn't he?'

'Yes. He almost looked white. It didn't occur to me to mention it.'

'Gibbs is white. Cabrera called Juan a "white angel." I thought it was a figure of speech, but I put that together with the missing piece of the address book and realized that he meant white-skinned.'

'It's not a lock,' Alan says, 'but it feels right. Hiding in plain sight. It's simple, it's smart, and it fits his MO.'

AD Jones shakes his head once, a gesture encompassing disbelief, frustration, and anger. I know just how he feels. 'So what's the problem?' he asks.

'Aside from the slight chance I'm wrong about this? No evidence, sir,' I say. 'No one besides Cabrera has seen his face. None of the scenes we're aware of have turned up anything probative or useful. Short of a confession, we have nothing to tie him to a crime.' I point to Callie and Gene. 'I'm going to have them scour this place from top to bottom, and hope something turns up.'

AD Jones shakes his head in frustration. 'Dammit.' He points a finger at me. 'Find something, Smoky. Enough is enough. End this.'

He turns and gets back into his car, leaving me nonplussed by his outburst. A moment later, it heads toward the gate and the growing throng of reporters.

'Well,' Callie says to Brady, 'I suppose you and I will have to continue this later. There will be a later?'

He tips an imaginary hat.

'That's affirmative.'

He saunters off. Callie ogles his backside as he goes.

'Ah, lust.' She sighs. She turns toward the house, winks at me. Callie is doing what Callie does: trying to lift the inexorable grimness of things, like the boom box and sunlight in my bedroom a lifetime ago. 'Are you ready to go to work, Gene?'

They go off together. I watch her reach into her pocket, pop a Vicodin.

I empathize right now. I want nothing more than a single shot of tequila.

Just one.

I wait. It's making me crazy.

Everything I can do is done. Gibbs is under surveillance. Cabrera is in custody. Theresa and Jessica are in a hospital, being examined. Bonnie, Elaina, and Sarah are safe. Alan is on the phone with Elaina, delivering the news about Theresa so that Elaina can pass it on to Sarah. Callie and Gene are inside, trying to balance speed with thoroughness. Thoroughness is winning.

All I can do now is wait.

Alan walks over to me. 'Elaina's going to let Sarah know. At least we can give her that.'

'What do you think, Alan? Even when we catch Juan, is there a happy ending? Or does he get what he wanted all along?'

I'm not sure why I ask him these questions. Maybe because he's my friend. Maybe because of all the people on my team, Alan is the one I feel I can look up to, subordinate or not.

He's quiet for a long moment. 'I think when we catch him, we're doing our job. We're keeping him from doing more damage. We're giving Sarah a chance. That's all. It may not be the best answer, but it's all we've got.' He looks at me, gives me a kind smile. 'It's all we're responsible for, Smoky. You want to know if Sarah's already dead inside, if he's murdered her spirit. The truth is, I don't know. The bigger truth is, Sarah doesn't know. The final truth is, we're giving her the chance to find out. And that's not everything, and it might not be enough, but it's not nothing, either.'

'And him? What about Juan?'

Alan's face becomes sober. 'He's a perp now. His days as a victim are long gone.'

I think about what he's said, and it comforts me and then doesn't, comforts me and then doesn't. My spirit tosses and turns, trying to sleep on a bed that's only soft in certain places. This is not a new feeling, and I let it wash over me.

Justice for the dead. It's not nothing. It's far from nothing. But it's not resurrection, either. The dead stay dead even after their killers are captured. The truth of this, the sadness of it, makes the job neither pointless nor fulfilling.

Acceptance and disquiet. Acceptance and disquiet. Two waves

that roll me gently, one following the other inside my heart forever.

I wait.

During my waiting, Tommy calls. I feel guilty and elated, two new waves. Guilty that I had not called him to check on him. Elated at the sound of his voice, at the truth that he is alive.

'How are you?' I ask.

'I'm okay. No major damage to the muscle. Cracked my clavicle, which hurts like hell, but I won't end up on disability. I'm fine.'

'I'm sorry I didn't call.'

'I'm not. You're doing your job. There'll be times I'll get caught up too. Nature of the beast. If we start keeping score, we'll be over before we begin.'

His words warm me inside. 'Where are you now?'

'Home. I wanted to call you before I took my pain pills. They can make me a little goofy.'

'Really? Maybe I'll have to come over and take advantage of you while you're all loopy.'

'Nurse Smoky giving me a sponge bath? I'll have to get blown up more often.'

The pressure inside causes me to react with a giggle. I clap a hand over my mouth, mortified.

'Anyway,' Tommy says. 'Get back to it. We'll talk tomorrow.'

'Bye,' I say, and hang up.

Alan glances over at me. 'Did you just giggle?'

I frown. 'Of course not. I don't giggle.'

'Ah.' We wait.

Callie and Gene are done with half of the home. They have a set of elimination prints taken from Cabrera that they're using for comparisons as they go. So far, nothing.

It's 3:00 A.M. The reporters and their helicopters are gone, maneuvered away by a skillful AD Jones. He'd made himself the source of information and they'd followed him like a herd of hungry vampires. I imagine that the story we want told has now

460

been splashed across television screens and Web sites, and will show up in the newspaper headlines of tomorrow. Cabrera found. Suspect dead. Case closed.

We wait.

My phone rings at 4:30 A.M.

'It's Kirby.'

The simple fact that her voice is serious and no wisecracks follow starts the alarm bells ringing.

'What is it?' I ask.

'Sarah's gone.'

60

I'm almost shouting at Kirby. It's anger driven by fear.

'What do you mean she's gone? You were supposed to be guarding her.'

Kirby's voice is calm without being defensive. 'I know. I was worried about people on the outside trying to get in, not her trying to get out. She wasn't snatched, Smoky. She left. I went to the bathroom. She walked out the door. She left a note, said, *There's something I have to do.*'

I pull the phone away from my ear. 'Son of a bitch!' I yell into the sky. Alan's been inside the house. He comes running out.

'Do you know where she might be going?' Kirby asks.

I stop, poleaxed.

Do I?

The voice in my head replies, accusing.

Of course you do. If you'd been listening, you would have been ready for this. But you were too busy with yourself, weren't you?

The truth I'm trying to reveal to myself appears.

Sarah, memorizing him. The way he talks. Saying she'd never forget his voice.

Sarah, taking a phone call from Gibbs the other day, supposedly to 'verify' she was fine with us going into the home.

462

I grip my temples with one hand. My head is spinning and my heart is racing.

He talked to her recently, the day he killed the Kingsleys. Then, he talked to her on the phone, in the hospital, as Gibbs. She knew the moment she heard his voice. He probably wanted her to know.

'I think I do,' I tell Kirby. 'Stay with Bonnie and Elaina. I'll be in touch.'

I hang up before she can reply.

She knew, and once she knew that Theresa was safe, she went off to do the one thing she wanted more than anything else in the world.

She went to kill him.

The endless cycle.

'What is it?' Alan asks.

I see the fear in his eyes. I can't blame him. The last time we were near the end of a case and I got a phone call that made me react this way, Elaina was in danger.

'Elaina and Bonnie are fine. Sarah's on the run.'

I see him thinking, his mind racing, watch as understanding hits home.

'Gibbs. She's going to kill Gibbs.'

'Yes,' I say.

The fear doesn't leave his eyes. It's not Elaina, it's not Bonnie, it's not me. It's not Callie or even James.

But it is Sarah.

I hear James's voice in my head: *Every Victim.*

'If we let her kill him, she'll never make it back,' he murmurs.

I unfreeze at this, snapping into motion.

'Get ahold of surveillance. Alert them, get the address. If they spot her, they're to detain her. Otherwise, they're to watch and wait for us to get there. I'm going to let Callie know we're going.'

I head for the house at a run. I find Callie in one of the bedrooms.

I tell her what's happening. Again, I see that fear. The same fear in her eyes that I'd seen in Alan's. It's odd to see on Callie, unsettling. No one's gotten away from Sarah's story without a scar to show for it.

'Go,' she says, grim. 'I'll handle things here.'

61

As it turns out, Gibbs – Juan – doesn't live that far away, in LA terms. In this early time of the morning, without traffic to slow us down, we should arrive at his house in the San Fernando Valley within twenty minutes.

On the way there, my phone rings again.

'Is this Smoky Barrett?' a deep voice asks.

'Who's this?'

'My name is Lenz. I'm one of the agents assigned to watch Gibbs. We got a problem.'

My heart beats even faster, if that's possible. 'What?'

'My partner and I were doing our thing, keeping an eye on the house. Pretty quiet detail. About five minutes ago someone took a shot at us. Well, at the car. Plugged holes through the trunk and one of the passenger windows. We dive down in our seats, pull our weapons, when we come back, we see a teenage girl beating feet to the front door.'

'Dammit!' I say. 'Did she enter the home?'

His voice is miserable. 'Yeah. Three minutes ago or less.'

'I'll be there shortly. Stay alert but stay back.'

It's a small home. Humble. A two-story built in older, some would say better, times. It has a small, treeless, unfenced front yard. The

465

driveway leads from the street to a detached single car-garage. The street is quiet. The sun is breaking somewhere on the horizon; we can see its glow climbing over the rooftops.

An agent I don't recognize is waiting. He comes to us as we get out.

'Lenz,' he says. He's fortyish, a little homely. He has the skinny look and sallow skin of a smoker. 'Really sorry about this.'

'You stay here,' I tell him. 'Keep your partner watching the back. We're going up to the front door.'

'You got it.'

They get moving. Alan and I do the same. We haven't drawn our weapons, but our hands rest on them. When we get to the front porch, I hear Sarah. She's screaming.

'You deserve to die! I'm going to kill you! Do you hear me!'

A voice responds. It's too low for me to make out the words.

'Ready?' I ask Alan.

'Ready,' he says, my friend that I secretly look up to. No questions asked.

We're at the tipping point. I can hear it in Sarah's voice. There is no time for finesse, only time for action.

We move to the front door. I check the knob. It opens under my hand, and I throw the door wide. I enter first, gun drawn. Alan follows.

'Sarah?' I call. 'Are you here?'

'Go away! Go away go away go away!'

It's coming from the kitchen, toward the rear of the house. It's not far; I reach the doorway in a few quick strides. I look into the kitchen and stop.

It's small. Old-fashioned and efficient. The dining table sits away from the stove, clean but battered, with four old chairs around it. Stark. Functional.

Juan is sitting in one of the chairs, smiling. Sarah is standing, facing him, about four feet from him. She has a gun pointed at his head. It looks like a thirty-eight revolver. It's an obscenity in her small hands. Something that doesn't belong.

466

I almost don't recognize Gibbs. He's missing his beard and moustache.

They were fake, dummy.

He turns, sees me, smiles.

Eyes aren't blue, either. They're brown. He was wearing contacts.

'Hello, Agent Barrett.' His voice is humble, but his eyes are bright. He's dropped the pretense, let the madness inside him shine. 'Are you the good side of what I've become?'

'Shut up!' Sarah screams. The gun trembles in her hands.

I glance back at Alan, shake my head. Telling him to wait. I lower my gun without putting it away.

Sarah had begun to unravel earlier. Now she's come undone. Looking at her face, I understand, finally, what it was that Juan as The Stranger had been striving for.

Her face was the face of an angel, its wings shorn, as it fell away from the sight of God. The absence of hope as a totality.

A Ruined Life.

I look at Juan and see that he's sucking down the horror of it, and that this, for him, has become a kind of ecstasy. He told himself once that it was all about justice, and maybe, at one time, it was. But he had changed, in the worst and most fundamental way, until it was only about one thing: The Joy of Suffering.

He'd set out to punish evil men, and in doing so, had become an evil man.

'This is not the ending I had planned,' he says, ignoring me now, 'but God's will is all, and I see, I see, what he is doing here, in his infinite wisdom, praise be to Him. He set me on the path, to make you over in my own image, and that can only be completed, I see, I see, by my death at your hands, praise be to Him. You will kill me in the name of vengeance, you will kill me because you think that it is right, but, I see, I see, that you will only be killing me because you want to, praise be to Him.' He pauses, angling his head down. 'You will not kill me to save Theresa. She has been released, she is unharmed. You will be killing me because you yearn to spill my blood, a need so sharp and huge and terrible that it burns your skin like a bright blue flame. And where does that need come from, where does that flame come from?' He nods and smiles with his mouth open. 'It is the flame of God, Little Pain. Don't you see? I was an angel of vengeance, sent by the Creator to destroy the men who hide behind symbols, the demons that caper through the world in pressed suits, proclaiming their goodness while eating the souls of the innocent. I was sent by God to cut a wide swath, a bloody swath, a swath that drowns both victim and oppressor, the innocent and the guilty. What are the deaths of some who shouldn't die in the name of the greater good? I was sacrificed so that I could be made into the Lord's weapon. And I have sacrificed you, I see, I see, so that you can become me and take my place, praise be to Him.' He leans forward, closes his eyes, his face blissful. 'I am ready to meet God. Hail Mary, full of Grace.'

I enter the kitchen, ignoring Juan, watching Sarah. I move toward her, not stopping, coming up next to her. She doesn't react. She can't tear her eyes away from Juan's face.

She sees, I realize. Like I see. Like James sees. Like that poor FBI agent who'd blown her head off. Sarah sees Juan, and understands.

Her agony is his orgasm. But the reasons behind it are all tragedy and madness.

I can feel her need coming off her, a burning. Her finger trembles on the trigger, and she stands, poised in the moment. She wants him dead, but she's afraid. Afraid it won't be enough. That it won't last long enough. That it'll be over too fast, and that none of it will fill the hole.

And she's right. She could kill him for an eternity, and in the end, she'd only lose herself.

What do I say to her? I'm going to get one chance. Maybe two.

Juan continues to pray, fervent, certain, proud.

Insane. He'd started out organized, but Dr Child had been right. The lunacy had been there, waiting and latent, like a virus.

I drown out his voice with my own thoughts, my eyes fixed on Sarah's angel face.

Falling, but not yet fallen.

Theresa, Buster, Desiree. Loved and loved by. Goodness and smiles and . . . gone. Where was the key? What would pull her away from the edge she was about to tumble into?

It comes to me softly, feathers, not thunder. A ghost-kiss.

I lean forward and put my lips to her ear. I whisper to her and I put the force of my own self into my voice, my own pain survived. We're both wingless angels, scarred inside and out, bleeding from wounds that fight not to heal. The decision is not about goodness or evil, about happiness or sadness, about hope or despair. The decision is the simplest of all: the decision to live or to die. To gamble that as life continues, suffering will abate, and *something* better will eventually abide.

I put Matt and Alexa into my voice, and hope that they will carry my words into her heart.

'Your mother is watching you from the clouds, baby. Forever and always, and she doesn't want this. The only place she lives is inside of you, Sarah. That's the last part of her. If you kill him, she dies for good.' I straighten up, move away. 'That's all I'm going to say, honey. It's your choice now. You choose.'

Juan narrows his eyes at me. He examines Sarah. Smiles like a snake lapping up milk mixed with sugar.

'You've already chosen, Little Pain. Do you need my help? Do you need me to remind you, to fan the flame inside so that you can do His will?' He licks his lips. 'Your mother? I touched her body after she died. I touched her private places. I touched her *inside*.'

Sarah freezes. I freeze too. I wait for her to kill him. A dark part of me, the place where I keep my own killer's eyes, forgets my purpose and wants her to kill him. Instead, she begins to shake.

It starts as a small quivering, like the tremors that precede an earthquake. It moves from her hands to her arms to her shoulders. Down her chest, to her legs, a terrible shaking, till it almost seems like she should fly apart, and then – she freezes.

Her head goes back and she howls.

It's awful.

It's the sound of a mother who woke up and realized that she rolled over on her baby in her sleep, suffocating him. It drills into my heart.

As she howls, I see Juan, and I get to witness his exaltation. Watch him quiver, see him shake, watch as his upper body pitches forward, as his fists clench and his hands curl. Hear his groan. Long, low, full of slithering things and the rolling, stinking, sticky dead. It harmonizes with the sound of Sarah through discordance, demonic. Juan's fall is complete. He's no better now than the men who made him this way.

Sarah falls to the floor and curls into herself, tighter, tighter, tighter. She continues to howl.

'Don't move,' I tell Juan.

He ignores me. He can't tear his eyes away from Sarah's agony. When he speaks, his voice trembles in wonder:

'*There* I am.'

In The End:
The Things That Glow

62

'Are you sure about this, honey?'

Bonnie smiles up at me, serene.

We are about to enter an interrogation room. Juan will be there. Bonnie has demanded to see him, for reasons she won't share with me. I had refused, at first. I even got angry about it, something I'd never been with Bonnie.

She'd remained resolute.

'Why?' I had asked. 'Can you at least tell me why?'

She pantomimed handing something to someone.

'You have something to give? You have a gift?'

She nods. Hesitates. Makes a motion of handing something to me, then handing something to – she points to the name on the paper. Juan.

'You have a gift for me and for Juan?'

A smile, serene. A nod.

She will not let it go. I've relented. I'd hoped that Juan would save me from this by refusing to see us. To my surprise and unease, he'd agreed. So here we are.

Bonnie has a notepad under her arm. She carries a marker in her hand. They wouldn't let her bring in a pen – too sharp. It took some arm-bending to get them to allow the marker.

We enter the room. Juan is already there, cuffed at wrist and ankles, secured through a link bolted to the floor. He smiles as we enter. It's a broad smile, a lazy smile, a dog in a nice patch of sun. The sinner, for now, not the saint.

I'm told he moves back and forth between these two temperaments. He spent one recent afternoon in the prison chapel, on his knees, arms spread wide to God. That same night he raped his cellmate, chuckling as the young man screamed. Juan does all of his praying in solitary confinement now.

'Agent Barrett. And little Bonnie. How are you both?'

'Fine, thank you,' I reply, trying for dispassionate.

Once he had realized he was going to live, Juan had spilled the beans on everything. He was, of course, proud of his accomplishments. He was righteous, and now, he had an audience to preach to. We hung on his every word and let him hang himself.

It had taken him some time to establish with certainty which of the two task-force members had betrayed him.

He'd spent years tracking down and documenting the flow of money from its original source. He'd managed to get proof on Tobias Walker first, over a decade ago. The FBI end of things was more difficult – Jacob Stern had been smart. Juan found out that Stern had come to the FBI via the LAPD, and had, in fact, served in the same precinct as Walker at one time. This had raised Juan's suspicions. His ruthlessness and persistence eventually got him the information he wanted.

Walker had been the primary contact with the underworld, the real Judas of the act. Afterward, he'd needed Stern's assistance in covering the money trail and so had brought the agent in on the scheme. Juan had proof of Stern's complicity, of Walker's sins. They were sitting on Michael Kingsley's computer.

'I was going to give you the password and let you extradite Stern. Once he was here' – Juan had smiled with too many teeth showing – 'I would have taken my revenge. It would have looked like an accident, of course, as I was supposed to be "dead," but I could have lived with that. The important thing is that the world would know, would understand that symbols mean nothing, the soul means all.'

In this, I suppose, he's succeeded. Stern *is* mid-extradition. I hope he dies a horrible death in prison. I hold him and Walker most responsible for everything that has occurred. They made this monster, and if Juan had settled for visiting himself on just the two of them, I would have considered justice served. Instead, he wreaked indiscriminate destruction over many lives and numerous years. He destroyed the innocent and I can't forgive him for it.

We asked Juan about AD Jones. He'd revealed a surprising streak of pragmatism. 'Too risky, killing an Assistant Director. I was willing to wait to kill him at a later date.'

All of this explains why he had come out into the open. It was a confluence of events, designed to lead us to Cabrera and to expose Stern. Once Stern was here . . .

It gives me a chill to think of how close he came to pulling it all off.

Juan blamed everyone on the original task force for not 'seeing' Walker's and Stern's true colors. In his mind, they were supposed to protect him. They failed. They deserved to die.

He was more merciful to the women because they weren't a part of the original betrayal.

'But they were harlots, blind to the inadequacies of their husbands' souls,' he pointed out with calm rationality.

They failed. They deserved to die.

It was about failure, I'd realized, all of it. Juan had been failed, probably from birth, and so he'd grown up to become a killer with no mercy for failure.

When Juan talked about Walker, I knew I was witnessing the closest thing to pure hatred I'd probably ever get to see. His face would go calm, but his eyes would crackle and his voice would vibrate with poison and death.

'He escaped my hand, but not his children or their children,' he'd said, gloating and hating simultaneously. 'I destroyed the Langstroms. You should have seen their *sorrow*. It was *magnificent*!

And their death was my *justice*. Do you know why? Because I ensured they went to hell!' His eyes had been almost all pupil and black. 'Do you understand? They committed suicide. Whatever else happens to me, they're burning in hell right now for all eternity!'

And he'd laughed and laughed and laughed. Madness.

I'd been curious about his change of MO. He'd shot Haliburton after forcing him to write a poem, and he'd tortured and castrated Gonzalez.

'It wasn't about ritual,' he'd explained to me. 'It was about suffering. I tailored their deaths to bring them the most agony before they died. The physical was important, yes, but their spiritual pain was most important of all, praise be to God.'

Sarah was, of course, *him* – but only *to* him. He'd been busy twisting her life, creating betrayals, giving her a taste of the living nightmare he'd gone through, in the certainty that she'd become what he was when all was said and done. He remains convinced that that's exactly what happened.

But I know better. Sarah isn't well, but she isn't Juan, either. Juan is evil. Sarah is good. I rarely get to think in such black-and-white terms in my job, but it's warranted here. Her soul is scarred, not gangrenous.

The 'Mr You Know Who' mentioned in the Vargas video was no longer living. Juan had long ago seen to that. He'd escaped his captors when he was fifteen. Four years later he'd hunted them down, one by one, killing them all in various horrible ways. The video had been a red herring, designed to occupy and confuse us. Juan had paid Vargas to make it.

'He was so far gone,' Juan had said, 'that he didn't even wonder why I wanted it, or remember who I was. Can you believe that? Junkies are truly bereft of God's love.'

Now we're here, and I'm wondering why. I don't want to be here. Juan is a lost cause, worthy of both my pity and my rage.

He turns those overbright eyes on Bonnie. 'Why did you ask to see me, little one?'

Bonnie has remained serene throughout. She appears untouched by Juan, by what he is, the presence of him. She opens the pad on the table in front of her and begins to write. I watch, captivated.

She finishes and hands the pad to me. Indicates that she wants me to read what she's written.

'She wants to know if you're familiar with her story.'

Juan nods, really interested now. 'Of course I am. That was an inspired act of pain. Forcing you to watch as he raped and killed your mother. Tying you to her body. Masterful work by a true artist of suffering.'

'You fuck,' I say, trembling with rage.

Bonnie puts a hand on my arm. She takes back the notepad. I glare at Juan as she writes some more. He smiles back at me. She hands me the notepad again. I read what she's written, and my heart stutters.

'She . . .' I clear my throat. 'She wants to know if you'd like her to tell you why she doesn't speak. The real reason. She thinks you'll appreciate it.'

I turn to Bonnie. 'I think we should go. I don't like this.'

She pats my arm again. Serene, serene.

Trust me, her eyes say.

Juan licks his lips. A corner of his mouth twitches.

'I think . . . that I would like that very much,' he says.

Bonnie smiles back at him, takes back the notepad, and hunches over it, writing. She hands it to me, but before I can read from it, she catches my eye. I see concern there. I see a little bit of wisdom. Too much for a girl her age, I guess. I also see more of that unending serenity.

Brace yourself, but don't be afraid, she seems to be telling me.

I read what she wrote and understand why. My eyes go wide. My breathing stops. A moment later, a tear runs down my cheek against my will. I feel like I am falling.

My pain is blood in the water for Juan. His nostrils flare.

'Tell me,' he says.

I look at Bonnie, numb. Despair creeps through me.

A gift to Juan? True enough. He was going to love this, that evil part of him. Why would she want to give him this terrible, terrible thing?

She reaches up and wipes the tear from my cheek.

Go on, her smile says. *Trust me.*

I take a breath.

'She says . . .' I stop. 'She says that she decided if her mother couldn't speak, then neither would she.'

Juan is as affected by this as I was, for very different reasons. His mouth opens and he sits back. He blinks rapidly. His breathing is shallow.

The Joy of Suffering.

I look at Bonnie. 'Can we go now?' I ask. I feel hollow. I want to go home and climb under the covers and weep.

She holds up a finger.

One more thing, she's saying.

She turns to Juan and smiles that wonderful, beautiful, serene smile. It's everything Sarah's face in the kitchen wasn't, and it makes Juan frown. It makes him uncomfortable.

'But I've changed my mind,' she says, her voice clear and distinct. 'I've decided it's time to speak again.'

I stand up in my chair so fast it crashes backward.

'Bonnie!' It comes out as a scream.

She stands as well. She tucks her notepad under her arm and takes my hand. 'Hi, Smoky.'

Now I'm the one who's speechless.

'Let's go home,' she says. She turns to Juan. Less serenity, now. 'Burn in hell, Mr Juan.'

He regards her, angered and yet contemplative.

Does he see? I wonder.

In this moment, in some ways, Bonnie was the angel Juan had once been. Un-conflicted and pure, she had no pity for him, no concern for what he was, only certainty of what he'd become.

478

She'd given him a gift of despair, and taken it away by giving me a gift of triumph.

I was happier, standing in that interrogation room with that evil, damaged man, than I'd been in a very, very long time. Which was her point to me, to us, to anyone:

However bad things may become, evil men only triumph in the most important ways when we let them.

That was also the moment I realized I wasn't going to take the offer of Quantico. I was done running. In that moment, once again, life began to glow.

It always will. You just have to let it.

63

I sit in the chair in front of Matt's computer, and I stare at the screen. I have a shot of tequila in my hand, ready and willing to help me. Liquid courage.

I glance at the glass and frown.

Bonnie sleeps. I think of her strength compared to my weakness and I feel ashamed.

I put the glass down. I stare at the computer screen.

1forUtwo4me.

Five days. That's how much time passed from my first meeting with Sarah to Juan's capture. More days have gone by since then, but it's the five days that stick with me like they were years.

I carry a new scar, Sarah's scar. It isn't visible, but the deepest cuts are the ones unseen, the march to death *inside*. The body ages and withers and dies. A soul can age as well. A six-year-old can become sixty in the span of a heartbeat.

Unlike the body, the soul can reverse this process, and become, perhaps not young again, but vital. Alive.

Sarah's journey cut me deep. My own journeys have aged me, too far, too fast. But scars are more than reminders of past wounds. They are evidence of healing.

I accept as a truth that I will always have moments of pain when it comes to Matt and Alexa. That's okay. The only way to be free of them forever would be to forget them, and I won't give up a blessed moment.

I accept that I will have moments of great fear when it comes to Bonnie, and I accept that this may never go away. All parents fear for their children, and I have more reason to fear than most.

I am flawed, I'm not unharmed by the past, but I am alive and I'm pretty sure I'll be happy more often than I'm not. Pretty sure parts of my life will continue to glow.

More than that, I cannot ask. Hope for. But not ask.

We finished packing away the house, Bonnie and I. We had converted Alexa's room into Bonnie's studio, a fitting memorial.

The last thing, now.

1forUtwo4me.

I've come to realize that my fear of this is not just the fear of what I might find.

You love a person, you live with them, you marry them. You spend your whole life getting to know them. I learned something new about Matt every day, every month, every year. Then he died, and the learning stopped.

Until now.

If I invoke 1forUtwo4me, and look through that folder marked *Private*, I may learn something good or bad, but however it goes, it will be the last new thing I'll ever learn about my husband.

I'm afraid of that finality.

Maybe I should save it. Save it for a day when I'm old and gray and I'm missing him.

I ignore my tequila, and I lean forward and click on the folder. I enter the password and gain access.

I see the icons that indicate that the files are photographs. They're all numbered. I poise the mouse-arrow over one, and pause.

What am I going to see if I click this?

For a moment, just a moment, I consider deleting it all. Letting it go.

I click the first, and it opens before me. My jaw drops.

It's a picture of me. Me and Matt. Having sex.

I squint, looking closer, remembering. The picture was taken from the side, so that our bodies are in profile. My head is back, and my eyes are closed in ecstatic concentration. Matt is looking down on me, his mouth slightly open.

It's not artistic, but it's not anatomically explicit, either. It looks like an amateur photograph. Which it is.

Matt and I went through a period, a time I've learned many couples do. Where sex becomes a subject of concentrated fascination and exploration. You try things, experiment, leave your comfort zone a little. Eventually you find your middle ground, a place that contains the balance of the things that excite you without shaming you. It's a fumbling time, full of mistakes. It requires trust. Exploration is not always graceful. Sometimes it can be mortifying.

Matt and I had explored taking pictures of each other nude, and of some of our sex together. It excited us at first, but it didn't last. It wasn't something we were ashamed of, it was just something we were done with. We tried it, it was interesting, we moved on.

I move through the photos, opening them one after the other, remembering each moment. There are photos of me by myself, trying to be saucy (but looking silly). I find one photo of Matt, sitting on the bed, back against the headboard. He's grinning. I close my eyes. I don't need the photograph. I see the grin, I see that mussed-up hair, the twinkle in his eyes. I can see his cock, and I remember thinking once that I knew it better than any woman anywhere, it had been in me and on me and against me. I had touched it and giggled at it, and I had gotten angry at it when it was too demanding. I had lost my virginity to it.

My eyes are stinging. These, I think, are moments that will never come again. I don't know what my future will bring in terms of love and companionship. I do know that I'll never be that young again, that I'll never feel the need to explore that particular thing again.

Matt and I had covered that ground. We'd fucked and fought

and laughed and cried and learned, and that curiosity was done and gone.

This was his, only his.

'1forUtwo4me, babe.' I smile, tears running down my cheeks.

Matt doesn't reply. He smiles at me. Waiting.

Say the words, that smile says.

So I do.

'Good-bye, Matt.'

I close the folder.

64

'You ready to go?' Tommy asks.

'Zip me up and then my answer will be yes,' I say.

He does so and then pulls me into him with his one good arm. He kisses my neck. It has a familiar, comfortable feel.

I hear the sound of footsteps. My precocious daughter appears in the doorway. She rolls her eyes and makes an icky face.

'Geez, can't you guys give it a rest? I want to go see Sarah.'

'Yes, yes, munchkin.' I smile, disengaging myself from Tommy. 'We're ready.'

A month had passed. Sarah had stayed curled into herself for a week. A week after that, she began speaking again. Theresa and Bonnie and Elaina spent hours by her bedside in the hospital, coaxing her away from her despair.

It was Cathy Jones who'd finally gotten through to her, though. Callie had brought the cop to the hospital. Sarah had seen her and burst into tears. Cathy had gone to her and grabbed her up and we left them alone.

Theresa was as wonderful and resilient as Sarah had described her. She hadn't had much interest in getting better or being coddled. She wanted one thing and one thing only: to see Sarah.

She had a strength to her, a warmth, that Juan had failed to extinguish, and she gives me hope for Sarah.

Last week, I got the call. Sarah was coming home. Really coming home – the home she'd had to leave so many years ago. The irony of this gift coming from Juan wasn't lost on any of us. We didn't care.

Cathy had moved in, at Theresa's request. Theresa had cleaned the place from top to bottom, had thrown open all the shutters and let the light in again. She'd hung the painting on the wall above the foot of Sarah's bed.

I'd had an idea, as well, a possibility. With Theresa's help, I checked it out and found it to be true. We had a homecoming gift that we were all pretty sure Sarah would like.

'Are we almost there?' Bonnie asks.

'Pretty close,' Tommy says. 'I just need to remember which turn to take. Darn snaky Malibu streets.'

'It's a left,' Bonnie replies, patient. 'I memorized the map.'

I sit back and enjoy hearing the sound of Bonnie's voice. It is magic to me. Music.

'Here we are.'

We pull up. Elaina and Theresa and Callie come out to greet us, followed by a surprise guest – Kirby.

'Is she here?' Bonnie asks, running up to them.

'Yes.' Elaina smiles. 'She's inside, resting.'

Bonnie heads toward the door at a dead run.

'I see where we stand in the order of things now,' Callie says. 'We are uninteresting, honey-love, uninteresting and old.'

'Speak for yourself, Red,' Kirby chirps. 'I'm going to be young forever.'

'That's because you're going to die before you get old,' Brady drawls, appearing from inside the house.

He and Callie are dating. I remember her telling me about her problems with relationships, about how 'her cup runneth under,' and wonder if this is changing. I hope so. Her hand still strays to her jacket pocket for the Vicodin more than I would like, and that outcome is uncertain, but there are different kinds of pain, and the hurt of loneliness well . . . there are no pills for that one.

It swoops down on me from nowhere, not a bat or a dove but something in between. Alan, haunted by the sounds of a shrieking mother. Callie, perfect on the outside, delicately maimed within. Me and my scars. I realize we trade pleasures and pains, back and forth forever, eating our donuts as we search for the glow near the watering hole.

And that's okay. That's life. Still the best alternative to death.

'So,' Theresa says, excited. 'Are you going to go get it?'

I grin. 'Right now. I'll meet everyone inside.'

The group heads indoors. They'll be joined before too long by others that are coming. Callie's daughter and grandson. Barry Franklin. People who had been touched by Juan, or who simply wanted to give Sarah hope. People who wanted the cycle to end at Juan. To ensure that Sarah was not, in fact, *A Ruined Life*.

I go next door and knock. A moment later, it opens. Jamie Overman is there, and she invites me in. Her husband appears next to her.

'Thanks for doing this,' I tell them. 'And not just this. Thanks for making it possible.'

John is a shy man. He smiles and says nothing. Jamie nods once. 'It's our pleasure. Sam and Linda were good neighbors and good people. Let me get her for you now.'

She wanders off and in a moment she comes back with what I want. Something from the past that I think will give Sarah some hope.

I look down at the Hope Giver, something alive from a long dead past. She's older, slower, grayer. But I see a spark of dumb love and expectancy in her eyes that makes me grin.

'Hey there, Doreen,' I say, squatting down so that we're at eye level. She wags her tail and she licks my face.

Hi back and I love you and what are we doing?

'Let's go, sweetheart. I want to reintroduce you to someone. She needs you.'